Praise for the Crime of Fashion mysteries

Designer Knockoff

"Devilishly funny. Byerrum intersperses the book with witty excerpts from Lacey's 'Fashion Bites' columns, such as 'When Bad Clothes Happen to Good People' and 'Thank Heavens It's Not Code Taupe.' . . . Lacey is intelligent, insightful, and spunky—a thoroughly likable, if quirky, investigator. . . . Interesting plot twists."
—*The Sun* (Bremerton, WA)

"The supporting characters—a hairdresser, a fortuneteller, and a lawyer with a jones for conspiracy theories—are humorous accomplices to Lacey's sleuthing. It's a pleasure to watch Lacey, stunningly attired in various vintage outfits, skillfully uncover what looks like a deadly deception. Clever wordplay, snappy patter, and intriguing clues make this politics-meets-high-fashion whodunit a cut above the ordinary."
—*Romantic Times*

"*Designer Knockoff* is full of fashion tips, vintage fashion lore, and long lost romances. Compelling. . . . Lacey is a spunky heroine and is very self-assured as she carries off her vintage looks with much aplomb."
—The Mystery Reader

"Ellen Byerrum is a very talented writer with an offbeat sense of humor and talent for creating quirky and eccentric characters that will have readers laughing at their antics. There are some very good fashion tips spread throughout. . . . A great beach read."
—The Best Reviews

continued . . .

Killer Hair

"Cut-wrong hair mingles with cutthroat Washington, D.C., in Ellen Byerrum's rippling debut. Peppered with girlfriends you'd love to have, smoldering romance you can't resist, and Beltway insider insights you've got to read, *Killer Hair* adds a crazy twist to the concept of 'capital murder.' Bubbles may have to visit."
—Sarah Strohmeyer,
Agatha Award–winning author of *Bubbles A Broad*

"Ellen Byerrum tailors her debut mystery with a sharp murder plot, entertaining fashion commentary, and gutsy characters. I'll look forward to the next installment."
—Nancy J. Cohen, author of the Bad Hair Day mysteries

"Chock full of colorful, often hilarious characters. . . . Lacey herself has a delightful catty wit. The book is interspersed with gems from her *Crimes of Fashion* columns. . . . A load of stylish fun even if you don't know anything or care to know anything about fashion."
—Scripps Howard News Service

"Lacey Smithsonian is no fashionista—she's a '40s starlet trapped in style-free D.C., with a feminist agenda, a cadre of delightfully insane friends, and a knack for stumbling on corpses. . . . Lacey slays and sashays thru Washington politics, scandal, and Fourth Estate slime, while uncovering whodunit, and dunit and dunit again."
—Chloe Green, author of the Dallas O'Connor Fashion mysteries

"Lacey Smithsonian skewers Washington with style in this new mystery series. *Killer Hair* is a shear delight."
—Elaine Viets, national bestselling author of *Dying to Call You*

HOSTILE MAKEOVER

A CRIME OF FASHION MYSTERY

Ellen Byerrum

A SIGNET BOOK

SIGNET
Published by New American Library, a division of
Penguin Group (USA) Inc., 375 Hudson Street,
New York, New York 10014, USA
Penguin Group (Canada), 90 Eglinton Avenue East, Suite 700, Toronto,
Ontario M4P 2Y3, Canada (a division of Pearson Penguin Canada Inc.)
Penguin Books Ltd., 80 Strand, London WC2R 0RL, England
Penguin Ireland, 25 St. Stephen's Green, Dublin 2,
Ireland (a division of Penguin Books Ltd.)
Penguin Group (Australia), 250 Camberwell Road, Camberwell, Victoria 3124,
Australia (a division of Pearson Australia Group Pty. Ltd.)
Penguin Books India Pvt. Ltd., 11 Community Centre, Panchsheel Park,
New Delhi - 110 017, India
Penguin Group (NZ), cnr Airborne and Rosedale Roads, Albany,
Auckland 1310, New Zealand (a division of Pearson New Zealand Ltd.)
Penguin Books (South Africa) (Pty.) Ltd., 24 Sturdee Avenue,
Rosebank, Johannesburg 2196, South Africa

Penguin Books Ltd., Registered Offices:
80 Strand, London WC2R 0RL, England

First published by Signet, an imprint of New American Library,
a division of Penguin Group (USA) Inc.

First Printing, August 2005
10 9 8 7 6 5 4 3 2

PUBLISHER'S NOTE
This is a work of fiction. Names, characters, places, and incidents either are the product
of the author's imagination or are used fictitiously, and any resemblance to actual
persons, living or dead, business establishments, events, or locales is entirely coincidental.
    The publisher does not have any control over and does not assume any responsibility
for author or third-party Web sites or their content.

This book is dedicated to the
teaching Sisters of St. Joseph of Carondelet.

ACKNOWLEDGMENTS

The process of getting a book published still sometimes seems like a mystery to me. But one thing is certain: It would never get far without the help of a large cast of characters.

I would like to thank my sisters, Barbara Price, Jacqueline Byerrum, and Diane Yeoman, for their good humor. It is only fair to point out that Lacey Smithsonian's sister, Cherise, is not even remotely based on any or all of my sisters, although they all have a fair share of perkiness, as well as other fine qualities. I thank them, and my brother and sister-in-law, Jim and Mary Byerrum, for their sibling support and solidarity. I also want to point out that Lacey's mother bears no relation to my late mother, Doloris Achatz Byerrum, who was intelligent and fun, had wonderful taste, and was a great cook. I will always be grateful for her wit and wisdom—and love.

I am very grateful to Lloyd Rose, who has listened to me chatter through countless lunches and helped me find answers to questions of plot and character.

Thanks also go to my agent, Don Maass, and to my editor, Martha Bushko, and Serena Jones at Signet.

And of course, to my husband, Bob Williams, who honors me with his keen insight, thoughtful critique, and ability to see comedy in the darkest moments, when inspiration has gone on strike and nothing but hard work will do, I owe so much more than thanks. But don't worry; I'll tell him all about that later.

chapter 1

It was a sign, all right.

Lacey Smithsonian wasn't sure what it meant. Her thoughts were momentarily blocked by soul-shattering thunder. And the lightning bolt that struck the neon Krispy Kreme doughnut sign had also knocked her flat on her butt. From the rain-soaked ground, she watched in horror as the steel-girded doughnut monolith wavered to and fro before crashing down on Harlan Wiedemeyer's brand-new Volvo. The Volvo she had stepped out of less than one minute ago.

I ask for a sign and what do I get? A giant neon sign of doom.

Trujillo's words came back to her: "Watch out. Bad things happen when you hang out with that guy."

The "guy" in question was Harlan Wiedemeyer himself, who had insisted on giving Lacey a ride home from her office to Old Town Alexandria, and then abruptly detoured on a whim to the Krispy Kreme doughnut capital of Northern Virginia.

Wiedemeyer? A jinx? But surely he couldn't be blamed for the storm that brought the lightning that struck the sign that stood on Route 1 that fell on top of the car that Harlan drove? Could he? she wondered. She wiped the dripping curtain of hair out of her face, struggled to her feet, and turned her attention to Wiedemeyer, just emerging from an oily mud puddle.

The little man shook his fist at the sky and shouted, "Missed me!" His thinning brown hair stuck to his head, perspiration mixing with the raindrops. His round belly gave evidence of his love of doughnuts. Some thirty-odd calorie-packed years of doughnuts, Lacey guessed. He looked as if misery hugged his shoulders like a well-worn sweater. He turned to Lacey. Out of his thunderstruck agony, Lacey glimpsed a sliver of triumph.

"Missed me again! Hey, Smithsonian! Did you see that?" A

maniacal grin lit his face in the next flash of lightning. "Why, that sign would have taken our heads clean off if we'd been one minute later! How many poor bastards, do you suppose, die just like that? It's a sign. That's what it is. We're the lucky bastards today! Let's go get some doughnuts."

Lacey could see shapes swarming behind the shop's steamy windows, faces pressed against the glass, staring in shock at their beloved HOT DOUGHNUTS NOW sign, which was now balanced upside down on the crunched roof of the Volvo. The lightning strike had darkened all the lights in the parking lot, but had somehow missed the shop itself. It was still bright and cheery. Lacey shook the excess water off her trench coat. It didn't help. She was sore and soaked to the skin. But hot coffee and a hot glazed puff of calorie heaven were calling to her. She thought she had never needed a doughnut more in her entire life.

"You know, Wiedemeyer, most people would take this as a sign to stop eating doughnuts," Lacey said.

"Stop eating doughnuts? Why, that would just be crazy." He held the door for her. A wave of doughnut aroma washed over them.

Harlan Wiedemeyer was a new *Eye Street Observer* reporter who covered what Lacey's newsroom called the "death-and-dismemberment" beat. He relished telling the world every day how some "poor bastard" died in a freak accident or grotesque workplace disaster. Untold poor bastards drowned in vats of chocolate, were ground up in the gears of heavy machinery, were turned into sausage. So when he escaped the blind wrath of the wayward Krispy Kreme doughnut sign, Harlan Wiedemeyer knew one thing: He was one hell of a lucky bastard.

Lacey Smithsonian, on the other hand, didn't feel quite so graced. Tony Trujillo, her buddy on the cops beat, had warned her not to ride home with Wiedemeyer because he was a Jonah, a jinx, a bringer of bad luck, and if she accepted his offer, woe betide her. She told Trujillo it was a malicious lie, a superstition, a remnant of Dark Ages thinking. And not an hour later she had barely escaped the Krispy Kreme doughnut sign of doom. *Wiedemeyer strikes again,* people would say.

"Pretty damn lucky, huh?" Wiedemeyer elbowed her in the side as the crowd milled around them.

"I'd hold your horses, if I were you, Harlan." Lacey was wondering how she would get home. If Wiedemeyer hadn't insisted on being chivalrous, she would have taken the Metro and been home already, warm and dry and doughnut-free. "I'm not feeling that fortunate right now."

"Yeah, damned lucky, I'd say. Lucky we weren't inside my car. Lucky we weren't squashed like bugs, lucky to be alive," he said with relish. "We should get a couple of dozen doughnuts just to celebrate." He rubbed his hands in anticipation.

"We could have been killed." *Thank you very much*, she added silently, *you Jonah, you*.

"We escape death on a daily basis, Smithsonian. A daily basis, if not an hourly one." His weird mix of fatalism and optimism grated on her last nerve. "Some other poor bastard's number was up today."

She felt a chill that had nothing to do with the storm. Up until now, the October weather had been deliciously warm, but the day had turned cold in a matter of hours. She gave up trying to talk to Wiedemeyer and ordered that cup of coffee and a doughnut, breaking her vow to eat healthier. "Nothing like a little caffeine and sugar to steady your nerves," she said. The sarcasm didn't faze him.

"Good idea, and I'll need a tow truck. You got a cell phone? Mine's in the car. Of course, it may be a while before they lift that sign off my Volvo. Every safety feature known to Swedish science, and look at it. It's totaled for sure. Poor bastard. Ready to be cubed." He observed the damage, clicking his tongue on his teeth before calling his insurance adjuster, with whom he was on a first-name basis. Lacey figured they had a long history.

A Fox Television network van slammed on its brakes outside. A broadcast reporter ran out of the van and through the rain into the Krispy Kreme store, demanding to know whose car lay smashed beneath the doughnut sign. "We were just cruising back from a story to get some hot doughnuts! Pretty lucky, huh?"

"We're all pretty damn lucky tonight," Lacey murmured. She visualized a headline: "Fashion Reporter's Brush with Death—and Doughnuts!" She tried to clean away a streak of mud from her raincoat with a napkin, but succeeded only in adding a streak of doughnut glaze.

A small Asian woman at the counter waved her hand for the Fox newsman like the star pupil. "I saw it. I saw everything. You put me on television?"

The reporter trundled Wiedemeyer and the counter lady outside for a live news bulletin, while Lacey called for a taxi on her cell phone. The dispatcher told her to sit tight, that it would take a while because of the storm. As she hung up, it jingled. *That had better not be Yellow Cab telling me I'm out of luck,* she thought.

"I don't care!" she snapped without even checking the number on her phone's display. "I still need a taxi!"

"Smithsonian? Are you okay? You took a ride from that lunatic! I told you not to do it, Lacey. Now bad luck is going to follow you like a boomerang until you shake him off."

"And a good evening to you, too, Trujillo."

"I guess you're alive, in spite of the Wiedemeyer Effect. So you weren't in the car when it happened?"

"How do you know what happened?" Lacey demanded.

"It's on the news right now. How does Fox do that?" She heard Tony snort into his phone. "It's always something with that guy. A lightning bolt heads straight for Wiedemeyer, misses him, but gets everything around him. Why did he want to take you home anyway?"

"Maybe he's a nice guy," she said, but she knew that wasn't the answer.

"Yeah, sure. The real reason."

"He was pumping me for information about Felicity." She grimaced to herself at the very thought of Felicity Pickles, *The Eye*'s food editor and part-time copy editor. Lacey's least favorite person in the newsroom had just returned to work after a short leave of absence, following the well-publicized demise of her minivan in an explosion outside *The Eye Street Observer*—an explosion meant for Smithsonian. Everyone had known Felicity was back by the aroma of freshly baked brownies and the crowd of hungry reporters swarming around her desk. Felicity Pickles used food as a weapon and a lure, but her ultimate goal, Lacey was certain, was to fatten up everyone in the newsroom until they all looked like Felicity Pickles. With her long, straight auburn hair, round china-blue eyes, and creamy complexion, Felicity had a strange doll-like look. A chubby child's doll with a hidden evil side, like something out of a bad horror movie.

"No kidding? Felicity?" Lacey could almost hear the gears turn in Trujillo's head. "I remember Wiedemeyer was starting to hang around her just about the time her van blew up."

"You're blaming Harlan for the minivan explosion?" That cheered her up, since she'd blamed herself for that.

"Well, no, everyone still blames you, Lacey. But I put my money on the Wiedemeyer Effect as a contributing factor. Wait till everyone hears how he got Krispy Kremed!"

A torrent of rain was still gushing out of the sky, and more curious onlookers were flooding the store and lining up at the counter, strangers who were now bonding over another stranger's misfortune. And hot doughnuts. "Tony, how did you know it was his car?"

"It's on TV. The 'poor bastard's' license plate." Harlan's Virginia plate read PRBSTRD, in honor, he said, of all the poor loser bastards in this world with no one to memorialize their passing but Harlan Wiedemeyer. "Besides, he just talked to the Fox reporter. On camera."

She groaned. Wiedemeyer was trudging back into the store and making a purchase at the counter. "I have to go, Tony. My jinx is here. I'll catch you tomorrow." She hung up.

Wiedemeyer pulled up a chair next to Lacey, took a moment to contemplate his doughnuts, then popped one into his mouth and swallowed it whole. He moaned with audible pleasure. Lacey averted her eyes and looked at her watch.

"You're not sorry you let me drive you home, are you?" he asked.

"Well, Harlan, I'm not dead. But I'm not exactly home either." She closed her eyes and sipped her coffee, hoping he would be gone when she opened them. He was looking a little worried, as if he knew what Trujillo had said.

"I know what they say about me. It's not true, you know. I am not a jinx. Someone probably told you that, right?" She opened her eyes. He was still there. "I mean, who knows how these silly rumors get started?" Another lightning bolt lit the sky, followed by a tremendous crash of thunder. Wiedemeyer flinched. "It's just ridiculous to say something so ignorant in the twenty-first century. I mean, that's like saying some poor bastard here is going to fall into a vat of hot doughnut grease just because I walked into the store, right?" He reminded her of a chubby-cheeked chipmunk. He might even be considered cute by some women. *If they closed one eye,* she thought. *And if they thought Sleeping Beauty was a fool not to hook up with one of those cute single dwarves. Harlan's dwarf name would be Lucky.*

"Better gulp down that doughnut, Harlan. Some poor bastard's heading for the grease right now."

He laughed, took another bite, and followed his own thoughts. "So I was wondering, Smithsonian, what is . . . um . . . what is Felicity Pickles really like?"

Oh, here it comes again. "I'm not really the person to ask." *I can't stand her. The less I know about her the happier I am.* "I don't really know her."

"But you sit right next to her," Wiedemeyer insisted.

"Remember when her minivan exploded last month, Harlan?"

He nodded. "Boy, that was something, wasn't it?"

"She blames me for that."

Relief washed over Wiedemeyer's round little features like the rain on the windows. "You're kidding! I was sure she blamed me! Because of . . . well, you know." Lacey stirred her coffee. "I guess you're telling me you're not the best of friends."

"She was trying to steal my beat and it backfired on her. Scratch one minivan."

"Who wouldn't want to steal your beat, Lacey? It's dangerous and exciting."

"It shouldn't be. I'm the fashion reporter. Remember? Danger is *not* my business. It's yours."

"Yeah, but you make it so much more. All those killers! Felicity probably just envies you all the excitement."

"Not anymore. Felicity hates my guts."

Wiedemeyer sighed. "Felicity." The way he caressed Felicity Pickles's name made it clear he did not see her as the malevolent cookie pusher and vicious copy slasher with whom Lacey was only too well acquainted. "She is such a substantial woman. And she's got such a big . . . Well, she's substantial."

That's one word for her, Lacey thought, but did not say. She merely nodded. It struck her then that Harlan Wiedemeyer was one poor love-struck bastard. And it was probably the last thing on earth he would want anyone else to know.

"She's just got such a big . . . such a great big well of sweetness waiting to be unleashed," Wiedemeyer mused. Lacey nearly choked on her doughnut. She did not want to see any part of Felicity unleashed. "Is she . . . is she seeing anyone at the moment?" He inhaled another doughnut.

"No, I don't think so." Lacey really had no idea. She and her nemesis never chitchatted, though inevitably she overheard a few tidbits. The only personal information she recalled was that Felicity lived alone with a couple of fat, lazy felines named Custard and Mustard or Brownie and Blondie or something like that. "Oh, Harlan, you really like her, don't you?"

Wiedemeyer ducked her glance and stared intently into his coffee while Lacey watched his rather large ears turn red. "I don't know . . . she's, well . . . What would she see in me?"

Lacey turned her gaze to the ceiling and rolled her eyes. "Or vice versa. You're too good for her, Harlan. Too . . . um . . . nice."

He reached for another chocolate-sprinkled doughnut.

"You're right; she's out of my league." He was a miserable man. "I'm such a dumb bastard."

"That's not what I meant, Harlan. You *are* too good for Felicity Pickles. That is exactly what I mean." At the sound of a taxi honking, Lacey touched his arm lightly. "My ride is here. I'll see you tomorrow." She gathered up her things. "Maybe you should just ask her out."

"I don't know. A woman like Felicity . . . Gee, this has been great, Lacey. Can we talk like this again?"

Lacey ran for the door as another thunderbolt rattled the windows.

chapter 2

"Lacey, *cher,* you there? Marie Largesse here, y'all's friendly neighborhood psychic."

Lacey braced herself for whatever wacky prediction du jour her friend Marie had left on the answering machine. Usually it had something to do with the weather.

"I'm feeling in my bones a heavy storm's gonna knock you on your fanny—so to speak. Maybe you should wear those padded bike shorts. Ah, that's not your style, is it?"

"I doubt it," Lacey said aloud to her machine. She shook her head and squeezed the moisture out of her hair and realized her knees hurt. She lifted her skirt to see that they were scraped and her hose were torn. "Kneepads would be more like—"

"And here's the thing," Marie's recorded voice continued. "I'm feeling there's some kind of jinx whirling 'round your head, trying to latch onto you, so you be careful, hear? I know you don't believe me; sometimes I don't believe myself. But there you go. A jinx grabs onto your astral body, it's got to be redirected back from whence it came. Like a lighting bolt hitting a mirror."

"Thanks, Marie." Lacey shook her head and reminded herself that Marie was usually wrong, and besides, she was never quite sure what on earth the soothsayer meant.

"Y'all come on by the Little Shop of Horus; I'll do a reading for you. With Halloween around the corner it's a madhouse, but you're always welcome. Maybe I'll start carrying those bike pants. Bye-bye now." The machine beeped to end her message.

Lacey rolled her eyes and willed Marie's words out of her head. She was a dear, but after dodging the lightning bolt with Wiedemeyer, Lacey was anxious just to forget it all. Besides, Marie's psychic warning was too late—and too cryptic—to help.

Lacey turned from the answering machine to watch lightning

strikes hitting the Potomac River. There was a lovely view from the French doors of her balcony. But her soaked clothing was sticking to her skin, and she was desperate to get into something dry. She stripped on her way to the bedroom and tossed her wet clothing into the tub. She slipped into some jeans and a soft red sweater, grabbed a towel for her wet hair, and then stood by the windows and allowed herself to be mesmerized again by the drama outside. In between thunderbolts and lightning, she heard a knocking at her door. Aware that she might look like a drowned cat after her rainy afternoon's adventure, she wiped her face, hoping her makeup hadn't streaked.

Through the peephole she saw the one man who could give her heart palpitations without an actual lightning bolt required. Vic Donovan.

He would choose this moment to show up. When I'm feeling about as seductive as a mud puddle, she thought, but she smiled to herself anyway. Lacey opened the door with one hand and held the wet towel in the other. Vic Donovan took her in with one long, dangerous look. His grass-green eyes were amused, his cocky grin revealing beautiful white teeth. His hair was wet, and his dark locks curled enticingly on his forehead, like a Heathcliff who had just ridden in from the rainy moors.

"Get caught in the storm, Lacey?"

"That keen private-eye observational skill slays me every time."

"You're dripping. I'd be happy to help towel you off." She chuckled and backed away. "That's no way to greet a weary traveler," he said. "By the way, you'd look beautiful in nothing but a wet towel."

She pulled him inside the apartment and closed the door behind him. "Shut up and kiss me, you wet fool." Sprinkling her with rainwater from his curls and clothing, he swept her into his arms and tightened them around her. Vic Donovan kissed her like a cowboy back from a long, hard ride on the range, and he looked like one as well in his tight jeans and scuffed cowboy boots. Under his beat-up black leather jacket, he wore an old blue denim shirt. The buttons were strained taut across his chest.

Lacey never really felt small until she was wrapped in Vic's arms and looking up at him. She was five-foot-five in her stocking feet, next to his muscular six feet. She pulled away and tossed him the towel.

"A call would have been nice."

"And ruin the surprise? I just wanted to make sure you hadn't gotten into any more trouble since last week."

"What kind of trouble could I possibly get into?"

He cocked an eye at her. "I'm sure I'll find out. Did you know the front door of your building is wide open?"

"Broken. Just try getting something fixed around here."

They had just come to the decision to revive their long-frustrated romance and try to take it to another level. But Vic's business was getting in the way. There always seemed to be something pulling them apart. And he was unhappy about her recent accidental involvement in crime solving. "Leave it to the professionals," was Vic's rule.

He had recently returned from Steamboat Springs, Colorado, where he sold his home to his ex-wife, who was now divorced again—and available. At the thought of Montana McCandless Donovan Schmidt, Lacey could feel her upper lip curl. Vic had made it back from Colorado just in time for Gloria Adams's long-delayed funeral the previous weekend, a funeral that Lacey had sworn would be a new beginning. And Vic Donovan was a big part of Lacey's new personal love-life makeover plan.

After years as a small-town cop and finally chief of police, Vic was now working for his dad, who had retired from the Pentagon to set up one of the most well-connected security firms in the Washington area. Vic was involved in running a big project that made huge demands on his time and pulled him away at odd hours. Worse, he said he couldn't discuss it. Lacey assumed it was contract work for the Department of Homeland Security, but she couldn't drag a word out of him. She made a mental note to revise her interrogation methods. They had been doing way too much talking anyway.

"Before I make a fool of myself, Lacey, I want to get one thing straight. About Jeffrey Bentley Holmes. Is he going to get in our way?"

"We were just friends." She didn't know what to think about Jeffrey. "And it's rather awkward after the rather untidy exposé I wrote about his family." She winced at the memory.

"You have to factor those things into the risk assessment when you date a reporter."

"Oh, really." She raised an eyebrow at him. "What have you factored into your risk assessment?"

"That the benefits outweigh the risks. I think."

"Very funny."

"About Holmes . . ."

Lacey had received a letter the other day from Jeffrey Bentley Holmes, nephew of the famous designer Hugh Bentley, following her latest story on the Gloria Adams murder. He said it was painful for the family dirty laundry to be aired in public, but it had been done before and no doubt would be again, and he held no grudges. She wasn't sure whether she believed him.

Mother is hospitalized under psychiatric care for the foreseeable future, Jeffrey wrote. *Uncle Hugh has decided it would be better that I distance myself from the Bentley name, Cousin Aaron no longer talks to me, Aunt Marilyn refuses to speak my name. Only the lawyers are speaking to other lawyers, and there has been talk of my disinheritance. So, as you see, things are looking up. My retreat here at the monastery has offered a most needed respite, but I soon will have to decide what to do next.* Lacey hadn't written back yet. She didn't know what to say.

Vic waited for her answer.

"Darling, there is nothing between me and Jeffrey."

"I saw you kiss him."

"He kissed me. There is a difference, and besides, you hadn't called or written for months while you were out of pocket in Steamboat. What's a girl to do?"

"I'm not a letter writer," he protested. "And we're talking about *now*. Next time I'll be sure to use the Pony Express." She raised her eyebrow again. "And e-mail. I'll e-mail. But Lacey . . ." His green eyes were warm as he reached and pulled her into a kiss so deep that she forgot what she was doing. "Don't go around kissing anyone but me, okay?"

"Okay." *Who else would I want to kiss?*

A tremendous bolt of lightning flashed outside. Vic moved swiftly through the living room. He opened the French doors to the covered balcony to take advantage of the stunning view of the sheets of rain and the sky still bright with beating thunderbolts, their clean white strikes arcing into the river. He stepped outside. "Some storm, huh?"

"I ordered it special for you." She stood at the open door.

Vic took hold of her hand and pulled her next to him, holding her close while she shivered. "I've been thinking, Lacey. We should really get away for a while."

Her heart jumped. "You want to get away? *You* and *me?* Are you talking about you and me—*together?*"

"I think it's time, don't you?" He tilted her face up and met her eyes. "I want us together pretty badly, and I get a feeling you do too." There was no denying that she wanted to be with Vic, but she had never heard him say it so plainly before. "We've waited long enough." He leaned in and kissed her forehead, then her cheek and her neck, raising her temperature and sending chills through her at the same time. "And if we don't do it soon, I'll be up to my ears in this new contract. And then we'll both, you know—explode. It'll be messy."

"Well . . ." She hesitated. It was complicated. Although he had flirted with her mercilessly the entire two years she worked in Sagebrush, Colorado, they had never dated there. Back then he was the chief of police, and she was the cops reporter on the tiny daily newspaper: a slight conflict of interest. There had been enormous sexual tension between them, but Vic was in the middle of a divorce from the infamous Montana—and Lacey refused to consider him while he was married. "Straitlaced," he had called it; "high standards," she had replied.

"I've waited for you for six years, Lacey."

"Technically, I'm not so sure you've been waiting, Vic Donovan," she countered. "And I certainly haven't been exactly—"

"Now you shut up." He kissed her again.

Catching her breath, she said, "Okay. What exactly did you have in mind?"

"Something romantic, preferably somewhere you can't run away from me."

"Me? Run away?" Of course, she had run away once from a man—not Vic—who asked her to marry him, and they were probably still talking about it back in Sagebrush.

"You'll like it." He grinned at her and his hands moved up the small of her back. "We'll go away for the weekend. Before Halloween." She opened her mouth to speak, but he cut her off. "I know a place. I'll take care of everything. You think you can stay out of trouble until then?" He kissed her neck.

"What do you mean, trouble?"

"Oh, you know, dead bodies, crazed killers, running with scissors, that sort of thing."

"Those were just freak occurrences. Besides, it's going to be a very simple week. I only have to interview one diva supermodel introducing her new line of clothing, which I very much doubt she had anything to do with. A major snoozefest. How dangerous can it be?" Then she thought of something else, and a look must have crossed her face.

"What? What is it?"

"Well, it's only a rumor, but this supermodel, Amanda Manville, has kind of a reputation."

"As what?" He was wearing his cop face. He looked suspicious.

Lacey didn't want to say, *Amanda Manville has a reputation as a killer.* It might set him off. She cleared her throat. "Nothing. I'm sure it's nothing."

"Lacey, I'm waiting," Vic said, his green eyes locked on hers. She could see how suspects would spill their guts to him.

"There's a rumor, and it's never been confirmed, probably because it's not true, right? It's totally a supermarket-tabloid story, and there never has been a body or charges or indictments or anything, but Amanda Manville is supposed to have, um . . . killed, um . . . an old boyfriend."

"You're making this up," he said, doubt still wavering behind his eyes. "You're yanking my chain."

"Your chain should be so lucky, big fella. And I try not to make up what I report. I work for *The Eye Street Observer,* after all. Not *The New York Times.* But I thought you would like to know about Ms. Manville. As I said, it's only a rumor. Completely unfounded, I'm sure." *I hope. I'll call Miguel in New York tomorrow. He'll know.*

"Are you sure, Lacey?" He stroked her cheek with his fingers. She marveled at how such large hands could be so gentle. "Because I really want to see you in one incredibly sexy piece by the end of the week."

"Incredibly sexy?" He kissed her so hard her toes curled. "Silly boy, what could possibly happen?" *Indeed, how many murders could possibly happen in one lifetime that I could possibly get involved with? I figure I'm done.* He kissed her again. *Incredibly sexy, huh?*

Vic laughed. "What could happen? With you on the story? Oh, darlin', don't get me started." He gave Lacey another kiss and then zipped up his jacket. "I have to go."

"Go? You can't go now!"

"It's tearing me up, honey, but there's this last-minute job I have to take over, a big surveillance for Dad."

"But you just got here. Come on, you're exhausted. You need to rest. Lie down. Prolonged bed rest is what Dr. Smithsonian orders."

"Smile and think of me, Doc. And be careful." He turned and

kissed her again before walking out the door. She admired his well-muscled flanks as he sauntered down the hall. He turned and saluted her, flashing a devastating smile before stepping onto the elevator. "I'll be thinking of you."

Isn't that just like a man? Gets you all hot and bothered and then waltzes right out the door.

chapter 3

"How do you do it, Smithsonian? The attack of the killer dough-nut sign, and there you are, right alongside the staff trouble mag-net!"

Douglas MacArthur Jones's deep voice greeted her. Lacey's boss, "Mac" to everyone who knew him, held up the front page of *The Eye Street Observer,* featuring a photo of the famous HOT DOUGHNUTS NOW sign, angled upside down, looking like a piece of modern sculpture rising out of Harlan Wiedemeyer's vanquished Volvo. Wiedemeyer was standing next to it, holding several boxes of Krispy Kreme delicacies and wearing a silly grin on his face.

"Great photo, Mac. So I'm not the staff trouble magnet any-more? Wiedemeyer stole my title?"

"You're trouble, all right. But compared to Wiedemeyer, you're small potatoes." Mac was wearing a blue ink stain below the pocket of his peach-colored short-sleeved dress shirt, where a pen had exploded. The purple madras-plaid tie didn't quite go with the shirt or the ink stain, and his pants were an inexplicable bright blue, as though they'd been cut from a beach umbrella. Though he was in the presence of the newspaper's resident fashion expert, or what passed for one in Washington, she knew he wouldn't appre-ciate her advice. Mac, who was editor of *The Eye,* merely shook his head and handed over the newspaper. He always reminded Lacey of a black G. Gordon Liddy, similar in mustache and eye-brows and polished dome, but the polar opposite in politics.

"It was Harlan's car, not mine. He gets all the glory. This time." Lacey headed to her desk while Mac followed.

"Too bad you weren't in the photo. We could start a collection. The Smithsonian portfolio."

"Sure. All I need is another ridiculously silly photo of me in the paper."

"You got fans. I'm not so sure about Wiedemeyer. Not even all those 'poor bastards' he keeps talking about. Of course, most of them are dead. But you, Lacey—you take a good picture."

Lacey was still smarting from her last picture. Taken by her hairstylist, Stella, of all people, it had appeared on the front page of her paper the previous month. She was caught wearing a great designer dress and brandishing an antique Victorian sword cane, technically known, she'd been told, as a "flick stick," while fending off an enraged killer at a prestigious fashion gala. *I looked like a maniac. Great dress, though.*

"That Stella could have a new career," Mac goaded.

"It was sheer luck," Lacey said. Stella was still glorying in her moment of fame.

"She has a talent for being in the right place at the right time."

"What about me?"

"You somehow always manage to be in the wrong place at the wrong time."

Unfortunately, that seemed true enough. The photo was a sensation on DeadFed dot com, the local all-conspiracy-theories-all-the-time Web site that had a host of crazed devotees, including her best friend, Brooke Barton. The photo had even reached Colorado and elicited an urgent long-distance phone call of concern from her mother. Lacey tried never to upset her mother, who inevitably offered a little unasked-for advice. *Unasked-for, uncalled-for, and unending.*

"Too bad, circulation went up with that one," Mac said. "Speaking of which, that photo for the head of your column—"

"We weren't speaking about it, Mac. It's an unspeakable idea." Lacey settled down at her desk and turned on her computer, all the better to ignore her e-mail.

"We need to speak about it." Mac made himself comfortable perched on the edge of her desk. "*The Eye* is getting a makeover, in case you hadn't heard. A whole new look. New layout. New graphic design, new features, new columns, new beats. Our consultants tell me all columns are to feature a photo of the writer at the head. Next to your byline."

"That's not new, Mac! It is so 1950s, and I hate the Fifties, the era of female bondage. And a reporter's copy ought to stand on its own two feet, not on who has the cutest little yearbook photo next to their name. Besides, it'll make us look like a bunch of boring talking heads, like one of those yammering news-talk shows this town is infamous for."

He leaned close in confidence. "Now, I personally think this makeover nonsense is a stupid idea, and an expensive idea, but those high-priced consultants have sold the idea to our boss lady."

"Claudia?" Lacey liked Claudia Darnell, the publisher, but once she had an idea, it was pretty much cast in concrete. "Why on earth—"

"They say it will put a friendlier face on the news. Warmer. Fuzzier."

Lacey growled at the very idea.

"That's not a friendlier face." Mac chuckled. Lacey ignored him and looked for a fresh notebook and her favorite pen. "With your 'Crimes of Fashion' column, maybe you could wear a trench coat, deerstalker hat, magnifying glass, stalking the wild fashion criminal, that sort of thing." Mac was most dangerous when he was being creative.

"No picture, Mac." She glared at him. *He is getting all the wrong ideas about my fashion beat,* Lacey thought. *And my column.* "I mean it."

"Think about it; you'll like it. Besides, you're, what's the word? Photogenic. You'll have the best picture in the paper. As long as you keep your eyes open." Lacey snorted. Mac suddenly inhaled deeply and turned at the aroma of freshly baked cinnamon muffins approaching from behind him. Felicity Pickles, food editor and carbohydrate pusher, chose that moment to offer Mac her platter of cinnamon muffins. Wearing a wilted, faded pink, sleeveless organdy dress, Felicity looked like the last rose of summer. Mac selected the largest one with the most icing. He favored her with the kind of smile he rarely gave to Lacey. A sugar-high smile.

Mac's wife, Kim, was trying to get him to watch his weight and his blood pressure. But Kim wasn't there, and Felicity's muffin was. He munched off down the hall. Lacey knew he would blithely ignore any good advice she might offer. So she didn't try.

Felicity offered her wares to Lacey with a crocodile smile and those glassy blue eyes. "Try one. You'll like it." It was nearly impossible for Lacey to keep in shape, especially in Washington, where work kept most people's butts in their chairs all day, and stress and long working hours encouraged bad eating habits. And there was Felicity, making it a little harder. Fresh air and exercise seemed to be for other people, like the President and his Secret Service detail, forever pounding around the White House running track in their sweats. *He thinks he's got stress,* Lacey thought. *He doesn't have Felicity.*

The cinnamon buns were just a symbol of the war between them, as the food editor sought desperately to win friends and fatten them up in one fell swoop, Lacey surmised. *Before dragging them off to her gingerbread house in the woods.* In that case, Wiedemeyer would make a tasty morsel for Felicity, the Gingerbread Witch. Lacey shuddered at the thought. Of course, with the Wiedemeyer Effect in the picture, could an exploding stove be far behind? *Headline: "Mysterious Blaze Guts Gingerbread House in Woods. Fire Investigators Blame 'Bad Luck.'"*

Lacey couldn't mistake the hostility behind the gesture and Felicity's recent attempt to steal her beat. Felicity couldn't forget that her minivan was bombed because somebody thought she was Lacey Smithsonian, even though it was her own fault for trying to steal a story from Lacey, and the effort blew up in her face, so to speak.

"No, thanks, I'm trying to quit," Lacey said. She thought again of Harlan Wiedemeyer and his forlorn crush on Felicity. "Why don't you offer one to Wiedemeyer?" She waved down the hall toward the death-and-dismemberment beat.

It was an offhand comment, but Felicity blushed and turned away quickly. *A blush? Could it be that Felicity likes Harlan Wiedemeyer?* But Felicity just said, "Harlan already brought in a box of doughnuts."

"I guess you two have something in common then." *Food and destroyed vehicles,* Lacey thought. "Maybe you could trade."

"I don't think so." Felicity snatched up her goodies and scurried away, clearly hoping to find someone more grateful than Lacey Smithsonian.

She turned her mind to work and pawed through her desk looking for her notes. Interviewing Amanda Manville, the famous celebrity model who was introducing a new line of clothing that she allegedly had designed herself, was slightly intimidating. Ms. Manville was certain to be a masterpiece of physical perfection, no doubt wearing some wispy outfit that flattered her tall yet supermodel-svelte body.

Next to a perfectly manufactured beauty like Amanda, Lacey was afraid she'd look short and frumpy. She needed both to look her best and to be on her guard, particularly if the celebrated supermodel was also a manslaughterer, as rumored. And Vic's reaction to her nervous babbling had reminded her just how little she really knew about Amanda Manville.

She called Miguel Flores, her fashion-industry-insider friend, who was freelancing as a clothing stylist for fashion shoots in New York. He had worked for years for the House of Bentley, and he knew everyone. He would have the inside skinny on any skinny supermodel Lacey could name.

"Hey, doll! What's up? God, I've missed you! And how's Stella? Sorry I couldn't make the funeral, but I hate funerals anyway. All those little black dresses, and not a cocktail in sight."

"Missed you too, darling. Stella is Stella, as always. And I've got a question for you. What's the dish on Amanda Manville?"

"Ah, the *prima* prima donna. Would you like that dish baked or barbecued?"

"How about the straight story?"

"Please, how dull. And straight is *so* not my forte. Besides, when it comes to Amanda, who knows what's fact or fiction? She goes through stylists, hair, clothes, and otherwise, as if they were Kleenex. Use once, throw away. Everybody up here has some outrageous Amanda story, even people who usually have to make them up."

"So she's temperamental?" Lacey leafed through her files to find the press release on Amanda Manville's collection.

"Some people think that. Personally, I think she's a screaming psycho. Between you and me, she's a bitch slapper, and that hasn't been popular with underlings since indentured servitude went out of style."

"But she always seemed so sweet on TV."

"Ah, but that was before the makeover. Apparently she got a new soul as well. Or she sold the old one."

"Could make for an interesting interview. Will I need a bullet-proof vest?"

"And a sword cane. You *are* uniquely qualified to interview her, come to think of it."

Lacey laughed. "So, her new collection. Did she really design it herself?" She was jotting down notes as they talked. She found the errant press release, with her note on the time and place for her interview, and stashed it in her purse.

"Oh, please. Do politicians write their own books? And you, of all people, should know how designers—some designers, that is—launch their careers. Thieves, the lot of them. Though I hear the collection cost her investors enough, it should at least be worth seeing."

"And Miguel, what's the story on the old boyfriend? Caleb

Collingwood, I think the name was. The one she's supposed to have killed?"

"Everyone swears it's true, only no one knows anything."

"No corpse?" Lacey asked.

"No corpse, no cops, no charges. But we certainly enjoy making it all up."

"What about motive? For getting rid of him?"

"Too ugly to live. I'm serious."

"What? That's terrible."

"It's just what they say. Don't blame me for being shallow; I'm a product of my environment. It's the rumor. Or one of them, anyway. Suicide is another popular theory. Too boring, I say. Anyway, after she had the surgery, he didn't measure up anymore. Amanda was, like, instant Ariel, and he was still the same old Caliban. He wouldn't go away, so he had to, ahem, go away. So they say— Yikes, my client is here early! That never happens. Gotta go. Kiss-kiss."

Lacey stared at the phone for a moment after Miguel hung up. She had chosen that morning to go with a vaguely 1940s look, her favorite. Her hairstylist, Stella Lake, once pointed out that the Lacey Smithsonian signature style was a combination of Rosie the Riveter and *His Girl Friday*: "Brains, beauty, and no bullshit," in Stella's memorable phrase. Lacey had to admit that Stella had her number. She had selected her vintage forest-green wool-gabardine suit, nipped in at the waist, with a delicate lace hankie tucked into the pocket and secured with a porcelain rose pin. She wore her three-strand pearl necklace and pearl studs in her ears. Her soft light brown hair, highlighted with blond strands, swung around her shoulders, a look reminiscent of early Lauren Bacall, but with more volume and presence. Stella was so good at this cut that Lacey had started to call it "the Bacall," although Stella herself just called it "the usual." Lacey thought she'd pass inspection with nearly everyone; everyone except, perhaps, the perfect psycho, Amanda Manville.

I'll just have to stay out of slapping distance, she told herself.

Lacey bent over her bottom desk drawer and heard another familiar voice mocking her.

"Hey, Lois Lane, still in one piece? I see we are wearing our vintage bravado today." Her glance traveled from the desk drawer where she kept her notebooks to the black lizard cowboy boots that stood by her desk.

"Morning, Trujillo." She straightened up in her chair. Tony Trujillo looked good, as always, with his inquisitive almond eyes and beautiful New Mexico copper skin.

"You win the prize for making it through the night after a trip home with the Wiedemeyer."

"He didn't actually take me home. I gave that pleasure to a Yellow Cab."

"Smart move. I was worried, Supergirl."

Lacey appraised his expression. Perhaps he *was* a bit worried underneath the sly smile, which revealed his perfect set of straight white choppers. "I'm fine, Tony. Really. Thank you for your concern. By the way, do you know anything about this Amanda . . ."

The aroma of the cinnamon-spiced air hijacked Trujillo's attention. Felicity had returned bearing her tray of buns. He reached for a gooey glazed treat and dazzled her with his smile. "Ooh, *muchas gracias!* I've missed you, Felicidad."

Felicity melted. "Oh, Tony. Take another."

Lacey decided she'd schmooze Trujillo later, after his carbohydrate buzz wore off. But before she left for her interview she wanted to know something.

"Felicity, what are the names of your cats again?"

"Hansel and Gretel. They were orphaned in the woods, and I found them and lured them home with a trail of tuna." Felicity practically purred with pride. She indicated their framed photos on her desk.

Aha! I knew it. She is *a gingerbread witch.*

"Oh, Lacey, you'd love them; they're just adorable."

And so well fed, I'll wager. Here, kitty, kitty, time for dinner!

Lacey retreated to the staff kitchen for a cup of coffee and ran into the newspaper's new resident storm cloud, Cassandra Wentworth, the latest addition to Mac's oh-so-important editorial writers at *The Eye.*

Cassandra was helping herself to a sort of herbal swill, something that would obviously be good for her but taste worse than medicine. She had no time for pleasure. She dealt with the more important issues of the day. Ms. Wentworth raised an eyebrow at Lacey's presence, but politely said hello anyway. Lacey was reaching for the brackish, though caffeinated, brew that passed for coffee at *The Eye.*

"That stuff will kill you." Cassandra made a nasty face.

Just the sort of face you want to see first thing in the morning. Lacey lifted her cup in a salute. "To each her own."

Peter Johnson, *The Eye's* congressional reporter, stumbled into the kitchen with his usual grace, wearing a sloppy khaki suit. His tie was askew and boldly sported various shades of mud and eggplant, and possibly a bit of breakfast. His permanent-press shirt was wrinkled. *How does he do that?* Lacey wondered. He glared at her through glasses sliding halfway down his nose, then turned his back on her.

"Morning, Peter," she said. "What, no news on Capitol Hill?"

He ignored her while searching for a clean cup in the cupboard. He found a dusty one and blew the dust out before helping himself silently to the java. "They're in recess," Cassandra said, her eyes following the slumped-over curve of Johnson's back with a look of unmistakable admiration and longing. She appeared to stifle a sigh.

What? Lacey wondered. *Cassandra, prophetess of doom, with a crush on our cranky congressional reporter?* The high-and-mighty Johnson was single, and so was the serious Ms. Wentworth, but the image of the two of them together was too weird for Lacey to wrap her brain around.

"That's right, Smithsonian," he growled. "Recess. Guess you can't trespass on my beat this week."

"You wound me, Peter. But I am charmed that you think your beat is so special," Lacey replied with a smirk. "And that you consider me a threat."

"You're no threat. You're a menace."

"Oh, you're so wrong, Peter. I'm both."

He was about to sneer some limp retort when his eyes met Cassandra's, who quickly tore her eyes away from him and gazed down into her poisonous herbal goo. Johnson seemed to forget all about Lacey and to lose the ability to speak. But when she caught him staring at Cassandra with what seemed to be fond affection, he grabbed his coffee and bolted. His rapid exit left Cassandra sighing out loud as she stared at his retreating figure.

Was it really possible that these two unlikely specimens *liked* each other? Lacey wondered. *Mixed signals? Furtive glances? Halting words? Ah, yes, romance is in the air, D.C. style. Call the Pentagon; the pheromone jammers are down again.* But was it her job to set these two straight? Of course not.

"So what's on the fashion agenda for today?" Cassandra said *fashion* as if it were a week-old fish Lacey was mysteriously required to gut. "Something important? The height of hems? The new black? The old black? Plum lipstick is the new pink blush?"

"Sounds like you're more up-to-date than I am. I thought pink was actually pink. Silly me."

Lacey did not blame Cassandra for her disdain. She had felt the same way before she inherited the accursed fashion beat from the former fashion editor, Mariah "the Pariah" Morgan, who had very inconveniently died in her chair at her keyboard and practiced her rigor mortis for some hours before anyone noticed she wasn't typing, or moving, or breathing, or finishing her feature for the next day's edition. Just as Mac was realizing the ramifications of not having a warm body in the fashion chair, junior hard-news reporter L. B. "Lacey" Smithsonian had wandered through his field of vision wearing something that looked like an actual style statement: instant fashion reporter.

Mac had no conception of fashion, other than dreadful descriptions of dreary Washington dresses wrapped around department-store advertising. But he also was a man of swift decisions, and Lacey was soon shanghaied to the fashion beat, kicking and screaming, where she demanded at least the dignity of a chair in which no one had died. Now she had the pleasure of listening to others who thought they were superior to her because they had better news assignments and loftier moral opinions—and prematurely serious wardrobes in festive shades of beige, gray, and taupe. And Mariah's death chair was still there, floating around the newsroom like the Ancient Mariner. The last time Lacey had seen it, Wiedemeyer had commandeered it for a meeting.

However, after a few years on the fashion beat and some exciting forays into the darker side of dressing oneself, Lacey was beginning to understand her beat on a new level. Fashion could be a kind of peephole into a person's psyche.

Lacey examined Cassandra's style vibe over her coffee cup and saw that she was all about being taken seriously, from her straight middle-part haircut to her horn-rimmed glasses and shapeless burlap-brown sack of a dress that hid her thin frame. Heaven forbid that makeup should offend the intellectual purity of the sallow complexion, the pale lashes, or the lily-livered lips. She was plain to start with and clearly proud of continuing the tradition.

"I'm interviewing Amanda Manville." Cassandra looked blank, so Lacey continued. "She was a noted ugly duckling who underwent some radical plastic surgery on *The Chrysalis Factor,* that reality makeover show a couple of years back. Now she's a celebrity supermodel." Cassandra blinked, wide-eyed, and for just a moment Lacey thought that perhaps a makeover might uncover even her hidden attributes. But then Cassandra's eyes narrowed in suspicion. *Nah. Hidden too deep,* Lacey concluded.

Cassandra shuddered. "That is just so wrong on so many levels."

"What, being a supermodel?"

"The whole plastic-surgery-on-television thing, mocking people for their looks, turning women into these plastic caricatures of themselves."

"It changed her life."

"And what does that tell us?" Cassandra editorialized. "That we have to be beautiful to be successful?"

"But those shows have done other things, good things. They've corrected birth defects, cleft palates, facial deformities," Lacey protested, wondering why she was even bothering to argue with Cassandra. *It's the caffeine talking.*

"For the cheap entertainment of millions." Cassandra's disdain was palpable.

Lacey stared into her hot coffee. She remembered her eyes tearing up when a woman on *The Chrysalis Factor* saw her beautiful new mouth and teeth for the first time in her life. *You're a wuss, Smithsonian,* she scolded herself. And Lacey had cried for the women who had reconstructive surgery after breast cancer. She suddenly realized she had cried over Amanda Manville's amazing transformation as well. *Too wussy to be a hard-news reporter?*

"It is immoral," Cassandra stated plainly. "God, Smithsonian, how can you be so complicit in this evil?"

"I'm being paid for it. But what about our innate love of beauty? It's hardwired into our brains," Lacey protested. "Even yours." *She'll love that one.*

"Speak for yourself, Ms. S." Cassandra Wentworth had enough moral superiority for an entire newsroom of reporters, Lacey wanted to say, but didn't. She figured it was tough enough being Cassandra: Everything she did, or said, or put into her mouth presented a morally or politically correct decision—whether to eat white bread or wheat, take the Metro or drive, buy animal cruelty–free products or torture small furry creatures for the sake of a little blush on her cheeks. And her editorials, did anybody read them? *Not even Mac on a slow news day, I bet.*

"Have a pleasant day, Cassandra," she said to the rigid figure who was stalking out of the kitchen in righteous indignation.

But before she left, Cassandra turned to her and moaned, "How can you be blithe when there is so much poverty in the world?"

Lacey shrugged and returned to her desk to reread a file of news clips about Amanda Manville—and to try to banish Cassandra's depressing oracle of the moral depravity of wanting to bring the world a little more beauty. Lacey's snarky "Crimes of Fashion" column certainly had more readers than Cassandra's editorials. But if Cassandra Wentworth was the new look the paper was going for, Lacey knew her fashion beat was in no danger of ever being taken seriously at *The Eye Street Observer.*

Lacey felt like exploring Cassandra's lament with a small bite of copy, a "Fashion Bite," to be exact, which allowed her to toss off brief and brash fashion opinions in print. She was sure her editor thought of these as "bite-sized" fashion columns. Lacey preferred to think of "Fashion Bites" as a complete sentence, with a subject and a verb.

"Makeover Madness" wasn't quite enough to fill a whole "Crimes of Fashion" column, Lacey decided, but it would be perfect for a "Fashion Bite." Maybe, she thought, she should thank Cassandra for the inspiration? *Nah, no way.*

Lacey Smithsonian's

FASHION BITES

Makeover Madness: Knowing When You've Gone Too Far

Make-me-over madness is running rampant through the land, on television and in magazines and newspapers. Now, nobody likes a good makeover better than I do. Whether it's new clothes, fresh makeup, or a dramatically different hairdo, discovering a brilliant new style can give you a new lease on life, open up your horizons, and unleash your true creativity. At least it can make you feel like a different woman, and sometimes that's all a gal needs, right?

A great makeover can help a woman discover her potential, look more appropriate at her job, and realize how attractive she can be. The perfect haircut can help her appear dramatic, or sexy, or more professional. Great makeup can emphasize the cheekbones and eyes and define the mouth: *Wow, I'm really Greta Garbo after all.* And the right clothes, as a saleslady once said to me, can cover up your negatives, honey, and really show off your positives. Thinking positive is good, right?

But suddenly, going too far is never far enough. People are going mad for the full-body makeover, from tip to toe, and maybe we should be wondering: Are we turning ourselves into better versions of ourselves—or just blander versions of everyone else?

How do you know when you've gone too far?

- You look like an android. And all the androids want to look like you.

- You can no longer move the muscles in your face. Smile!
- Children ask where you got the clown lips, but you can't answer because your lips won't move.
- Your pets no longer recognize you. When your dog runs away, you're in trouble.
- You look just like everybody else, and it feels like an episode of *The Twilight Zone.*

A makeover should be about discovering the real you, a better you. It should not be about obliterating your individuality and leaving a plastic doll in your place. A face that has a charming idiosyncrasy is the one we find beautiful. A woman who is interesting, mysterious, and intelligent is more attractive than a Barbie doll. (And what's the real reason she and Ken broke up?) How interesting would it be if we were all perfect in every way? Not very.

My advice: Think about what *you* need, whether it's a Washington weatherproof haircut, a professional wardrobe, makeup that's a little more glamorous. Concentrate on small and smart changes that won't scare the hamster. And above all, find a way to be yourself, not someone else.

Why not uncover a little more of the unique person you are? Remember: What's the big moment on those reality makeover shows always called? It's not called "the conceal." It's called "the reveal."

chapter 4

Amanda Manville was the quintessential ugly-duckling-into-swan transformation. On Lacey's beat that was newsworthy enough. But of particular interest to a Washington fashion reporter, as oxymoronic as Lacey knew that phrase to be, was that Amanda came from a neat and green neighborhood in Northwest D.C., and she had returned home to the District to unveil her new line of clothing, rather than doing the usual runway debut in New York. Her collection was called Chrysalis in honor of the TV show that had changed her life. Lacey figured her debut might raise the glamour level of the habitually seriously dressed District of Columbia. *This week, anyway. Next week it'll be back to beige.*

Amanda was a modern-day miracle, a testament to what could be done with willing raw material, a team of highly skilled surgeons, and unlimited network-television money. Of course, if she had stayed plain, gawky Mandy Manville, she would be checking groceries at the local Safeway and living in the shadow of her pretty older sister, Zoe. But the magic of *The Chrysalis Factor* happened instead. The news stories in Lacey's clipping file recapped Amanda's unexpected journey to supermodel. Amanda's publicist had also sent her a video press kit on DVD, but thirty seconds of jump-cut images and thumping disco had threatened to cause a migraine, so she pulled the plug and returned to the clippings.

Although Lacey was not a fan of reality television shows, she had gotten hooked on the endless waves of ultimate-makeover shows, the ones in which the plain and homely, left behind because of their looks, were offered the chance to change their appearance and their lives for the better, presumably forever. *The Chrysalis Factor* had been one of the most sensational—and sentimental. It was like *This Is Your Life* meets the surgeon's scalpel. Lacey remembered the episodes that featured Amanda's transformation.

In high school Amanda suffered with the nickname "Ostrich." The crueler kids taunted her to hide her face in the sand. Her sister, Zoe, pretty in a wholesome, blond, and freckled way, was a cheerleader, while Amanda never had a date until college. Zoe Manville told the TV audience it was terrible to listen to the taunts her sister endured. It was so hard to be "the pretty one." They wept together for the cameras.

Amanda's pain was so naked on TV that the nation (and Lacey) wept with her. And she was so sweet. Amanda worked as a volunteer at a battered-women's shelter, and she even had a boyfriend, Caleb Collingwood, who loved her, he said, "for her beautiful soul." Caleb was a gentle guy, just as homely as Ostrich. They met while dishing up soup side by side at the shelter. With his oversize hawk nose, receding chin, pale hazel eyes, and scraggly mud-brown hair he was a perfect match for her. As Miguel had said: "Too ugly to live." They were already engaged when Amanda was being considered for the show, so she was selected from among thousands of hopeful applicants for one of a special series of episodes: the "Wedding Belle Makeover."

The premakeover Amanda was nearly six feet tall and skinny as spaghetti, except for a rather disproportionate bottom. On top, she was a double-A bra size—when she inhaled. Her skin was blotchy, her teeth wandered around her mouth in a Picasso-esque way, her eyes were hooded, her nose enormous, and her chin nonexistent. The doctors chipped her nose down to size. They cut away the extra skin from her eyes. They also implanted a pert chin and a pair of solid C-cup breasts, and sculpted her bottom with liposuction. The smile makers restored her teeth. Dermatologists tackled her skin with scalpels and lasers, and stylists selected her wardrobe, dyed her hair, and applied her makeup. She weathered a rocky postoperative stage, with massive bruising, swelling, and lingering infections. She was not a pretty sight, and she often wondered aloud if she had made the right decision, a poignant uncertainty that the cameras caught for the sniffling television audience. Lacey knew she wasn't the only one reaching for another tissue.

She recalled the moments leading up to the "big reveal." The distinguished and handsome lead plastic surgeon, Dr. Gregory Spaulding, said he had never seen such a dramatic change through surgery. Captivated by his own work, Spaulding called Amanda his masterpiece in front of the cameras, which also captured the first hint that Amanda had fallen in love with her surgeon.

Amanda's infatuated glance traveled from her image in the mirror to Spaulding to Caleb Collingwood—and a sudden shock of dismay showed in her eyes. She quickly covered it up with her new big, white porcelain smile. But Lacey and everyone watching saw that look and knew in an instant that it was all over for him. Caleb Collingwood dropped out of sight, and the wedding never happened.

The misshapen larva disappeared and Amanda emerged from her chrysalis as a butterfly. She was an instant out-of-left-field sensation on magazine covers and on the runway at Fashion Weeks in Paris and Milan. Partly it was her curiosity value, the "freak factor," but she also seemed to represent the possibility of change for even the plainest person. But would she really be that beautiful off-camera? Lacey wondered. And could she really have been as homely as she first appeared on *The Chrysalis Factor*?

Lacey caught a cab from *The Eye*'s office at Farragut Square to a new boutique known as Snazzy Jane's on Wisconsin Avenue in Georgetown to interview Amanda Manville. In spite of the occasional downpour, October in D.C. was generally well behaved. And this day did not disappoint, with its hint of apples and turning leaves in the air. The sky was bright blue and clear. Lacey was comfortable without a coat, but on the street there was the usual mix of costumes; short shorts and sandals and exposed pierced belly buttons, along with the Washington uniform of civil servantdom, those bundled up in their trench coats and mufflers as if marching off to war instead of the office.

Snazzy Jane's occupied one of the narrow Georgetown town houses that had been redeveloped, like many of its neighbors, into a long, thin sales space with a second-floor balcony that hovered over the store's entryway. Large plate-glass windows tempted passersby with a glimpse of the interior. The effect was oh-so-cool—at least, cool for D.C. And the message was, *If you're not oh-so-cool, don't bother stepping into* this *store.*

From the sidewalk Lacey could hear popular retro numbers from the Fifties. What she could see of the decor, while sleek, had an air of knowing irony, something like a cocktail party in a vintage Airstream trailer. To herald Amanda Manville's premiere Chrysalis collection, large butterfly wings in gauzy pastels were suspended from the second-floor balcony.

Because of the media interest in the hometown-girl-turned-supermodel, Snazzy Jane's was closed to the public this afternoon, and the staff and Amanda were fielding interviews and allowing a sneak peak of the collection for the media. It would open later that evening for a cocktail party for invitation-only guests.

Lacey stepped up to the front door just as a broadcast reporter and her cameramen were leaving and the caterers were buzzing around. The reporter was giving his camera guy notes to take some shots for the B-roll. Lacey could see that the black-and-white-clad waitstaff inside were setting up tables and covering them with pastel linens.

A young woman posted outside the boutique checked Lacey's credentials and was just ushering her through the door when someone came out of nowhere and rudely muscled his way in ahead of her, pushing Lacey aside so roughly that she hit the doorjamb and caught her shoulder bag on it. For a minute they were all three wedged into the opening together.

"Oww! Hey, who do you think you are?" she said.

"Amanda!" he yelled, "I need to see Amanda!"

"Sir, are you on the list? Sir?" the gatekeeper shouted after him, but the man, small but seeming to take up a lot of space, pushed past them and into the store with all the panache of a process server in a panic.

"Amanda! Amanda Manville!" he yelled. "Where are you? Show me your phony face, Amanda!"

"Security!" the gatekeeper called out. "Security!" Lacey checked to make sure her suit hadn't been damaged. She glared at the man's back, noticing that his brown hair was thinning and his shirt was wet with sweat. He was about to dart up the stairs when a huge man suddenly appeared from behind a clothes rack, grabbed the intruder, picking him up like a suitcase, and evicted the man from the store, brushing past Lacey with a face as calm as a man putting out the cat. All the while the little man was shouting about having to see Amanda on a life-and-death matter.

Something about the huge security man was very familiar. Lacey realized she had met him once, and knew him only as "Turtledove," a code name. Lacey watched them briefly through the store window, though she couldn't get a clear view of the intruder. He trudged off morosely as Turtledove stood resolute, his arms crossed and a scowl fixed on his face.

Lacey turned away as a woman called her name. The woman approached with a studied nonchalance, but Lacey caught her taking a deep breath before speaking. For her part, Lacey made an effort to refocus on the fashion aspects of her assignment, while wondering what the hell Turtledove was up to. And who was the little intruder, what did he want, and was this a more interesting story than all the pretty dresses?

"Hi, I'm Yvette Powers. Sorry for the disturbance." She put out her hand. "Welcome to Snazzy Jane's. This is my store." Yvette looked exactly like the prom queen who had made all the right choices in life. Or perhaps, Lacey thought, life had made them for Yvette. A silky sheet of straight ultrablond hair hung obediently to her shoulder blades. She wore a sleeveless deep-beige linen shift dress that emphasized her lean, athletic build and punishing beige stilettos. She was tanned the same shade. *Wow, she's been dyed to match her shoes,* Lacey thought. *Pretty chic.* Nevertheless, Yvette looked tired, and makeup could not quite disguise the shadows under her eyes.

"Lacey Smithsonian. I write the 'Crimes of Fashion' column for *The Eye*."

"*The Eye Street Observer.* Of course. And you're the one who got, um, *involved* with that adventure with the House of Bentley. So nice of you to come."

Lacey had to give Yvette credit for poise. Only the slightest rise of her eyebrows indicated she was less than thrilled that a reporter from *The Eye Street Observer* was here to interview Amanda, or that a crazed intruder had nearly made an entrance on her coattails. After *The Washington Post,* which everybody said they read, and its conservative counterpoint, *The Washington Times,* which fewer people admitted to reading, many people refused to acknowledge that they had ever heard of *The Eye.* However, its rising circulation numbers told a different story.

"How did you decide to showcase Amanda's collection here first, at Snazzy Jane's?"

Yvette gave a little wave of her left hand, indicating the store, as well as showing off a perfect two-carat emerald-cut diamond set in a platinum wedding band. "Oh, we're old friends. We went to high school together."

"You and Amanda Manville?"

"I went to school with both Zoe and Amanda."

"So you're all friends from way back?"

"Yes. I was actually in Zoe's class. Amanda's a year younger." Strain showed on Yvette's face. "Zoe and I always planned to do something exciting. And Amanda wanted to come back home to showcase her talents. Then the collection came together. And here we are."

Lacey was about to ask how Zoe fit into the business, but Yvette said, "We're so glad you could come today." It was a dismissal. Yvette's assistant arrived on cue. "Oh, there you are, Fawn. Please show Ms. Smithsonian to the interviewing area." Fawn took over resignedly as Yvette turned and spun on her pointy high heels and nearly ran right into a third frazzled female. "Zoe! What are you doing out here? What's the trouble now?"

"Amanda says she needs a few minutes. So it will be just a moment. Or two." The woman shot apologetic looks at Yvette and Lacey.

With a shock, Lacey realized this woman must be Zoe Manville, the "pretty sister." But between her sister's famous makeover and the present, the blond and freckled former cheerleader had put on about fifty pounds. The weight had puffed out her features and given her an unfortunate set of jowls, only partially disguised by a voluminous Hermès-like scarf. She also wore a powder-blue sleeveless dress, something from the Chrysalis collection, Lacey presumed. A mistake: She had the arms to match the jowls.

"That's ridiculous! She knows we have back-to-back interviews all afternoon," Yvette snapped, and pulled her away from Lacey.

Zoe lowered her voice. "She just found another letter taped to her mirror and . . . um . . . had an episode."

"Oh, my God. How did that happen?"

"I don't know. We're mopping up the damage now."

"What the hell is that bodyguard for? I thought he was supposed to keep those things away from her." Yvette's patience appeared ready to snap.

Zoe shrugged helplessly. "I've called him back inside."

At that, Turtledove wordlessly appeared behind Zoe. The three of them moved to the back stockroom. But before disappearing again, Turtledove caught Lacey's eye and winked.

"Everyone's a drama queen," said the sweet-faced assistant, Fawn, who had also eavesdropped on the scene.

"What about the man who tried to get in? Who was he?" Lacey asked.

"Sorry. Must've missed that episode. Oh, darn." Fawn smiled slightly. "Don't worry; I'm sure there'll be more."

"Well, then, tell me this: Who's the queen drama queen?"

"Our celebrated supermodel diva of the day, but don't quote me. Deep background," she said, demonstrating to Lacey that in Washington, D.C., everyone learned how to play the media game young. Fawn wore a black miniskirt and turtleneck sweater with short-heeled ankle boots and a completely unnecessary Burberry scarf in that bland beige Burberry plaid that had seized D.C. by storm and still had it in a stranglehold. Fawn's bed-head was a wildly layered haircut delivered by an out-of-control stylist with a dull razor; it made her head resemble a feather duster. Looking at her, Lacey positively longed for the not-so-distant days when the legendary Washington Helmet-Head haircut reigned supreme in the Nation's Capital.

Fawn led her upstairs and left her with a nice thick press packet, with photographs of Amanda and her clothing, and the usual puffery about how fabulous it all was. The press release revealed the hitherto unknown information that it was actually Zoe who created most of the designs, while Amanda oversaw the colors and fabric selection and personally approved each item. Reading between the lines, it was apparent that Amanda's fame and connections got the Chrysalis Collection off the ground, not her talent.

Fawn retreated, Burberry scarf tossed over her shoulder, as Zoe drew near. The "pretty sister" who had seemed so confident on TV approached Lacey almost shyly. "Hi, I'm Zoe Manville. Amanda will be just a few more moments. Do you have everything you need?"

"No, actually, I don't. Can we talk? I didn't realize the designs were yours. Aren't you the one I should be interviewing?" What Lacey really wanted to ask was, *How does it feel to be the pretty sister all your life, then be pushed aside?*

A pained look crossed Zoe's face. "It's a collaboration," she said. "But of course, you're interested in meeting Mandy, not me."

True, Lacey *was* interested in meeting Amanda, who apparently was the Evil Queen from *Snow White*. *"Mirror, mirror on the wall, who's the supermodelest of them all?"*

"But I'm interested in your story, too. So you two design together? It must be great to have so much in common with your sister," Lacey said. *My sister and I are about as alike as Snow White and Rose Red. I'm Rose.* "When did you decide to undertake this venture?"

"I used to design clothes for my dolls, and my teddy bears, and then myself. When I was old enough, I took classes at the Fashion Institute of Technology in New York," Zoe said, then remembered

to include her famous sibling. "Of course, Amanda is key. She has
such a great eye for . . . for details and color combinations. It really
has worked out. Wonderfully." Zoe looked away and caught her reflection in a nearby mirror. She looked slightly dismayed and
smoothed a wrinkle where the skirt crept up over her ample hips.
"I'll just check on Amanda," she said, running for the back of the
store.

Lacey was left to linger at the balcony and enjoy a view of the
Georgetown sidewalk scene, a parade of wealthy foreign tourists,
university students, and the ladies who lunched. The occasional
panhandler crossed into view, equal parts despair and salesman-
ship, asking for dollars, not change, and being polite, as required
by D.C. ordinance. With a bird's-eye view of the action, Lacey noticed a man stride boldly into the salon as if he owned it. In fact,
Brad Powers did own it, with his wife, Yvette. Lacey recognized
him from his photos in the social and business pages.

Belying his expressive blue eyes, his shiny shaved head and his
silk suit gave him the air of an expensive thug. His skull had the
first hint of a five-o'clock shadow: From the balcony Lacey could
see exactly where his receding hairline stopped.

Powers called for his wife and took her by the arm. Lacey could
not hear them, though their gestures and expressions betrayed an
argument. She noticed that he and Yvette were the same buttery-
tan color. *Dyed to match,* she thought. *The fashionable postmodern couple.* They moved out of view.

She turned her attention to the delicate wisps of fabric that fluttered from their hangers, the chic little dresses of Chrysalis. They
were arranged in small artistic groupings and equally small sizes.
It was October outside, but it seemed to be some sort of springtime
of the mind inside. Chrysalis, of course, was the perfect symbol for
Amanda Manville, the pupa transformed into a butterfly. The colors ran from pale pinks, blues, and lavenders to jewel colors of
sapphire blues and deep greens, in velvets, silks, and polished cot-
tons. Many of the dresses were cut on the bias, a mixture of velvet
and chintz, offbeat yet with a winsome charm.

The clothes were affordable, Lacey supposed, if you were a
Georgetown University student with a very healthy allowance. Or
a TFB, a trust-fund baby, like so many Washington interns and
staffers. And heaven knew, there was no dearth of wealthy university students and interns. They could be seen everywhere, net-
working on their cell phones in their Volvos and BMWs. A skirt
that cost $300 and a simple cotton dress that topped $550 were

nothing to them, though it would certainly strain a reporter's paltry budget. At least a reporter who worked at *The Eye.*

They were the kind of dresses that *The Washington Post* fashion editor would probably lament as being "pretty enough" and then muse somberly whether it was "enough to be pretty." As far as Lacey was concerned, Washington fashion could always use a little prettying up. The city itself, she reflected, with its malls and monuments, was always stunning, although choked with traffic and burdened with its odd mix of tourists, lobbyists, lawyers, bureaucrats, wonks, and weirdos.

The question was, Would women in Washington buy them? It did seem that a small conspiracy of color had recently taken hold of the retailers. Everywhere display windows featured pink and blue and yellow, as if to slap back at the troubles pressing in on the nation. Perhaps even in Washington women craved clear blue skies, the rosy dawn of optimism, blazing yellow sunshine, and Code Green days. And a few brave men had even been sighted wearing pink preppy shirts.

Occasionally Lacey sighted one of these color rebels. Just the day before, there was a young blonde on the Metro wearing a black coat and shocking-pink Wellingtons, even though it wasn't raining. But maybe she was just a tourist from California, the land of neon.

Lacey made her way back to the staging area for the interviews, where pale curtains hung behind a semicircular stage. Giant photos of the beautiful Amanda framed the space. Angular modern gray chairs, ugly and painful, were set next to a clear Lucite cube. She sat down gingerly. *Perhaps designed to keep the interviews short,* she thought. Lacey was rummaging through her bag for her trusty reporter tools when she heard a voice behind her.

"Another scribe waiting for Amanda?"

She glanced up at possibly the most handsome man she had ever seen. "Lacey Smithsonian, *Eye Street Observer,*" she said, offering her hand.

"Hi, I'm Tate Penfield." He had glossy black hair and a beautifully sculpted chin and full lips. Lacey estimated his age at about thirty. A loud crash came from behind the stage. The sound of breaking glass made her jump. Penfield smiled. "Another mirror bites the dust."

"Do I need a bulletproof vest for this interview?"

"Only if it comes from Amanda's collection. Don't worry, it was probably an accident."

Lacey noticed that Penfield was burdened with cameras and photo equipment.

"You're here to take photos of Amanda?"

"Yeah." He mounted a video camera on a tripod and set down a large bag of cameras and lenses. "Some stills, and also I'm filming a documentary on Amanda. Her life, her startling transformation, her fabulous career, that sort of thing. I'm always shooting extra footage."

"You've been around her awhile then?"

"On this project, about six months."

"Sounds like a long time." Miguel had told her that Amanda went through people like tissues.

"Not for a documentary." Penfield seemed rather distracted, trying to be polite and concentrate on his work at the same time. It gave her a chance to take another look. He wore blue jeans, Top-Siders without socks, and a well-worn fishermen's knit sweater that was fraying at the sleeves, which were pushed up his arms. Somehow it looked perfect on him. If he had dressed more slickly he would have come across as a self-obsessed metrosexual. This way he looked comfortably male, even if absurdly handsome.

"I like your sweater. Looks well loved."

"Thanks." He stroked the sweater. "It's a sentimental favorite."

"So, a documentary. You're including Amanda's life before the big makeover?"

"I'm doing my best, trying to get something that she hasn't said before." He moved the giant photos of Amanda out of his field of view.

"How long have you actually known Amanda?" Lacey asked.

"And lived to tell about it, you mean?" He laughed. "A couple of years. When Amanda decided to come back home to D.C. for this career move, I thought it would make a good story, documenting her rise to the top. It's a celebrity society. Everyone wants to be immortalized."

"And Amanda?"

"Especially Amanda." He adjusted the tripod. "So I've been working on this project and making money doing photos for the Chrysalis ad campaign."

"Then you know something about a stalker hanging around?"

He shrugged. "A guy's been writing her love letters. They've turned dark. And they show up in odd places. She's come unglued."

"Is it the same guy who tried to get through the front door earlier?"

"Someone tried to get through the door?"

"Not on the list," Lacey said.

"I didn't hear about that. Sort of an occupational hazard for people like Amanda. But the letter writer is probably some geeky little guy who imagines he's in love with her. My theory, he's trying to snag something personal of hers, like a pair of her shoes to wear. To sell on eBay maybe, or put under his pillow at night and stroke."

"Now you're messing with me." Lacey laughed.

"Better to let Amanda tell you." Penfield focused on her through his Hasselblad camera. He clicked the shutter.

"Hey, don't take my photograph. I'm a reporter, not a celebrity." She remembered the whole battle with Mac over her photographs, then smiled ruefully. Penfield clicked again. "I didn't say you could—" Again he snapped the shutter. "No more! I'm no model."

"No. You're not." He clicked one more photo and stopped. "That's a compliment, by the way. Beautifully real. I'm basically a freelance photojournalist. I prefer that, but this stuff pays better. For the moment."

Lacey squirmed around on the horrible chair to see if the long-delayed Amanda was coming. She stood up and stretched. Penfield grinned and put down his camera.

"She's usually late."

"No problem, I love waiting for prima donnas." Changing the subject back, she asked, "Have you sold anything to *The Eye*?"

"A few assignments." He seemed pleased by her interest. "I share some studio space in the city with a couple of news photogs who freelance on the side. Some of us still like darkroom work. You know one of them. He took photos of your 1940s hairstyles."

"So Hansen freelances? It's really amazing what we don't know about each other."

Fawn approached with a tray of delicacies and a single mug of tea for Lacey, which she set down on the Lucite cube, Snazzy Jane's version of a coffee table. Lacey perched again on the edge of the evil gray chair and sipped her tea, and just when she thought she could wait not one minute longer, the stage lights came on. The music changed to something ethereal and New Agey. Layers of gauzy curtains were suddenly backlit, revealing a multitude of pale-painted silk wings, like so many butterflies caught in a web. They parted and the magnificent Amanda Manville emerged, wearing one of her Chrysalis designs. It was showtime.

chapter 5

Really, I don't need the theatrics, Lacey thought, *I'm a print reporter.* But she enjoyed them anyway.

Amanda stood still for a moment, as if posing for a horde of photographers, or perhaps it was merely for Tate Penfield. He was handsome enough, and he was the official documentarian. She smiled at Lacey, revealing the perfect porcelain veneers she had been given. As beautiful and polished as her photograph, Amanda had her hair sculpted in a short geometric cut, in a magnificent dark red mahogany color that emphasized her cheekbones. Her skin was as pale as a snowflake. And perhaps it was just a trick of the light, but her eyes looked very large and lavender. Tall and impossibly thin, Amanda wore a sleeveless panne velvet dress in imperial purple with gold accented braid. The material flowed over her torso, the waistline dipped low on her hips like a flapper's, and the hemline flirted around her knees. At a towering six feet she didn't need the four-inch height of her gold stiletto-heeled sandals, but she wore them anyway.

Her eyes grazed over Lacey and zeroed in on Penfield setting up another camera in the background. Her eyes went wide, her lips curled back, and she shrieked at him.

"Tate! What are you wearing?! Why on earth are you wearing that ratty old sweater?! Take that horrible thing off *now*!"

Lacey wasn't ready for that entrance line. *I can give Miguel a new Amanda story! Screaming Psycho Diva, scene one.* Amanda's screeching voice had a curiously flat, nasal tone to it that didn't suit her exquisite looks.

"Chill out, Amanda," Penfield said evenly, and went on maneuvering his lenses and props. "I'm just part of the furniture, remember?"

"It's a disgrace, a total disgrace, and you're a disgraceful excuse for—"

"Then don't look at me. I like it." He had a decisive tone in his voice, and Lacey wondered if that was the way to handle Amanda. The supermodel snorted with derision and turned away, scowling, from the handsome photographer. Then she took a deep breath and composed herself before gracefully taking a seat across from Lacey. She smiled coldly. Fawn scurried in with a mug of tea for Amanda and quickly scurried out. Amanda gave Lacey the once-over with her startling lavender eyes. Lacey met her gaze and hoped her great vintage suit would be her suit of armor against the Evil Queen.

"And what on earth are *you* wearing? Oh, please! Vintage?" Amanda sneered. "It *is* vintage, isn't it? Is that what they're wearing in Washington now?"

"No, it's what *I* wear."

"And you write about fashion? Really? For *The Eye*?" Her tone was snotty diva to the max. Lacey would have to try to mimic it for Miguel.

"I write about style for real women." Lacey smiled, revealing her own even white teeth, which were natural. "Sometimes fashion and style intersect. A happy but rare occasion."

"Right." Amanda touched her forehead like she was rubbing the pain away. "Never mind. You're Lacey Smithsonian, right? The one who took on the Bentleys? Good, you're the one I wanted. So let's talk." She carefully lifted her steaming mug, took a sip, spat it out, and yelled for the unfortunate Fawn. "Damn it, Fawn, that's terrible! Where is that little bitch? She does this to me on purpose."

"Does what?" Penfield asked in a very soothing tone of voice from behind his camera.

She whirled on him. "I ordered Earl Grey tea! This is green tea! It tastes like a mowed lawn. It's a simple enough task; you would think any moron could do it." Her voice reached an unpleasant range. Somewhere porpoises were squealing in pain. "But apparently she can't. And what is she wearing? Burberry?! She's supposed to be wearing something from my collection!"

Yvette Powers swiftly moved in, her heels clicking on the polished wood floors. "What is the trouble now, Mandy?"

"Don't call me that."

Yvette deliberately took a long, slow breath. "*Dearest* Amanda, do tell me what is the matter?"

"That little idiot brought me the wrong tea."

"That's hardly enough to make a federal case over." Yvette stalked off and sent Fawn scurrying back with another cup of tea, presumably Earl Grey this time. Zoe crept back in and stood quivering, clearly upset.

"Amanda, honey, it's okay. We are all a little tense."

"What are you tense about, Zoe? It's worse for me! I'm surrounded by incompetent zombies." Amanda's gaze settled on Lacey.

It's going so well. Lacey knew she shouldn't be amused, but she was. Amanda was like one of those terrible thirteen-year-old girls who lived only to torment the less powerful. But Lacey had the power of the pen, in her case her favorite Waterman fountain pen, a green-enameled weapon mightier than the sword. *Well, at least mightier than Amanda's stilettos.* Lacey remembered Mac's favorite saying: "Never argue with people who buy paper by the ton and ink by the barrel." She gave a little wave with her pen and smiled, and Amanda got the hint. She was immediately back on good behavior.

Amanda's voice dropped an octave into a chummy intimacy. "I'm so sorry. It's just been a terrible day; you'll understand when I tell you," she said, including Lacey in her little club of mean teens.

"We all have bad days," Lacey agreed. *Kill anyone yet today?*

Zoe absentmindedly reached down for one of the small sweets on the tray, which did not go unnoticed by her bone-thin sister. "Go ahead, Zoe, sweetie," Amanda snarled. "What's another ten pounds?"

Zoe dropped the treat and backed into a rack of clothing, looking as if she'd been slapped.

Miguel was right. The makeover had unleashed Amanda's inner bitch. *Frankendiva. And she seemed so sweet on TV.* Lacey waved her green fountain pen again. Amanda paused.

"Let's start over, shall we? Ms. Smithsonian, you're the reporter who solved those murders. The hairstylist and the intern, what's her name? Esme something?" Lacey shrugged. *Solved* seemed to her a pretty high-concept term for her involvement in those stories.

"I just put two and two together and got lucky."

"Then you *are* the one who solved those murders, right?"

"My beat is fashion." Lacey marveled at how she could say that now without cringing. "But sometimes I seem to get in the way of a bigger story."

"I don't want you here because of fashion, for God's sake," Amanda said with another pointed glare at Lacey's beloved vintage suit. "I'm not even that interested in what you might have to say about my designs. Basically the collection will do fine without the help of your little newspaper. The celebrity media will see to that. I need your help for something else."

"What?" Lacey cursed her curiosity. She'd like to stand up and walk out. *Maybe I should have spent more time talking to Miguel.*

Amanda bellowed for her favorite target. "Fawn! Get me my bag!"

The girl scuttled out from where she was hiding, with a large leather tote bag. She thrust it at Amanda at arm's length, not daring to get any closer. *Smart girl. Stay out of the slapping zone,* Lacey wanted to say. Amanda opened the tote and withdrew a folder. Perhaps a half dozen articles from *The Eye* fell out. They were stories Lacey had written about the murders she had been involved in solving, and documents copied from DeadFed dot com. Amanda held up a front page of *The Eye* bearing Lacey's photograph.

"This is you, right?"

"Not my best angle."

"You found out who killed these women, didn't you?"

"Yes, but it sounds so braggy," Lacey said. "And I'm no detective. Amanda, I don't understand what you want."

"It's very simple," Amanda said, as if Lacey were intellectually challenged. "Someone is trying to kill me. If they succeed, I want you to solve my murder."

chapter 6

"Someone wants to murder you?" *Why do I get all the nutcases? And why am I not surprised?* Amanda was clearly not as lovable as her press releases would indicate, and there were deadly looks being exchanged behind her back among her own staff. *But murder?*

"Just humor me! Okay? Or this interview is over."

"Oh, that would be such a shame." Lacey was unable to keep her comment completely sarcasm-free, but her fatal flaw was kicking in and she knew it: She always needed to know the end of the story. Besides, this was going to make great giggle-time conversation with her friends. Miguel would simply eat it up, not to mention Brooke and Stella. And she owed Amanda at least one good comeback in return for her comments about her suit. Lacey just didn't know what it would be yet.

"Okay, sure." *So, you're a murder victim waiting to happen.* "Have you told the police? Tell me what's going on." *Keep your poker face on, Lacey,* she ordered herself.

"I have bodyguards." Amanda indicated Turtledove, who somehow once again seemed to appear out of the ether, and at her nod silently drew forward out of the shadows. A beautiful mixture of races, the dark man looked even bigger up close, wearing khakis and a short-sleeved black knit shirt that showed off his bulging biceps to maximum effect. He was very intimidating. Lacey took his hand, and Amanda made a cursory introduction. "This is Forrest Thunderbird. He's the day shift."

"Pleased to meet you, miss." Only Lacey could see the look of recognition on his face.

"Smithsonian. Lacey Smithsonian." He gave Lacey another wink and took her hand. "I feel as if I know you already," Lacey said.

"But can we ever really know each other?" Forrest replied.

"You're right. There are so many layers to uncover," Lacey deadpanned.

"An interesting proposition," he murmured.

Lacey cocked one eyebrow and blushed a little. She hadn't intended a double entendre. But Turtledove, a.k.a. Forrest, seemed to be enjoying himself, which irritated Amanda.

"Enough chitchat! Forrest, go check my dressing room to see how someone could have gotten in there past you and your so-called security experts."

"I can tell you, Miss Manville, that no one has breached security. Everyone who has entered has been on the list. If someone is leaving you notes, it's someone on the list. And I've been informed that the people on the list are not my concern." He set his shoulders back, nodded to Lacey, and gave a small salute to Amanda before sauntering off to fight her phantoms. Lacey was aware that Yvette was now standing close by, apparently to make sure there were no more scenes.

"You see? My security people are as incompetent as the rest of them," Amanda sneered. "I'm not planning on being killed without a fight, but if anything happens I want you to find out who did it and make sure they are brought to justice."

"Tall order. And I don't take orders from sources," Lacey protested.

"It's a good story, isn't it?" Amanda snapped. "Why doesn't anybody believe me?"

"Tell me about the stalker."

"Which one? The one in D.C. is just an overeager fan, a celebrity groupie. His name is Johnny Monroe, or so he says."

"Why don't you think he's a threat?"

"Ha! You should see him. He's just a nerdy little pipsqueak nuisance. But apparently someone else wants to see me dead. Here, if you don't believe me . . ." Amanda pulled a small note from a carefully concealed pocket in her dress. Lacey was impressed: a designer frock with pockets! Not having enough pockets was one of her pet peeves. Amanda thrust the note at Lacey. It was written in red marker on a small glossy photo of Amanda. Scrawled messily across her face was the message, *Pretty is as pretty dies. Sweet dreams, top model.*

"You don't think this Johnny Monroe wrote it?"

"No. He believes we could have a 'relationship.' He's desperate to see me. He has something to tell me, he says. But we can't let him get too close, because . . . well, you just don't want to encourage that sort of thing. He writes daily. And we've caught him trying to deliver another letter today."

So that's what the ruckus at the door was about?

"Forrest could break him with one hand. And he doesn't write these horrible things," Amanda said, pointing at the new message. Lacey wondered if this was all just an elaborate ruse to get more news coverage.

"Did you tell the other reporters this story?"

"The other reporters have not solved any murders, to my knowledge." Amanda sipped her tea.

"Let's say I believe there may be someone who wants to kill you. Let's narrow the field. Who do you think it is?"

At that, Lacey saw Zoe and Yvette trade a look that told her there was no shortage of people who might like to dispatch Amanda to the Big Runway in the Sky. She overheard Yvette whisper, "Kill the golden goose?" Fawn shot Amanda a look of pure hatred.

"I know who it is," Amanda said. "It's Greg. Greg Spaulding."

"Your fiancé?"

"Former fiancé. You know how to deal with killers. Can't you just stab him or something?"

"No, I can't just stab him!" *A couple of incidents with sharp-edged weapons and they never let you forget,* Lacey thought. She wondered why Amanda didn't suspect her unfortunate former boyfriend, Caleb Collingwood, of being behind the threats. Unless she knew he really *was* dead. Did she even have a hand in his disposal? But Lacey didn't want to interrupt the flow of Amanda's thoughts, especially if Dr. Spaulding was involved in a murder plot. So she simply jotted down Caleb's name in her notebook with a question mark. She couldn't print the mad ravings of Amanda Manville. Not ethically. Politicians were easy targets, but libeling private citizens, especially wealthy, influential ones? Very dangerous. Mac's eyebrows would have something to say about it. "And why on earth would Dr. Spaulding want to kill you?"

Amanda stood up and clutched her chest melodramatically. "To destroy his own creation. He made me what I am; he told me that. And now he hates me. He never should have fallen in love with me, he said, that it was wrong for a doctor to fall for his patient. He wants to erase me, permanently."

"What does it matter that he's finished with you? You've gone on to greener fields too. And new conquests," an angry Yvette cut in. "And you don't seem to care if your conquests are married or not."

And we've made a turn into new territory, Lacey observed.

"I told you, Yvette, it was just a fling with your darling Brad. It didn't mean anything. Not to me. And certainly not to him. Just look at him. Does Brad care about anyone but Brad?"

Amanda's gaze passed over their heads, and Lacey followed her eyes. Brad Powers was standing at the door, well within hearing distance. He looked like a man made of polished stone and gave no hint of what he might be thinking. *This chic Georgetown boutique crowd is really tough,* Lacey thought, taking mental notes. Powers turned and left without a word.

"It means something to me, old friend." Yvette spat the last two words at Amanda and stormed out of the room, followed by Zoe, who always seemed to want to smooth things over. Yvette stopped her cold. "Leave me alone, Zoe. And after tonight I want her out of here."

Zoe said nothing, but padded back morosely. She picked up a mug of tea and avoided the sweets. Amanda turned her attention back to Lacey.

"It's Greg; I know it is. He called me the biggest mistake he ever made." Amanda's eyes began to fill with tears. "He said he wished he'd never met me and that I would be better off ugly. Better off if he'd never made the first incision. Better off if I never met him." The tears began to slip down Amanda's cheeks.

"This wasn't the first time you were engaged, though, was it?" Lacey asked quietly. Everyone turned to look at her. Zoe rattled her mug on the table, narrowly missing a spill. "There was Caleb Collingwood."

Penfield clicked off a couple of close-ups with a Nikon, and Amanda waved him away.

Amanda sat down and looked at the floor. "That is ancient history, and we were talking about Greg Spaulding," she sniffed.

"But surely you're not in danger here in Washington. Spaulding's a well-known plastic surgeon. In Beverly Hills." At least, that was what Lacey remembered about Dr. Greg Spaulding.

"He's not in Beverly Hills. He's here in D.C. for a conference on plastic surgery. He's one of the speakers and organizers; he's been here for a week."

"What is his speech about? His work on *The Chrysalis Factor*?"

Amanda rolled her eyes. "How he miraculously saved poor

woebegone little Mandy Manville. How he deserves all the credit. He tells the world I'm his masterpiece. But he tells me I'm a monster."

"Oh, no, Dr. Greg has totally changed his focus," Zoe cut in, and absentmindedly took a chocolate off the tray. "Greg is delivering a talk about physicians who donate their services to help children with disfigured faces in third-world countries. He's raising money for them."

"He's no Mother Teresa, Zoe. He's a phony."

"He's not a phony, Mandy, he's not. And he's not the scourge of Beverly Hills either." Zoe faced Lacey. "He donates a couple of months every year to perform surgery on these children at no cost. Greg's actually a very decent and nice man." Zoe licked chocolate off her fingers, daring her sister to say something.

"A nice man who wants to see me die." Amanda leaped to her feet and paced the stage. She never gave up the floor for very long. "That's why he's here!"

"These surgeons change lives dramatically," Zoe told Lacey.

"He changed my life, and then he left me," Amanda screeched.

Lacey was beginning to think that Greg Spaulding had good reason to flee his creation. "If he's so busy, how could he find time to come after you and leave little notes?"

"He's hired somebody to do his dirty work. He's good at that."

"Amanda," Lacey asked, "did you arrange to be here while Greg Spaulding was in town?"

"No! Premiering Chrysalis at Snazzy Jane's has been on the calendar for at least six months. It was part of my plan all along," Amanda protested. "It's been my driving desire to premiere my clothes in my hometown. Next week I'll open—that is, *we* will show the collection on the West Coast, in Beverly Hills. Then New York. Saks is going to carry the line."

"Washington is the first stop on the tour?"

"Of course. I wanted everyone to see where I came from—and where I've ended up. Do I have anything to prove? You'd better believe I do."

And when you grow up, you get to be Joan Crawford in Amanda Dearest.

"We really wanted our friends around us for this happy occasion. We've worked so hard to get to this point," Zoe said. Lacey wondered if she were taking some kind of happy pills. "Greg and Amanda were still together when this was planned. Greg's speech for the surgeons' conference was on board even before that."

"They planned to be in D.C. together?" Lacey asked.

"He knew I would be here," Amanda said.

"Do you still love him?"

"That doesn't matter!" Her eyes teared up. Instead of answering, she waved one of Lacey's news stories on a dead intern named Esme Fairchild. "You found this woman's killer. And I want you to . . ."

"To what?"

"To find my killer *before* I die. Please."

That *please* was the only humble word Amanda had uttered, but it felt sincere.

"I've never been asked to do that before. How do you suggest I go about it?" This was going to make great dinner conversation. *But maybe not with Vic.* Yvette returned quietly, pretending to rearrange dresses on the racks.

"If you expose him before he tries to kill me, then maybe it won't happen."

"You want me to libel a prominent plastic surgeon who is leading other doctors to donate their time and money to fix the faces of poor disfigured children." *I don't think so.* "What about the note you found? Your bodyguard says no one breached security."

"Greg is smart. He paid someone to put the note here. Don't you see? It's not libel if it's true."

"You can't prove it, and if you can, you should bring it to the police."

"But you promised!" Her whine suddenly climbed into a shriek. "Fawn! I need a warm-up. And it's Earl Grey, not warmed-over hay!" But Fawn was nowhere to be seen. Lacey tried to bring things back to reality.

"Amanda, I said in the event something happened, I would look into it. I did not agree to libel anyone. It's hard to believe Spaulding would go after you so obviously. You're way too high-profile. And you have security."

Amanda sat down in a sulk, as if out of steam. Lacey straightened up and readied her pen.

"There's something else we haven't discussed," Lacey said. "What happened to Caleb Collingwood?"

Amanda stared at her silently.

"I don't know why you would bring him up now," Zoe said carefully. "He's been gone for years."

"I don't want to talk about Caleb," Amanda said.

"You broke his heart, didn't you?"

Amanda shifted uncomfortably, then bolted up out of her chair. "I know all about those insane rumors. I know that people still think—"

"That you killed him?" Lacey heard a camera whirring away and looked over at Penfield, who seemed completely absorbed in his work. *I guess I've put a little spark in his documentary.*

"It's crazy talk. The police even came one day." Amanda looked particularly wounded. "Because I'm famous now."

"The police cleared Amanda of any suspicion," Zoe interjected.

"Then Collingwood has nothing to do with these threats?"

Amanda closed her eyes momentarily. "Caleb is dead. And no, I didn't kill him. He committed suicide. If you must know, he left me a note that I gave to the police after someone spread rumors that I had something to do with him disappearing."

"What did it say?" Lacey asked and she was conscious of a heavy silence. The background music had stopped.

Amanda fixed her gaze past Lacey's head as she recited the note from memory. " 'Caleb Collingwood dies tonight by his own hand. Don't bother to look. You'll never find me.' "

"That's it?"

"He never did like writing."

"His body hasn't been found," Lacey pointed out.

"Don't be an idiot," Amanda cried, tired of the subject. "Of course he's dead, somewhere in the mountains of West Virginia. He said we'd never find him."

There's a location at any rate, Lacey thought. *If his bones haven't been picked clean.* She needed a breath of fresh air. "Where in the mountains?" Amanda merely stared at Lacey and crossed her arms. "Has anyone searched for him? Who has the note? Do you have a copy of it?"

"I'm not talking about him anymore. Caleb is dead and I'm alive. This is about *me.*"

"But there's no chance that he's alive?" Lacey pressed.

"I told you! What kind of dumb-ass reporter are you? I'm offering you a great story, a story that could make your career and what do you do? Dwell on the past and unimportant details." An ugly expression crossed her face. "So what are you going to do? Are you going to help me?"

Lacey wondered if she should tell Amanda what she really thought, but she was fed up with the Frankendiva's nonsense. "Let's see. You've sneered at my clothes, scoffed at my newspaper, called me an idiot, and demanded my help to solve a murder that hasn't happened yet. It simply doesn't bode well for a long-term relationship, Ms. Manville."

Amanda seemed to be, for a moment at a loss for words. Zoe looked stricken.

"Oh, and you don't care if I write a story about your designs, only your paranoia," Lacey continued. "So I think we're done here."

She heard snickers from Yvette and a booming laugh from Tate Penfield.

"What! Lacey Smithsonian! You're worse than all the rest of them. They're just incompetent. You of all people could help me, and you just quibble over trivialities." She turned and swept regally toward the door, leaving Lacey to calmly close her notebook. Amanda turned around to make a parting shot from the doorway. "Reporters! I hate you all!" Then she was gone.

Lacey reached for her mug of tea. It was cold. *I guess there's no point in asking Fawn for a warm-up.*

Zoe exchanged a look with Yvette. "Do you want to go after her?"

"Why should I? The whore slept with my husband. Not that she had to force herself on him." She clicked off on her stilettos in the opposite direction. So it was up to Zoe, once again, to smooth things over for Amanda. It seemed to be Zoe's main job, besides designing the collection. She tossed a look at Lacey and said, "That really wasn't necessary."

"It really was," Lacey said. "I've had my fill of insults today."

Lacey caught Tate Penfield's eye. He smiled and started packing up his cameras. Lacey picked up a petit four. *No use letting this go to waste,* she thought, closing her eyes and popping a small piece of nirvana in her mouth. She opened her eyes to see Brad Powers sitting opposite her on the ghastly gray chair that Amanda had abandoned.

"She's been under a lot of strain lately," he said.

Lacey could feel her eyebrow lift of its own accord. "Yvette or Amanda?"

He colored slightly and turned his baby blues on her. "Both, actually. They're old friends with a big misunderstanding."

"They seem to understand each other perfectly." *He's worrying about what I'll write,* Lacey thought, and looked at her fountain pen. *Such a small yet interesting weapon.*

"Let's just say Amanda's fears are a little hyper, and my wife is a little too eager to listen to idle gossip."

Lacey had seen Powers exchange a guilty look with Amanda.
"So no one wants to kill Amanda? Why on earth not?"

He laughed, then sobered quickly. "No, no one really wants to kill her, that I know of. But she has a real talent for cranking up the tension."

"Is this stalker any threat?"

Powers shrugged. "She's got bodyguards around the clock."

"And do you think Collingwood is dead? Did she kill him?"

"Your guess is as good as mine."

Lacey gathered up her things, feeling at a loss for something to write that wouldn't sound like a bad episode of *Days of Our Lives.* Of course, there were always the clothes.

"You won't mention her crazy idea, will you, Amanda? I mean, that she's going to die?"

"I'll certainly do a story on the clothes. But I try not to write about imaginary events that haven't happened, tempting as it is. It's not sensible reporting."

"Good. I knew you were a sensible reporter." Powers smiled with relief, and Lacey felt her eyebrow shoot up again.

Ha. He obviously doesn't know me very well. Would a sensible Washington reporter be caught dead in my fabulous vintage suit? Then she remembered that being "sensible" was part of her new Lacey's Love-life Makeover Plan. A little more sense and sensibility in her life wouldn't kill her.

Besides, Lacey thought, *I promised Vic: No more dead bodies. At least not until Halloween.*

chapter 7

She hoped that Turtledove would be willing to give her the body-guard's intimate perspective.

Lacey didn't have a chance to chat with him at Snazzy Jane's, where his job was to keep the diva in one piece. And it would be difficult to ask him right in front of Amanda whether she was a complete lunatic or if there was some truth to her fears.

However, Lacey hated the idea of calling the one person who would know how she could get ahold of the big guy. That would be his friend Damon Newhouse, editor of the dreaded Conspiracy Clearinghouse Web site, DeadFed dot com, who sensationalized everything and jumped to wacky conclusions at the drop of an e-mail. He was a cyberspace scribe, but he had the soul of a gonzo jazz-age journalist. Lacey visualized him with his press card in his porkpie hat shoved back on his hallucinating forehead. For DeadFed, it didn't matter whether the story was true; what really mattered was the creepy way it turned your world upside down. Back at her desk, she sent him a brief e-mail. She got back an im-mediate phone call.

"Smithsonian, what's up? Must be serious if you're calling me. Dodging any more errant doughnut signs? Lightning strikes, and Smithsonian is there. That's why I admire you so."

"Can the flattery. About Turtledove's phone number . . ."

"I understand you took a ride with your office jinx, guy named Wiedemeyer? I hear trouble follows him like an angry ex-wife with a bounced alimony check."

"It hasn't gotten him yet. And hello to you too, Damon. And be-fore you publish that I've captured the beauty secrets of an alien bigfoot, let me state for the record that this call is nothing serious. Just fashion, fashion, fashion. Girly stuff."

"It's never just fashion with you. I grant that it doesn't always come with dead bodies, not daily, anyway. But there's always subtext. What is it now and how soon can I post it on my Web site?"

Lacey groaned, put her head down on her desk, and smacked the phone three times before she protested into the receiver, "Really. It's a fashion story, Damon."

"Okay, sure, fashion. If you say so. But I like the beautiful-alien-bigfoot angle."

"They're shy because they just can't do a thing with their fur. Trust me; there's no story," she said. "Just a crime of fashion."

"Everything is a crime of fashion in this town. Did you see my piece on DeadFed about tiny microchips they're implanting in your clothes that tell the government where you shop—"

Almost any idea, no matter how tame, could transport Damon Newhouse to a state of inspired delusion. Lacey would like to blow him off, but he was in love with her friend, Brooke Barton, also a devotee of the grand conspiracy theory. The love-struck duo knew every rumor of a conspiracy behind every bush, down every alley, and, of course, in any dimly lit parking garage in the District of Columbia. Lacey couldn't fathom the appeal of this stuff, but it seemed to get them really hot. She cut him off.

"Focus, Damon. Your buddy, code name Turtledove? I need to get ahold of Forrest Thunderbird. Is that his real name? And before you get carried away, it's just for background on a fashion story. He's bodyguarding for Amanda Manville."

"Amanda Manville, the human Barbie doll?"

"Yes, Damon, the same."

"Is she missing? Dead? Kidnapped? A sex slave to a senator or a Saudi prince?"

"Chill, Damon. She's alive and well." *So far.*

"Have you heard she's a guinea pig for the government? They're turning out bionic combat superbabes under the guise of a tawdry plastic-surgery reality show, right before our very eyes. Manville is the prototype. I got an anonymous e-mail—"

"It's a theory," Lacey conceded. "Are you having fun?"

"I like it. There are rumors. And where there are rumors, there is some truth. So tell me what this is all about."

"How can I talk to you seriously, Newhouse? You take my words and twist them into something completely different."

"I improve them."

Unrepentant idiot.

"Are you going to give me the information?" He hesitated. "I'll call Brooke and she'll break your resistance."

"Indeed, I am Brooke's love slave. And she is my blond goddess." Damon gave Lacey a cell phone number for Turtledove. "But I get first Web links on any sensational stuff you unearth. And I'll follow up for my readers."

"I was afraid of that. But you get nothing until after *The Eye Street Observer* gets it." She signed off and pondered where to start on the Amanda story.

Who was Amanda Manville anyway? A plastic supermodel, a butterfly caught in a net, waiting only to impaled on a spike by the media and added to their collection of beautiful dead things? It was a dismal thought, and Lacey chided herself for it. She left a voice message for Forrest, a.k.a Turtledove. As soon as she hung up, the phone rang. *Wow, that didn't take long,* Lacey thought. Not expecting a call so soon from Turtledove, she was betting the call was from Brooke, and *The Eye*'s new caller ID confirmed it.

"Lacey, what's the story? Damon said you called."

"No court today?"

"Just doctoring some briefs. Boring. You're writing about Amanda Manville?" There was an air of expectation in her voice.

Lacey started keying in her notes on her computer while listening to Brooke. "A fashion story. She's unveiling a new line of clothing at Snazzy Jane's in Georgetown."

"Well, I'm sure you've already heard the wicked rumors about her." Brooke purred like a cat hoarding a bowl of juicy information.

"What rumors?" *That she's crazy? It's not a rumor.* "Tell me."

"About her old boyfriend. You know, the ugly one that was on that TV show."

"Caleb Collingwood?"

"Umm-hmmm. They say she killed him. As in murdering him, depriving him of life."

"Oh, that rumor. Sure, but she denies everything," Lacey said. "She says he killed himself. After meeting Amanda, I can see why he would."

"So the notorious supermodel can torment men to their death?"

"I think he ran away from her as fast as his long, tall legs could carry him. She's a mean girl, middle-school scary. If she's a killer it's in the grand tradition of Lucrezia Borgia." Lacey leaned back in her chair, knowing it would be a few minutes before Brooke would let her get back to her keyboard.

"She probably is a killer, and I bet it had something to do with the Bionic Babe Project."

"The Bionic Babe Project? Is this that conspiracy theory Damon was ranting about?"

"Why do you suppose she was never prosecuted for his murder?"

"Maybe because there was no body?"

"A technicality."

"Are we in 'Smoking Gun' territory?" Lacey knew that Brooke was also a devoted follower of that muckraking Web site.

"I'm afraid the rumors are not that reliable. But it's supposedly top secret."

"How secret can it be if you're blabbing about it to me?" Lacey had to bite her tongue to keep from laughing. "And how on earth does the government have time to conduct a Bionic Babe Project and install 'pheromone jammers' on the roof of the Pentagon and the White House and keep track of all the other conspiracies in the world while deciding whether the alert level is Code Indigo or Code Fuchsia?"

"I love that you're skeptical, Lacey; it keeps me on my toes. But someday you'll believe. The truth is out there. Anyway, some say Collingwood knew too much about the project and was terminated with extreme prejudice."

"Gosh, that is terribly entertaining, Brooke, but I need facts. My editor prefers them. Maybe the poor guy went into hiding because he was humiliated on national television. I mean, who could blame him? He's supposed to marry his ugly duckling, but she gets turned into a swan and dumps him like dirty laundry in front of the whole world. And I'll tell you one thing about Ms. Manville. She's a basket case. A complete psychotic diva."

"That or a cold-blooded bionic killer with superhuman strength. But maybe the guilt is getting to her. The diva part is a great cover. So what did she say about him?"

"That was it. She hasn't seen him in years. And she is tired of being a suspect."

"Exactly."

"Ah, Brooke, if only I wrote fiction, I'd love to use this stuff. Gotta go. Gotta write about fire-breathing fashion divas and their pretty sisters who sew."

"Okay, but keep me current. Lunch this week?"

"Sure." Lacey checked her appointment book. "Tomorrow I'm seeing Stella for lunch."

"Your crazed stylist? You know those salon chemicals have

probably damaged her brain. Your hair looks fabulous. Don't let her touch it." Brooke didn't care for Stella.

"This is not about hair."

"Stella's always about hair. Besides, she just gets you in trouble."

"Sometimes she helps me out."

"If you call taking that goofy picture for the front page of *The Eye* helping you out. Remember?"

Lacey remembered the picture very well and winced at the memory. She was wearing the Gloria Adams "telltale heart" gown, made especially for Lacey in morning-glory blue. She had found the original pattern in Aunt Mimi's wonderful trunk. Lacey was wielding the sword cane at her attacker when Stella arrived with her camera. "She did help me fight for my life after she took the picture, you know."

"A true friend would not have stopped to take a picture while you were being murdered." Brooke sighed loudly, as if Lacey would never get this obvious point.

"And where were *you* when I needed you? Looking fabulous in your grandmother's vintage gown? Flirting with Damon?"

"No fair. I had no idea you were in trouble. But I wouldn't have stopped to take a photograph. Maybe afterward—for DeadFed— definitely not before. Anyway, how about lunch Friday?"

After setting a date with Brooke, Lacey couldn't resist checking out the Web for gossip on the missing and presumed dead Caleb Collingwood, even though it added nothing to the story she had to write today. Maybe she could find a way to contact his family. Someone had to know if he was dead or alive. *Even a guy who planned his disappearance might not be able to resist calling home to tell the folks he's all right,* she thought. Instead, she found some old articles that indicated Collingwood had no immediate family. His father was unknown, and his mother ran off when he was young. Caleb was raised by an elderly alcoholic uncle in West Virginia, one Adam Collingwood. The Internet coughed up a telephone number, but when she called it, the phone was no longer in service.

She discovered a friend of the missing man, one John Henry Tyler, who had put together a Web site that led with an essay, "The Last Time I Saw Cal." Tyler had included a picture of Caleb and Amanda in her presurgery days, in matching denim overalls at the battered-women's shelter. The pair looked rustic and homely, but happy. "Rustic and homely" described Tyler's Web site too.

Following his famous dismissal on prime-time television, Amanda's boyfriend was "lower than a whale on Prozac," according to Tyler. He didn't come right out and say that Amanda committed murder, but he laid the blame for Collingwood's disappearance at her feet. Cal had told Tyler that Amanda was "killing him slowly, inch by inch." Caleb Collingwood vanished less than a year after being dumped on national television. He was going to visit a friend in Ohio and never showed up. His rusty old Honda Civic was found by the side of a dirt road. The keys were in the ignition, a suitcase on the backseat. The paper quoted a West Virginia state patrolman who theorized that the driver stopped to answer nature's call, but after that, no one knew. If there was a body, the elements and wild animals got to it first.

Tyler had met Caleb the summer after high school, when they were both working at a custom car shop in Winchester, Virginia, hometown of the late, great country singer Patsy Cline. They were hot-rodding and pool-shooting buddies. But then, Tyler said, Caleb decided he needed to see what life was like in the big city, and he had plans for more schooling. He went to D.C. and met Amanda.

John Henry Tyler offered a reward for information on Collingwood. And he posted an open plea to Ms. Manville: "Come Clean, Amanda Manville. Tell the World What You Know!" The site also featured a guest book where others had posted their theories. Collingwood had gotten lost, died from exposure, and been eaten by wild animals, according to one. He was a lovelorn suicide over the public humiliation of losing Amanda. He had been taken by aliens; he was apparently driving along a notorious alien abduction route. Another suggested snarkily that his disappearance was of interest only because he was a footnote to the career of the beautiful Amanda.

One popular theory was that Amanda had slipped him cyanide, then dissolved his body with quicklime at a construction site. This theory was sketchy on crucial details, like time and place. Lacey's favorite theory by far was that he had fled the country, changed his name, and was using his famously ugly face as a character actor in the films of Spanish director Pedro Almodóvar. Someone claimed to have spotted him in a crowd scene.

No wonder Amanda was rattled when I asked about the ex, Lacey thought. *I had no idea Caleb's disappearance was such a feeding frenzy for rumormongers.* But she wondered if the suicide story was true. Was Miguel right and Caleb had been too ugly to live—and could it somehow be a true Crime of Fashion? She imagined the headline: *"My Ugly Boyfriend Had to Die! He Couldn't Match My Makeover!"*

What did that say about our values in the new millennium? Lacey wondered. What if Cassandra Wentworth, *The Eye*'s gloomy editorial writer, had a point? Was the nation's makeover madness a sign of the incipient fall of Western civilization? Lacey shuddered at the thought. She personally thought everyone deserved a good makeover once in a while. *I could use a day at the spa right now.*

Perhaps there were others who might tell her what they knew about Caleb Collingwood. Perhaps Zoe Manville. But she was veering away from the topic she had to report on: the Chrysalis Collection. And the secondary topic: Was someone really trying to kill Amanda, or just having the nasty fun of torturing an already high-strung diva to watch her go ballistic?

She suspected she could get ahold of the distinguished Dr. Gregory Spaulding. Lacey checked the paper's electronic daybook, which posted upcoming news events around town, collected by Mac's assistant editor from a variety of wire services and other sources, as well as by the reporters assigned to each event. They rarely had anything to do with Lacey's beat, which she made up as she went along. However, she found that Spaulding was set to address a conference of surgeons the next morning at the tony Mayflower Hotel on Connecticut Avenue near Dupont Circle. She marked it down in her appointment book. Maybe he could spare a few words about his former paramour. In the meantime, Lacey tried to rough out a lead for her story for the next day. She was determined to give Zoe her due. "Celebrity Sisters' Fashion Act Sizzles at Snazzy Jane's."

She didn't get far before the phone rang again, interrupting the little dance with her keyboard. *What now?* "Fashion desk, Smithsonian speaking."

"Hey, beautiful." His voice was like warm honey, easing the tension in her shoulders.

"Hey, Vic," she said, her voice softening. "What's up?"

"Just thinking of you. When I saw you last night, you left out the part about escaping death by lightning strike and Krispy Kreme sign. Slip your mind?"

"I was too busy kissing you. It must have helped erase the painful memory."

"Lucky for me I have the front page of your paper to consult when you leave out a few salient details. You've turned me into a subscriber."

There's a mixed blessing, she thought. *The Eye needs every subscriber it can get.* "Let's not talk about lucky, okay?"

"Who is this Wiedemeyer character anyway?"

"Just a reporter. He handles what we like to call the 'death-and-dismemberment' beat."

"I thought that's what you've been doing."

"Hey, you're supposed to be saying sweet nothings to me, especially if you want to whisk me away this weekend."

"Sweet nothings, huh? I'd practice, but somehow jeopardy always seems to come between us."

"That's not a sweet nothing."

"I don't want to sound overly macho here, but damn it, Lacey, it feels like I should be there to . . . to protect you. To be there for you. To keep you out of harm's way."

"If this is your idea of sweet talk, sweetheart . . ."

Trujillo walked past and stopped, riveted by the word *sweetheart.* He perched on a corner of her desk.

"Look, I'm not saying you can't protect yourself." She heard Vic sigh in frustration and she almost laughed. "God knows you're pretty wicked with a weapon, especially blades. I'm just calling to make sure everything is okay," he said, "that you're not being pursued by errant lighting strikes. Or murderers. And that we're set for this weekend."

"So far. Lightning never strikes twice." She had a small moment of wanting to tell him about Amanda's lurid reputation, but she decided to let it slip by. "Where are we going, Vic?" He was silent. "Vic? Are you there?"

Vic's voice dropped to a near whisper. "Look, I'm on the move; I'll have to call you later. Stay out of trouble and away from falling doughnut signs." Vic hung up, no doubt surveilling someone. Lacey sighed. At least he hadn't quizzed her about any killers she might have brushed up against today. She turned around to find Trujillo grinning at her.

"This weekend?" Trujillo said, seizing this key nugget of information like a true reporter. "Is love finally in the air for Smithsonian?"

"You're a hopeless snoop, Tony."

"It's my job." He favored her with his lady-killer smile. She had witnessed the effect that smile had on Tony's girlfriends.

"Vic's in town? Your voice changes when he's around. A heightened state of arousal, I'd say."

"Shut up." She tried to smack him with a newspaper, but he dodged out of her way.

"The way you're grinning tells me he is. That's cool. Then *he* can worry about you for a while. I just dropped by to see if you were in one piece."

"Would you give it a rest, Tony? Wiedemeyer is not the bad-luck charm you seem to think he is." *Keep saying it; it might be true.* "There is no such thing as a jinx."

"Right. Have you talked with him today?" He sat down again on her desk.

"No. I've been busy visiting boutiques, interviewing an insane supermodel." Lacey handed him a couple of shots of Amanda from the press packet. "Ah, the glamour of dealing with a real diva. Amanda Manville. You'd like her."

"Trying to throw me over?"

"She's available, Tony. Between boyfriends."

"Yeah, and we all know why. *Señorita Matadora.* And she's too skinny. But a pretty face for a femme fatale, a very pretty face." Tony shuffled through the photos. "I take it you have been staying away from Wiedemeyer like the sensible Smithsonian I know, the one who hides inside your foolhardy Lois Lane exterior."

"Flattery from you, Tony? Well, that's just weird, that's what it is. And to tell you the truth, I'm not that fond of Harlan Wiedemeyer. Besides, he's fixated on Felicity. Possibly the only lucky thing I can think of regarding him."

"You're a wise woman. I'm on my way out; do you need a ride home? You can tell me how Vic plans to seduce you."

"That sounds like such fun, but I drove my car."

"The legendary Z? Wow, you never drive." Tony stood up and stretched. "I thought it was embalmed in the Z Museum."

It was true she usually took the Metro to work. Driving into Washington was a complete pain, not to mention the savage search for parking, but after her experience with Wiedemeyer and the Krispy Kreme sign the previous night, Lacey had craved the sense of security that driving her own car gave her. There were a limited number of spaces in the paper's garage, and most were reserved for the resident bigwigs, like Mac and their publisher, Claudia Darnell. But she'd arrived early and parked her vintage Nissan 280ZX in one of the few open spaces set aside for nonmanagement types.

She trusted her Z to ward off another encounter with the Wiedemeyer Effect.

"I'll walk out with you," he said.

Tony waited for Lacey to gather her things. She was congratu-
lating herself on having driven, but when they reached the garage,
her car wasn't there. It took Lacey a while to absorb the reality that
it was gone. Really gone, not just hiding behind an SUV. She and
Tony circled the garage three times, then she checked with the attendant while he circled once more. She kept hoping she'd simply
forgotten where she had parked her beloved silver-and-burgundy
280ZX, that she would turn one more corner and there it would be.
But it had vanished.

Someone had stolen her car right out of the newspaper's own
parking garage.

chapter 8

"It doesn't make any sense," she kept saying. "Who would steal my car? It's over twenty-one years old—old enough to drink."

"Maybe we should check the bars," Trujillo said. "It wasn't towed by mistake? What did the attendant say?"

"No tow trucks, and he didn't see anything unusual."

"Yeah, he was probably asleep."

"Why would someone take *my* car?" She found it hard to breathe through her disappointment. She felt tears lurking just out of sight in the corners of her eyes. "And I always lock the Club on the steering wheel! How could someone possibly steal it?"

"That Club is no big deal to a pro, Lacey. They can snap it in thirty seconds. I've seen 'em do it," Tony offered helpfully. "They probably just took the car for the parts." She glared at him. "It had alloy wheels. Then again, you let Wiedemeyer give you a ride last night. The Jonah of Eye Street."

"Shut up, Tony."

"Give you a ride?"

"Please. After I make some calls."

With Trujillo at her heels, Lacey stormed back up to the office to make a police report. The D.C. police verified that her Z, her lifeline to freedom, the car she'd had longer than any man in her life, had not been towed to an impound lot, so it apparently was stolen. Ho-hum. They took her whole report over the phone. They were bored. ("You know how many cars get stolen in the District every day, ma'am?") After that, she called her insurance agent and left a voice mail.

She was in an extreme state of distress when Wiedemeyer sidled over to her desk, the remains of a Krispy Kreme doughnut scattered down his tie. No doubt it had been a busy day for him on the death-and-dismemberment beat, reading such stimulating publications as CDC's "Morbidity and Mortality Weekly Report." For Wiedemeyer this always required lots of sugar. And, of course, he had to report to Lacey on the distressing workplace death of the day. With hand gestures.

"Another poor bastard dead on the Woodrow Wilson Bridge Project," Wiedemeyer announced proudly. "Right next to your place, right, Lacey? A construction worker. No hard hat. Of course, a hard hat wouldn't have helped him when the crane knocked him in the *cabeza*. It somehow hooked onto his tool belt, swooped him over the fence, and dropped him onto the Beltway. No hard hat. No fall protection. Smack. But he might have made it, except just then a Virginia Department of Transportation truck ran right over him. The vicious slime bastards." He took a deep gulp of air, like a fish out of water. "Poor little bastard never knew what hit him."

"Which ones are the bastards, Harlan?"

"Everyone's a bastard, Lacey. Everyone."

"Yeah. The crane. The Beltway. The truck. The bastards. We got it, Wiedemeyer." Tony distilled the report to its essence. "Now if you can stop listening to yourself talk for a few minutes, we got a situation here."

But nothing daunted Harlan Wiedemeyer for long. He was all chummy sympathy after hearing about her missing car.

"Jeez, I know how you feel, Lacey. First my car is totaled, and now yours is gone. I wonder how many poor bastards have to go through this every day."

"I don't care how many poor bastards lose their cars every day, excuse me very much, Wiedemeyer," she snapped. "At the moment, if you don't mind, I only care that mine is gone! My car. My beautiful 280ZX."

"I'd like to get my hands on that bastard! Who stole it?" Harlan was shaking with righteous fervor.

Lacey just looked at him. Wiedemeyer could barely wrestle down a doughnut, let alone a car thief.

"Hey, I know. I'll drive you home, Lacey. I've got a rental car," he offered. "We can stop for doughnuts." She had to stop herself from smacking him, because the words just didn't come. Trujillo stepped in.

"She's had enough of your help for a while, *mal de ojo*. Thanks all the same."

The little man retreated, but as he backed away from her desk, Wiedemeyer said, "I didn't have anything to do with this, Lacey. I wouldn't dream of it; you know that." He walked a few steps, then

turned around again and glared at Trujillo. "And I am not an evil
eye, a harbinger of bad luck. It's a crazy rumor. I have no idea how
it got started." He continued muttering back down the hallway.
The few remaining reporters in the newsroom steered clear of him.
Tony jingled the keys to his Mustang.

At home, Lacey dropped her bag on the floor and felt a scream
of frustration coming on when the phone rang. She didn't want to
answer, but she picked it up anyway, cursed by her insatiable curiosity.

"Lacey Blaine Smithsonian, you haven't called home in three
weeks. I just wanted to know if my eldest and most forgetful
daughter was still alive or if I should come to the funeral."

Oh, no, Lacey thought. *Please, no. Not now.*

Rose Smithsonian had a mother's instinct for calling at all the
wrong times. Lacey never quite knew what to say to her, because
she didn't quite feel related to Rose. She wasn't sure she ever had.
When she thought of her mother, she saw a relentless bulldozer of
a woman, albeit a small bulldozer, with an unbridled enthusiasm
for *projects*, the most important of which were her daughters. But
Cherise, Lacey's younger sister, was the blue-ribbon prizewinner
of Rose's projects, like a perfect soufflé: happy, fluffy, perky, and
just so darn sweet. Lacey was more of a fallen angel-food cake,
which could never rise to her mother's expectations and so had
never really been properly frosted and decorated, in Rose's esti-
mation. She would never bring home a ribbon. But to Lacey's cha-
grin, her mother would not give up on her, as other mothers with
better sense would have.

When she wasn't working on crafting the perfect daughters,
Rose devoted her life to decorating her house, in wild frenzies of
enthusiasm that would leave the whole family camped in the hallways like refugees for weeks at a time while every room was
stripped, scrubbed, painted, and wallpapered beyond all recognition. Lacey didn't know how she had ever lived through her
mother's Neon-Orange-and-Lime-Green Phase, which was followed by the Eye-Popping Primary-Color Assault, and capped by
the Dismal-Eggplant-and-Ochre Period. Lacey was convinced she
had nothing in common with Rose except the name Smithsonian.

Lacey long ago concluded she had been exchanged for the real
baby Smithsonian at birth, probably by wayward Gypsies. Even as
a small child, she had treated her family as a group of strangers
who had politely taken her in without understanding what exotic

manner of creature she really was. The only one she had resembled at all, in looks or spirit, was her Great-aunt Mimi, her favorite relative, who was now dead. She missed Mimi more than she could say, but she was grateful she had a few things to remember her by. Her mother, however, was still under the impression that Lacey was her responsibility and somehow related to her, despite the utter lack of a family resemblance.

"Hi, Mom, I'm still alive. How is every—"

"Lacey, honey, what's wrong? You sound funny."

"I'm fine. Really. Not funny at all." She tried to lighten up her voice, but the misery of having her car stolen weighed heavily on her.

"Lacey, something is wrong. A mother knows these things. Did you lose your job?"

"No, I didn't lose my job! But if you must know, my car was stolen today," she snarled, without meaning to. *Happy now?*

"Stolen?" Her mother's voice registered alarm and excitement. "Goodness gracious, haven't I always told you that Washington, D.C., is a terrible place? My poor baby. Stolen? By car thieves?"

Lacey, what have you done? You don't share personal information with Rose. "It's no big deal," Lacey said, trying not to sniffle.

"No big deal? I should say it is a big deal, young lady. I knew something like this would happen." She heard her mother call to someone else and relate the news. No doubt she had just made her mother's day. Now there'd be something shocking to tell the neighbors.

"Who's there?"

"Your sister and your father. We're just finishing dinner. I made my special meat loaf." Lacey's stomach turned over at the very thought of her mother's meat loaf. "They are shocked about this crime, let me tell you. Shocked."

"Mom, things happen. I'll be okay. I have insurance."

"And no car! I just don't feel right with you trapped all alone in that terrible place."

Lacey sank down in one of her striped satin wing chairs, unbuttoned her jacket, and slipped off her shoes. She hated being grilled by family members, even on the phone, where if necessary she could simply hang up. "Cars get stolen in Denver too," she protested.

"Not ratty old cars like yours. I mean, if they go about stealing a car as old as yours, what kind of danger would you be in if it were a good car?"

"It *is* a good car," Lacey protested. "I love that car. It's a classic—"

"Did you call the police?"

No. I'm brainless. "Of course I called the police, and the insurance agent. Everything is going to be fine." *Yeah, right.* She heard her mother groan in utter disbelief. "Stop worrying. How's Cherise, Mom?" Switching the subject to her sister, Cherise, was usually a surefire way to put her mother off track. It seemed to work: Lacey was informed that Cherise, the perfect one, was now dating a very nice young man who was an accountant or something. He seemed very "suitable." Her mother filled Lacey in on all the family news she would have heard in her obligatory twice-monthly phone call, which had apparently slipped to three weeks. But Rose wasn't ready to let go of Lacey's stolen car just yet. She urged Lacey to call if she needed anything.

"And I can fly out there tomorrow on Frontier. Your father wouldn't mind."

"No! Mom, I'm fine. I'm sure you've got other things to do. Like your big Halloween thing, right?" Rose agreed that her traditional Halloween open house was a top priority, but she still sounded dubious about Lacey's safety alone. Finally they exchanged good-byes. Lacey was thankful she had survived the Smithsonian Inquisition for another week—or three. She changed her clothes, ate some popcorn, and was about to call it an early night when her cell phone rang, startling her. Mac had forced it on her after Felicity's minivan explosion the previous month, but she rarely used it, and when she tried she often found the battery had been dead for days. "Hello?"

"Hello, Lacey? Turtledove here. I'm downstairs. You said you wanted to talk. May I come up?"

Wow, a gentleman, she thought. *Everyone else just troops in through the broken security door.* She made sure he remembered the apartment number and let him in when he knocked.

"Thanks for calling back, Forrest. But I didn't expect you to show up on my doorstep."

"It was on my way. Thought I'd swing by. It's been a long day with the— Well, it's been a long day."

"Do you prefer Forrest or Turtledove?"

"Only my friends call me Turtledove." His voice was deep and rich, and his brown eyes were amused. "So you can choose."

"I prefer Turtledove, if you don't mind. Thanks for helping me out last month, when you guys hid Mimi's trunk for me." She had been afraid the vintage patterns in her trunk would be an irresistible target for the fashion designer Hugh Bentley and his henchmen. Damon Newhouse and his conspiracy Web site crew, Turtledove among them, had helped her stage a diversion and moved the trunk to safety. Now he went over to the big old leather-covered and brass-buckled trunk and smiled slowly.

"I see you got it back. Looks nice there."

"I need it for the decor. And . . . well, I need it." Lacey glanced fondly at Mimi's trunk, now safely back in her living room in its usual place as her coffee table.

"Any more secrets in it?"

"Who knows? I hope so," Lacey smiled and offered him a beer and the last of the popcorn, but he just had a glass of cranberry juice instead. Lacey sat on the sofa and he took a chair. "This conversation is just between us, okay?"

He raised an eyebrow. "Of course."

"The reason I called is that I want to know if you think Amanda Manville is really in trouble."

"She thinks she is." He swallowed half the drink in one gulp. "My associates and I proposed doing the job right, at least while she's here in the District. State-of-the-art security for a high-threat, high-profile celebrity. Secure perimeters, around-the-clock controlled access, locked-down safe areas, multiple identity and credential checks, the works. But she didn't want that. She just gave us one photograph—Dr. Greg Spaulding—and orders to keep him away from her, and not to let the lovesick stalker near her, if he should show up. I think mostly she just wanted bodyguards for show, a big, flashy celebrity entourage. Maybe just to scare off Spaulding, or the stalker. Or maybe it's just a big old ego trip."

"She wants to get me involved," Lacey said. "With her idea that someone's going to kill her. She thinks I can solve it, or do something to stop it. Shows what she knows."

"Ms. Amanda's got everyone around her half-crazy with it. And pissed off. For all sorts of reasons."

"Yvette Powers?"

"Check."

"Brad Powers?"

"She's got a way with him," Turtledove said. "And he's not smart about women."

"Unlike you?"

His smile was back. "Any man can be a fool, but that woman is dangerous. She wants to show she's the alpha bitch, no matter what it takes. With women, she likes to scream."

"With men?"

"She uses sex. Or she tries."

"And with you?"

"Ms. Supermodel made me an offer. She said she'd do *anything* if I could just keep her safe." He leaned back in the chair. Lacey nodded. She could see the attraction.

"And?"

He laughed. "Reporters are as bad as detectives. But I'll tell you one thing, Lacey: It's my responsibility to keep her safe, or as safe as she'll let me, but 'love slave' is not in my job description. Believe it or not, getting personal can be an occupational hazard when you're in my line of work." Lacey could believe it. He smirked. "Besides, she's got way too much baggage."

"Do you think she killed her old boyfriend?"

"That's the rep. And I think she's capable, but . . ."

"But what?"

"If she actually killed the first guy and got away with it, why not take out the doctor?"

"Maybe because she's under a cloud of suspicion."

"Good point. But she could hire it done by a pro. She's got the money. And she's crazy enough."

"But who'd really want to kill her?"

"After today, I'd say just about anyone who's met her. If she dropped off the planet the staff at Snazzy Jane's would throw a big old party."

"What about the reported stalker?"

Turtledove shrugged. "She gave us a name, but no one's really sure what the letter writer looks like. Or if the stalker even is the letter writer. You saw me dump that scruffy little guy in the street today? We think he's the letter guy. Or one of them. He was nervous, sweaty, stuttering and stammering after I escorted him out."

"I hate to break it to you, big guy, but I think you'd get that reaction from any number of law-abiding citizens," Lacey said. Turtledove gave a little nod, taking the comment modestly. "Did you catch a name?"

"He wouldn't tell me. And there were reporters everywhere all day, so I couldn't very well shake him down in the street. Bad publicity."

"There's an image," she said. Turtledove could have shaken

him upside down with one hand. "What do you know about the let-ters?"

"I'm just the hired muscle for her D.C. visit. Part-time at that. But from what I've heard, the writer's gone from pleading for a few minutes of her time to demanding to see her on a matter of great importance." Turtledove drained his glass of cranberry juice, and Lacey brought him another from the kitchen. He looked like he could drink a gallon of it at a time.

"What about the note she found on the mirror?"

"It was nothing like the letters I saw. And I only saw a couple, but they're very controlled, small writing, in block letters. The note on the mirror was emotional, choppy, angry—scrawled let-ters. No one from the outside could have come in and slapped it on her mirror. Of course, there were lots of people with permission to run through the place. Could be someone she pissed off just wants to torture her a little. Someone from the catering crew, maybe. Maybe the makeup and hair people. Who knows?"

"What about Zoe or Yvette?"

"She treats them like dirt, and what's worse, she enjoys it. My opinion."

"What about Spaulding?"

"Not a peep out of him, far as I can tell."

"How much longer will you be there?"

"Just a couple of days. Amanda will be leaving, and life will go on pretty much the same."

"So you're a professional bodyguard?"

Turtledove smiled and glanced at Lacey's bookshelf clock. "Sometimes. We prefer the term 'protection agent.' What can I say? It's a gig. And I've got to go." He rose to his feet with grace. "I have another kind of gig going on tonight. I play the late set in a little band at Velvet's Blues."

Lacey sat up straight, surprised. "The jazz club down on King Street? Upstairs over that restaurant? I've been meaning to go there for ages."

"Come by some night if you like classic blues and jazz and swing."

"Duke Ellington and Glenn Miller? Gershwin?" Lacey asked as she stood up and walked Turtledove to the door.

"Absolutely. Everything from Satchmo up to early Miles. We play smooth and we play jazz, but we don't play no 'smooth jazz,' if you know what I mean."

"What do you play?"

"Trumpet."

"I had no idea you were so talented."

"Man of mystery. That's me. *Ciao,* Lacey. Call me if you need me." He handed her a business card with just his name, Forrest Thunderbird, a phone number, and a quote at the bottom:

> *"Truth is always strange."*
> —Lord Byron

Lacey had just crawled into bed when Vic called. He was unable to console her in person, being on some dreary stakeout somewhere, but he seemed appropriately sympathetic about Lacey's car theft. At least until he said, "Well, finally now you can buy a decent set of wheels."

"Hey! I love that car! It's a classic Z," Lacey protested.

"Sweetheart, it didn't run half the time."

"It would have, once I replaced all the moving parts," she said, and he laughed. "I was getting there. The only problem was that the parts were getting pretty expensive. And my mechanic had to swim to Japan every time it needed something," she said, feeling stranded and miserable.

"I'll help you find a new car."

"Promise?"

"A good car, I promise. Something safe, sturdy."

"I'm not buying a Jeep. Or a Hummer. Or a Sherman tank."

"Maybe we could look around this weekend."

"Car shopping on a romantic weekend. Just like a man. Doesn't sound romantic to me."

"Car shopping can be very romantic," he assured her. "Although I do have other plans to keep us occupied. How does a little inn in the Shenandoahs sound? Crunching in the autumn leaves? Intimate dinners and a cozy fire in our room?"

"Sounds perfect. I'll build the fire, Boy Scout." She could smell the leaves already. "You driving?"

"Apparently I am." His voice was lulling her into a deliciously relaxed state. But one thought was nagging at her.

"About your 'no dead bodies falling in Lacey's path' rule: Remember the woman I interviewed today?" There was a pause. "Amanda Manville, the supermodel?"

"The one that was chopped and channeled on TV by the plastic surgeon?"

"Still thinking about cars, Vic?"

"Course not. Amanda Manville's kind of spooky-looking. Too symmetrical. Nothing that nature intended."

"I think she's beautiful."

"No, she's freaky, plastic—not beautiful. You're beautiful, Lacey."

You think I'm beautiful? She imagined him reaching out, smoothing her hair out of her face. Then kissing that spot on her neck behind her ear, and then more kisses up and down, making little chills run up and down her spine. She willed herself to stop the fantasy, and sighed. "You say the sweetest things completely by accident, Vic. But about Amanda."

"The one who dispatched her old boyfriend to the great beyond, right?"

"Allegedly dispatched him."

"So you met her today. Is she dead yet?" He was waiting for the punch line.

"Not yet. The thing is, she thinks someone is out to kill her. Looks like a case of paranoia. However, in the event someone—"

"Kills her? I don't like the turn this conversation has taken."

"She wants me to find out who did it. I mean, in the event it happens. But it won't. Because she also wants me to stop it first. Not that I believe her."

There was a pause on the other end. She heard him groan. "Oh, Lacey, sweetheart, what is it about you that draws these wackos?"

"It's not me; it's her. She's crazy."

"Crazy enough for someone to want to kill her?"

"Hard to say." Lacey drew her quilt up around her. "But nothing is going to get in the way of this weekend. Just us. Together," she said as she snuggled down happily into her pillow.

"Lacey, if anything happens to that surgical freak, up to and including death, I want you to promise me you'll just stand there with your notebook like a responsible reporter and let the police handle it."

"I'm not sure I like your condescending tone, Mr. Let the Cops Handle It."

"And you are a responsible reporter?" he prompted her.

"Of course." She sighed. "I'll let the cops handle it."

But I did make a promise to Amanda too. Sort of.

chapter 9

"Dr. Spaulding, I think you might want to talk with me," Lacey said as she handed over her business card. "I'm a reporter with *The Eye Street Observer* . . ."

Lacey had waited to intercept Spaulding until after he had finished his presentation to the assembled surgeons at the Mayflower Hotel. She let the crowds of colleagues and admirers thin out before she approached him. She didn't mind waiting there in the lovely old building with its deep-rose carpets, touches of gold, and heavy chandeliers. She figured he would acknowledge her if she blocked his path, but Spaulding excused himself from the remaining hangers-on and ignored her and her offered card. He kept walking. She kept pace with him.

"I know you're busy, but Amanda Manville's been making rather reckless allegations about you," Lacey said. "I wouldn't want to print them without giving you the opportunity to respond, but—"

He stopped and turned to regard her. "How reckless? And just who are you again?" The distinguished-looking Spaulding, with his dark hair shot through with strands of gray, had been the featured speaker at the morning session of plastic surgeons. He wore a dark suit and serious steel-framed glasses, but they didn't disguise his classic good looks. He looked like an actor playing a handsome plastic surgeon on TV. Of course, Lacey reflected, he had already played himself on TV on *The Chrysalis Factor,* so his media-ready polish was no accident.

Lacey gave him a very abridged version of Amanda's rant.

"That certainly sounds like our Amanda." He took her card and sized her up in a glance. He pondered for a moment. "Look, I have a half hour or so before my next session. Is there somewhere we can get some coffee out of earshot of my colleagues?"

Lacey led him outside to the Dupont Circle Starbucks up the street. They ordered their coffee black. She would have liked to get a double latte with whipped cream, but she didn't want Spaulding to think she wasn't a serious journalist. *Lacey's law for drinking coffee with a source: If he drinks it black, then I drink it black.*

Sitting opposite him, Lacey found it difficult to believe Amanda's charges. The mild-mannered Spaulding removed his glasses and rubbed his eyes. They were pale blue and tired.

"Amanda's in town? In D.C.?"

Lacey nodded. "She's publicizing her new line of clothing. She knows you're here. She says you're plotting to kill her."

"Kill her?" He looked perfectly appalled. "I don't even want to be in the same room with her, let alone stay long enough to kill her. She's been unraveling for quite a while, but this—"

"Unraveling?"

"I'm not telling any secrets here, Ms.—" He pulled out her card. "Smithsonian. Amanda has been irrational, neurotic, paranoid, tyrannical, everything you'd expect in a celebrity of her ilk. But this sort of allegation is new."

"She seems convinced that you want to destroy your own creation. 'Erasing your mistakes,' she called it."

"Same sweet girl." He shook his head wearily and shifted in his seat. "But I don't know what to make of this murder-plot fantasy of hers. . . . Listen, my comments are for background only right now, do you understand?"

Everybody knows the game. "Yes. I'm not sure what I'm going to write. It may just be a superficial piece about one woman's journey in the pursuit of beauty here in the twenty-first century. And the fallout."

"For which we will all be damned in one way or another." Spaulding finally smiled outright, which unexpectedly revealed considerable charm. "I'm through with that kind of plastic surgery, you know. So extreme you don't even recognize the person underneath anymore. I don't think it's healthy—physically or mentally."

"Why does she believe you're going to kill her?"

"She may say it, but she can't really believe it. Amanda's still angry with me. The fairy tale didn't work out the way she thought it would."

"People are supposed to adore you when you're beautiful. They're not supposed to fall out of love with you," Lacey said. She suddenly thought of Vic. For a modern guy, he really had waited for her for a long time. *And last night on the phone he said I was beautiful. Was that really the first time he's ever said that? Or just the first time I really heard it?* "Zoe Manville said you've changed your focus."

"I always liked Zoe. Living in Amanda's shadow's been very hard on her, I think. It used to be the other way around." Spaulding reflected for a moment. "Yes, my focus has changed. In the beginning, plastic surgery for me was happy medicine. My patients weren't sick, and they were generally pleased with the results. I liked making people prettier. Sometimes it really turned their lives around for the better. Then I became involved with that show. It made me a TV celebrity. And it ruined my life."

"The Chrysalis Factor, you mean?"

"Yes. After Amanda and I became a couple. I didn't enjoy all of the media attention, the interviews, the paparazzi, my photos in those tabloid magazines, the appearances on all those stupid talk shows. In some ways it even damaged my reputation. She was one of the most desirable women in the world, and I was just the man at her side, and we were both going crazy. It was a brief madness for me. I realized I had to wake up."

"From a dream or a nightmare?"

"Good question. Both, I suppose."

"And now you're donating your services to disfigured children. Pretty impressive."

"I'm not noble. But when I look at these children with cleft palates, conjoined twins, major disfigurements, land mine victims, I have to try to help. Volunteer surgeons can give them a chance for a normal life, instead of an abnormal life, like Amanda's. It's been a long time coming for me. A form of redemption, if you will."

"Penance because of what went wrong with Amanda?" Lacey asked.

"Yes, in a way. That I took this poor homely girl and made her a beauty: That's the work of the press. She had a kind of beauty before we ever started. That's all gone now. I'm not blameless. I helped create this monster and it weighs on me." He wiped his glasses clean without looking at Lacey. "Generally speaking, there's a very strict psychological screening that the makeover candidates go through. But this time—"

"What does the screening do?"

"It's supposed to filter out the candidates with too many psychological problems to make the surgery worthwhile, to make the transition successfully, the ones who want it for the wrong reasons. For revenge. To get even with the world. Amanda claimed she was not counting on it to make her beautiful, just to make her normal. She was very good. She gave all the right answers."

Lacey wondered if Spaulding was just giving her all the right answers. He was smooth and convincingly contrite. But how much of that was his own media spin? *"I'm not really a mad doctor who created a monster; I just played one on TV."*

"But it did make her beautiful," Lacey said. "And changed her life."

"It changed both our lives. Catapulted us into a life we didn't expect. But she couldn't let go of the bitterness that she masked so well. She had an entire laundry list of people with whom to get even. I suppose I'm on that list now." He took a slug of the hot coffee.

"You thought she'd be happy," Lacey said.

Spaulding nodded. He seemed surprised to be bedeviled by these problems. No doubt he had done all the right things: the right schools, the right country club, the right persona for TV. He was certainly well turned-out. She could imagine him dashing into the elegant Thomas Pink store at the Mayflower to order expensive custom-made dress shirts. Yet he was seeking redemption using the same surgical skills that had led him to Amanda Manville. Or so he claimed. Public relations–wise, it was a very clever strategy.

"You should never fall in love with your patient," he continued. "And I'd like to make it clear that we never connected in that way until after the surgery." He took a deep breath. "I have no wish to see Amanda get hurt. I just want her out of my life." Spaulding gazed out the coffee-shop window at Connecticut Avenue, obviously wishing he was somewhere else.

"She's getting hate mail and threats."

"Not from me." He turned his attention back to Lacey. "But it's always something with Amanda. There always has to be something theatrical. She's unhappy without some crisis in her life."

"A drama queen and a diva?"

"She has a pathological need to be the center of attention. Maybe she never got any attention as a child, or too much of the wrong kind, I don't know. But I don't believe anyone is really after her."

"Are you saying she's writing death threats to herself?"

"Who knows? These lunatic charges against me are proof that she's disturbed. To be honest, Ms. Smithsonian, if I could do it, I would have her fade gently away out of my life, like an old photo washed out by the sun." He looked sad and resigned.

"Do you know whatever happened to Caleb Collingwood?"

"Who? Oh, Cal, the old boyfriend. I'd forgotten his full name. I have no idea. But I don't believe any of that nonsense about Amanda killing him. He probably went to ground, like I'm trying to do. Though it's possible he killed himself. I know that's what Amanda thinks. But murdered? The media are just out of control. They write stuff just to sell papers." Spaulding checked his watch, then stood up. "I have to go."

"Thank you for speaking with me."

"If you see Amanda, tell her— No, don't tell her anything." He smiled, tossed his trash in the can, and was gone.

Lacey threw the rest of her coffee away and rushed to make her lunch date, just a few blocks away. Stella was already inside the little bookstore/restaurant at Kramerbooks & Afterwords Café near Dupont Circle, sipping a Coke. One look at her and Lacey stopped in her tracks. Stella was wearing her Stylettos smock over a little purple leather halter number. That was to be expected, as was her short-cropped spiky hair, a sort of dark purple this week. It was totally in keeping with her profession as a hairstylist, along with the short, tight black skirt and fishnet stockings. But Stella, of all people, was carrying a plaid Burberry tote bag and wearing a pair of Burberry sling-back pumps. Lacey thought she couldn't have looked more incongruous if she were wearing a perfect Jackie Kennedy pillbox hat perched on her purple crew cut. As Lacey approached the table, Stella waggled one Burberry pump in welcome.

"How do you like my shoes, Lacey? I know they're, like, totally Georgetown old lady, but I think on me they're very *ironic*. What do you think?"

"Irony works for me. But you've never been big on irony. Your outfits are usually more like blunt instruments."

"Speaking of blunt, you never told me you were going to interview Amanda Manville." She was holding up the newspaper with Lacey's story on the Chrysalis Collection sister act.

"Stella, you're reading the paper. I'm so proud of you."

"Don't be a smart-ass. So what d'you know? Yours truly is doing her hair and makeup later today for a photo shoot."

"Lucky you. You know about her reputation?" Lacey settled into her chair, being careful not to knock anybody out of their own in Kramerbooks' cramped space.

"Totally. I called Miguel. She's a man killer, huh? But she only killed her boyfriend, so I should be safe, right?"

"How did you get involved?" Lacey asked, although she figured that Stella was just plugged into the universe that way. Things fell in her lap, like information, which she traded like a stockbroker. And men, whom she collected like little girls collect Barbies.

"The stylist, some punk from Stylettos Georgetown who was supposed to do it, bailed. And then Leonardo was supposed to do it; you remember Leonardo, Stylettos' resident temperamental artiste? He bailed. This woman's got a *rep*. So I got a call from a friend of a friend. You know how it goes." She took a breath and a sip of her soda. "So, what's she like? I hear she's really whacked. With a double dose of paranoia."

"I think she might run into trouble if she crosses you. So what's the photo shoot for?"

"Some ads for her new design line. Or I guess I should say her sister's designs, according to your little exposé. I hear Amanda wanted to do some location shots in the city, D.C. hot spots for backdrops, 'cause she's local, or ex-local. You know, Adams Morgan, Georgetown, the Ken Cen. And tonight they're starting with the fountain in Dupont Circle. Convenient."

"No kidding. Maybe I'll drop by and catch her in action."

"Cool. They're shooting at dusk. Whatever that means these days. It's getting dark early. I'm meeting her at two o'clock." Stella checked her watch. "So, Lace, is this a diva or what? My salon is right down the street, but no, she's got to have her own trailer. So we'll do it there, because she wants her privacy. But you know what? No woman is a paragon to her stylist."

Lacey thought using the trailer would probably make it easier for Amanda's security people, like Turtledove, to control the undesirable elements—stalkers, lethal ex-boyfriends. But she hesitated to stimulate Stella, the D.C. gossip hotline, with tales of imaginary murder plots.

"So are you going to mention me in your column? I'm looking fabulous and I'm ready for my close-up, Mr. DeMille." Stella blew a kiss to an imaginary director.

"Still a publicity hog, I see." Lacey grinned at her favorite stylist over her menu.

"Who always comes to your aid at the drop of a hat? I do."

"Whether I need it or not."

"Ha! You always need help. And what happened to your lipstick? Have you tried the all-day kind? You look like a ghost."

"Yeah, it dries out your lips, then cakes in the lines, and it doesn't live up to your expectations."

"Nothing is perfect. Have you tried kissing with it? Works like a charm."

The waiter came by and took their orders. Lacey got the crab-and-avocado salad, while Stella went for a cheeseburger with bacon.

"Wish me luck with Amanda. Hey, do you think she did it? Offed the homely guy, I mean." Stella's eyes were as big and round as golf balls, her spiky purple hair aquiver. "I guess the real question is, did he deserve it? Did he beat her? Cheat on her? Steal her money?"

"I never heard anything like that."

"I bet he did. Bet he was a brute, or he pulled that old passive-aggressive shit; that drives me nuts. Yeah, the bastard proba-bly—"

"Is everything okay with you and Bobby?" Lacey thought that Stella's current off-and-on guy, known affectionately as "Bobby Blue Eyes," seemed like a real sweetheart, looked like a schoolboy with a sexy secret, and seemed to keep Stella happy. *But you never know.*

"Sure, why?" Stella's countenance was benign. She munched her burger.

"It's nothing, but you did sound a little . . . I don't know . . . feminist vigilante just now."

"Oh." Stella swallowed a bite. "No, Bobby's fab, the man of the hour. But I've known some real assholes in the past. I have a col-lection of them. I was just thinking that guy . . . what was his name?"

"Caleb Collingwood. Old Cal."

"Yeah, I was thinking he might have been that way, and a woman who doesn't have as much self-control as I have could've knocked him off."

"Okay. There's something else you might want to know about Amanda Manville." Lacey leaned over the table, dangling her in-formation like a piece of bait.

"Yeah, what? Tell me."

"She might be a little more nuts than usual at the moment. More nuts than even Miguel told you." Stella leaned in close. "She thinks the Grim Reaper is after her and she's making life miserable for everyone around her."

"The Grim Reaper? As in the long good-bye, the big siesta, the last enchilada? Wow." Lacey now had Stella's full and undivided attention. Stella kicked off her Burberry pumps and pushed her lunch aside, hungrier for juicy details than for a juicy burger. "Spill it, Smithsonian, and I mean *everything*."

Lacey Smithsonian's

Fashion Bites

Attack of the Burberry Pirates; or, Invasion of the Plaid Body Snatchers

Please tell me I'm only dreaming. In this nightmare it seems that the Burberry empire has invaded the capital of the Land of the Free. The Burberry pirates respect no political divisions, and their mother ship flies a flag of Burberry beige plaid with a $500 price tag. Burberry to the right of me, Burberry to the left of me, into the valley of the dull rode the Burberry pirates!

Not a dream? I'm awake? *Oh, the horror, the horror.*

The awful truth is that a ghastly proliferation of Burberry bags, scarves, raincoats, umbrellas, and for all I know Burberry-plaid underwear has hit the D.C. streets like an invasion of the plain-plaid pod people, and too many otherwise sophisticated women are even flirting with the Full Burberry. One word: Don't! Drop the shopping bag and step away from the plaid *now.*

Grudgingly I admit that the traditional Burberry is in many ways the perfect plaid for Washingtonians. It is boring and bland and features the muted colors that this city holds dear. Black. White. Gray. Beige. More beige. And that tiny stripe of red adds just the merest rumor of color, the most muted possible thrill of whispered visual excitement. The tiniest thrill goes a long way here in the City That Fashion Forgot. But really, live a little, ladies (and gentlemen).

To speak of Burberry is to invoke thoughts of knee-length Bermuda shorts, sensible British trench coats, cheerfully overpriced merchandise, and items in beige plaid that were never meant to be beige plaid. Swimsuits! What were they thinking? And now there is the fresh horror of *pink* Burberry plaid, and the disturbing concept of Burberry perfume in a Burberry plaid bottle. Plaid perfume? Is smelling slightly *plaid* the stuff that preppies dream of? Perhaps so, but the saucier perfume bottles on your dressing table may be unwilling to make room for this plain-plaid interloper.

Surrender your affections (and pocketbook) to the Burberry pirates if you must, but remember:

- A little Burberry goes a long way. The Full Burberry—plaid coat, plaid scarf, plaid bag, plaid shoes, and plaid umbrella—is a one-way ticket to the lower circles of the Fashion Inferno, the circle reserved for leisure suits, Nehru jackets, and *Flashdance* leg warmers.
- There are other plaids in the universe, plaids that are full of color, mystery, romance, heritage, and did I mention color? Ask any Scotsman, if you don't believe me.
- Go ahead and wear Burberry, if you love it, if you really, truly love it. But don't wear it just because you think it will impress all the K Street lawyers and lobbyists. And for heaven's sake, don't wear it just because it's expensive and everybody else is wearing it. Why not just wear the price tag instead? Afer all, the latest fashion fad will be over in a minute, but expensive price tags never go out of fashion. Do they?

chapter 10

"Long Lens" Hansen, one of *The Eye*'s staff photographers, sprawled in Lacey's chair, his legs propped up on her desk. He was leafing through Amanda Manville's press photos when Lacey got back to the newsroom after lunch with Stella.

"Make yourself at home, Hansen. Can I get you anything? A blanket? A pillow?" She swung her bag onto the desk and reached over him to see if her voice-mail light was on.

He straightened up and smiled at her, easing his lanky legs down. He held up a sultry photo of Amanda. "Tate Penfield does nice work."

"Yeah, the photograph is beautiful. But she's a lot of trouble."

"Look at the composition," Hansen said, dwelling on the picture.

"Taking notes?"

"Sort of. Mac told me to sweet-talk you into a head shot for your column. I'm doing all the columnists. Part of *The Eye*'s big makeover."

"Really? You planning any of those up-the-nostril shots, or mouth-open-tongue-out-fingers-in-ears kind of photos you guys are so fond of?"

"Nah, no candids. Mac would kill me—right after you did." He grinned. "I'll even let you comb your hair. Besides, those up-the-nostril shots take a lot a practice, if you must know. But I find they're important if you want to get a politician looking appropriately silly."

Hansen had his own rogues' gallery of candid shots tacked up outside his darkroom, photos deemed too embarrassing for even *The Eye Street Observer* to publish, Democrats and Republicans alike snapped unawares in funhouse poses, tongues wagging, features exaggerated, clothes awry. Candidates stuffing their faces with regrettable food. Senators captured making lewd gestures and moronic faces. Congressmen caught leering at the busts of nearby females. Lacey could just imagine her future place of honor on Hansen's Wall of Shame.

"Okay, consider your message delivered. I'll think about it," she said.

"You're lying, right?"

"Yep. No photo. No way."

"Well, then, I've done my job." He unfolded himself to a standing position. "Let me know when Mac succeeds in pressuring you into knuckling under. We can do it at the studio I share with Tate. He's teaching me all the glamour-photog tricks. I promise, you'll look like a movie star."

"Why don't I believe you?"

"Or we can just select one of those Forties hairstyle shots we did last month."

"That was a weak moment," Lacey said. Stella had talked her into trying a different 1940s hairstyle every day for a full week to see what would go best with the Gloria Adams gown for the Fashion Museum gala. Mac thought it would make a nice photo feature, and a way to turn the fashion tables on his pet fashion reporter. His style sense was lacking, but his editorial-imperative senses were keen.

"How about the one with the snood?"

"Over my dead body. Go back to your dark kingdom, Hansen."

"Your wish is my command." He bowed theatrically and strolled off. Hansen waved at Felicity as he passed the food editor in the hall.

Felicity returned from a long lunch to her desk across the aisle from Lacey's, and sat down to do whatever it was she did to produce her food column. She looked up at Lacey with her strange, blank blue eyes.

"I heard the terrible news that your car was stolen." Felicity was oozing with faux sympathy. "I am so sorry, Lacey. Your poor little sports car," she said in a tone that made it perfectly clear that she felt the universe was merely evening up the score between them. *One minivan, one Z. Love all.*

"I appreciate your kind words, Felicity." *Why don't you just shut up?*

"Perhaps it's for the best, after all. It was getting kind of long in the tooth, wasn't it?"

"That's one way of looking at it." *Bitch.* "I'm sure when your minivan blew up, you realized it was all for the best. It was getting a little broad in the butt, wasn't it?"

Felicity slammed the drawer shut. "That explosion was meant for you!"

"Because they thought you were me! Fancy that. How on earth could that have happened? The amazing resemblance? Or maybe because you were nibbling on my beat like a mouse on a stolen cookie?"

Felicity jumped up from her seat, grabbed her coffee cup, and marched out in speechless fury. Mac passed Felicity on his way over to see Lacey.

"Are you two squabbling again?" He glared at Lacey.

"Are we breathing?"

Mac looked toward Felicity's desk for today's sweet and fattening offering. "It's not going to work, Smithsonian. I am not separating you. Learn to play nice. This is the LifeStyle section, and the girly beats go together."

"That's a nice offensive take on things," Lacey responded. "You know, there's a desk open near Wiedemeyer. Felicity could move there. Or he could move here. Make a nice change. Part of the big makeover. Move me to news."

Mac grabbed an iced oatmeal cookie. "Not gonna happen, Smithsonian; we like Felicity. Sitting her near Wiedemeyer? It's not a good idea."

"Because you think he's a jinx."

"No, I don't believe in that. No such thing as a jinx. However, it's a known fact that bad things mysteriously happen to Wiedemeyer and the people who hang out around him."

"Like a jinx?" Mac rolled his eyes. "But Mac, Felicity likes Harlan and he likes her. She's already had her car blown up. What else could happen?"

Mac looked over at Felicity's desk. The plate of cookies was calling, and he took a couple more. "I'm not interested in finding out." He cleared a spot on Lacey's desk and leaned against it. "I am, however, concerned that your car was stolen out of *The Eye*'s garage yesterday. And our publisher is furious."

"Is Claudia going to buy me a new car?"

"Nice try. But you will be glad to know we're putting together new security procedures."

"Closing the old barn door after the horse is stolen. Good strategy."

"By the way, you got a 'Crimes of Fashion' column for me this week?"

"I'm working on it." It was Wednesday, the deadline for her Friday "Crimes of Fashion" column. She was still hammering away at "Make Me Over: The Mad Pursuit of Beauty in the Twenty-first Century." But there was quite a ways to go. "Better leave me alone or you'll be running blank column inches." Mac grabbed another cookie and ambled off.

The weekend couldn't come fast enough, as Lacey found herself dwelling on pleasant thoughts of Victor Donovan. He was broad in the shoulders, narrow in the hips, and had muscular arms that made her melt. Getting out of town alone together would be the perfect antidote to all this nonsense about supermodels and their paranoias and her beloved car being stolen and the paper's big makeover and being badgered about a cutesy little photo to go along with her column. She couldn't stand it one more second. She gave Vic a call. Anything to hear his voice and relive the promise of seeing him later.

"Howdy, stranger," she purred. "Can I buy you dinner?"

"That's hard to pass up, lady. By the way, who is this?"

"Smart-ass. First I have to finish this accursed column, and then I'm going to see Amanda Manville in action at a photo shoot in Dupont Circle. But I can meet you later."

"Is this the knucklehead model who wants you to solve her much-anticipated murder?"

"The very same."

"In that case, we'll go together. I'll meet you at the paper."

"It's sweet of you to care."

"Lacey." His voice was a caress. "I've loved your mind and your soul for a long time. But right now, I'm pretty darned interested in your body, and I'm going to protect that cute tush of yours, no matter how many weirdos try to trap you in their sick head trips."

"Ooh, you think I have a cute tush?"

"The cutest."

"Sometimes, Vic, you're adorable."

"Prove it."

Thrills danced up Lacey's spine. "Prove it?"

"This weekend. And remember what you're going to say if anything, much less the worst, happens to Ms. Manville?"

"I'll let the police handle it, Chief." *I'll let them handle their end of it, anyway.*

*　　*　　*

Lacey felt his presence before she saw him. *There really is something to those pheromones.* She smiled to herself; then she looked up from her computer screen and there he was, sexy smile and all.

"How did you get through security?"

"I'm a professional." His skin was still dark from the Colorado sun, his jade eyes telegraphing his desire for her. His faded jeans molded to his body, and a black sweater pushed up on his forearms revealed curly dark hair. Goose bumps and a few other hot, sweaty feelings distracted her. Good thing she had finished her work. Her friend Brooke's fantasy "Pentagon pheromone jammers" that were allegedly derailing Washingtonians' sexual desires certainly had no effect on Vic. "You look beautiful, Lacey."

This is what men are good for, she thought. *Among other things.* Lacey had no idea how she looked today. Yesterday she had dressed to impress. Today, dressing for comfort, she simply wore black slacks and a fitted red jacket with black buttons, but one word from Vic made her feel beautiful. She ran her fingers through her hair as she gave him a slow smile.

"Maybe we could start our weekend early," she flirted.

"I can make a phone call," he said. "Take Thursday and Friday off."

"Oh, darling, I can't," she said, "but maybe tonight we could . . ."

Trujillo chose just that moment to pass by on his way to the staff kitchen. "Get a room, you two."

"Reservation's already made," Vic said. Tony grinned, and they slapped hands. Lacey blushed.

"Get out of here, Tony," she said.

"It's quitting time; we all should get out of here. Then later Vic and I can swap stories," he said, ducking a paper missile that Lacey launched at him. Lacey gathered her tote bag, grabbed her leather jacket, and sneaked a kiss with Vic.

The sun was an orange ball low on the horizon, lighting pink and lavender clouds in the dusky Washington evening. A hint of wood smoke perfumed the air, and it was just crisp enough to kiss the cheeks with a hint of colder weather to come. Just crisp enough for her black embroidered shawl and gloves. Lacey held Vic's hand as they approached the park and the Navy Memorial fountain at Dupont Circle. It was a pleasant oasis tucked inside the city's most irritating traffic circle, a setting that always reminded Lacey of Paris, or at least the Paris of her imagination, the one she had seen only in the movies. The green ring of shrubbery around the fountain was a perfect setting for a painting—or a catalog photo. Scarlet, orange, and yellow blossoms glowed in the dimming light. A few leaves fell as if on cue.

Lacey spotted Hansen, obviously working freelance for Amanda, along with some other guys from the paper, checking lights and equipment for the photo shoot. A mob of Amanda's fans were milling around, waiting for a glimpse of America's makeover queen. There was an air of excitement among them, young women of every shape and description.

Amanda's trailer was set up on P Street, on the east side of the Circle. Stella emerged from the trailer in her Stylettos salon smock and spied Lacey and Vic sitting on the edge of the fountain. She waved and dashed through the ever-chaotic Dupont Circle traffic to join them.

"You survived Amanda," Lacey said, meeting her halfway. Stella looked uncharacteristically beat. Her makeup was doing a disappearing act, and her usual sparkle was fizzling out. Even her spiky purple crew cut seemed to be drooping.

"She's a trip. Amanda Manville makes the evil queen of Stylettos, Josephine Radford, look like a lamb. Can you believe that bitch said I look cheap?" Stella took off the smock and showed off her outfit, especially chosen to impress her client. "Vic Donovan, you tell me, does this turquoise-leather catsuit look cheap? And let me tell you, these turquoise chandelier earrings cost me a small fortune. They are, like, totally authentic Native American, and there is nothing cheap about that." She was deeply offended. Vic tried not to smile. He consoled her with a pat on the back.

Lacey perched on the edge of the fountain. "It's okay. She sneered at my green gabardine vintage suit. She said vintage is *so over*."

"Just goes to show she knows nothing about real style for real people, like you and me, Lacey."

"Maybe it's because she's not real anymore. So how does she look now?"

"Gorgeous, thanks to me, but a little weird. Plastic, you know? Doing someone's makeup I'm always trying to balance the two sides of the face, 'cause everybody is a little asymmetrical, right? But not her; she has, like, mirror-image symmetry. Creepy. And I'm not sure she can move all of her features."

"Maybe she's Botoxed. Although she's really too young, mid-twenties."

"You're right. Definitely Botoxed. And she should really be Prozacked as well, and maybe chloroformed," Stella continued. "I think maybe her teeth are too big. Veneers, you know. And she has too many of them, in double rows like a shark. And I swear they glow in the dark." The exhausted little punkette stylist, with her own makeup smeared, sank down next to Lacey.

"Did she mention her big fear?"

"That she's being stalked by the killer plastic surgeon? Oh, yeah. You know what I think? It's a freakin' miracle no one's knocked her off yet."

"Do we get to see this mythical creature anytime soon?" Vic wanted to know. "Does she levitate off the bed? Does her head spin around?" He laughed, but the sound of a high-pitched shriek made them turn in unison and look toward the east side of the Circle. Amanda had emerged from the trailer.

"Stella!" It was a bellow worthy of Stanley Kowalski on amphetamines. "Who told you to take a break? I didn't say you could leave. This lipstick is all wrong! I need you to fix this *right now!*"

Stella stood up, spoiling for a fight. "She said she was wearing the gold dress. That lipstick was right for the gold dress. Now look what she's gone and done!"

Amanda was a vision of shrieking loveliness, wearing a long dark red panne velvet gown. It was a Christmas fantasy of a dress, featuring a hood trimmed in white faux fur. Deep, wide cuffs on the bell sleeves were also trimmed in white fur. She had selected this evening gown for the Dupont Circle shoot for her premiere winter catalog. Against the autumnal parkscape of the Circle it would paint a serene picture and play to the fantasies that encourage women to buy those perfect dresses they never wear. But Amanda was anything but serene as she marched across the street into the park to yell at Stella. Stella, menace in her heart, trudged over to meet her. Amanda towered over the small stylist.

"Where did she get that voice?" Vic asked, grimacing at Amanda's nasal flatness. "You know who she reminds me of? The robot in *Metropolis,* the Fritz Lang movie."

"Don't say that. Damon Newhouse thinks she's part of a government Bionic Babe Project or something."

"Ah, Newhouse. He's a lunatic, but I like him." He nudged her shoulder. "And he could be right."

"Don't encourage him."

"He likes you."

"He likes to make things up about me. And make me look like a lunatic, too."

They turned to take another admiring look at the alleged Bionic Woman in full cry. It was quite a tableau, Amanda pointing and screeching, Stella gesturing wildly, terrorized underlings scurrying everywhere, when suddenly three loud *pops* rang out. It sounded like a car backfiring, but much louder. At first Lacey didn't realize what it was. But Vic knew.

Before the second shot was fired Vic threw Lacey to the ground beside the fountain and covered her body with his. They hit the cement with a smack. Vic whispered in her ear, "Damn it, Lacey. I think she was right. Don't move."

"I can't; you're smothering me." He adjusted his position slightly so she could breathe. She peeked out from under Vic's protective arm. Stella had fallen to the ground, but Amanda had not. Amanda stood still for a moment, looking confused, and then gazed down at her chest. A dark stain seeped out through the red velvet of her dress. Amanda took a step and brushed against the stain with her sleeve, and the white fur came away bloodied. She looked shocked, but she kept walking toward them. She slowed down, wavered, and took one more step before she collapsed and fell to the ground.

It was as if Lacey were watching the scene in slow motion. As Amanda slowly fell to the sidewalk Lacey saw a familiar blur of color careen past, behind the supermodel's falling body. Its tires squealed as it rounded the Circle and disappeared. *Oh, my God. That's impossible. A drive-by shooting—and the shooter is using my car?* She didn't want to believe that she had seen her stolen Nissan 280ZX speeding by, but how many silver-and-burgundy versions of that car could still be on the road? Lacey had a sudden hot jolt of nausea hit her, her heart was beating double-time, and tears sprang to her eyes. *It can't be true; dear God, don't let it be true.* She wanted to jump up and run after her car, but she knew she had to stay safe. She prayed that the others were safe too.

There were no further shots. Vic let her up, and they ran to where Amanda had fallen. People were crowding around the victim, and Stella was kneeling by her side, unhurt. No one seemed to know what to do. Someone was screaming and running through the traffic in the Circle. She thought she saw Harlan Wiedemeyer at the edge of the crowd, craning his neck at the spectacle. Young women were hugging each other and crying. All the bike messengers who had been peacefully hanging out at the Circle were taking to their bikes at once in every direction, not wanting to hang around for the police to arrive. Lacey wondered where Turtledove was and whether he was even on duty. She looked in vain for Dr. Greg Spaulding; she even wondered briefly if he was behind the wheel of her stolen car. Lacey focused on Amanda. *Maybe she saw who shot her. Maybe there's still time. . . .*

Amanda's eyes were glazed. Vic was trying to stop the bleeding from her chest wounds. She was still breathing, but not responding to questions. Soon they heard the police sirens, and an ambulance screamed around the corner, stopping almost on top of them. Paramedics jumped out and took over smoothly from Vic. Lacey was unsure how much time had elapsed, but it seemed like an hour. She saw Zoe running for the ambulance, Yvette and Brad Powers following her. She hadn't remembered seeing them before. More sirens pierced the night. Vic snuggled Lacey protectively into his arms and whispered in her ear.

"Lacey, honey, just a word of advice here. You don't have to confuse the boys in blue by volunteering everything you know."

"Just what are you suggesting?" she whispered back as a very intimidating boy in blue approached her.

"If they don't ask," he said, kissing her quickly, "I would leave out the part about how being something as benign as a fashion reporter has led you into a double life as an independent righter-of-wrongs and freelance killer magnet. They wouldn't understand."

"Take it back. I am not a killer magnet."

He gave her a look, then put his finger to his lips. Clearly he was not taking it back.

Lacey and Vic were quiet while waiting their turn to talk with the police. She wondered briefly whether she should call Trujillo to tip him off, but she realized he was probably already on it. *Tony's got such great cop sources, he'd get it before* The Post *anyway.* Besides, the photographers were still clicking shutters and rolling tape and Hansen and Penfield were there, so *The Eye* was covered. Passersby were watching curiously from the many street corners that ringed the green circle. Turtledove came into view. He was dangling a small man from his mighty arms, and his prisoner was squealing loudly.

"Hey, you cannot hold me. I have not done anything," the man protested. He struggled while Turtledove dropped him in the lap of a couple of cops. He turned to Lacey and Vic.

"Shit, man, I missed the whole thing. Amanda sent me to

follow this squirt because he was hanging around, harassing her stylist." Turtledove pointed to Stella, who was braced by two cops and looked small and cold and scared to death. In the spring, when they were looking into the death of one of Stella's stylists together, Stella had told Lacey she didn't "do well" with cops. *Oh, no,* Lacey thought, *she's really in for it now. But at least she's alive.*

"I wish I could talk to her now," Lacey said to Turtledove. She took a closer look at the little man. "He's the stalker? Is that the same guy you threw out of the boutique?"

Turtledove shrugged.

The man seemed to be resisting the officers' attempts to talk with him, and they had limited patience. Something about his pinched, thin face was familiar. Then it hit her: John Henry Tyler, the man with the Web site calling on Amanda Manville to tell the truth about Caleb Collingwood. The cops were leading him to the ambulance when he twisted away from them. He ran to where Amanda was lying on the gurney and spat in her face. The cops had enough. He was handcuffed on the spot and hustled into a cruiser. The two cops came back and headed toward Vic and Lacey, and she realized it was now their turn.

And I passed up the chance to start my weekend early, Lacey thought ruefully.

chapter 11

Detective Broadway Lamont was as big and broad as a bull, but he didn't look like he would take any from Lacey. She could imagine him locking horns with Babe the Blue Ox—and winning. A middle-aged African-American with cocoa-colored skin and salt-and-pepper hair, he wore khaki slacks, a pink knit shirt, and a brown tweed jacket that hugged his broad shoulders like a wet suit.

The detective looked like he would just as soon throw her up against the wall as talk to her. Lacey checked the wall for any recent body imprints. It was too dirty to tell. Lacey never actually had a burning desire to know what the D.C. Violent Crimes Branch looked like, and yet here she was, among the witnesses to Amanda Manville's shooting who had been taken to this police facility in Southeast D.C. for questioning.

Broadway Lamont was not in charge of Amanda's shooting; he was just assisting the lead detective. Lacey figured that meant she was among the second tier of witnesses. She didn't know exactly where Vic was; they had been separated for individual interviews. Stella, who was closest to Amanda when she was shot, and Forrest Thunderbird, otherwise known as Turtledove, the bodyguard, were presumably in line to talk to the head guy, one Detective Steve Rogers. Stella would no doubt keep him on his toes. As for John Henry Tyler, who knew where he was? And had he really shot Amanda? And what on earth was Lacey's missing car doing at the scene of the shooting? And who was the driver?

Detective Lamont fixed his skeptical dark brown eyes on Lacey. One eyebrow went up and the other went down. Based on years of reading her editor Mac's expressive eyebrows, Lacey took this to be a don't-mess-with-me look. He had a face that was fierce even at rest, achieved presumably from years of staring down bad guys, but his voice was a rich, creamy baritone. He started with an insult. "So you work for that rag, *The Eye Street Observer*?"

"Yes, I cover fashion. For that rag." It came out as a squeak. But as intimidated as she was, she was also curious to see a real, live D.C. homicide detective in action.

He snorted. So she and her paper didn't impress him. That was apparent. Lacey assumed his manner was meant to be intimidating. At least, that was what she told herself in order not to be intimidated. He began the interview standing and paced the floor while she sat. His badge was attached to his belt, along with a cell phone. He removed his jacket to reveal his bulging biceps, and if they weren't enough to make someone think twice, there was the shoulder holster with the black nine millimeter.

"I am Detective Broadway Lamont," he introduced himself. "And I don't sing and I don't dance. I don't tell jokes. I'm not here to entertain you. We are here to dialogue. We start with introductions. I have just told you who I am. And you are . . . ?"

"Lacey Smithsonian." *He knows who I am. Is this a test?*

"That's quite a name. And in my family we know all about having fancy names," his deep voice rumbled. He didn't look convinced. "You putting me on?"

"Nope." She cleared her throat. "That is my name. My legal name, and the family name is a long story. No relation to the museum." She fumbled in her pocket and produced her congressional press pass, the one with the really awful photograph, to prove both her identity and her profession.

"Lacey Smithsonian." He squinted at the picture, then at her. "I guess that's you. You look better in person. Now that the pleasantries are out of the way, let's make this simple. Tell me what you saw, what you heard, and what may have occurred to you at the time Ms. Manville was shot."

"Is she still alive?" The vivid picture kept playing in her head; Amanda looking puzzled, trying to continue walking with three bullets in her chest, then falling.

"You know what I know. She was breathing when they put her in the ambulance." He shrugged. "Three shots to the chest. Course, miracles do happen."

Lacey repeated what she heard and saw, though she thought she couldn't possibly have seen anything that would help the police. She also tried to follow Vic's advice not to volunteer confusing information. But the accusatory voice of Amanda rang in Lacey's head: *"You promised!"*

She sighed and looked up at Detective Broadway Lamont. She didn't know if she could trust him or not. Probably not.

"I interviewed her yesterday for *The Eye*. She told me someone was trying to kill her," Lacey said in a small voice. "I didn't believe her." *Would it have changed anything if I had?* she asked herself. She knew the answer was no. And now she was stuck with a promise to find out what she could. Lacey consoled herself with the thought that she had never actually agreed to find the killer. After all, Amanda told her whom she suspected. And besides, Amanda was still alive.

Lamont stopped pacing and paid close attention to her for the first time. "Say what?"

"She asked me to help her." Lacey put her face in her hands, willing herself not to be emotional. *I'm not going to cry. Reporters don't cry.* "I couldn't."

The big man grabbed a chair, turned it backward, and sat down slowly, hoisting one leg over the seat and resting his elbows on the back of it, facing her. "Say all that again." Lacey repeated it all while Lamont stared intently at her.

"She told you that out of the blue? Yesterday? To a complete stranger? Why?" he asked when she finished.

You are a complete stranger and I'm talking to you, Lacey thought rebelliously. "People tell reporters surprising things sometimes. Like cops, I imagine."

"Just like that." He glared at her. "'Hello, Lacey Smithsonian, someone is trying to kill me'?"

"Pretty much."

"I don't want pretty much; I want exactly."

Lacey walked through it several more times, growing increasingly testy. "I told her to call the police."

"What did she say?"

"That she had bodyguards."

"Did she happen to say who was going to do the deed?"

"Dr. Gregory Spaulding. He's the one who performed the plastic surgery on Amanda. And they were engaged for a while. But it ended recently. Not well." Lacey's throat was suddenly very dry. She needed something to drink.

"The surgeon giveth and the surgeon taketh away? Interesting."

"But that's just crazy. He's a famous guy, and he's doing charity work now."

"Many things seem crazy, Smithsonian, and yet they happen. Every damn day of the week. And you know what? Even though it's supposed to look like just a random drive-by shooting, it's most likely someone close to her. Nobody ever wants to kill you more than your nearest and dearest; I guarantee it. So, Lacey Smithsonian, in your professional journalistic opinion, leaving aside motive, would this famous doctor have an opportunity to do it?"

Lacey shrugged and wrapped her jacket around her in the cold room. "He's in town for a conference of plastic surgeons. At the Mayflower Hotel."

"At the Mayflower. Nice place. You ever notice how doctors and lawyers always get to go to the finest places? The rest of us? Some wretched Holiday Inn off the Beltway." He snorted again. "The Mayflower." He didn't say anything for a while. "Do you think it's possible Spaulding shot her?"

"I talked to him this morning." She rubbed her eyes. "He seemed convincingly appalled by her accusation, but I don't know. You're the detective; what do you think?"

"I don't think nothing at this point. And I'm not the lead detective on this one. I'm just gathering information," Lamont said. He shrugged his giant shoulders wearily. "But anything is possible."

"What about Caleb Collingwood?" Lacey asked. "The old boyfriend that she humiliated on national television. The one they say she murdered? She says he killed himself, but his body's never been found."

"And you think he's alive, just like Elvis, and orchestrating this whole thing? Yeah, I'd expect that kind of story from a reporter," he snorted. "Leave the investigating to the police. Anything else?"

"What happened to the little guy the police took away?"

"I do believe he was arrested for resisting an officer. And no doubt is being questioned at this very moment. Maybe not so friendly, like you and me."

Lacey didn't want to know what "not so friendly" was. "And do you know where my friend Stella Lake went?"

"Smithsonian, if you're gonna ask me pointless questions, we'll be here all night. The questions are my job, got it?"

"No singing or dancing?"

"That's right. I ain't no Broadway song-and-dance man, no matter what my mama named me, so don't give me no song and dance. Now, is there anything else you saw, heard, smelled, or even imagined at any time before, during, or after the shooting?"

Lacey sighed deeply. "Oh, there is one little thing." She put her head down on the table. "This may not mean anything."

"I'll be the judge of that. And look at me." She straightened up and stared back at him. He looked like a judge to her. A hanging judge. She said nothing. "I'm waiting," Detective Lamont said.

"My car was stolen yesterday in the District while I was at work. I reported it to the police. But I think I saw it tonight. When Amanda was shot."

Showing some mercy, Lamont didn't ask her to repeat that. "What kind of car? You could be mistaken. Dull-gray Hondas you womenfolk drive, they all look alike. And exactly when, in relation to the shooting?"

Dull-gray Honda! What does he take me for? "It's a Nissan 280ZX. Last model year they made them, 1983. It's silver and burgundy. Not as much rust as you'd expect. And I think I saw it speeding around Dupont Circle just as the shots were fired. But I couldn't see the driver."

"Hell, Smithsonian! That almost sounds like a clue to me. And you said you were clueless. See how much better this works when I ask the questions and you just tell me everything you know?" But Lamont didn't look happy about it. His big neck was bulging against the collar of his tight pink knit shirt. *Uh-oh,* she thought, *the bull is back, and he's snorting and pawing the ground.* "Let me get this straight, Lacey Smithsonian. This woman you don't even know tells you someone's trying to kill her. She wants you to find out who it is, although in the next breath she tells you it's her former fiancé. You don't believe her, you tell her to go to the police, but you question the accused would-be killer anyway. Then someone steals your car and may have used it in the drive-by shooting of the woman who told you she was a murder target. And you say you don't know anything useful to assist the police in our little investigation."

"That pretty much sums it up."

"I don't like it. I don't like it one damn bit. I just hate it when a witness, and a reporter to boot, plays dumb and then turns out to be all wrapped up in the damn thing."

She refrained from telling him she didn't like it much either. But she kept quiet.

"Reporters. Lord have mercy. You'd think they'd want to tell you the damn story, but it's always like pullin' teeth." Lamont snorted several times. He went over it again to confirm all the details, and he made her write out a statement and sign it. He noted every phone number and address she could ever be reached at, muttering darkly about "reporters." Finally, he let her go. It felt like the middle of the night. She felt like she'd gone ten rounds with the Spanish Inquisition.

chapter 12

This night couldn't get any worse, Lacey thought. But of course it could. And it did.

When she finally got home at nearly midnight the message light was blinking on her answering machine. Hoping it was Vic or Stella or Brooke, or at least not bad news about Amanda, she hit the button.

"Lacey, this is your mother. I have a surprise for you. Your sister and I are flying in on Friday. Isn't that wonderful! Let me see here—" There was a pause and the sound of rustling papers. "—Yes, to Ronald Reagan National Airport. That's close by you, isn't it? I know you'd say not to, but I feel that this is your hour of need, and your sister and I are going to be there for you. . . ."

"No! No, no, no! Mom, this is no time for you to go all maternal. I have a life. I have plans." She thought of her plans with Vic, but talking back to the machine did not help. Lacey listened in horror as Rose rambled on about the details of their flight and her plans to come to Lacey's aid in the citadel of evil that was Washington.

". . . and we can look at cars for you while we're there," her mother's voice continued, "something big and safe, like, oh, I don't know, your father and I have always had good luck with Oldsmobile station wagons; can you still get those in Washington? And I haven't seen Washington since your Great-aunt Mimi died. Good Lord, how long ago was that? It's a shame we can't go visit the White House anymore. But we must go to the Smithsonian! It's a Smithsonian family tradition; it will be such fun. . . ."

"I can't believe this. You can't come here." *This is my city.*

". . . and don't think you're talking us out of this, dear. The tickets are bought. Cherise wants to buy a Smithsonian sweatshirt

and maybe one of those cute little caps. And so do I. See you on
Friday." Her mother hung up.

Lacey slid into a chair in shock. She couldn't imagine her family invading her personal space. The only saving grace was that at
least they weren't dragging her father along. She remembered him
as the invisible man behind the newspaper, who emerged only occasionally to tend to matters of plumbing, electricity, and basic
auto repairs. He had just retired, and he was enjoying hanging out
with his buddies, mulching the lawn, watching football, playing
golf, having "tailgate parties," whatever those were. Lacey
wouldn't know what to do with him. But then, she didn't know
what to do with her mother or sister either.

She looked around her rather shabby chic (though not on purpose) apartment, with its great French doors and balcony. It had an
amazing view of the Potomac River from every window, which
she loved, but it lacked any modern amenities, like a dishwasher
or disposal, and the vile washers and dryers were in the skanky
basement and only worked half the time. To make it cozier than the
typical anonymous apartment, Lacey had painted the walls a soft
French blue. She had inherited a few pieces of Great-aunt Mimi's
furniture: her cherry dining room set, her blue velvet sofa, her
leather-bound trunk. But her mother, who imagined herself a great
decorator, had often expressed her disdain for "Mimi's old things."
And her sister had a definite preference for the interchangeable
anonymity of IKEA catalog furniture.

But it was Mimi's trunk, leather-bound and brass buckled, full
of patterns and secrets, half-finished clothes from decades past and
all their mysteries, that was Lacey's personal treasure chest, a
treasure that she lovingly excavated from time to time, finding a
fabulous vintage pattern for an evening gown, clippings from the
1940s, letters with a little insight into Mimi's life. When she was
stressed-out and world-weary, Lacey usually wound up at the
trunk, wandering through its patterns, fabrics, old photographs,
and little snippets of Mimi's legacy. She occasionally selected a
pattern from the Mimi collection to have finished for her own
unique wardrobe, which was leaning heavily toward styles from
the fabulous Forties. They suited her curvy, petite figure, and her
Rosie the Riveter–meets–Rosalind Russell attitude. She didn't
wear these vintage finds all the time. But they gave her a certain
confidence. She now wished she had worn vintage today. Maybe
she would have handled Broadway Lamont differently, dressed
like a self-confident femme fatale out of a Bogart movie.

The thought of her mother and sister pawing carelessly through her things was unbearable, particularly Aunt Mimi's trunk. Her sister would just think they were silly and glue herself to the TV. Her mother, on the other hand, might decide to throw everything out in a cleaning frenzy.

It was late, but the trunk was calling out to her. She gave in and opened it, inhaling the faint aroma of satin-and-lace sachets placed there decades before by Mimi. Running her hands over a length of emerald-green crepe, once intended for an evening gown, Lacey smiled. Her aunt had great ambitions with her sewing, but erratic follow-through. A note pinned to the fabric indicated a complicated *Vogue* pattern from the late 1940s that she had planned to use for it. But the pattern lay uncut in its package under the material. The dress would be lovely, but Lacey knew that nothing could rival the Gloria Adams dress that Miguel Flores had made for her from a pattern hidden in the trunk's lining.

Lacey had been wondering if there were more designs by Gloria hidden away in the trunk, and she started to lift some of the materials out to look. Then she stopped. She would have time to get to the bottom of the trunk later, after her mother and sister had come and gone. The trunk was hers and hers alone. Mimi had wanted it that way, Lacey told herself, and she couldn't risk their pawing through it. Besides, her mother couldn't care less about vintage clothing. To her, vintage was merely old. Lacey didn't dress for her family; she dressed to please herself. But every once in a while, those voices of maternal discouragement came floating through her subconsciousness: "You're not really wearing that old thing, are you?"

Lacey dug up Mimi's old padlock, made sure she had the key, and secured the trunk. *Calm down, Lacey,* she told herself. *It's a weekend, one tiny little ruined weekend. How bad could it be?* She grabbed a piece of paper and started making a list. She would have to buy groceries for the fridge and clean sheets for the new trundle bed that she had bought for the small second bedroom, the room she generally used as an extension of her closet. And she would have to make the sofa bed too, in case the two of them wanted their own spaces. Lacey wondered why Cherise was coming along. Her little sister had been the perfect child, which Lacey generally thought was a good thing, because it let her off the hook of being perfect. But she hadn't seen her sister in years, except for the occasional mandatory visit home.

They couldn't be more different, she thought. Cherise had been the head cheerleader for Denver's Geronimo High School in her senior year, cementing her position as favored child. She was tall, thin, and blond with blue eyes, and she had never in her life done anything wrong—except once. It was the one thing that made Lacey sympathize with the stressful life of Cherise, the perfect sister, the chosen one. And it always made Lacey laugh, because it proved that Cherise was actually human. Nevertheless, it had become the incident of which the family Smithsonian never spoke.

It happened at the state championship football game between Geronimo High and some rival high school from Pueblo or Lamar in Cherise's senior year, Lacey's freshman year at college. The Geronimo High cheerleaders were dressed in their unique gold-suede fringed Indian vests and matching suede skirts with black turtlenecks and tights, outfits they wore only for the most special occasions, like state championships and homecoming. Lacey, who had refused on principle to participate or even attend any sports events, was bullied into coming home from college for the weekend and watching the game. It was a command performance; the entire family was there. Lacey had no interest or aptitude for football and was positive she would never understand it, even with subtitles and a program book, like a bad opera. But she was there to see Cherise, the golden one, do her thing.

Cherise was always totally focused on her cheerleading, but never more so than this game, achieving a Zen-like state of perfection. During the halftime show she was completely in the cheer zone: Jump! Turn! Cheer! Kick! Do it again! At the same time, Tommy Rutland, the dim-witted star quarterback for the Geronimo High Apaches, started goofing around with the cheerleading squad, mimicking their kicks, looking up their skirts, and generally clowning around for the crowd. Cherise, intently counting out her beats, never even saw him as she executed her killer high kick, and Tommy never saw it coming. Her right foot connected with his chin and knocked him out cold, to the horror of everyone, including, most especially, his coach. The other team, however, went wild. With Tommy out of the game, the Apaches were doomed.

Tommy revived late in the second half, and despite the humiliation of being drop-kicked through the goalposts of dreamland by a mere cheerleader, he went back in and made a heroic effort—and the winning touchdown in the last thirty seconds of the game. Then Tommy collapsed with a concussion and a broken jaw and was carried off the field.

Cherise's instant nickname quickly evolved from "Lucky Foot" into "Lethal Feet"—and then stuck. The team was ordered to stay strictly away from her and the other cheerleaders during games and practices. The joke around school was that to win the big game all you needed was "Lethal Feet Smithsonian" to give you that lucky kick in the head. In the halls for weeks afterward, you could hear kids yell, "Hey, Lethal Feet! Kick me, I need a touchdown!" "Right in the jaw, Lethal Feet, I got a big math test today!" Though separated from high school by more than a decade, Cherise was still a little sensitive about the whole episode. Lacey often pointed out to her that even in screwing up big-time, Cherise had managed to be, once again, *perfect.* "You go, Lethal Feet," Lacey said whenever she really wanted to bug her sister.

Unfortunately, now "Lethal Feet" was about to kick her weekend in the head, and Lacey didn't see any way to recover in time for the big touchdown.

And how was Lacey supposed to entertain them? "I'm not even supposed to be here this weekend!" She knew in her heart that her plans had been thoroughly sabotaged by her mother and her sister. She felt like she'd been ordered to sit through the big game all over again, with Cherise as the star of the show.

How could she tell Vic? After the police interview, Vic had found her sitting in the hall at Violent Crimes and had driven her back home in silence. They were both too tired to talk. She had kissed Vic good-night and sent him home. She thought she wanted to be alone. But now, in her apartment without him, and confronted by the impending disaster of her mother's visit, she longed to feel his arms around her. She didn't want to admit she felt scared, but she did, a little.

What is he thinking right now? she wondered. She would bet he was trying to sort out the shooting as if he were still a cop, comparing his methods with those of the Metropolitan Police.

She went to bed and tried to sleep. It wasn't happening. The phone rang a few minutes later. It was Vic.

"I was halfway home when I realized I was crazy to leave you alone after this night."

"It's okay."

"No, it's not. I'm at your door. Let me in. Please."

She raked her hands through her hair and glanced in the mirror before going to the door. No makeup, but she was wearing a favorite black silk robe over a white nightgown. She wasn't a pajama girl. She was sure she looked like a stressed-out mess after tonight, but there was only one soft light on, so it would be okay. She opened the door. Vic looked troubled and sexy, with an unruly curl falling over his forehead. He cracked a sheepish grin. "Hey, beautiful."

She felt herself smile. "Come on in; you look beat." She pulled him in and shut the door. He wrapped her in his arms in a hug. "Did you straighten out the cops?"

"They know where to find me. It's no fun being on the other side of the table in a witness interview," he acknowledged. "And you?"

"I didn't announce the killer-magnet part. He's going to have to find out on his own."

"Good. Let him work for it." Vic turned and made sure the door was double-locked, and he slipped the chain on. "I don't like it, your being pulled into this. The Manville woman and her obsession is one thing—"

"She was right; someone was trying to kill her."

"Stealing your car and using it in this attack is another thing altogether. It's really loony." He took off his leather jacket and draped it over the back of a wing chair. "Contrary to popular fiction, most killers don't lay out their work in some twisted pattern to send a message and impress the police with their brilliance. But this guy's got an agenda."

"And you think I'm part of it?"

"You are now. I don't want you to be alone until this jerk is put away."

"Don't worry, I have bad news."

"More bad news? Did someone else get shot?" He started to glower, and she fell onto the sofa in exhaustion.

"Worse. My mother has announced she's coming here for the weekend. With my sister. They'll be here on Friday, thereby killing our plans for a romantic weekend."

"You can't stop her? Put her off for a week or two?"

"Can you stop a locomotive barreling down the tracks at a hundred miles an hour?"

"But why now?" He put his arms around her. "To stop you from running away with me?"

"Because of my car being stolen. She kept repeating something about comforting me in my hour of need. As if that were possible. She doesn't know anything about you."

"You haven't told her about me?" He paused. "Not even in passing?"

"Good God, no. I don't tell my mother anything important."

"Finally an admission from you that I am important." He chuckled. "It's always something, isn't it?"

"Are you hungry?"

"Not really. You?"

"No, I was just going to bed."

"Mind if I join you?" She must have looked startled. He added, "To sleep, that's all. I'll bunk on the sofa. I have before. Trust me, this wouldn't be the right night for our big romantic moment."

"The sofa won't be necessary, Vic." Lacey led the way into her bedroom. He kissed her, then sat down on the bed to remove his boots.

"I'll just go and turn out the lights," Lacey said, her heart beating fast. By the time she returned, he was sound asleep on her bed, one boot on, one boot off. She didn't disturb him; she just pulled off the other boot, threw a blanket over him, and turned off the bedside lamp. She crawled under the sheets next to him and kissed his cheek.

"I think I love you, Victor Donovan," she whispered softly.

chapter 13

"Smithsonian. In my office. Now," was Mac's first order of the day Thursday morning.

Lacey had suspected she would need a little extra moxie that day, so she selected her black Gloria Adams suit, the original prototype of a famous Bentley's suit from the Forties. It hugged her curves and gave her an extra measure of sass when she needed it. She wore it with her black suede tango shoes, so she could dance on men's hearts if the occasion called for it. And it might. She quelled her nerves, squared her shoulders, and swaggered into her editor's office.

Mac noted her bravado with one raised eyebrow and gestured for her to sit down. The phone interrupted with a shrill, insistent ring. Mac picked it up, placing his hand over the receiver, and said, "Relax. Sit."

She had to clean a stack of newspapers off the extra chair in order to use it. She plopped the papers on a large pile of files precariously perched on Mac's desk. Then she sat on the edge of the chair while he listened. She couldn't relax. He hung up and looked at Lacey.

"That was Trujillo. Amanda Manville just died. Never regained consciousness."

"She's dead? Damn." It hit her like a leaden blanket thrown over her, cutting off her air supply. *It's not your fault,* she told herself. The detective had said it didn't look good. And Amanda was a perfectly unpleasant person, but still, a human being who desperately wanted to live. Mac leveled his eyes at her.

"Talk to me, Smithsonian. Tell me what I don't know that you're going to tell me now so that I'm in the loop." It was an order. *Might as well,* she thought. *He'll read all about it in my story anyway. Eventually.*

"I was there last night in Dupont Circle," Lacey began hesitantly. "I saw her get shot. I was just there to follow up on my interview with her." She could tell that Mac was about to say something snarky, so she quickly continued. "But that's not the worst of it, for me. Remember my car? Stolen out of the company garage? It was used in the drive-by, I'm sure of it. I told all of this to the police. Tony probably has it all written already."

"Damnation, Smithsonian!" He said it so loud that nearby reporters looked up from their desks, where they were playing solitaire and surfing the Web. Mac moved swiftly to shut the door and pull the blinds over the glass windows. Lacey suspected that reporters were tiptoeing to the door to listen. It was what she would do.

"You're telling me the shooter stole your car and then used it in the attack? On purpose? It's not some insane coincidence?"

"Well, that would be nice, Mac. But it's about as likely as another 1983 silver-and-burgundy 280ZX just like mine being driven by the shooter."

"There's something else, isn't there?" *How does he know?* "I'm waiting, Smithsonian."

"Amanda Manville told me someone was trying to kill her. I didn't believe it."

He took a deep breath and wiped his hands across his face. "I don't need to know why, Smithsonian. No one knows why things happen. But what I'd like to know is how you do it. Get yourself all jammed up in these murder stories. It's not like you're a war correspondent or a police reporter, or even an obituary writer, for Christ's sake. You're the fashion reporter. It just doesn't make any sense."

"It doesn't make any sense to me either." She stared at the high pile of papers on his desk; it was threatening to fall. If she moved a little to the left, she could almost hide behind it, but he'd probably find her. *Eventually.* "Maybe if you switch me off the fashion beat, the killings will stop."

Mac actually laughed. A good sign. "Very funny. But this is another fine mess."

"It's not my fault, you know."

He looked at her with a glare that sent shivers down her spine. "Right. Maybe it's Wiedemeyer's? It is never your fault, Smithsonian. But there you are. And before you open your mouth to protest"—he put his hand up to stop her from talking—"I'm not ordering you off the story, even though my blood pressure is off the charts. You'd find a way to get mixed up in it anyway."

"Thank you, Mac." She was going to say something when he interrupted.

"However, you'll cover the fashion angle. Sequins and satins, buttons and bows, colors and quips. Got it?"

"But this is a murder."

The glare was back. "I'm sure you can dig up some fashion angle, right? Tony is covering the police angle," he said. "And Lacey, this next part I have to say because it's my job and I do care, and because maybe if I say it enough times, my words will mean something to you. Be careful, damn it! *The Eye* does not ask its reporters to endanger their lives. My motto: Get the story, but don't get killed doing it."

"Maybe you could have cards printed up and just hand me one every time I get into trouble," she offered.

"Not funny, Smithsonian."

"Duly noted, boss."

"Get back to work. Write a story about her fears, the terrors of sudden undeserved fame, America's love-hate relationship with celebrities, whatever. You'll pull it together. And unless she went around telling every reporter in Washington that she was pursued by a killer, you've got an exclusive."

"A fashion exclusive?"

"Find a way."

She stood up quickly before he could get any more bright ideas. She opened the door, and several reporters quickly scattered, acting like they hadn't been glued to the door listening. They were such bad actors, it almost made her laugh. But she was determined to behave as if everything were under control. She sashayed back to her desk. After all, the Gloria Adams suit and the tango shoes deserved it. At times like this, looking put together and polished was an antidote to the storm of emotions swirling inside.

Luckily, it was still early. Felicity hadn't yet begun her daily ritual of offering calorie-laden, sugar-soaked snacks to everyone. All it would take for people to stop encouraging this would be one good case of food poisoning, Lacey thought. But Felicity didn't want to hurt anyone; she just wanted everyone to be fat and unhappy.

Lacey tried to keep her mind on the story, but the picture of Vic, sweetly sleeping on her bed that morning, kept distracting her.

They had both overslept, and he was out of there like a jackrabbit on speed, but not before offering advice in true cowboy-hero style.

"I could lend you one of my guns."

"No, Vic. You know they're illegal in D.C."

"That doesn't stop every punk criminal from having one."

"Even you don't carry a gun, Vic," Lacey pointed out.

"Not usually. But I also don't get involved with the wrong sort the way you do."

"The wrong sort like you?"

"We need to go to the range again anyway. You need some practice." He kissed her good-bye, then paused on his way out the door. "I'll be back."

Hurry, she thought.

After turning on her computer at her desk, what she needed, she decided, was some java to jump-start the old brain. She made her way to the small staff kitchen.

"Well, well, well. I guess that trading her integrity for unlimited free plastic surgeries in search of a new face and body didn't help the ultimate makeover queen," Cassandra Wentworth, editorial gunslinger, said as she crossed Lacey in the lair of the coffee drinkers.

"Working on some pearls of wisdom for the next edition, Ms. Wentworth?" Lacey rinsed her cup and sniffed the pot of coffee. It smelled slightly bitter, with an odd overtone. *Worse than burning truck tires, but better than battery acid,* she decided. *It will have to do.* She took her chances and poured.

"For Sunday actually. It is a rare day that I get such a clear-cut and dramatic example of America's rotting moral fiber." Cassandra said it with relish. "With the exception of Congress, of course. What are you writing about it? That it's a tragedy for retailers and trendy young anorexics?"

"Not quite. But I will be putting Amanda's demise in a fashion context." *Somehow.*

"How do you plan to do that?"

"She lived for fashion," Lacey said. "Maybe she died for it."

Cassandra finished stirring something disgusting and herbal into her cup. It smelled as bad in its own way as the coffee, but the aroma was more *Swamp Thing* and less industrial sludge. "I guess the killer preferred the original Amanda, the one who had a heart, who handed out bowls at the soup kitchen, to the plastic doll she became."

"It sounds like you know a lot about her, Cassandra. I could swear you've been reading my fashion magazines."

"Research," she protested. "Just good research. Know thine enemy."

"Still, being shallow and superficial and going to extremes to be beautiful are no excuse for murder."

"Hmmph. I guess not." Cassandra took her steaming cup of ooze and turned to leave the kitchen, deep in her fevered editorial dream. She bumped head-on into *The Eye*'s Peter Johnson, the scourge of Capitol Hill. He was just as surprised as Cassandra, who slopped some of her herbal porridge on Johnson's ugly tie du jour. Lacey thought it did no harm to the tie, but Cassandra was unexpectedly distressed.

"Oh, I'm so sorry, Peter." She turned scarlet and began to mop away at the tie with her free hand.

"No, it's okay." He grimaced and then strained to turn it into a smile. "Smells good; what is it?"

Smells good? Lacey thought. *Like low tide on the Potomac smells good.*

"Oh, you know, a little echinacea, licorice, ginger, cumin, green tea . . ." Cassandra rattled off a few more incompatible ingredients, but Lacey was concentrating on their body language.

"You actually drink that sludge?" Johnson asked, apparently trying to be funny, perhaps even flirtatious. The odd couple's pheromones were dancing in the air for one brief moment; then they came crashing into the cupboards and falling messily to the floor, as Cassandra bristled and Johnson looked away, embarrassed. "Oh, Peter . . ." Cassandra stopped herself, on the verge of tears, and ran out of the kitchen, spilling her herbal swill in every direction.

"What did I say?" Johnson asked himself, then he turned and saw Lacey. "I don't get it."

"Date much?" she asked.

He glowered and she exited quickly, trying not to laugh an unkindly laugh. *Not their fault: Echinacea one, pheromones zero.*

Lacey returned to her desk to find an urgent call from Brooke. "Meet me at the foot of Farragut at ten thirty. We must talk." Brooke meant the statue of Admiral David Farragut poised heroically in the center of Farragut Square across the street from *The Eye*'s offices, not far from Brooke's posh gray flannel law offices. She also had a message from Miguel Flores: "Is it really true about

Amanda the Terrible? Call me!" She left a message on his voice-mail.

Lacey took Brooke's call as a cue to read DeadFed dot com before dashing over to the Square. Sure enough, Damon had risen early. "Supermodel Gunned Down in Dupont Circle." The first subhead mentioned Lacey. "Fashion Sleuth Smithsonian Witnesses Amanda's Fall." *Oh, yes, the early bird caught the worm.* She didn't tarry to read the story. It was enough to know she once again had been made to look like a comic book character, thanks to Damon's yellow cyberjournalism. *If only I had Wonder Woman's wardrobe. And figure. And those great bracelets!* Besides, Brooke would fill her in.

Lacey considered her cup of caffeinated sludge. She set it down, picked up her purse, and was out the door. Passing by Mac's office she saw him raise an eyebrow. She waved gaily on her way out.

Three minutes later she spied Brooke tapping her foot impatiently at the statue in the square. She looked like the up-and-coming K Street lawyer that she was, wearing a tan suit and carrying a Burberry tote and matching umbrella, despite the lovely weather. Her long blond hair was braided down her back.

"Oh, my God, you *are* alive. I was worried to death. Did you get my voice mail last night?" Brooke asked. "I left it on your cell."

"I never pay any attention to my cell phone," Lacey replied. "Did you need a midnight consultation on the wisdom of wearing Burberry?"

"It's nice, isn't it?" Brooke held up the tote. "Cost an arm and a leg, though."

"As far as I know it isn't a requirement of the Bar. Or is it a new rule? Did you ever stop to think that the government is slowly brainwashing the populace into buying Burberry? Note the subtle changes in the plaid. Could they be a code for secret treaty details with the Galactic Federation, or a road map to alien body storage in Area 51?"

Brooke took another look at her new Burberry tote, loving it all the more. "Lacey, if I could wear the price tag on the outside, I would. Or just the tag alone, as you suggested in *The Eye.* That's all my colleagues care about."

"That is appalling."

"I'm not like you. I can't find that perfect offbeat treasure in a no-name vintage boutique. You either have the talent or you don't."

Great suit, by the way. Is that the Gloria Adams? I thought so. But if it's not new and expensive, it just doesn't work for me."

They walked to the Firehook Bakery for coffee. Once there, they gave in and bought chocolate croissants, then strolled back out to enjoy the spectacular autumn day in the square.

"If you think we lawyers are boring dressers in D.C., you ought to see what the Commonwealth of Virginia sends to court. Even I was surprised."

"Really? Tell me more." Lacey removed the notebook from her bag and lifted her pen in anticipation while Brooke indulged her. "I need some inspiration."

"Are you willing to trade information for my very own little 'Fashion Bite'?"

"Maybe."

"Yesterday I steamrolled some neophytes from the Virginia attorney general's office. The lead attorney wore a sleeveless light-blue tattersall dress with white tights and black vinyl slingbacks. It was just so wrong: summer dress, winter tights, shoes from Kmart. Hair defeated before she even began by some off-price stylist at Shags-R-Us," Brooke said. "Her assistant was worse. Too old for long, stringy gray hair, bangs falling into her eyes. Suit a size too small, maybe two sizes. Gaping open across the tummy. Shoes from the Dumpster behind a Goodwill. You and your column are definitely right on the money sometimes, Lacey. Didn't you write something like, 'It's hard to rise to the occasion when you're not dressed for the occasion'? Case in point. Her look was shabby, and her argument was shabbier."

"Did it impress the judge?" Lacey enjoyed fashion barbs launched at people who could and should be able to take it.

Brooke shook her head and licked latte off her lips. "Judges generally don't like to be told what the statutes say and what they can and can't do, even when they don't know. I, on the other hand, know how to get the judge on my side, even when the law isn't." She and Lacey sat down on a park bench with their lattes. "Smart and beautiful beats dull and shabby every time. No surprise. But right now I need to know what *you* were up to last night. Have you seen DeadFed? Is that how I have to find out things about my best friend?"

Lacey was about to ask how Brooke's boyfriend, Damon Newhouse, found out she was there, but of course—Turtledove was there, and he was a personal friend of Newhouse's.

"I don't know, Brooke. DeadFed seems pretty efficient. Unless you want to know the truth. And what Damon can't confirm he merely makes up. The government's 'Bionic Babe Project'?"

"Details to follow. It's a legitimate theory. And you're confirming that you were there when Amanda was gunned down in cold blood?"

Lacey nodded yes, leaned back on the bench, and closed her eyes. She hadn't realized how weary she was after her late-night tête-à-tête with Broadway Lamont. She inhaled the coffee aroma, then sipped the brew slowly to enjoy it.

"And you made a statement to the police without me?" Brooke smacked Lacey in the arm with the Burberry umbrella. "I am your attorney. Haven't I taught you anything?"

"Yeah, but it's much more fun watching you go crazy." Lacey wrestled away the umbrella, and Brooke glared. "And you are not supposed to assault your clients. Besides, *I* didn't shoot her. However, this is privileged information, and you can't tell Damon."

"No fair." Brooke groaned. "Okay, talk to me, Lacey."

Lacey sighed. "This is the rundown. The privileged rundown. Two days ago I interviewed Amanda Manville, who told me someone was trying to kill her." Brooke opened her mouth, but Lacey stopped her. "I'm sorry, but if you interrupt me, we'll never get through this. Sometime that day, my 280ZX was stolen from the company's garage. Yes, I know I never drive, but I did that day. What do the two events have to do with each other? Wait and see. Yesterday Amanda was shooting photos for her winter collection in Dupont Circle. I know this because Stella Lake did her hair and makeup for it. Small world, D.C., isn't it? I decided to wander over, watch the photo shoot, and ask Ms. Manville some follow-up questions. She was shot before I could talk to her. That's when I saw my car zoom away from the Circle. I think that's where the shots came from. My poor little Z." Lacey took a breath and a sip of coffee and held up a finger. "One more thing. Amanda Manville died this morning."

"Oh, my God, Lacey. You're involved in another murder." Brooke sounded a little too eager. Lacey gave her a look. "I'm so sorry about your car. Don't worry; we'll go car shopping. But right now, what do we do next?"

"Next what?"

"To investigate, of course. Surely Amanda told you more than you're telling me. Who's the suspect? What about surveillance? I've got a new pair of night-vision binoculars. And I'm dying to test them out."

"I'm sorry, Brooke. I forgot two salient points. Vic, with whom I was planning a romantic weekend, doesn't want me to get involved with any more killers. He thinks it's dangerous. Not to mention that I don't want to get involved with any more killers. Because it *is* dangerous."

"It's not like you're dating them."

Lacey ignored her. "Amanda is, or was, a total nutcase. And to put the cherry on the top, my mother is coming this weekend. She thinks I need her, because my car was stolen. Perfectly good weekend plans destroyed. Bad weekend looming. Boyfriend bummed. Me too."

"Good heavens, Lacey, have you been jinxed? Cursed by Gypsy fortune-tellers? I heard something about that little man in your office. I'm really sorry; there are a lot of obstacles here. But we shall overcome. So how are we going to go about our investigation?" Brooke lifted her latte in a salute.

"I'll think about it and let you know. But for now, we'll have to reschedule lunch. Duty calls."

"Lacey, call me before you say anything else to the police again," Brooke pleaded.

"You're an alarmist, but you're sweet."

"Consider yourself warned by counsel."

"And assaulted by counsel. Watch who you're whacking with that umbrella." She waved good-bye. They walked in opposite directions, Brooke toward K Street and Lacey toward Eye Street. She caught a glimpse of Trujillo crossing the Square, which gave her a chance to pump him for any extra details he may have discovered. He waited up for her. In her tango heels she was walking a little more sedately than usual.

"Tony, do you know if the police questioned Spaulding about Amanda Manville?"

"Hey, Lacey, how's it going? Nice suit and shoes," he said, evading the question. "Isn't that your truth-justice-and-the-American-way suit?" His eyes took it in, and he smiled his approval. She loved that Trujillo was one of the few men in Washington, D.C., who could frankly appreciate a woman and get away with it. *No pheromone jammers for him.*

"Is that another Lois Lane reference, smart guy?"

"Always. What would life at *The Daily Planet* be without its comic-book heroes?"

"Well, you're one of 'em, Jimmy Olsen, but I want information."

"Is this a trade?"

"Sure, why not."

Tony laughed and slapped her on the back. "I might know a thing or two. And I'm not Jimmy Olsen. Hanging out on the police beat and all. Then there's the additional perk of it being a high-profile case, what with the late Ms. Manville being the famous makeover supermodel. I had to fight my way through the entertainment press and other riffraff to do my job. You know, she's not the only crime in this city."

"Come on, spill it. Did they interview Dr. Gregory Spaulding, Amanda's former fiancé?"

"I love it when you beg." It turned out, Tony said, that the police had indeed picked the surgeon up at his hotel and questioned Spaulding into the wee hours of the morning, but they eventually cut him loose. "He has a whole Mayflower Hotel full of alibis."

"Broadway Lamont didn't tell me anything," Lacey complained.

"You dueled with the big guy? He wouldn't. He doesn't know you; he doesn't know if he can trust you. You know cops take a while to warm up to us. Some never do. And Broadway Lamont is a hard case."

"Not a song-and-dance man?"

"He'll dance on your head if you're not straight with him."

In some ways, cops were the same everywhere, Lacey thought, big city or small town. But not in every way. It had taken a fair amount of time back in Sagebrush, Colorado, for Lacey to gain Vic's trust when she was the police reporter and he was the chief of police. And that was aside from all the raging hormones, Vic's pursuit of her, and Lacey's rejection of Vic because he was married, although he was going through a divorce at the time. He was free now.

"And Smithsonian . . ." Tony yanked her back from a brief reverie.

"Yeah?"

"When he finds out your particular history, I predict our Detective Broadway's not gonna be happy."

"Can't be helped; he's not a happy man. And he can't stop me from writing about it. It's a really hot crime of fashion."

"If you're going to be that way about it, we can always tag-team this one."

"Okay." She brightened up. "You know my byline rule. Smithsonian before Trujillo."

"Yeah, sure. Damned alphabet."

"Mac already informed me you've got the cops part. As for me, I need to ask some questions. Fashion questions. Among other things." She took a beat. "Tony, what do you know about a guy who may have been stalking Amanda? John Henry Tyler is a possible name; Johnny Monroe is another."

"I heard the Tyler name, not the Monroe. A 'pissy little twerp,' according to my sources. Said the cops let him cool his heels most of the night, then questioned him this morning. He lawyered up and swears he had nothing to do with her death. And one of her bodyguards was apparently collaring him just when the shots were fired, so he's alibied, too. They had to let him go this morning."

"Really. I saw him spit at her after she was shot."

"That lacks dignity, man."

"To say the least." Tony headed for the lobby, but Lacey suddenly decided against going back to the office. Instead she waved Tony on and caught a taxi back to Snazzy Jane's in Georgetown.

Last time Snazzy Jane's was expecting me, she thought. *Let's see how snazzy Jane looks when she's caught by surprise.*

FASHION BITES

Reckless Dressing;
or, Road Rage Meets Fashion Fury

Pull over, lady! You got a license and registration for that out-fit? The charges are reckless dressing, dressing while ability impaired, dressing under the influence of a fad—oh, yeah, you're going downtown for this one. You get one phone call. Make it a good one.

Is this you? Guilty of reckless dressing? Leaving the scene of a collision at the intersection of style and fashion, not knowing which way to run? Relax; we've all been sideswiped by a speeding trend only to be dissed by the snotty fashion-istas in the fast lane, who rule that your look was *so over* two and a half minutes ago.

I understand. You want to scream. I call it Fashion Fury. Fashion magazines, which I love, sometimes do that for me. What, fuchsia gloves are *out*? Already? I just bought mine! Go-go boots are coming back? No, they're not? Yes, they are? Is fashion all just a cruel joke? Sometimes it seems that way. What fashion-conscious woman hasn't been entrapped into wearing the cool-for-one-minute top with the hot-for-one-second skirt, and oh, yeah, the big hair, the clown makeup, the look that was *it* for a heartbeat, and now has been enshrined forever in somebody's bad photograph? We've all been there. When you get your one phone call, call me.

Maybe it wasn't the skirt; maybe it was the pants you thought were long enough, but somehow when you arrived at the office, they were hugging the tops of your ankles and traveling upward. Welcome to Geek City. Perhaps it was the brocade jacket that would be fabulous in the royal court at Versailles, but is somehow *too much* for your oh-so-democratic life in the twenty-first century. And why, oh, why did you buy it in mustard? It was a mistake and you know it. You want to give up. You want to wear a uniform, something out of a bad science-fiction movie where everyone wears matching Mylar jumpsuits with that cute rocket-ship logo. At least they all match.

Get ahold of yourself! It doesn't matter what the fashion flaw was—it happened—but that's no reason to give up on attempting to look put-together and professional. Nothing is worse than giving up on yourself. This doesn't mean you have to follow fashion when it jumps off a cliff; you just have to discover your own style and figure out what looks good on you. Remember the Fashion Police are out there, cradling their fashion radar guns, waiting for you to cross the double yellow line. So many moving violations, so little time.

- **Dressing in the dark.** Of course you didn't mean to do it, but you reached blindly into your closet and grabbed the first thing. Unfortunately, it was the outfit you were giving to Goodwill. Might look good on Will, but it doesn't look good on you.
- **Dressing fifteen in a thirty-five age zone.** Step *away* from the juniors rack, ma'am. Please, leave the rebellion to the teenagers. Pink hair, overalls, grunge, or whatever they latch onto this week. Let them latch on without you. Realize that it's fun for them to wear outrageous clothes because they're finding their own style. Find yours. Besides, they really resent it when you steal their latest look and paint your lips blue and shave your head in a spiral. If you think dressing young necessarily makes you look young, you're mistaken. It can look like a case of arrested development. Don't let it put you under fashion arrest.
- **Following fashion trends too closely.** That's just what retailers want you to do. So you'll buy more clothes to hide in your closet when they go out of style with the speed of light. This is probably okay for trust-fund babies and conspicuous consumers, but wouldn't you

rather have a few classic pieces that are always appropriate? Wouldn't you rather look smart than like Paris Hilton? (Don't answer that. Anything you say may be used against you.)

chapter 14

Lacey slipped unobtrusively into Snazzy Jane's with the crowd. She found the store just as hip and colorful as before, but the atmosphere had changed. The staff was overwhelmed with customers clamoring for a piece of Amanda's brief celebrity. They wanted anything they could get their hands on from the premiere, and now presumably final, Chrysalis Collection. She overheard a woman of about twenty at the counter with a stack of clothes in her arms and a credit card in her fist, just waiting to be charged. She wore a Levi's jean jacket over a cream-colored cashmere sweater and slacks. Tiny square black spectacles perched on her tiny nose.

"These are *so* going to be collectible," she said to the woman next to her. "You heard she died, right?"

"You are, like, totally gruesome," her friend said. "The woman is dead. How you can think of money?" She looked like a student in sloppy oversize clothes, but she held a delicate Chrysalis dress in her arms.

"Commerce is cruel," the fashion entrepreneur said, signing the charge slip and examining her sales ticket. "Perfect, it has today's date, the day Amanda Manville died. Trust me, this stuff will *kill* on eBay." Many others were also lined up, their arms full of pretty dresses, skirts, and tops from the Chrysalis Collection. *They weren't buying yesterday, but they're buying today.*

A very plain young customer was crying. "I felt like her friend, you know?" she said to Fawn as she charged a violet dress from Amanda's collection. "Like she understood how it feels to be plain underneath it all?" Fawn withheld her true opinion of Amanda, murmured something soothing, and rang up the purchase. She folded the item and placed it in a special Chrysalis Collection bag, clear plastic sporting the butterfly logo. An instant collector's item.

In a mirror positioned above the cash counter, Lacey caught a glimpse of Yvette Powers, looking hard-eyed. Today Yvette was wearing a sapphire-blue dress from the collection with clean princess lines in wool crepe with a faux Persian lamb collar and cuffs. She also wore a pair of stilettos in the same blue. She wore her sleek blond hair in a chignon and looked terribly chic, under the circumstances. Lacey approached Yvette gently. "Yvette, Lacey Smithsonian from *The Eye Street Observer*. We met the other day."

Yvette turned her glance to Lacey, nodding her acknowledgment. "You were the only reporter who gave Zoe credit for her designs. The other papers only mentioned her in passing and gave Amanda all the glory," she said with just a trace of bitterness. She collected herself. "That's a stunning suit. Is it designer?"

"Yes, vintage."

"They don't make them like that anymore. Except in couture, because of the labor involved. It's beautiful."

"Thank you." Lacey silently thanked her great-aunt, who had left her the suit. She looked around the crowded store. "This place is a madhouse."

"They're all here for the Chrysalis Collection. If this keeps up we'll be sold out by five," Yvette said, leading Lacey up the stairs to the second floor. "I suppose all the reporters will descend on us now."

"I'm sorry," Lacey started to say, but she realized that Yvette was counting on that; she was calculating the effect of Amanda's tragedy on sales. The racks held only about a third of the clothes that were there the day Lacey interviewed Amanda.

"Don't be sorry. I know it's your job, and Amanda was terrible to you the other day. She was terrible to everyone. I almost lost Fawn, and she's my most reliable associate. We all thought Amanda had gone around the bend with the stress. But please don't quote me on that."

"When she said someone was trying to kill her?" Lacey prompted.

Yvette sighed and rubbed her arm. "I need a cigarette, not this damned patch." She tapped her heel on the floor. "She's really gone. Nobody believed that someone was going to kill her. We all thought Amanda was just crying wolf."

Lacey pulled out her notebook and pen. Yvette did not protest. "How long had she been talking like that?"

"I don't really know. But certainly since she hit town last week. Brad would know better. He's had more *contact* with her." Yvette

bit her lip and sucked in her breath, then let it out in a sigh. "I was
stuck in D.C. while he was in L.A. last month, working out the
business end of things." She snorted, and looked away. "And apparently a lot more. When he came back, I knew he'd been warm-
ing her bed. And she wanted me to know. It was exactly what the
bitch wanted. Oh, God, don't put that in the paper."

"I don't understand. Weren't you all friends?" Lacey put the
notebook down before it could inhibit the conversation.

"Friends. Oh, yes." Yvette laughed bitterly. "We had it out yesterday afternoon. I never realized how much Mandy hated me.
Ever since high school. That's what she said. To me, she was just
Zoe's little sister. I was the one who started calling her 'Ostrich.'"
Yvette blinked back a memory. "Mandy looked like one, you
know, a sweet, big-eyed ostrich. I didn't really say it in a mean
way. One of those silly things that just pop out. And then it was so
funny. Amanda laughed as much as anyone. We were just kids, for
heaven's sake. Lots of kids get tagged with nicknames. We called
Zoe 'Stringbean' at one time, and I was once known as 'Kansas,'
as in, 'flat as Kansas.' Until I, you know, developed. But the name
Ostrich really stuck. So sue me."

Yvette must have been one of the favored girls who never felt
the sting of awkward adolescence, Lacey realized. One of the original alpha girls, a vicious little vixen at thirteen or fourteen who always hit the mark and then protested, "I didn't mean it like *that*."
Who knew how long Amanda had waited to even the score by
sleeping with Yvette's husband? If Yvette hadn't found out, it
wouldn't have counted.

Shrugging her shoulders, Yvette added, "Amanda never acted
like it bugged her. She was just a nice kid, before."

Amanda knew that showing pain would just have egged you on.
Lacey's thoughts must have translated to her face.

"You're shocked that we were partners?" Yvette continued. "It
actually was all Amanda's idea. Like I said, she never seemed
upset about the old days. Life goes on, and suddenly our little Ostrich was this makeover miracle and a famous fashion model. It
was like some magic act, changing brass to gold. But it was really
the other way around. Amanda was gold before and brass afterward. Although she turned into a solid-gold bitch."

Lacey refrained from saying that Amanda must have studied
Yvette and graduated with honors: mean girl cum laude.

Yvette moved to one of the racks and straightened out the disheveled remains. "You're not going to write all this, are you?" Lacey said nothing. "We're not going to stop, you know."

"Stop what?"

"The Chrysalis line. The clothes are really ninety percent Zoe's anyway. Her ideas and her designs. Amanda had control—or I should say, demanded control—over some of the details, fabrics, trims, colors, but she took full credit. Oh, we didn't argue about that. Amanda was the famous one that everyone clamored for. It was her name that raised the financing and sold the line. But Zoe has the talent, and she can still design the line. And we have the rights to Amanda's name and likeness for marketing."

"When did you decide all this?" Lacey inquired. She wasn't shocked, but it seemed a bit cold. Yvette picked up a gold velvet top that had fallen to the floor, her ultrablond hair glinting in the light from the window.

"At the hospital. We were there most of the night with Zoe. But it's what Amanda would want. You can write that the Chrysalis line will continue in Amanda's memory. As a tribute," Yvette added, as if she were testing it out to see how it sounded.

"How is Zoe handling all this?"

"She's a wreck, but she'll mend." Yvette looked straight at her. "I've always been her friend, and I'll be there for her."

"I'd like to talk with her."

Yvette looked doubtful. "You'll mention that the Chrysalis Collection will continue?"

"Of course. It's news. Fashion news."

Yvette walked to the counter, picked up a card, and borrowed Lacey's pen to write on the back. She handed the pen and the card back to Lacey.

"That's Zoe's number at home. At their parents' house, where they stay when they're in town. She took something to help her sleep, and she's probably still out. I'll talk to her first and tell her you'll be calling later."

"Thank you." Lacey tucked the card in her purse.

Yvette looked at her watch. "Don't call her till after two."

"No problem." Lacey was distracted by Brad Powers, who had just emerged from the stockroom with some papers in his hands, which he tucked into his inside suit pocket. He came up behind his wife and laid his arm around her shoulder. Yvette didn't react; she merely stared at the depleted racks of clothing. "They can have a shipment here by tomorrow," he said.

She nodded silently and removed his arm. "Is that all you need?" she said to Lacey.

"For now, thanks. Please tell Zoe I'll call this afternoon."

Yvette walked off without looking at her husband, who tried to disguise his discomfort. "Is there anything I can do for you?" He put his hand on Lacey's arm. *A hands-on kind of guy.* She shrugged his hand off as delicately as she could, refraining from slapping him and telling him to back off. Powers looked a little irritated. She quickly shifted gears.

"The shipment coming tomorrow, is that more Chrysalis clothing?"

"Yes, I'm afraid it's the last I can get my hands on, for now." There were shadows under his eyes; his chin and his head were both stubbled. Obviously time for a shave. "The California boutiques and department stores have locked down their supplies for their own premieres next week."

"What about the line for next season?"

"At the factory now. Contracts are filled for the spring. After the debut, the girls planned a sort of limited-edition collection for the holidays. That was what the photo shoot was for last night. Ads for the holiday collection." He mused on something, perhaps wondering if he could increase orders now that people were clamoring for the clothes. "Zoe's working on sketches for next fall."

"Zoe really is the design machine behind Chrysalis?"

"Well, Amanda had her role. A major role with the media and the image and all. But Zoe is the woman with the original ideas."

"How did the opening reception go?"

"Positive. Very positive. But with Amanda gone now, who knows?"

"Were you in love with her?" *Is that out of line?*

He looked at Lacey sharply. "Love? What I did with Amanda was so stupid and . . . and I'm not going to talk about it."

"All right. Next question. Where were you when Amanda was shot?"

He didn't seem to think it was an odd question, perhaps because the answer had been polished by police questioning. "It's been tense lately. We were having drinks at Childe Harolds, the three of us, Yvette and Zoe and I. Amanda hated having us all milling around before a shoot anyway; it made her . . . um . . . too nervous. We were just going to wander over to see the shoot later, after a glass of wine. Someone ran into the restaurant and started shouting to the bartender about a shooting in the Circle. Zoe ran out, followed by Yvette. I had to stay for a minute to pay the bill. By the time I got out there, the police and ambulance and paramedics were all over her. I couldn't get past them."

"I see." Lacey said, writing it down, realizing that she might never know the actual truth. Brad Powers excused himself before she could ask another question. *Everybody lies.* But then, she reflected, a journalist was obligated only to attribute the right statements to the right speakers, whether they were lying their heads off or not. *You simply have to make sure the lie is correctly quoted.*

From her vantage point on the second floor, Lacey saw Powers greet a camera crew heading into the store, no doubt wanting a pithy news bite, so vital now that supermodel Amanda Manville was dead. *It doesn't take long for the vultures to gather,* Lacey thought, knowing that she too was guilty of seeking the story first, wanting a scoop, and knowing that her take on the matter would be unique. The eyewitness account. She slipped out of the store quickly, feeling like a vulture, but a vulture with a scoop.

The crowd in the store was getting thicker, but today there was no security for crowd control. She wondered where Turtledove and the other bodyguards were. *Out of a job?* She passed by a group of about ten young women holding a sort of vigil at the door, Amanda fans comforting each other.

On her way back to *The Eye*, Lacey asked herself what Amanda would really want. She didn't want to die, but would she care that her clothing line would survive? Or would she want it to end with her? Lacey wondered. Amanda couldn't speak for herself now, but the survival of the Chrysalis Collection was a good story. And a good spin on Amanda's death, for those who would still profit from her name.

chapter 15

The cab dropped her off on Eye Street across from her office, and Lacey longed to linger in stately Farragut Square. It was one of those brilliant jewel-like fall days that make the city of Washington a picture postcard. The square was wrapped in deep green foliage, accented here and there with a few scattered gold and orange leaves previewing the fall. Crimson flowers greeted the day. Autumn tarries in Washington, but there was no rest for this reporter. Waiting at the front door of *The Eye* was Detective Broadway Lamont. She sighed and trudged across Eye Street to meet him.

He seemed out of place there, and it took her a moment to gather her manners before she said, "Detective Lamont. How nice to see you." She had hoped she'd left him behind at the Violent Crimes Branch.

"Smithsonian," Broadway said by way of hello. "I've been reading all about you." He displayed some old copies of *The Eye Street Observer*. "Courtesy of your boss."

"You've met Mac, then." *Wonderful. The two of them would make a great song-and-dance team.*

"You'll excuse me if I don't read your newspaper. There are so many I have to skip reading before yours. Generally I start my day by not reading *The New York Times*; then I don't read *The Washington Post*, and I certainly don't read *The Washington Times*, except occasionally. You can see that I hardly have time to not read *The Eye Street Observer*."

"Yeah, it could fill your day, not reading all those papers. How can you tell when you're done?" He made no move to open the front door, so she did.

"I gotta ask you one thing, Smithsonian. You got a yen for weird-ass situations, or what?"

"Referring to what exactly?"

He held the front door for her and followed her in. "Putting yourself in harm's way. That Razor Boy character last spring who killed those hairstylists? And messing around with the Bentleys on that missing intern? Esme Fairchild, just last month. I know you had a hand in catching the guy, but anyone ever tell you that this stuff is dangerous? Going around stabbing people with sword canes? That's a nasty weapon. We don't see too many of those on the street, I'll tell you."

"Self-defense."

"I'm not arguing the point. You ever take up fencing?"

"No."

"Maybe you should start."

Lacey wondered. She always liked those dashing fencing outfits they wore. "Fashion is a tough beat, Detective. Not for sissies. At least here at *The Eye*." She hit the elevator button. "I write 'Crimes of Fashion.' Some people just take it more literally than others."

"So I hear. Mac Jones is a font of information," he said, as if that were big news.

"Yeah, in seventy-two point type." She never knew what Mac would say about her. *The tattletale.*

"Says you're trouble, but decent fashion reporters are hard to find. I understand the last one died at her desk. Another fashion-related death?"

"It was natural causes, or so they say. And if you must know, Douglas MacArthur Jones is stingy with praise. Editors are like that." The doors opened up on her floor. "What can I do for you, Detective?"

"Take my advice, Smithsonian. On behalf of the Metropolitan Police Department, I'd like to encourage you to stay the hell out of this one. You've been lucky so far—you haven't been killed, maimed, or kidnapped—but your luck can change. Reporters tend to think they're indestructible, but it ain't necessarily so."

Lacey was tired of people telling her what to do and what not to do. She strode to her desk in the newsroom in a hurry, the big detective in lumbering pursuit. Felicity Pickles intercepted them in the aisle, a plate full of hot apple tarts in her hands. Broadway Lamont brightened considerably at the aroma.

"Try one, Lacey," Felicity said. "Down Home Barbecue on U Street gave them to me. I'm running the recipe this week." The tarts' crusts were glazed and topped with a dusting of sugar. They looked sinful enough to tempt a saint, but Lacey declined.

"Sorry, I just ate something. Really."

Felicity also offered one to Lamont. "Please help yourself," she simpered to the detective.

Lacey noticed Lamont eyeing them. "Go ahead; she lives for the attention. Felicity Pickles, food editor." To Felicity she said, "This is Detective Broadway Lamont from the Metropolitan Police Department."

"Oh, Lacey, are you in trouble again?" Felicity asked, and the detective laughed, a booming guffaw that made people stare.

Lacey turned her back on this heartwarming little scene, flung her purse into her bottom desk drawer, and waited for Broadway Lamont to focus on whatever he wanted to tell her. She had to listen to several big "mmms," some lip smacking, and Felicity's fawning and giggling.

"Do you really like them? Are you sure there's enough cinnamon?" Felicity urged a second tart on the big man and they seemed to share a warm moment. *Perhaps a spark?* It would take a lot of food to feed Broadway Lamont. But Felicity, no doubt, would be up to the task. "I'm so glad you like them. Here, take one for dessert tonight."

Gag me. Lacey turned back in time to see Harlan Wiedemeyer duck behind a cubicle, witness the cozy scene between the object of his affections and this huge unknown stranger, and slink away dejected. But Harlan wasn't her concern at the moment, and she had to butt in to retrieve the detective's attention. "Did you want something else, or was the friendly warning the gist of your trip?"

Lamont swallowed the last of the tarts and wiped his hands on a napkin offered by Miss Felicity Pickles. "Here's the gist. We found your car, a 1983 Nissan 280ZX, silver and burgundy? No plates. Matched the VIN number, though."

"What? My car? Oh, my God. Is it okay? Where? When can I get it?" She held her breath, trying not to sound too excited.

He put out one long arm of the law. "Hold on a minute." He grabbed a nearby chair, the one in which the former fashion editor, Mariah "the Pariah" Morgan, had died, pulled out his notebook, and sat down. "They found it behind the Source Theatre on Fourteenth Street, in the alley. Funky neighborhood." He paused and rubbed his chin. "And 'okay' is not the word I'd use for it. It was stripped."

"Stripped? As in . . . ?" She fought the vision of her poor Z stripped.

"Wheels, stereo, the usual. It's a parts car now."

And so fate delivers another dropkick in the head. Lacey was a little dizzy and a lot upset. She had to sit down. She couldn't talk; she merely looked at him, hoping for it all to be a bad dream.

"And no, you can't have it back yet."

"When?" She tried to contemplate a fitting burial.

"Couldn't say, but I wouldn't hold my breath. If I were you, I'd just call the insurance and total it."

She sucked in some air and tried to shake the cotton from her skull. "Was it used in the attack on Amanda Manville?" She hoped fervently that it wasn't. But she knew it was. Why? Sheer implausible coincidence? The Wiedemeyer Effect? Or some sick bastard deliberately entrapping her in this mess?

"It's been impounded, and crime-scene forensics are gonna take a look, see if it was the shooter's car. Might be prints, powder, shells, receipts, body fluids, all sorts of good stuff."

"My poor little Z."

"Just be glad it was your car and not you that got roughed up. But somebody finds your car, they can find you, so watch your back." She didn't respond. "Cheer up, Smithsonian. I'm leaving now." He made no move to go.

"You're not going to tell me what to write? Or what not to write?"

"Does that work?" He looked at her with interest.

"No, just asking. Some people don't feel the conversation is finished until they tell me how to do my job."

"I suppose that means you're going to spill your guts in this rag."

"So to speak."

He shrugged his giant shoulders. "I'll try not to read it. At least you're not *The Post.* It's harder to avoid."

"Nice backhanded slap, Lamont," she said.

He rose from the seat and loomed over her. "I'll show myself out. Y'all stay safe." He paused next to Felicity's cubicle, and Felicity was instantly back on full boil. "And if you think of anything else, call me. I'm a good listener." He walked a few more steps. "Even the off-the-wall stuff you write about. Guess you call it fashion clues, Smithsonian."

"You don't think they're crazy?"

"Sure I do. Lots of things are crazy. I hear crazy shit daily. But whatever works." He left with a hint of a smile on his face and an apple tart wrapped in a napkin from Felicity Pickles.

Lacey whirled around to her computer and contemplated what

to write about the late Amanda. She typed the words, *"I don't want to die."* *Those words were nearly the last thing Amanda Manville said to me.* But just then the office mail cart came by, and it turned out that Lacey was wrong. The mail brought another wrinkle, a letter from the dead model, written the day before, perhaps just hours before Amanda was gunned down in Dupont Circle. The letter was almost an apology—almost, but not quite. Apologies were apparently not Amanda's style. Lacey held the paper up to the light. It looked like there were tearstains on the light-blue stationery that bore a watermark of Amanda's interlaced initials.

> *Dear Ms. Smithsonian,*
> *I could tell that you didn't believe me yesterday. Even my bodyguards don't believe me. But I promise you someone is going to try to kill me. I found another note after you left. It said, "Time is running out for Ostrich." The police can't do anything because it's not someone "out there" that they can take care of. It's someone close to me, someone who knows me. Someone is trying to drive me crazy. If you don't believe me, talk to Tate Penfield.*
> *After the reception last night, I went back to the house. Someone had touched my things, photographs of me. He or she replaced them with hideous pictures of me, the way I was before. In the kitchen, on the bathroom mirror, taped to the walls, and on my pillow. I tore them into a million little pieces, although I suppose that was the wrong thing to do.*
> *I know that lots of people hate me because of the TV show, because I changed. It's a weird thing—the people who liked me before, hate me now. The ones who hated me want to be my friend now. But this is important: No matter what happens, I'll never regret doing it. A moment of being beautiful is better than a lifetime of being ugly.*
> *All I ask is that if something happens, find out who did it. You didn't give up till you found out what happened to those other women. Don't give up on me. Don't let them get away with it. Help me.*
> *Amanda Manville*

Damn! Lacey thought. *How do I duck a promise when a dead woman begs for my help?*

chapter 16

Lacey highlighted the single line she had typed and hit Delete. Tapping Amanda's letter in her hand, she wondered what to make of this. There was no question now of giving up. Besides, she always needed to know how the story ended. But where could she start? Was this evidence that would interest the police? She read the letter again. Broadway Lamont might be interested in it, and he would tell her again to stay the hell out of it. Lacey slowly smiled and remembered that Mac was fond of telling her to trust her editor. This was the kind of sticky situation in which she found that advice valuable: passing the buck.

Lacey approached Mac with the letter in one hand and grabbed one of Felicity's tarts to offer him, in case he had a bad reaction. She handed both the letter and the tart to him without a word. He read it silently and glanced up at her. "You've still got that trouble-magnet thing, don't you? Go make copies of this for us. The original will go to the police. We're going to cooperate with them on this. As much as possible. Don't step on their toes—that's Tony's job—but stay on it." Lacey smiled and said nothing. Mac turned his attention to the tart, and she exited for the copy machine. He was munching away when she returned and slipped the Manville letter and a copy on his desk. She returned to her own desk with a copy of her own.

Her brain was as blank as her computer screen, but luckily she was distracted. Her cell phone rang inside her purse, inside her bottom desk drawer, surprising her with a call from Gary Braddock, an FBI agent with whom she had dealt before. He had recently rescued a pair of her shoes—insanely expensive shoes, purchased in a fit of madness—and saved them from a fate worse than death; an FBI evidence locker. After a brief hello, he said,

"Broadway Lamont is one of the good guys, Lacey. Be nice to him."

"Word travels fast, Agent Braddock."

"What kind of agent would I be if I hadn't heard about your latest adventure?" He chuckled. "Besides, you're all over DeadFed dot com. Part of my daily fringe pseudonews diet."

"It's not exactly my adventure. And Lamont's not the lead investigator on this case."

"No. But he's the smart one."

"You don't care for the lead investigator, Detective Steve Rogers?" Lacey knew only that the lead detective on Amanda's investigation was by reputation a flashy dresser. She hadn't dealt with him.

"The Bureau does not comment, but off the record—"

"You can tell me, Braddock."

"He's an arrogant bastard who couldn't crack a case with a crowbar. Looks good on TV, though."

"Are you working on the case?"

"Not yet. No jurisdiction. We're waiting to be asked for our help. And that is not a quote."

"When will that happen?"

"When the case goes unsolved for so long that it gets embarrassing and dead cold and next to impossible to solve."

"So why are you calling me?"

"Little bird told me you're in it up to your neck. Did Manville really ask for your help?"

Amanda's letter was just about burning up in her hand. "You can read all about it tomorrow. But between you and me and very shortly the Metropolitan Police Department, she sent me a letter to that effect."

"When?"

"After I interviewed her and before she got killed. It arrived in the mail today."

"Interesting. I'll keep that in mind if we catch the case. Be safe, Smithsonian." He paused, then added, "I mean that. You know how you are with sharp implements."

"Someone's always got to be a wise guy," she said.

He hung up laughing, no doubt clipping his cell phone back on his belt, one of four she remembered he carried there. She made a batch of phone calls and left a message on Zoe Manville's voice mail, asking for a few minutes of her time.

As for the possible stalker, John Henry Tyler, she found his Web site again. It hadn't been updated for a week; however, there was an e-mail address. Lacey wrote a brief message saying she knew he had been questioned and that she saw him spit at the dying Amanda. She offered him a chance to tell his side of the story and left her office e-mail address and phone number.

Lacey didn't know how to get ahold of Tate Penfield, Amanda's documentarian, but she figured Hansen would, so she hiked over to the photography department. *The Eye*'s photographers were beginning to rely more and more on digital images, but there was still a busy darkroom stocked with chemicals where the traditionalists hung out.

She found Hansen looking over his photos of Amanda in Dupont Circle on his computer screen. "Hansen, do you know where I can reach Tate Penfield?"

The photographer nodded. "Sure. He's in there." He pointed toward the darkroom as Penfield emerged with a couple of proof sheets. Penfield smiled when he saw Lacey, and she was struck again by his good looks, though at the moment he looked tired. For that matter, she thought, so did she.

"I didn't expect to see you here," she said.

"Hansen and I both took photos last night at Dupont Circle. Hell of an evening." He set the proofs on a light table and bent over to examine them. "We were both freelancing for Amanda, but it turned out to be a news shoot instead. *The Eye* got some photos, and your editor wants more," he said. "We've got digital and film, and he's putting some on the Web—"

"Right," Lacey said, not needing a photo play-by-play. "Tate, I was wondering if I could talk to you about last night, for my story."

"Sure." He kept his attention on the pictures. "What do you want to know?"

"Where were you when Amanda was attacked?"

"Lousy timing. I was late for the shoot—it feels odd to call it a 'shoot' now. The Metro was delayed. I was stuck on the Red Line. When I arrived the police and ambulances were on the scene." He straightened up and stretched, obviously weary. "Once I got there, I started taking pictures. Video and film. I know it sounds cold that all I could do was take photos, but it's an automatic response."

"Yeah, and Mac wants to see them soon," Hansen chimed in.

"You heard that she died today?"

Tate rubbed the back of his neck. "I heard. It's terrible news."

Hansen picked up his camera. "Hey, Lacey, as long as you're

here, why don't we take a couple of candids and keep MacArthur Jones quiet on the old column-photo front?"

"Very funny, Hansen."

"No, that's a great idea," Penfield said, grabbing his camera. "Let me take a couple." She demurred. "Come on, that's a beautiful suit. You wear it well."

"He's really good, Lacey," Hansen said.

"He's a flatterer." She gave Penfield a look of disgust. But she did love Aunt Mimi's suit, and it gave her an extra measure of confidence. And Mimi certainly would have liked it preserved in a photo. "And I look tired."

"Don't worry. Penfield is the glamour man," Hansen said. "Or you could get stuck with me, and you know what I can do with nostrils."

Lacey was exasperated, but she figured this was a losing battle. "A couple of shots, if you promise to tell me anything else that you remember about last night and Amanda." She gave Hansen a look. "But that doesn't mean I'm going to okay a photo on my column."

Penfield asked her if she wanted to comb her hair. She did, and she took a moment to touch up her makeup, allowing him to highlight her cheekbones with blush and offer her a couple of tips on enhancing her features for the camera. He took her over to a window where the light filtered in softly. "I'm not going to bite," he said.

"Be careful, I might," she said.

"You look so serious," Hansen said.

"No, it's perfect," Penfield told her. "You don't need to smile if you don't feel like it."

She tried to look pleasant, but she felt troubled, and she was sure it showed. It was the best she could do at the moment. She relaxed a bit, endured a few more shots, and soon it was over. He wasn't a shoot-the-whole-roll kind of photographer; he knew the look he wanted and he got it.

"Okay, your turn, Tate. Talk to me. What do you remember?"

He set the camera down on the desk, then leaned against the wall, arms folded. There were shadows under his beautiful brown eyes. "I was taking the Red Line from Woodley Park. There was some sort of train delay. You know the Metro—it happens all the time; they never tell you what it is. I got off and walked down Connecticut to the Circle, but by then it was all over. I heard sirens, and people were running away, not wanting to get involved. I ran toward it." He straightened up and took her arm. "Here. It's easier for me to show you."

He led Lacey to the light table and pointed out the photos: Amanda lying on the stretcher, her eyes open but in shock. Zoe being restrained by a policeman. In another, pain and disbelief apparent on her face. And amazingly enough, John Henry Tyler also appeared in a couple of the pictures, lurking in the corner.

"That's the guy they think was stalking her," Lacey said, pointing to the proof sheet.

"Where?" Penfield asked, and he and Hansen crowded around her. Tyler's gaze was focused on Amanda; her blank eyes were glazed over as she was being lifted onto a stretcher. Tyler's body was obscured by a policeman whose back was to the camera, yet his eyes looked feverish even in the picture. "Good eye, Lacey."

"I'll show these to Mac along with my shots," Hansen said.

"What happened to the guy?" Penfield asked.

"He was in police custody last night, but they let him go. I'd like to get ahold of him," Lacey said. "Is there anything else you recall?"

"It's kind of a blur. I'm sure I'll remember more as I think about it," Penfield mused. "The pictures help reconstruct it for me."

Hansen gathered photos and proofs and tapped Penfield on the shoulder. "I'm off to see the wizard."

"Watch out for the winged monkeys," Lacey said. "Oh, and Felicity is peddling tarts today."

"Great, I'm hungry." He disappeared.

"What do you think, Lacey?" Penfield asked. "Amanda stepped on a lot of toes. And you saw her in action. Not quite at her worst, but a typical day."

Lacey leaned against Hansen's desk, remembering. "Yes, it was pretty much, 'Hello, I'm Amanda, let me insult you.' Did she ever mention Caleb Collingwood?"

"Oh sure, Cal. Cal Collingwood. The ex-boyfriend before Dr. Frankenstein. The kind of guy you feel sorry for; God knows I do. I asked Amanda the whatever-happened-to-old-Cal question for the documentary, but she never wanted to talk about him. Of course"—he tapped Lacey's arm—"you've heard all the rumors. Collingwood died in the woods. Amanda killed him. He killed himself to spite her. And so on. And you heard how crazy it made her to talk about him."

"Do you think she had anything to do with his disappearance?"

"Boy, any suggestion of that just drove her out of her mind. She denied everything. And she said she hadn't heard from him since that last note, the one she told you about."

"I remember. The smoking-gun suicide note." Lacey eased herself into Hansen's chair. "I tried looking up Caleb Collingwood on the Internet and made some calls, but no one seems to know much about him. Except for Tyler's little homemade Web site. If he died, no one knows where he's buried."

"The Internet is such a reliable source of information."

"I know, a pack of lies at the speed of light. For instance, I didn't find that much on you," she teased.

"Oh, please," he said, mock offended. "There are at least ten Web sites with my name all over them. You know, ten thousand words on Amanda, and on me, one line: 'Photo by Tate Penfield.' But some poor slobs have no links at all."

"Well, your high school yearbook is posted on the Web. I read that Tate Penfield was very shy. It said he was cute, didn't talk much, instead 'he spoke with his camera.'"

"He was very shy, but he's not so shy now."

"You grew up in West Virginia?" Penfield nodded. "And you didn't know Collingwood?"

"The state is not as small as you think, Lacey. We don't all know each other. We aren't all even related, or marry our first cousins. But a fair number of us do wind up in Washington. No jobs back there."

"I guess you're right," she said, remembering that people often assumed she knew everyone else in Denver.

"But don't worry; I'm working on building those links. We can't all be the darling of Conspiracy Clearinghouse, like you."

"Oh, Tate, you don't really read that Dead Fed nonsense, do you?"

"Before I read the sports page."

Lacey groaned audibly. "You know it's all wildly exaggerated, don't you? It's the Web equivalent of the *National Enquirer* crossed with *News of the Weird*. 'Government Coverup: Aliens Abduct Pregnant Bigfoot from Pentagon!'"

"I'm shocked. I didn't know she was pregnant!" Penfield's eyes twinkled at her. "So are you going to try to find this guy, like Amanda wanted?" Lacey looked at him questioningly. *Does he know about the letter?* "I was there, remember? I heard her ask for your help."

She sighed and shrugged. "All I can do, and all I ever promise, is that I'll ask questions."

He leaned against Hansen's light table and looked her in the eyes. "But you have bumped into killers before?"

"One thing led to another. That's all."

He nodded and tapped her shoulder in a friendly way. "Go get 'em, tiger. Be careful."

"You be careful yourself; you look beat."

Tate rubbed his face with both hands. "I was up all night. I'm trying to see if I can salvage the documentary. Amanda would want me to, as long as it ends with the killer being caught."

Lacey glanced once more at Penfield's proof sheet before trudging back to her cubicle. Luckily the tarts were all gone when she passed by Felicity's desk. The woman had been in a cooking frenzy since returning to work after her minivan blew up. *Be kinder to Pickles,* she told herself. *It's just the way she deals with stress. But does her stress relief have to make the rest of us fat and stressed-out?*

Lacey heard a low sound, like someone gargling. "Hey, Smithsonian." It was Wiedemeyer, looking perhaps a little more miserable than usual. He peered around for Felicity, the object of his misplaced affections.

"Why are you whispering, Harlan? She's not even here. Probably off browbeating somebody into wolfing down four times their daily calorie allotment," Lacey said, immediately breaking her resolve to be nicer.

"I gotta know if she's seeing that guy, you know, that big guy who was here earlier eating her tarts!"

"You're kidding!" *Harlan's jealous of Broadway Lamont? Oh, no.* "Felicity has never even seen the guy before. He's a detective, and he was here to talk to me." Ignoring him, she sat down at her computer and called up the file she had been working on.

"He was affected by her," he whined. "Attracted to her. I could tell. God, how many poor bastards have fallen at Felicity's feet?"

"Get a grip, man! Just ask her out if you like her. Tell her you long for a taste of her hot, sweet buns." Wiedemeyer's jaw dropped in horror. "I'm serious! You may not get lucky, but at least you won't go hungry."

"Ask her out and risk being shot down by the warmest, most fascinating, most beautiful woman I've ever known?"

He looked as though Lacey had suggested he jump from the roof of *The Eye.* If only she could just shake some sense into him, but Wiedemeyer made her a little queasy, and she really didn't want to touch him. "I'm getting tired of this alternate reality we're in here, Harlan. Please go back to your daily disasters beat."

"You're right. I have another one that'll curl your toes." She pointed the way to his desk. "Another poor bastard got his ticket to eternity punched at one of those monster hardware stores on Route One. Right near you, Lacey. Out of nowhere, lawn tractor falls fifteen feet off the top shelf and crushes him to death."

"That's too bad, Harlan." She turned away, seeking refuge in her blank computer screen.

"I'll say, and he wasn't even looking for a lawn tractor. He was in the wrong aisle. He'd been wandering in there for hours, looking for air purifiers, and he made a wrong turn at plumbing supplies—"

"Good-bye, Harlan."

"Poor bastard would be alive this afternoon, if he'd only turned left through the power tool aisle instead of right through—"

"Turn left, Harlan. Or turn right. Just go away."

"Sure." He didn't move. "Only keep me in the loop on the fair Felicity Pickles?" He started musing to himself. "Felicity rhymes with complicity. Pickles rhymes with tickles."

"Yuck! I don't have any more cars to lose, Wiedemeyer! Go. Now."

His eyes registered shock and dismay. "That was harsh, Smithsonian. Really harsh."

At this rate, she would never get her story written. She jumped out of her seat, pointed his way down the hall, and snarled, "I'm on deadline here!"

He moved quickly now, but he was not one to hold a grudge. "In the loop. Keep me in the loop, Lacey," he pleaded. "In the loop? About Felicity?"

Wiedemeyer was finally gone, but Lacey still felt as if she were caught up in a tornado of events swirling around the murder of Amanda Manville. The facts kept dancing like feathers in the wind, and she couldn't catch them all. And that was before Trujillo, animated with the juices that flowed when news happened and deadlines pressed, sailed down the aisle with another news flash.

"Hey, Smithsonian, remember that Spaulding guy, the surgeon boyfriend of the dead model?"

"He's been arrested?"

"No, he was gunned down on the street outside his hotel."

"What?" She jumped out of her seat. "When?"

"Hang on, Lois Lane; you can't fly without Superman."

"Spill it, Clark Kent."

"This story's got you awfully wired."

"Everything's got me wired! I deserve to be wired. And Wiedemeyer was just here looking for his dream girl."

"Wiedemeyer? Now you've got me spooked." Trujillo looked around cautiously. "As long as you don't take any favors from him, you should be okay."

"Accepting a ride from him was no favor. It's turned out to be more of a punishment. He thinks we're friends and I'm his lifeline to Felicity Pickles, and now he just won't shut up." She expelled a deep breath and shook her shoulders, trying to expunge Wiedemeyer from her consciousness. "But you digress. Back to Spaulding, Tony. Is he dead?"

"No, he's at George Washington Hospital." Tony perched on his favorite spot on her desk.

"When did this happen?"

"This morning. Apparently he was taking a break from his conference. He took the probably inadvertent precaution of strolling outside with several colleagues. All doctors, I hasten to add. They applied immediate first aid, and, no doubt, saved his life."

"Lucky break."

"Yeah, and he gets a professional discount. He's in surgery now."

"Do they know who did it?"

"Nobody knows nothing, Smithsonian. Except that it was someone on the street. Drive-by, walk-by, bicycle-by? Maybe one of the docs saw something, but I haven't heard about it yet."

Lacey put her elbows on her desk and her chin in her hands. "At least it wasn't my car; the D.C. cops found it dumped behind Source Theatre. A dramatic choice. So, does this exclude Spaulding from suspicion in the murder of Amanda Manville?"

Trujillo stood up and scanned Felicity's cubicle, looking for sweets. "Unless he had a disgruntled accomplice. Or someone else wrongly believed he was the shooter and decided to apply justice without due process."

Lacey flipped open her notebook. "I interviewed him over coffee yesterday."

"*Bruja!* Why didn't you say so?" Trujillo shook her shoulders.

"I just did. After Amanda insisted she was a target and he was the one who wanted her dead, I thought I'd see what Spaulding had to say."

"And what did he have to say?" Mac rumbled, appearing out of nowhere on little cat feet. *How much did he hear?* she wondered.

"That he had nothing to do with any threats to Amanda. Though he did take credit for turning her into the beautiful monster she was. With apologies." She faced Mac. "If he was involved with her death, he didn't do it himself."

"He was alibied for the shooting. The cops let him go," Trujillo said.

"Write it, Smithsonian," Mac commanded. "Everything you know, but split your angles with Tony; he'll do the police stuff. By the way, this will be your 'Crimes of Fashion' column for tomorrow. Front page."

"But I already wrote my column for tomorrow."

"And I'm your editor. It'll keep. You'll be one column ahead. You're apparently the only one who interviewed both victims, and this is too hot not to jump all over it while it's still sizzling."

She knew better than to protest too loudly. After all, it was the front page. "I can write what I want?"

"Within reason." An eyebrow danced, and he and Tony left, discussing the hard news story that Trujillo would write. Lacey started over again. She typed the working title that suddenly struck her as comical and creepy at the same time. *Not to worry,* she decided, *Mac will just change it anyway.*

CRIMES OF FASHION

Supermodel's Happy Ending Terminates in Hostile Makeover

By Lacey Smithsonian

Growing up, Amanda "Mandy" Manville wanted just one thing: to be pretty like her older sister, Zoe. For a homely teenager the other kids called "Ostrich," that was the impossible dream.

But America's love affair with reality-makeover television made the impossible possible, the dream a reality—or was it a nightmare? After extensive and very public plastic surgery that accomplished that goal, she decided she wanted to be a model. America made her a supermodel. Still later, she wanted to be a clothing designer. All of which she achieved by the time she was in her mid-twenties. For Amanda Manville, suddenly everything was possible.

We know now that Amanda won't achieve any more of her goals. Someone fatally gunned her down Wednesday evening as she was preparing for a photo shoot to showcase her designs amid the monuments of her hometown, Washington, D.C. She was determined to be a success. Even after three bullets were drilled into her chest, she kept walking toward that happy ending. And then we watched her fall, never to rise again.

However, her goals came at a terrible cost to Amanda herself as well as those around her. She found a dazzling match in her plastic surgeon, only to see the relationship succumb to all the dangers of celebrity love affairs. Dr. Gregory Spaulding soon decided he couldn't live with his plastic creation. Now he is fighting for his life after being shot down on the street this morning. Yesterday he told this reporter that Amanda had become strident and tyrannical, and she drove herself and her associates with a gritty determination to succeed, something little hinted at when she was a gawky teen, meekly handing out meals to battered women and the homeless.

Acquaintances said she changed after the plastic surgery that transformed her face, her body, and her life. They said she made others miserable in her quest for success. Perhaps as miserable as she had been as a child.

But in spite of being unhappy in the midst of her success, she wanted to live. How do I know? Because she told me so. She said that someone was trying to drive her crazy, perhaps even to kill her. I didn't believe her. Nor did others who knew her much better than I. They called it a delusion, celebrity paranoia, perhaps even a little self-aggrandizement. We were all wrong. . . .

Lacey poured out everything she knew about Amanda Manville. She gave Mac more column inches than he could probably use. *It's the front page; I might as well press my luck.* In addition to the column, Lacey composed a sidebar on the pandemonium she witnessed at the boutique that morning: "Shoppers Storm Snazzy Jane's for Chic Chrysalis Clothing."

It was nearly four o'clock when Lacey finished, and she was tired and hungry and increasingly bothered by something that had been nagging at her all day, just below the surface. She had thought it was just her normal deadline stress, plus the added stress of her life falling apart, but it wasn't. It was something underneath the deadline anxiety, a dizzy, panicky feeling, like suddenly realizing she'd left her purse somewhere last night, who knew where, and now it had been missing for hours before she'd even noticed it was gone. What could it be that was eating at her?

"Oh, my God! Stella!" Lacey leaped to her feet and shouted at the half-empty newsroom. "What the hell happened to Stella?"

chapter 17

Stella hadn't called. Lacey hadn't even seen her since just after Amanda's shooting last night, when the D.C. detectives had separated all the witnesses before trundling them off to the Violent Crimes Branch for interrogation. Lacey's stylist was pretty much the unofficial voice of Dupont Circle, especially when she was an eyewitness to a crime. It was unthinkable that after the experience she had gone through the previous night, Stella wouldn't have called Lacey. *Probably at dawn.* Now she wondered with rising concern if Stella was okay, if she made it home safely, or if she was still in custody for some weird reason.

That can't be it, she thought. *If Stella were in jail, the whole world would have heard about it by now.*

Lacey had a hard enough time herself dealing with Detective Broadway Lamont, and she hadn't wasted much time thinking of anyone else, except Vic. Now guilt washed over Lacey like a cold shower.

Maybe she's in trouble. Lacey thought about the times Stella had come to her aid. *My God, why haven't I thought about her till now?*

She called Stylettos, but the new receptionist said that Stella hadn't shown up or bothered to leave a message that she wouldn't be in. It seemed that the temperamental Leonardo, of all people, was covering for her. Did madam want an appointment with Leonardo? *Not on your life. I want Stella.*

"Gosh, do you think maybe something's wrong?" the woman asked blithely. "I thought she just spaced us out. Happens, you know."

Lacey then tried Stella's number at home, but there was no answer. She dashed out to Eye Street and caught a cab that took her up Connecticut Avenue toward the National Zoo, where it became a veritable canyon of apartment buildings. She would have told the driver to step on it, but she didn't know the translation in whatever his native language might be. Lacey knew the building, but she had never had been inside Stella's place. Her stylist preferred to visit Lacey's apartment in Old Town Alexandria, sometimes unexpectedly and unannounced. Lacey was certainly curious about how Stella lived and how many leather outfits she actually owned. But the closer the cab got to the building, the more nervous she became.

Stella dwelled inside a large older brick building with a small circular drive. As she opened the heavy oak front door, Lacey was blasted by the scent of pine cleanser. Dread mixed with the overwhelming pine smell and made her slightly sick to her stomach. The concierge made a call to Stella's apartment and got no answer. Having no interest in checking it out himself, he signed Lacey into the building and said that if something was wrong to call him and he would call someone.

The hallway beyond the antiseptic lobby smelled musty, and the washed-out green paint looked like it needed a fresh coat beneath the forty-watt bulb. Lacey marched on to Stella's place on the third floor. She knocked. There was no answer. *Please, God, no awful surprises. Please let her be okay.* Lacey knocked again. "Stella, it's Lacey." She pounded louder. She waited one full minute, her stomach turning over in panic. She pounded again. "Stella! It's me! Anyone there?"

This time the door opened a crack. The inside chain was latched. "Lacey? What are you doing here? Hang on." Stella closed the door, undid the chain, and opened it again to let her into the dark apartment, which had what looked like black drapes closed tight against the late-afternoon light. Stella's face was smeared with dried tears and day-old makeup. Black smudges spread like spider legs down her cheeks and up toward her forehead. She wore only a large black T-shirt that reached her knees and proclaimed, I LIKE MY ATTITUDE PROBLEM!

"New look?" Lacey inquired, leaning back against the door because her legs felt rubbery. She felt terribly relieved that Stella was alive. She could have hugged her, black smudges and all.

"I kind of fell into bed after I got home." She rubbed her eyes, making the smears worse.

"Are you okay?" Lacey couldn't tell from the looks of Stella or her apartment. Clothes were tossed on nearly every surface, and there was a prevailing sense of gloom. *Or maybe it's just the black drapes. Is it always like this, or is today special?*

"Sure, I'll be okay. Right? It's just freaky. You know? The cops kept me out really late."

"I know. Me too."

Stella looked a little surprised. "Right. You were there too. I totally forgot, what with all the pandemonium."

Lacey moved cautiously deeper into the apartment. "I got interviewed by the second-string guy," she said. "You got the lead detective."

"That Rogers moron? What an asshole. And cops and me . . . Well, this shit isn't supposed to happen, you know?" Stella's eyes started watering, and she rubbed her hands through her longish purple crew cut. She picked up a hand mirror from a stack of hair-styling magazines perched on the coffee table. "Wow, I'm a total mess. I look like a hard night at the 9:30 Club."

"Have you eaten?" Lacey asked. "I'm starved; maybe we could catch a bite to eat. I'm buying." The ambient gloom was getting to her.

"Yeah. Sure." Stella was uncharacteristically subdued. "A shower, gotta have a shower. And . . ."

"What's the matter, Stella?"

Tears threatened to spill down her face. Stella shook her head as if to clear it. "What time is it?" She squinted at a digital clock that sat on top of a television set. "Oh, my God, I missed work! Oh, Lacey . . ."

Lacey dropped her reserve and wrapped Stella up in a big hug that smeared her makeup even more. "It's okay. Leonardo covered for you. I'll call them and let them know you're all right."

"Thanks. I could really go for a Coke and some breakfast." The tears finally fell. "I'm so freaked out, Lacey. I mean, she got shot right in front of me. And the television said she's dead. I mean, I've seen dead people before, but I haven't seen them go down. And she was right next to me. I could've been killed too. What if it was me he was aiming for? What if it was supposed to be me?"

"He wasn't aiming for you."

Stella stumbled around, picking things up and tossing them back down. "I keep seeing that look on her face. The only time she didn't look like a total bitch on wheels. God, I know that sounds terrible. But all of a sudden she looked like a little girl who didn't know what was happening to her. And she just kept walking; that was the worst."

"What did the police say?"

"I don't know what it is about cops, but they always start in on me, like I got some kind of label on my ass that says, 'Kick Me.'"

"Do you have a history with cops, Stel?"

"Christ almighty. I never told you?" Stella started picking up a few magazines, then, without a clue where to put them, tossed them back on the black leather sofa. "They always came to my house when I was a kid. Every Saturday night, like clockwork. My folks were always fighting. Or beating on me. Or both. The old man thought using his belt was a competitive sport: Olympic Synchronized Whipping. Anyway, the cops never did anything about it; they blamed us, blamed my mother for setting the bastard off, blamed my brother and me for being bad kids. I know all about how helpful cops are. And you know why? My freaking dad was a cop. Ex-cop. Those cops were all his buddies. Sticking together. Pricks." Stella collapsed on the sofa and curled her feet under her. "Then this jerk-face cop last night, he tells me maybe I'm the target, and not Amanda Manville, maybe it's all my fault. So I start thinking, Maybe he's right; maybe I'm next."

"Maybe I should open the drapes," Lacey suggested. The place was closing in on her.

"No, no, no, what if the shooter's out there?" Stella looked around the apartment and clutched her throat. "I gotta get out of here, Lacey."

"The shooter isn't after you, Stel. Amanda told me someone wanted to kill her. Remember?"

"Yeah, but what if the shooter thinks I can ID him and now he's after me? Hey, can I stay with you tonight?" Stella looked hopeful for the first time. "I don't want to be alone. Bobby Blue Eyes is out of town, but he'll be back tomorrow. Staying by myself, I just keep thinking all these crazy thoughts. Like I might be next." The tears were a steady stream now. "I can bunk on your sofa," she pleaded. Stella had bunked there before.

Lacey couldn't bear Stella's crying. "Of course you can stay over, Stella. And you don't have to use the sofa this time. I bought a trundle bed, pulls out, sleeps two. You'll be my first customer at Motel Lacey."

"About time, I say. What's the use of having all that extra room without a bed?"

"I have to buy some sheets first, and they have to be washed." Lacey didn't want to admit that she had refrained from buying an extra bed for so long because it would just attract family members to D.C., and apparently it had. "There's another thing. My mom and my sister are coming tomorrow, but you can stay tonight."

"Your family? Wow. That's so nice. You have a family. I thought you were an orphan or a refugee or not on good terms or something. How long are they staying?"

"Over the weekend. They leave on Tuesday." *If I'm lucky. And if I live so long.*

"Cool. You can tell me all about them. We'll have a slumber party." Stella wasn't listening anymore. A little of her old spirit was returning. "I know, we'll do face masks!" She headed to the bathroom. "I'll pack some girly stuff. Make yourself at home."

As if. Lacey looked for a light switch and turned it on. The room was still dim. Stella apparently believed in mood lighting. When she looked closer, Lacey realized the drapes weren't black. They were dark brown, and the walls were a deep taupe, something the Addams Family would have selected. A monument to gloom. The living room made her uncomfortable, so she took a tour and peeked into Stella's small bedroom. The queen-size mattress sat directly on the floor and nearly filled the room. Outfitted in red and purple drapes and matching bedspread and sheets, the bedroom was also in a state of disarray. In one corner there was a small pink aluminum Christmas tree adorned with silver balls and pairs of silver earrings, sitting on top of a violet dresser. It was only October, but for all Lacey knew, the tree could have been up all year. A small pink spotlight was pointed at it. *Yes,* she thought, *Stella would have a pink aluminum tree dressed with earrings.* The room was garish, but much more cheerful than the living room, and on the whole, Lacey preferred it. She found the phone under a pillow by the bed and called Stylettos. The blasé receptionist seemed pleased, but not at all surprised, that Stella was all right.

Lacey heard the shower turn off and she made her way to the tiny kitchen, where every surface was painted in too many coats of standard apartment off-white. And it looked like the painters had simply covered everything in their path, including specks of dust and what appeared to be marching columns of embalmed ants.

"I'll just be a minute," Stella hollered from the other room.

Lacey put a kettle of water on and made herself a cup of instant hot chocolate and another for Stella, who was trying to decide which provocative suede or leather outfit would be appropriate for a quiet night in Old Town Alexandria. Lacey wandered back to the bedroom and handed the cup to Stella, who was clad in a giant beach towel. This time she noticed something new. Hanging on the open closet door was a long white gown in cheap satin. Next to it on a small stand was a black wig with hair piled high on the crown, perhaps five inches or more. Rising from each temple was a white streak that looked like a lightning bolt.

"What's with the Bride of Frankenstein getup?" Lacey asked.

"You noticed! Isn't it great? It's from Backstage Books, the costume shop." Stella glanced fondly at the outfit and stroked the wig protectively. "It's my Halloween costume; you ought to see the makeup I'm doing. Eyeliner out to here." She pointed to somewhere near her ear.

"A little early, isn't it? I mean, Halloween is still a week away."

"No! If you don't have your costume by now, you're absolutely sunk. They are totally gone by Halloween. Besides, we get to dress up in the salon every day for a week before the big day."

"How charming. We don't do that at *The Eye*." *Thank God.*

"You don't know what you're missing."

"What reporters wear is scary enough. Trust me." Lacey longed for the days when Halloween was meant for children and not every adult who refused to grow up. "You don't think you're going to frighten your clients with hair like that?"

"Are you kidding? Half of my clients are going to want this exact style when they see it on me." Stella hoisted the wig on quickly to show Lacey. She was beginning to seem more like her old self. She grinned impishly. Then she hissed, exactly like the Bride of Frankenstein when she first laid eyes on her intended mate. "I'm practicing. Gotta get into character."

"Thanks for the warning. And the outfit is very fetching. But how can you wear that to the salon? With perm solution and color stains and that sort of thing?"

"Oh, the dress is for a big party on Halloween that I'm going to, bunch of stylists. But I'll wear the hair and makeup with my Stylettos smock. I'll be the Stylist of Frankenstein." Stella lifted the wig off her head and settled it back with a friendly pat. She emitted another hiss. Then she selected a red leather miniskirt, black sweater, and tall heels.

"Pretty subdued." Lacey had seen Stella wear more provocative clothing to a funeral.

"Yeah, well, I guess it's just us girls tonight, right? And I'm kind of worn out." She grabbed her black leather jacket with its full complement of zippers, a big satchel, and the hot chocolate, and took a sip. "Hey, you forgot the Amaretto!" She ran to the kitchen, where she kept her liquor, opened a bottle of the amber-

colored liqueur, and poured a slug into both her mug and Lacey's.
"It's really better this way; trust me. So, are we taking your car?"

Lacey sighed. "My car was stolen, Stella." Stella yowled in surprise.

"Oh, my God! And you've been holding out on me? I can't believe it! Who stole it?"

"It's been a very busy few days, Stella. I'm having a hard time
keeping track of what I've told everyone. And what day it is. And
where I've left my friends. Okay?"

"Okay. You're forgiven. Drink up. And finish mine too, I'm
driving. We'll take my Mini and you can tell me what happened.
Everything that happened. Every little detail. Make up what you
don't know. You owe me." Her loud, chunky heels clattered down
the hall, picking up steam as she went. Lacey trailed behind
wearily, but very happy to see Stella back on her high-heeled feet.

"No, Stella. I am not buying black satin sheets or red satin
sheets or any color satin sheets for my new trundle bed. Besides, I
have to buy two sets of everything."

"But Lacey . . ." They were in the middle of a big bed-and-
bathroom-accessories store that held a thousand temptations for
Lacey, but satin sheets weren't among them.

"My mother is sleeping on that bed, and she wouldn't understand." *She'd think I live in a bordello.*

"Vic would like them, I bet." Stella batted her eyelashes.

"I don't think Vic cares about the sheets. A man once told me
that, of course, men prefer to sleep on manly sheets, rather than
girly sheets. But if it comes down to sleeping alone on his brown-
plaid duck-hunter sheets or with a woman on her pink floral girly
sheets, he'll take the girl with the girly sheets every time. Besides,
if you ask me, the girly sheets are probably clean and have a higher
thread count."

"Well, duh! Guys will sleep on a bed of nails if there's a girl in
it. If she's on the bottom, that is. A straight guy anyway. So speaking of sheets and getting nailed, have you guys done it yet?" Stella
was way too interested in Lacey's love life, and as usual she
wanted all the juicy details. Lacey had no comment, which, of
course, told Stella everything. "You haven't? Holy cow, Lacey!
Retarded! The two of you. I swear I think you're both sexually
brain-dead, or maybe dead a little lower down. I give up. Be a nun.
Just don't expect Vic Donovan to share your vow of chastity with

you." Stella fingered more sheets thoughtfully. Then she stopped. "Oh, my God, Lacey!"

"What?" Lacey looked around to see if they were being followed, if somehow the shooter was in the store with them, perhaps hiding behind the goose-down-pillow display.

"What if he's, like, actually been interested in guys all along, and he's not really, you know, as big and macho as he seems? I mean he totally comes off like a testosterone-driven hetero *hombre,* but you never know. I know lots of gay guys who are totally buff and macho-looking, and Vic could just be one of—"

"He's straight! Okay? Straight. Trust me. We just have a few issues to work out."

"Issues? A few?" Stella rolled her eyes. "Whatever."

Lacey grabbed several sets of light blue and cream sheets with delightfully high thread counts and equally high prices. They were for her mother and sister, she rationalized. "These, Stel. I'm getting these. Okay?"

Stella looked them over and nodded. "Okay. Not hot or sexy, but they're okay. They're pretty. They're actually kinda girly. Ooh, Vic'll love 'em." Lacey elbowed her gently in the ribs.

By ten o'clock, Stella's red BMW Mini Cooper was full of sheets, pillows, groceries, and other necessities for Stella's overnighter—and Lacey's mother and sister. "That wasn't so bad now, was it, Lacey? We should go shopping together more often." Stella seemed invigorated by their surgical strike to the shopping mall at Pentagon City, but Lacey felt like a zombie.

"I can't move. I'm so tired."

"You're not up for a nightcap?"

"Please take me home. I still have to wash the sheets. I'd rather not be hungover for the trial by family I am about to endure."

"You are such a drag sometimes. Got anything to drink at home?"

"I'm clean out of hot cocoa and Amaretto, but there's some gin and tonic."

"Well, then, make mine a double."

The Mini Cooper was sailing down Washington Street when the cell phone in Lacey's purse rattled her with its jaunty tune. "So answer it already," Stella said.

"Hello?" Lacey moaned from sheer exhaustion.

"Sweetheart, are you all right?" Vic's deep voice instantly warmed her.

"Vic, I'm not going to live through my mother's visit."

"Is that Vic?" Stella asked. "Hi, Vic!"

"Stella's with you?"

"I forgot to call you," Lacey explained. "She didn't want to be alone after . . . well, you know, the interrogation. She's sacking out at my place tonight." She remembered then that Vic didn't want Lacey to be alone either after the Amanda Manville shooting. Maybe he had planned to come over himself? *Damn. My trundle bed isn't even made up yet, and already I need a reservation book.*

"That's good," he said.

"Why good?" Lacey asked. Stella glanced over, trying to figure out what was being said.

Vic hesitated a moment. A moment too long. "Montana is in town tonight and . . . and she wanted to get together. With me. You know, for a drink."

"What?!" Lacey yelled and Stella slowed down the Mini. "Montana McCandless Donovan Schmidt, your ex-wife, excuse me, your *ex*-ex-wife, is here? In town? And you're going to buy her a drink?"

"Oh, Lacey, I'm so sorry," Stella said. "I guess he isn't gay after all." But her look said that Vic obviously must not be as hot for Lacey as she had thought.

"I just wanted to make sure you're not alone tonight."

"How very damn thoughtful of you. But of course, you're not going to be alone either. Montana! That backstabbing little . . . I thought you left her behind back in Steamboat Springs." *For good.*

"Now, Lacey, calm down. Seems she's got a job lobbying for the Colorado Cattlemen's Association and she's in town to sweet-talk a senator or two before some committee vote on some range bill; I didn't get all the details."

Lacey bit her tongue to keep from saying something about inspecting meat being the perfect job for a man-eater like Montana.

"Lacey, are you okay?" Stella asked softly.

"Are you there?" Vic asked.

"I'm here. Where are you?"

"I'm picking her up at the airport. We'll probably just have a drink somewhere before I take her home."

Lacey sat bolt upright in her seat. "'Home'? Back up, cowboy. Where exactly are you taking your ex-ex-wife?"

"What's he saying?" Stella was leaning over to hear Vic's side of the conversation.

"Stella, watch the road," Lacey whispered.

"I mean I'm taking her to my mom and dad's place, not mine.

I tend to say 'home' when I mean their home. My place is just a rest stop."

"And you'll be staying where?" Her heart felt like ice.

"At my place. Alone. Damn it, Lacey. Anyway, this trip came up so suddenly, Montana didn't get a chance to make a reservation, and my folks really like her, so . . ."

Better and better, Lacey thought. *His folks still dig his ex. Great. I haven't even met Vic's folks. And I never will at this rate.*

"Vic, are you really a private investigator? Because any rookie knows this town is lousy with hotels! She could walk into any one of them day or night and snag a room, and probably some rich old geezer with it. For free."

This sounded like fun to Stella. "Is he on a hooker case now?" She pulled the Mini to the curb.

"Come on," Vic pleaded. "She's a small-town gal who doesn't know her way around Washington."

"Ha! She's a big-time operator, and she knows her way around you, Vic Donovan!" *And what about me?*

"Listen, honey, we shouldn't fight when we're both tired. You take care of yourself and Stella tonight, Lacey. I'll come over to-morrow night to meet your mother and we'll start over."

"Don't you dare come over! You stay away from my mother and my sister! I'll talk to you next week, if you're not remarried to Montana McCandless Donovan Schmidt *Donovan!*"

"Lacey—"

"Good-bye." She pressed the Off button on him. It wasn't as satisfying as slamming down a real phone.

Stella looked over, dying for more information. "Wow. Is Vic getting married again?"

"Just drive, Stella. Okay?"

The Mini Cooper roared back to life and they were off.

chapter 18

If Lacey was afraid that her heart would stop beating over Vic's apparent dalliance with his ex-wife the previous night, she needn't have worried. Conspiracy Clearinghouse, a.k.a. DeadFed dot com, had her heart thumping away in no time first thing Friday morning as she read:

TOP SECRET BIONIC BABE AMANDA MANVILLE SLAIN IN DUPONT CIRCLE
Fashion Scribe Smithsonian's Car Used in Drive-by Attack; Grisly Coincidence or Message From a Killer?

By Damon Newhouse

Most of America is unaware that one of their favorite supermodels, the late Amanda Manville of *Chrysalis Factor* fame, was allegedly part of a secret government project known unofficially as the "Bionic Babes," sources have told Conspiracy Clearinghouse.

In fact, none of the artificially beautiful women in the project were aware that they were being used for clandestine purposes. Or that they were cybernetic surgical prototypes for a superstrong bionic female warrior to be deployed in combat in the near future. Their various implants and prostheses were made with weapons-grade silicones and plastics, manufactured in secret laboratories in Delaware, packed with classified nanotechnology devices. They are not available on any open market for civilian use.

The Babes had not given their permission to be part of any experiment, nor did they know how special they were—or that their every move was being tracked. Global position-

ing systems were embedded in their breast implants to allow
a rogue group of so-called government scientists to keep tabs
on their human science projects. . . .

Lacey snorted in disgust. "Newhouse, how do you get away
with this drivel?" But she kept reading his Amanda Manville story,
which had nothing in common with the one she had written except
the name Amanda Manville.

Manville had recently undergone a severe personality
change, attributed to toxic chemicals from the highly experi-
mental implants in her body, which used nanotechnology,
sending microscopic machines coursing through her mem-
branes and into her brain like a kamikaze cocktail. Our
source hypothesized that she had to be eliminated before she
became completely unstable and brought too much attention
to herself and the project. That may also be the reason for
the attack on Dr. Gregory Spaulding, the TV plastic surgeon
who was duped into using classified government-provided
materials in this ghastly lab project. . . .

Lacey couldn't read any more. She reached for the phone and
dialed. Damon Newhouse answered immediately. "Where do you
get this stuff, Damon? Do you just make it up, you sorry excuse for
a journalist?"

"Whoa, Smithsonian, a personal call. I am deeply honored. To
answer your question, I have highly placed sources, Lacey." He
chuckled. He was annoyingly calm.

"Who hang out in the psych ward at St. Elizabeth's Hospital, no
doubt."

"A history of institutionalization would not necessarily mean
your information is false."

"Spill it, Damon. Do you guys just get high and cook this stuff
up? Do you take turns inventing the wacky conspiracy of the week,
and then call each other your sources?" Felicity looked over at
Lacey to admire her tirade. "And who do you think the shooter is,
in this comic-book conspiracy theory of yours?"

"A quasi–government agent. Probably an untraceable subcon-
tractor."

"Of this secret rogue Bionic Babe agency?"

"That's right."

"Lunatic!" Lacey was so animated she knocked over her coffee cup, which was not full, but it splashed a little onto her sweater. Fortunately she had worn black slacks and a black V-neck sweater, because she knew she would need to be comfortable to dash around all day. She also had a new sleek black leather jacket to combat the coolness of the October air. After sopping up the coffee with a paper towel, she focused back on Newhouse, who was still blathering away into the phone, something about "rogue nanotechnology, deep background, and secret documentation."

"Then why kill her in Dupont Circle, in front of everybody?" Lacey cut in. "If she's got GPS transmitters embedded in her implants and you can track her anywhere, why not just kill her quietly in the middle of the night?"

Felicity stopped any pretense of work and simply stared, as did Peter Johnson and Tony Trujillo, riveted in their tracks on their daily goody run to Felicity's desk.

"Because," Damon said, "this way it looks like anything *but* a top-secret government conspiracy."

"It's *not* a top-secret government conspiracy! Amanda Manville died because someone who knew her intimately hated her and wanted her dead. And the bastard used my car, Damon, which makes it very personal for me."

"Is that a quote? 'Cause I really like it. I'm using it."

"No, it's not a quote!"

"It is if I put quote marks around it. It's good talking to you, Smithsonian. I liked your column, by the way. Responsible, but with some feeling."

"Don't you sneer at responsible journalism, you kook; you write for the funny papers. Look, Newhouse, I realize that you fancy yourself a rogue pirate on the high seas of the information superhighway, and you can write whatever jumbled, sleep-deprived fantasy you want, because it's your Web site, but . . ." She tried a deep, cleansing breath. It didn't work. It never worked.

"I'm putting you on speakerphone here. Is that okay?"

Lacey ignored that; she knew he usually worked alone. "Just for the record, I'm glad you make Brooke happy, but please leave me out of your paranoid hallucinations. Do not connect the name Smithsonian with these crackpot stories."

"Don't worry about it, Lacey. Half the people who read my Web site just think you're a wing of the museum. You know, the Lacey Smithsonian Crime of Fashion Wing, right between American History and Air and Space? Gotta run. 'Bye." He sounded a little too damn cheerful for Lacey's taste this early in the morning.

She hung up, wondering if Brooke could be saved from the clutches of this madman. She doubted it. Brooke was a true conspiracy-theory believer, and she trusted that Damon had broken through the "pheromone jammers" mounted on top of the White House and the Pentagon just for her. And he was pretty damn cute for a crackpot. In other words, Brooke was a fool in love.

The phone rang again, jangling her nerves. Her audience returned to their own quieter pursuits. She was hoping against hope for a last-minute reprieve from her mother's visit. Lacey prayed that Rose Smithsonian had suddenly decided that there were oh-so-many things to do before her traditional Halloween party for the neighborhood, where she served hot apple cider and cinnamon doughnuts, and no doubt was planning some wild new creation involving Wheaties, chocolate chips, maraschino cherries, and four-and-twenty blackbirds baked in a pie. And she would save her visit for later. *Maybe ten years later?*

"Lacey Smithsonian," she answered, forgetting to even look at her caller ID.

"My God, I thought you were dead!" It was Miguel. "Gunned down along with the horrendous and deserving Amanda Manville! What other reason could you have for not calling me? Me, your dearest friend, your personal couture stylist, who would rush to your side at your merest call."

"Miguel! Is that you?" she teased. "I'm sorry, it's been really crazy. I left you a message." She realized she hadn't spoken with him since Amanda's murder, and if Stella was the voice of Radio Free D.C., then Miguel was the Mouth of Manhattan.

"A very uninformative message. I promise to forgive you, but only after you tell me everything, absolutely everything, every little detail. Leave nothing out."

"You sound just like Stella, you know. Demanding this, demanding that." Lacey smiled at his high dudgeon. "I desperately want to share everything with you, Miguel, but I have another crisis. My mother is coming to town, and I can't let her find out about any of this."

"That is so sad, dear, and I promise not to rat on you to your mama, so you can tell me all," he pleaded. "I can't believe that Stella was there and I wasn't, the minx! Who did it? Have you figured it out yet? Are you in danger? Do you need me to help bring the bad guy down like I did last time?"

"You're my hero, Miguel, but I think I'll be okay. More than okay—I'll be surrounded by my mother and my sister, but I'll be lucky if they don't aggravate me to death. Or vice versa."

Lacey took a few minutes to bring him up-to-date and promised him an in-depth gossip session soon. She knew Miguel would be entertaining the New York fashion world with juicy tales of how *his* friend had seen Amanda go down.

She dreaded her next task: informing Mac that she had to leave early because company was about to descend on her, and she had to rent a car in order to pick them up at the airport. She'd forgotten to clear it with him.

"Who is coming to town?" Mac inquired. "Your family?" He looked suspicious, as if he didn't believe that she could actually have a family. *Well, I'm with you on that one, Mac.*

"My mother and my sister," she said, eager to get out of his office and finish her work. "Really. It's the truth."

"Two more Smithsonians?" Mac squinted at her. "Does this mean trouble times three?"

I'm so amused by you sometimes, Mac. But this is not one of them. "For your information, they are extremely nice people who never get into trouble." *Which is possibly why they don't understand me one little bit.*

He chuckled and bit into an oatmeal cookie, heavy on the cinnamon, courtesy of Felicity Pickles. Obviously the specialty of the day. It smelled delicious. "Be my guest. By the way, Smithsonian—and I say this only out of habit, you understand—stay out of trouble."

"You have no faith, Mac."

"No, but I have a lot of experience with you. What's your mother like?"

"She likes meat loaf," was all that Lacey could think of saying. She knew Mac liked meat loaf. "And she collects wallpaper patterns."

"Doesn't sound too dangerous."

"My job is to chauffeur them to the museums so they can buy Smithsonian souvenirs." *And avoid anything unpleasant, like having them mess with my life.* "It's bound to be a boring weekend."

"It sounds perfect to me. Are you planning to do any work today?"

"Zoe Manville has agreed to talk with me. I'm meeting her at ten o'clock."

"Fashion?"

"It could be fashion."

Mac rustled some papers on his desk, then leaned back in his chair. "You know, Lacey, no matter what that crazy dead woman said, you don't have to try to solve this thing yourself. That's actually the cops' job." She said nothing. "I hate the jerk for using your car," he added.

"Thanks, Mac. I hate him too." Neither of them believed that the use of her car was a coincidence. She stood to go. "Just another day in happy valley," Lacey said as she dashed out of his office.

The Manville family home was an unprepossessing row house in an untrendy area of Northwest D.C. far above Georgetown, a two-story edifice with a front porch painted white.

Zoe met Lacey at the door, weepy and red-faced, without makeup. She wore a long white shirt over black slacks, and her feet were bare. Neither she nor the shirt had any starch left. She ushered Lacey in, shutting the door against the bright sunshine as if it were an insult to her grief.

The small house was immaculate, and roomier inside than it appeared on the outside. Wooden floors gleamed against creamy walls and were topped by dark-red-and-blue Oriental carpets. A full complement of sturdy mission furniture completed the polished look.

"Thank you for seeing me," Lacey said.

Zoe's eyes measured her. "Can you find out who did this terrible thing?"

Lacey shook her head and shrugged helplessly. "I'm not a detective; I'm just a reporter. I just write stories."

Tears squeezed out of Zoe's eyes. "I heard that the killer used your car."

Is she accusing me? Lacey wondered. "Someone stole it from my office the day I went to Snazzy Jane's. To send a message, I guess. And it worked." She felt as if they had all been cast in a play without having been given scripts, and now they were stumbling blindly around the stage. Zoe did not offer her coffee or tea. They stood awkwardly in the foyer. "This is a lovely house," Lacey said.

"It's where we grew up. Our parents won't move. They always insisted this house was good enough, even though Amanda was always after them to upgrade."

"Where are they now?"

Zoe's red eyes watered. "They were on vacation in Switzerland. They're flying back to Dulles today. The first time they've ever traveled overseas." She rubbed her eyes. "Mandy paid for it as a treat. She wanted them out of the way of all the chaos when we came home, and we could have the house to ourselves as our base for the premiere at Snazzy Jane's. It was kind of fun, like being kids again, teenagers with the folks out of town. Until the threats started."

This was one of those times when Lacey's words failed her, which happened more often than she liked. "I am so sorry."

Zoe started sobbing, loud, painful, unearthly sobs that racked her frame. "My folks are coming home! What am I going to tell them? I was her big sister." She swayed as if she were going to fall. She gasped for breath, and Lacey helped her to the sofa in the living room. "I was supposed to protect her. Oh, God, oh, God, what will I tell them?" She sounded panicky, catching her breath now in short gulps that sounded like hiccups.

"Tell them nobody thought it would happen."

"Mandy knew it would happen, and I didn't believe her."

"There was nothing you could have done to prevent it."

"I should have. Somehow." Her voice rose painfully, like that of a child in trouble.

Lacey sat on a chair next to her. "Do you believe that Spaulding had anything to do with the attack? He was Amanda's only real suspect."

Zoe shook her head, took a few breaths, and blew her nose before speaking. "Greg didn't really seem to have any passion about Amanda, one way or the other. At least not after they broke up. As horrible as this was, it had to stem from passion." She tried to speak more clearly. "His lack of feeling seemed to make it worse for her. The angrier she got, the more withdrawn and formal and sad Greg became."

The personal storm that had rocked Zoe had subsided, and she leaned her head back against the sofa and wiped her eyes. They looked painfully swollen.

"Why don't I get you a washcloth for your face?" Lacey asked.

"That would be nice. Thanks." Zoe pointed to a small half bathroom down the hall, near the kitchen. Lacey padded to the small room, which was painted a warm coral. She rinsed a washcloth under warm water then wrung it out and picked up a small bottle of lotion that sat on the vanity. When she returned she found Zoe in the same position, staring at the ceiling. Lacey handed her the cloth and the lotion to soothe her chapped skin.

"You know that Dr. Spaulding was shot? That he's in the hospital?" Lacey asked quietly. "He was critical yesterday, but his condition has been upgraded to serious."

"I don't understand it. Any of it." Zoe covered her face with the washcloth.

Lacey sat down on a nearby chair. "What is he like?"

Zoe moved the cloth away from her mouth, but kept it covering her sore eyes. "Greg is a nice guy, despite what Mandy said about him. He just couldn't deal with Amanda the Diva Supermodel. Sometimes I think he's kind of like me. He doesn't like conflict. He doesn't like to fight, and he didn't like scenes. He likes making people happy, I think, and Amanda just couldn't really be happy anymore. Like she couldn't be beautiful and happy at the same time. That's what ruined it for him."

"And Amanda liked to fight?"

Zoe removed the cloth from her eyes. "She was the sweetest thing before the surgery, the best sister anyone could hope for. But somehow, afterward, she needed reassurance all the time that she was beautiful, that she was loved, that she was . . ." Zoe stopped.

"She was what?"

"I was going to say 'better than me.' I don't know, like Mandy held some big, silent grudge all her life and it exploded after the makeover and the television show. All that attention really wasn't good for her. She liked it too much—and she needed it too much. She had to be the prettier sister, the thinner sister."

Amanda must have encouraged Zoe to eat, like Felicity on one of her cupcake campaigns. And then, Lacey imagined, she probably tormented Zoe when she got fat. "Yvette said you are going to continue designing the Chrysalis clothing line."

Zoe just looked weary and closed her eyes again. "I suppose. Yes, of course I will. We have contracts. And investors."

"If they were your designs, why did you let Amanda take all the credit?"

"She was the important one, the famous one. She had backers ready to jump on the bandwagon. She had a good eye and she did have talent. No matter what Yvette says, I didn't mind. Nobody would have backed me without her."

"I received a letter from Amanda yesterday," Lacey said.

"Yes. I got your message. Then Detective Rogers showed up. He wanted to know if it was true that someone had replaced her photos with the B.S. pictures—Before Surgery, I mean. It was true, but I don't know who could have done it, although the house was guarded only when Amanda was here. I even had a moment when I thought that maybe Amanda had done it herself. Some twisted desire for more attention."

"Did the police find anything?"

"I don't know. They took some empty picture frames from Amanda's room, to test for fingerprints, I guess. At one point the detective insinuated that I had tormented Amanda." Zoe laughed for a minute, a high, shrill, nearly hysterical laugh. "As if I would goad Amanda into one of her special tantrums, so she could scream at me for an hour or two, and taunt her with those old photos of her when everybody called her Ostrich? Never in a million years."

Lacey didn't want to admit that Conspiracy Clearinghouse's insane story of Bionic Babes Gone Berserk was sounding a little more plausible. Amanda really had changed radically, and not just on the outside. "May I see her room?" Lacey wanted to know more about Amanda, and her bedroom seemed like a logical place to look.

Zoe put her hands on her knees and pulled herself to her feet like an old woman. Lacey followed her up a narrow stairway to the second floor, where there were three bedrooms, one good-sized room for the parents, and two rather small, cramped rooms for the daughters. They passed Zoe's room, which was decorated in lavenders and blues that flattered her blond complexion, and moved on to Amanda's.

The room was white on white, with a double bed and an iron headboard, also painted white. The bed was covered with expensive linens and pillows in soft golds and moss green. An armoire hid a television set and dresser drawers. Sheer white curtains fluttered softly at the window, which was open a couple of inches. It was a spare and serene room, the only other furniture a cushioned rocking chair next to the window, taking advantage of the light. Beside the chair was a large basket filled with colorful balls of yarn. A pair of large knitting needles was stuck in a ball of crimson wool yarn that sat on top. They were attached to an unfinished piece of work.

"I forgot that she knitted," Lacey said. That fact had been mentioned on the makeover show, but who would imagine Amanda the Supermodel as someone who would have the patience to sit and knit to pass the time?

"She said it helped her think. The faster she knit, the faster she talked. It was almost a family joke." Zoe sat in the rocking chair and picked up the needles. Every remembrance required an enormous amount of Zoe's energy. "I love to design clothes, but

Mandy's passion was really fabrics and fiber arts. Knitting and crocheting. She wanted to introduce a line of knitwear. Little sweaters and cloche hats."

"Like a 1930s kind of look?" Lacey could imagine neatly tailored sweaters over the bias-cut gowns, or over the straight long skirts already featured in the Chrysalis Collection.

"We were thinking of next fall, a year from now. I have some sketches. They were going to be so much fun." Her voice fell. "We just wanted to bring a sense of play back to what people wear." She opened the door to the closet and pulled out an emerald-green bolero sweater with full sleeves and deep cuffs, while Lacey took notes. There was also a green-and-white-striped knit hat with a white knit rosette raffishly set off to one side.

"I love these," Lacey said. They were playful and retro and classic, all at the same time. They would make a delightful and, yes, sassy outfit for fall days and football games, a look for the homecoming royalty and kisses in the swirls of autumn leaves. A wave of sadness hit Lacey, and she had to take a deep breath. She had a real glimpse of the woman behind the model, the one who liked to be bundled up in cozy sweaters and knit and have fun. Amanda, with her dramatic coloring, her lavender eyes and auburn hair, would have looked especially pretty in these clothes.

"Fall was her favorite season," Zoe broke into her thoughts. "Until this year."

"There are no photos of Amanda in here."

"No. There were four or five that were switched with the ugly photos. She tore them up. Those were the frames that the police took."

"When did the threats begin?"

"About a month ago, I think, but I couldn't really say. There was always the occasional crude letter, a stalker or two. Ever since all the publicity started, the TV show, the makeover, the magazine covers." Zoe brought out something else for Lacey to see.

"A wedding gown?" Lacey asked.

"Beautiful, isn't it?" The full-length ivory dress was a delicately crocheted gown with long bell sleeves, designed to be worn over a colored underslip. Pearls had been sewn into the lacy bodice-work, giving it an even more elegant texture. Romantic, with a definite medieval influence, Lacey decided. Something that Guinevere might wear. The sleeves had an intricate pattern of interlocking initials: A. M. and C. C., for Amanda and Caleb, Lacey assumed. It was an older dress, and Lacey thought it was interest-

ing that Amanda had kept it, but then it represented hours of hand-
work.

Zoe suddenly hung the dress back up and shut the closet door,
overcome with memory. "I'm sorry; I can't look at it now. Have
you seen enough?" she asked without looking at Lacey.

"Yes, thank you." Zoe steered Lacey out of the bedroom, closing the door softly, and led her back down the stairs. "When did
Amanda fall in love with Greg Spaulding?" Lacey asked.

"The first time she saw him, I think. At the first consultation for
her surgery. You can even see it on the videotape of that show. She
came alive in a way I'd never seen before."

"What about Caleb Collingwood?" Every answer she had heard
about Caleb was unsatisfactory. Surely Zoe must know something
about him, have some insight into what happened.

"She didn't kill him, if that's what you mean. No one knows
what happened to him. I do think he's dead. I wish I'd never heard
of him. The rumors were even harder on my parents. You're not
going to ask them about him, are you?"

How am I even going to meet them? Lacey wondered. *I have my
own planeload of family to take care of.* "No, I just thought . . .
well, he's part of her history, isn't he? It wouldn't hurt to talk about
him, would it?"

They turned in to the living room, and Zoe collapsed on the
sofa again, tucking her bare feet under her. She couldn't seem to
stop herself from sighing. "I really didn't know him very well. I
was in college at the time, in Philadelphia. Then I took classes in
New York at the Fashion Institute of Technology. Mandy was
going to school here because she didn't want to leave home for a
new environment. High school was pretty hard on her." She
reached for the wet cloth and wiped her eyes again. "I met him
only at holidays. I was dating Brad at the time."

"Brad Powers, Yvette's husband?" *Small world?*

"Yes. Funny how things happen, isn't it? It wasn't really serious. The point is, I had better things to do than hang out with my
little sister's goofy boyfriend."

"What about his family?"

"He didn't seem to have any. None that he mentioned, but
maybe I wasn't paying attention. He was just a skinny guy with
really bad teeth. It was kind of hard to look at him. They were a
matched set, Cal and Mandy. I hate to admit this, even now, because it was something no one ever discussed, but I was a little embarrassed by my sister. I wanted her to be normal-looking. The

makeover show seemed like a godsend, because we never would have had the money for the surgeries. No one expected a superstar to emerge. She really never was normal-looking."

Lacey was suddenly conscious of being short on time. And she needed to pick up the rental car before going to the airport. She pulled out her cell phone, apologizing to Zoe, and made a quick call for a cab to pick her up.

"Mandy thought I was a complete snob. She resented the whole cheerleader thing." Zoe reflected. "I was pretty then, a cheerleader." She stood up and glanced in the oak-framed mirror that hung over the gas fireplace, staring at the bloated and tear-streaked naked face that peered back at her. "Not that you would know it now, fifty pounds heavier."

Lacey didn't know how to respond. A shadow of the pretty woman was still there, and Zoe was desperate to hear that she was still young, still pretty, still desirable. But everything Lacey could think of to say would sound hollow. "When is the funeral?" she asked instead.

"Next week. It will be private, just the family. But there will be a big memorial service Sunday afternoon. There's been a huge interest from Amanda's fans, and the media will be invited. I'll make sure you're on the list." Zoe sighed deeply. "I'm not sure of the details. Brad is taking care of it. We want to accommodate the people who . . . loved Amanda."

And possibly hated her, Lacey thought. "There should be a large crowd."

"Yes." Zoe's voice turned bitter. "You know, *The National Enquirer, Access Hollywood,* and *Entertainment Tonight.*"

A knock at the door startled both of them. Zoe peered out from behind the curtain to see who it was and then opened it. Yvette stepped in the foyer and threw a brief inquisitive glance at Lacey. She was wearing a brown tweed jacket, a camel-colored sweater, and matching slacks. She carried a rich brown leather tote bag from Coach, and her sleek blond hair was tucked into a chignon. She looked casually elegant and completely composed. Yvette eyed Lacey coolly.

"I'm just leaving," Lacey said. To Zoe she murmured, "Thank you for seeing me. I'll be happy to attend the memorial." *What will I do with Mom and Cherise? Send them to the mall? Bring them along? Lock them in my apartment?*

Yvette turned her attention to Zoe. "Oh, dear, you look terrible. Let's go take care of you. You must do something with your face."

"There were always the two of us, Yvette." Zoe began to cry again. "We had our problems, but we were a team. I had a sister. I can't be the only one left now."

"You and I are still a team. You have to pull yourself together, Zoe. We're picking up your parents in two hours. Go on up and take a shower. I'll find something nice for you to wear."

Zoe hesitated for a moment. "I don't know what to do."

Yvette hugged her and gave her a slight push toward the stairs. "Go, Zoe. I'm here now. I'll take care of everything."

A purple cab pulled up at the curb, and Lacey shrugged on her jacket. "Good-bye. Take good care of her."

Yvette nodded. She held the door open and watched until Lacey climbed into the backseat of the cab.

chapter 19

The knot in her stomach throbbed as Lacey waited outside the security gate at Reagan National Airport. She had driven like a maniac to arrive on time after picking up the pathetic rental car. She had been promised a midsize, but they were out, so she had been downgraded to a tiny Toyota Echo. It felt cramped and cheap, except for the daily rental rate, which was exorbitant. Compared with her late, lamented 280ZX, it felt like she was driving a tin can, a flimsy tin can that probably cost more than $15,000. What was worse, it was beige with a gray interior, but Lacey hoped this bland color scheme would be soothing to her mother.

She watched as the first passengers came out, followed by the middle-row passengers, before there was any evidence of her family. Finally Lacey's mother bobbed eagerly into sight, looking cheerful in her neon-green nylon jogging suit, which featured hot-pink stripes up the sides. A huge purple-and-yellow tote bag hung from her shoulder, and her sunglasses perched on her head. Rose Smithsonian might just as well have worn a neon sign that spelled out TOURIST! in sequined letters. Lacey closed her eyes and made a mental note not to let any cabdrivers take her mother for a ride. They would take one look at her and charge her triple fares.

"There she is, Cherise," Rose said. "Lacey! Lacey, darling, we're here!"

Lacey opened her eyes and managed a weak smile. "Hi, Mom." She offered a cheek for her mother to kiss. Rose left a lipstick print that Lacey had to smudge off with her hand. Her mother looked trim, fit, and attractive, and way too happy to have landed in Lacey's life with both Nike-shod feet.

Her mother took a good look at her. "Dressed for a funeral, dear?"

Lacey looked down at her all-black ensemble. "I just wanted to be comfortable today."

"You couldn't just wear blue jeans?"

"I had to work this morning." Changing the subject. "You look good, Mom."

Rose smiled. "I have to keep up, you know."

Lacey did know. Peer pressure to be fit was brutal in the Mile High City from whence she came. Denver, Colorado, was the thinnest and fittest big city in the United States, and no Smithsonian woman worth her mettle was going to endanger that record. "With you girls out of the house, I've been taking up sports," she said. "A little golf. A little tennis."

"We're not girls anymore." Lacey had been saying that since she turned eighteen.

Her mother gave her a quick hug. "You'll always be my girls. Right, Cherise?"

"Hey, big sis!" Cherise said with feeling as she gave Lacey a smothering hug. Lacey focused on her sister, who was younger by just a year, but from a vastly different universe. An aura of well-scrubbed perkiness surrounded Cherise like a halo. She wore tight, faded jeans and a snug bubblegum-pink fitted T-shirt, in all her blond and tanned glory. Her longish hair was pulled back into a ponytail held by a pink fuzzy scrunchy. A dab of mascara and lip gloss was all the makeup she wore. Cherise was still single, though she was always on the lookout. Lacey remembered her as perpetually dating some athletic and respectable but slightly dull young man or another, who generally lived up to Rose's expectations, if not quite up to Cherise's.

Please be tired so I can just tuck you both into bed. "I'm sure you're exhausted after the flight," Lacey said.

"No way, I napped on the plane," Cherise said. "What is there to do in this town?"

"Oh, this and that. How about I take you home and get you settled?"

"Okay. Then we'll go out, right?" Her motor was still running. "I want to see everything! It's been ages since I was here last, visiting crazy old Aunt Mimi."

"Cherise, we're not here to run Lacey ragged," her mother offered.

"Sure we are." Cherise smiled deceptively. "It's Friday; I'm sure Lace wants to get out and party. Girls' night out, right? Look out, D.C.; here come the swanky Smithsonians!" There were aspects of the head cheerleader that would never desert Cherise. She would have a frantic agenda of whirlwind sightseeing planned. It was her nature.

Once a cheerleader, always a cheerleader. If Lacey didn't act fast, they would be racing from monument to monument, museum to museum, to coffee shop, to boutique, to dinner and dancing, and to utter exhaustion. "Let's start with baggage pickup. This way, ladies. And then we'll load up my rental car."

"It's so sad about your ratty old car, Lacey, but on the plane I was thinking," her mother began. "Actually, Cherise and I were talking, dear, and we decided you should take her old car."

"Her minivan?" Lacey nearly choked. The very idea of driving a minivan was deeply offensive to her. Felicity Pickles drove a minivan, for heaven's sake. *And just look what happened to hers.*

"You'll like it, Lacey," Cherise jumped in. "It's big and roomy. You can haul the whole gang around. It's like a dorm room on wheels. And it has a great sound system."

"Every car you ever touched had the curse of the lemon," Lacey shot back.

"All except the minivan," she said. Lacey knew this was stretching the truth. "Anyway, I'm buying an SUV hybrid next."

"How ecological of you. How did you ever wind up with a minivan, anyway?"

"It was Mom's, before she got her SUV."

"Mom's minivan?!" *Do you hate me that much?*

"It can pack a lot of equipment. You know, your skis, your bike, your golf clubs, your camping gear . . ."

"None of which I have, or need. Thanks for thinking of me, but I don't require any more hand-me-downs from the Smithsonian lemon orchard of ungrateful automobiles."

"But it's the perfect solution, Lacey," her mother said. "You don't have a car; Cherise needs to get rid of this one. You could fly home and drive it back. We could even drive with you, make it a cross-country family vacation. Like when you two were babies. It would be fun."

A perfect scenario for disaster. "I'm sure you can pawn it off on some homeless person in Denver."

"Well, we don't want any unpleasantness now," Rose said. "We'll talk about the car later." Her mother paused a beat before starting another thread of conversation. "But I do have a little bone to pick with you, Miss Lacey Blaine Smithsonian."

The middle name. Uh-oh. Only criminals and little kids in big trouble ever hear their middle names.

Lacey figured the knot in her stomach could not get any tighter. "You might as well pick away, Mother." They arrived at their baggage carousel, which was still empty. The Smithsonian luggage was nowhere in sight.

"What is this nonsense about your being involved with killers?"

"Killers?" Lacey wondered for a moment whether to just play dumb. She had hoped her stolen car was the only problem that Rose would plan to solve. She intended to keep Vic undercover— unfortunately not her own—and any and all of her friends and acquaintances as far away from her family as possible while they were in town. And she promised herself never to discuss her job.

Her mother always protested that she was proud of her daughter's journalism career, but Lacey didn't believe it. Reading newspapers only depressed and confused her mother, and when Lacey sent her clippings of her column, which was seldom, Rose was of the general opinion that Lacey was a little too judgmental, and who really cared about clothes anyway? Rose rarely bought *The Eye Street Observer*; it was carried only at a few out-of-town newspaper outlets in Denver, and always a few days late. The thought that Rose knew next to nothing about her eldest daughter's life was comforting to Lacey. She actually had settled on two relatively benign subjects for discussion, movies and food, and she had stocked her apartment with both. But here was the *killer* question. "I don't know, Mom. What do you hear?"

"Our neighbor—Mrs. Dorfendraper, you remember her; she's our precinct committeewoman? She found your name all over the Internet. I'm far too busy to fool around with your father's computer, but are you aware that there is some sort of terrible thing called the Conspiracy Clearinghouse on that . . . oh, what is it called, Cherise?"

"That Web site?" Cherise said. "DeadFed dot com. It's pretty wild."

"Mrs. Dorfendraper has nothing better to do than Google my name on the Web? The woman needs a hobby." *I forgot, she has a hobby: gossip.*

"That Web site has the most unbelievable stories. Why, it's worse than reading those crazy tabloids in the supermarket, and your name seems to be attached to some of them," her mother continued. "I tell you, Lacey, there are days when I wish our family name were still Smith. I mean, just how many Lacey Smithsonians do you think there might be?"

"Good old Mrs. Dorfendraper, the eyes and ears of central Denver." Lacey could picture Mrs. Dorfendraper. She was the very picture of a concerned neighbor, with her sensible shoes, her practical haircut, her old-fashioned glasses, and her nose in everybody's business. What fun it must be to be able to do her busybody business in cyberspace now. Especially when she'd never worked a day in her life. "So she has a computer now? It must make spying on the neighbors so much easier."

"Don't be unkind, dear." It was an automatic mother response. "She doesn't have any family."

"You know you can't believe everything you read on the Internet."

"And I suppose that picture of you waving that sword thingy was phony," Rose said.

Ah, the infamous picture, again. Lacey shrugged and said nothing. *Actually, I was aiming the sword thingy, not waving it.* "We already talked about that, remember? It was all blown out of proportion—"

"It was a sword *cane,* Mom," Cherise kicked in. "Like an antique, or something."

"Thanks for the news flash, Lethal Feet." Lacey made a direct hit with the lethal nickname. Cherise sniffed and backed off. "Really, Mom, the story was all about the dress I was wearing. Events just happened to . . . unfold."

Her mother continued in a lather. "I couldn't even read it all. It was just too upsetting. Did you really have to stab that poor man in the foot?"

"It was him or me. Don't worry, Mom. He'll walk again. In prison." *Lacey caught with unsavory playmates; how fun.* "Those are really old articles," Lacey said in her defense. *Almost a month ago. Ancient history. Thank you, Mrs. Dorfendraper, for bringing it up again; I'll Google you sometime, too.*

"You know that I don't tell you how to live your life," her mother continued. "I am not that kind of mother. But I will have none of this tracking-down-killers business while I am here."

"We'll only be here for a few days." Cherise smirked. "How much trouble could she get into?"

"I don't want my girls involved with any killers or murderers or kidnappers or politicians or any other unsavory characters." It was the lament of mothers everywhere.

"At least not while we're here," Cherise said, and winked.

"We won't be visiting my office then," Lacey said, wondering how she could fit that in if it became necessary. She did not want to be involved with the aftermath of Amanda Manville's death, but she had made a promise to the deceased. She had found that trouble didn't always seek an appropriate slot in her agenda. What if the idiot who stole her car planned to send another message? "A quiet weekend is my fondest wish," Lacey promised. "And where on earth did they send your luggage?"

"You were a police reporter in Sagebrush, which was bad enough, and you never got into these kinds of situations, at least not that I'm aware of. I may not know a lot, Miss Lacey." Rose turned to scan the slow-moving baggage carousel for their tardy luggage. "But I do know that fashion reporters do not solve crimes or write about them."

"Just 'Crimes of Fashion,'" Cherise said. "And you know Lacey has an opinion about everything, Mom. She probably even has a snarky opinion about what we're wearing."

Lacey spied a tourist on their left holding a copy of *The Eye Street Observer*, its front page blazing with headlines about Amanda Manville—and Lacey's latest "Crimes of Fashion" column. She moved to the right to draw their eyes away from the paper.

"I do have an opinion, Cherise, and I love your touristy outfits. You'll fit right in at all the museums."

"Mom plans to buy everything she can lay her hands on that has the name Smithsonian on it," Cherise pointed out. "And so do I."

"We'll get right on that." Lacey breathed a sigh of relief as the bags finally hove into view on the carousel and pulled their attention away. "But Cherise, I'm not sure they have those seven-days-of-the-week Smithsonian bikini underwear you've been longing for."

"Very funny. I'll settle for the T-shirt. And the sweatshirt. And the baseball cap, and the tote bag, and the umbrella, and . . ."

Lacey's rent-a-tin-can barely held the three of them and their motley collection of neon-colored luggage, but Rose commented favorably on Lacey's sensible choice in transportation. Soon they were motoring sedately down the George Washington Memorial Parkway toward Old Town Alexandria. Lacey pointed out various scenic attractions as they passed: the Potomac River on their left; the memorial to the Confederate dead in Alexandria, with the grieving Rebel soldier facing South, turning his back on the

Union; the bustling Beltway; and the war zone near her apartment building, where the Commonwealth of Virginia was building a new Woodrow Wilson Bridge practically in Lacey's hip pocket, a project which she despised even more than Harlan Wiedemeyer did. *The vicious bastards!* And then they were home.

Now all Lacey had to worry about was how she could get rid of them for an hour or so in the morning, in order to make her interview with Spaulding, who was listed in improved condition at George Washington Hospital. She had called him earlier on the off chance he'd talk to her. Spaulding was in good spirits; he said he wasn't going anywhere, he was sleeping a lot. She took that as an invitation and made an appointment to see him Saturday.

Her mother's main concern, a car for "poor Lacey," was resurrected on the way home in the rental car, at the grocery store buying the additional supplies Rose insisted she needed, and in the elevator going up to her apartment. Her mother finally conceded that maybe Cherise's minivan wouldn't work for Lacey, but another plan bubbled to the surface. "You know, your father and I have been thinking about buying a new car. You could take your father's Oldsmobile station wagon! He only uses it these days for hauling those big sheets of plywood, and deer hunting, and it still runs like a top. It's built like a tank; I've always felt very safe in it."

The very thought of piloting that immense faux-wood-grain gas hog full of venison carcasses sent shivers down Lacey's spine. "Mother, it's very sweet of you to care. And I remember Dad's *Battlestar Galactica* fondly. But I'm an adult. I will decide what kind of car I will buy. If it turns out to be a mistake, it will be my mistake." The elevator doors parted and she steered her family down the hallway.

Lacey unlocked the apartment door, and much to her surprise Stella was there. Had she returned, or had she never left? Even stranger, there was the intoxicating aroma of cookies baking, chocolate-chip cookies. Stella rushed to greet them with a big smile.

"Oh, Lacey. This must be your mom and your sister. Hi, I'm Stella. Come on in; I've just been doing a little baking." She was wearing the only apron Lacey owned. Never before worn, it was a gag gift from some friend long ago. It said, KISS THE COOK! The matronly white garment nearly covered up a red miniskirt and a revealing red sweater that displayed the startling cleavage Stella was so proud of. *A punk Martha Stewart.*

"Stella, you didn't have to do this." Lacey was puzzled, sure that Stella had gone home to the gloomy little apartment where the hairstylist had evidenced nary a trace of such domesticity. *This can only mean danger.*

"It's my pleasure." Stella grabbed an oven mitt, opened the oven door, and removed a tray full of perfectly browned chocolate chip cookies. She set them on top of the stove as efficiently as a voluptuous purple-haired Betty Crocker.

"Lacey, introduce us to your charming friend," her mother said. Stella had once told Lacey she was good with mothers; other people's mothers, that is, not her own.

"Mom and Cherise, this is Stella. She's my hairstylist. And my friend. And my cookie baker." She raised an eyebrow at Stella. *And full of surprises. What are you up to?*

Cherise unloaded milk cartons from a grocery bag and started pawing through the cupboards. "Where are your glasses, Lacey? We have to have cold milk with hot cookies," she said, just like a little Girl Scout.

"It's so nice to meet one of Lacey's friends," her mother said, exactly as if Lacey were ten years old on a play date.

"Same here, I'm sure." Stella launched into a compressed explanation for her bizarre behavior. "Anyway, this is just a little thank-you for Lacey. I was so freaked out over being grilled by the cops that I was, like, totally convinced that crazy drive-by shooter would get me next, and my boyfriend was out of town, so Lacey let me stay here last night. I also got to help pick out the sheets you're going to break in on her new trundle bed. They're totally cute, even if they are really tame, if you know what I mean." She winked at Rose and tossed a meaningful look at Lacey, who felt like sinking through the floor.

"Drive-by shooter?" Rose looked nonplussed. "Is that some sort of new drink?"

Cherise had poured cold milk for four and was sliding hot cookies onto a pretty hand-painted china plate that had belonged to Aunt Mimi. She set everything down on Mimi's cherry dining room table.

"Cookies and milk, everybody! Get 'em while they're hot!"

chapter 20

"Lacey, what's a 'drive-by shooter'?" Rose Smithsonian asked again, clearly hoping this was some new slang term, perhaps for a happy-hour special at a drive-in.

"Guys, it's time for cookies and milk," Cherise announced again. She ushered everyone into the dining area, then decided it would be nicer to sit down in the living room. She moved them again.

"Lacey didn't tell you?" Stella chirped. "That's because she is so modest. You can read all about it in *The Eye Street Observer* or maybe on the Internet. Check out DeadFed for the inside story."

"It's nothing," Lacey said to her startled mother. "All in a day's work."

Cherise set the cookies down on Aunt Mimi's trunk, and Lacey quickly slid coasters underneath everyone's cold glasses. "Wow, you still have this funny old thing," Cherise said, meaning the wonderful trunk that Lacey considered her dearest and most important treasure. "Might be worth something at an antique store. If you like that kind of thing. Did you ever consider selling it?"

"No, I like this kind of thing. That's why I have it, that's why Aunt Mimi left it to me, and that is why I will never sell it."

Cherise shrugged. "Just a thought, sis. Ever hear of eBay?" She tried to open it. "Hey, it's locked."

"Oh, my God, if you only knew what we have gone through for that trunk," Stella said with a dramatic flourish of her cookie. "Lacey would never part with it." Lacey shot Stella a look that said, *Stop now.*

"What's in it?" Cherise asked.

"Nothing. Just Aunt Mimi's patterns."

"Sewing patterns? You don't sew. Nobody in our family sews. Besides, they'd be, like, a million years old."

"Exactly," Lacey said. "So you don't have to look at them."

"Still, they might be worth something."

"They are priceless. To me. Okay? This trunk is going nowhere, okay?"

"All right, all right, chill out. It's just a bunch of dumb patterns."

Her mother tried again. "About the latest trouble you were in, dear. A drive-by what?"

"You don't need to worry with Lacey on the case," Stella burst in, while Lacey made hand signals to stop her talking. "She's too modest, so I'll tell you."

"That's not necessary," Lacey said, panic setting in. She knew all too well that there was no stopping Stella when she was wound up. "Have another cookie. Everybody. Stella, have another."

Stella put up her hand. "Not for me, ladies. I must have eaten half a bowl of cookie dough, and believe me, I'm stuffed. So anyway, I'm going to tell this story, okay?"

Rose Smithsonian settled into her chair comfortably. "Please continue, Stella, and don't leave out anything interesting." She picked up a cookie and took a sip of milk.

"Lacey always leaves out the good parts," Cherise interjected.

"Don't I know it." Stella took a deep breath. "You know that supermodel, Amanda Manville? The one who supposedly killed her old boyfriend, but they never found his body, so she was off the hook?" Heads nodded in unison. "The one who used to be, like, really ugly, known as Ostrich in high school, but then she got all remodeled on that plastic-surgery change-your-life show, *Chrysalis Factor*? Well, they totally made her over so as to be a beautiful bride when she married her really ugly boyfriend, her fiancé, the one who died, that maybe she killed. And that was also going to be on television. I mean the wedding that didn't happen, not the killing that maybe did. You with me so far?"

Lacey noticed that Rose and Cherise were concentrating very hard on following Stella.

"But the wedding fizzled, 'cause she was, like, too gorgeous now for the homely homeboy," Stella continued, "and 'cause she had a sudden urgent thing for her doctor, you know, the one who redesigned her face? She fell in love with him, because he, like, gave her a new chin, 'cause she really didn't have much of one, and some great new boobs, and took away that humongous honker of a nose. Well, of course she was grateful. Duh. I know I would be." Stella tapped her own pert little nose.

Lacey stole a glance at her mother, who seemed way too inter-ested in Stella's story. Cherise was blissing out on hot cookies and cold milk.

"So she comes out of surgery gorgeous, especially with the makeup and the wardrobe," Stella said. "I mean, what would you do if you're suddenly gorgeous after being a gargoyle all your life? Marry the scary ugly boyfriend, or the babe-alicious doctor hero? Obviously you dump Mr. Ugly, become a supermodel, and grab the handsome doc. Right? Wedding plans ensue, only the plan goes all screwy, Amanda turns out to be way too high-maintenance—believe me, I know this from experience—and the doc dumps her. Meanwhile, death threats, stalkers, the works, the price of fame, you know?"

Stella took a breath, inhaled part of a chocolate chip cookie, and resumed her narrative while Lacey nibbled nervously. The cookies were terrific. *Where did Stella learn to cook?*

"As I was saying, death threats. Oh, and she's a fashion de-signer now too, like she didn't have enough going on in her life al-ready. Anyway, she tells Lacey, who is there at Snazzy Jane's, the snotty boutique, only to write a fashion story, that she is in the crosshairs of a crazy killer, Amanda, not Lacey, but *this* is where Lacey really comes in. And it happens all the time to Lacey. Any-way, Amanda Manville, supermodel, asks Lacey Smithsonian to find out who it is. The killer. The killer-to-be, that is. If he does. Even though Amanda thinks it's the doctor, she's not a hundred percent sure. She asks Lacey, so justice can be served, and as luck would have it, it's a crime of fashion too. So it totally fits with Lacey's job."

"And what happened to this Amanda Manville?" Rose asked.

"Oh, geez, I thought you heard! It was all over the TV, but then you've been on a plane all day; what am I thinking? She got killed, just like she said she would, just the other night. She was shot three times right in front of me, but she lingered for a while before ac-tually dying." Stella was winding down. "She died the next day. And now Lacey is going to find the killer, just like she always does, well, a couple times now, 'cause she, Lacey, has, like, this amazing sense for stuff like fashion clues that the dim-bulb cops are too clueless to pick up on. Isn't she great?"

Stella looked at Lacey with admiration. Rose and Cherise were silent.

What's the worst that can happen? Lacey wondered, though she actually didn't want to find out. *Maybe they'll disown me in a huff and leave town.*

"Me and Lacey were there! We saw it all happen! I was *this* close to taking a bullet myself, even though I was just there doing Amanda's hair and makeup, and speaking of makeup, if you don't mind my saying so, Mrs. S.—"

"Call me Rose." Her mother looked a bit adrift, trying to digest Stella's tale.

"Rose, I could do your makeup for you. It would be my pleasure. I'm just over at Stylettos salon at Dupont Circle, near where Amanda got killed. I could show you the exact spot. Lord knows you're a beautiful woman like your daughters, but maybe you need just a little update?"

"An update?" Rose appeared to consider the offer.

"So Lacey is looking for the killer?" Cherise asked, proving she had been paying attention to something besides cookies.

"Lacey, you promised. No killers," her mother said, as if that were just another teenage dating rule. *No drinking, no staying out past curfew, no killers.*

"My job is just to talk to people and write what they say."

Stella's eyes opened wide. "Oh, no! She does way more than that. Don't you worry about Lacey, because she's got this total, like, talent for this kind of thing. Trust me," Stella said. She stood up and took off the apron, revealing her red miniskirt ensemble, looking ready for some hot Friday-night action. "Come to the salon anytime. Stylettos, Dupont Circle, in the District. We'll make room for you. And Cherise, you gotta lose that ponytail. It's totally a first-day-on-the-Hill intern look. Don't you just love a good makeover?"

Cherise stroked her hair, considering. Before Rose could cross-examine Lacey, Stella's boyfriend, affectionately known as Bobby Blue Eyes, knocked at the door. His choirboy face and Cupid curls distracted the women as he collected his wild little crew-cut stylist. Stella ran her fingers through Bobby's curls and gave him a huge welcome-home kiss that made Lacey long for Vic. But her heart sank at the thought of his spending the weekend with Montana. Forcing these thoughts away, she knew a crisis was brewing right here at home. *Maybe if I simply take a flying leap from the balcony they will forget the entire story.*

However, after Stella slipped out with Bobby, the family Smithsonian did, remarkably, what they did best. Denial. They said nothing. And Lacey said nothing. They went on with their evening as if nothing at all had happened. Rose and Cherise inspected the apartment at length and murmured here and there. They oohed and aahed over the balcony and Lacey's famous view down the Potomac River toward Mount Vernon. They shook their heads sympathetically over the lack of closet space. Lacey had done her best to clear the spare bedroom for company. It looked less like her personal dressing room, office, library, and walk-in closet, and more like a guest bedroom. And she had shoved her computer, Tony's old laptop, under her own bed for safekeeping. *Let 'em Google me when they get home.*

They swore they liked her trundle bed and that it would do perfectly fine. Cherise chose the lower pullout bed, and her mother the upper. Yet there was room for improvement, her mother said. "Lacey, if we just turn everything around and put the beds over there, the sunlight won't wake us in the morning. This direction is east, isn't it?"

Lacey excused herself and ran to the bathroom, which was full of new fluffy, clean towels and French milled soaps. She opened the medicine cabinet and cracked open a bottle of Advil for the tension headache that was squeezing the back of her neck like a vise.

"Are we driving you crazy?" Cherise followed her in.

"No, no, just sinuses," Lacey fibbed. They returned to the living room.

"You know, dear," her mother said, "if we just rearranged the furniture in here, we could create intimate conversation areas."

"I like it the way it is, really. Open. Spacious."

"Don't be such a stick in the mud," Cherise said. "And you know, everything is brown this year. Naturals are back; what's with all this blue?"

"Has it been outlawed? Are there blue laws?" No one laughed. They didn't get it. "Anyway, I'm not a brown sort of person."

"You could be a little more open-minded." Cherise sniffed. "How about sage?"

"Maybe we could just move the furniture around to get an idea of what it might look like," her mother offered.

Cut them off at the pass, Lacey thought, *or they'll trap you in a box canyon.* "Maybe later. Why don't we think about dinner?" A loud knock on the door interrupted her. *Now what? And when will they fix the front door?* "I'll get it." She started for the door. "Why don't we call for pizza? The Domino's number is on the fridge. No weird stuff, like pineapple." Cherise was just the type to inappropriately slap fruit on top of a pizza because it was *healthier* that way.

"I could just whip up something homemade," Rose said. "My meat loaf—"

"No!" Lacey nearly yelled, then added, "You're not here to slave in the kitchen, Mom. Pizza's always a treat." *Nothing but evil carbohydrates.* The knock came again. She looked through the peephole at her visitor, opened her eyes wide, then opened the door and slipped into the hall, quietly closing the door behind her. "What are you doing here?" she practically hissed at the man who usually made her toes curl.

"Meeting your family, of course." His wavy hair was wind-tossed, and his eyes danced with amusement.

"Why? I haven't met your father. Or your mother."

"Name the date, sweetheart. They'll be crazy about you." Vic gave her a lazy smile and leaned against the doorjamb, temptingly close to her. "I brought you some flowers." He handed her a lovely bouquet of day lilies, peach-colored roses, and white daisies. The first flowers he'd ever given her, she realized, and they should have made her happier. But with the kind of day she was having, he would have to offer to run away to Paris with her on the spot.

"The flowers are beautiful," she said, then shook her head. "Men, you just never pay attention, do you?"

"Don't you want to see me, Lacey?"

Vic stroked her face. He leaned in for a kiss. She leaned in too. His leather jacket was slung over his shoulder, and he was looking damn good in his jeans. His soft blue chambray shirt was open at the neck, and the sleeves were folded back, exposing his tanned muscles. She was also aware that he smelled good. But the mood didn't last. "What about Montana?"

"She's at a hotel in the District. Dad drove her in today."

"I'm so glad you found a room at the inn for that poor shy girl, stammering around strangers the way she does." Lacey remembered Montana from Sagebrush, Colorado. Montana was no shrinking violet; she was aggressively blond and busty and leggy, and she had a reputation as a hard-partying good-time gal, especially when she was divorcing Vic. Lobbying for Colorado's cattlemen was probably a good use for her, although Lacey could think of a few other good uses. Lacey folded her arms and leaned against the door. "I can't believe you came over here."

"How could I ignore the challenge you laid at my feet?"

"What challenge?"

"To meet your family. Why, Lacey? What haven't you told me about them? Do they have two heads, green scales, cloven hooves? What kind of sniveling coward would I be to run away from your family of fire-breathing dragons?"

"You wouldn't be a coward to honor my wishes. And to answer your question, they're like everybody else's family. They drive me crazy, they want to run my life, and they ask too many questions. And after Stella spilled the beans about the Manville murder, which really thrilled my mother, I don't need any more complications, thank you very much."

He moved in closer. "So I'm a complication?"

She stood her ground. "And how. My mother doesn't need to know these things. Besides, you're always busy doing God knows what to protect the national security, and now suddenly you have a whole evening just for me?"

He looked serious and gave her a hug. "No, I don't have a lot of time. I'm sorry about that, Lacey. I just came to show you that the idea of your family doesn't scare me. And to say hello to them."

"And cause trouble."

"What kind of trouble? Lacey, let me come inside. Besides, they always tell you to get a good look at your girlfriend's mother. As a preview."

"They? Who are they?"

He was about to push open the door behind her when Cherise stuck her head out the door.

"Lacey, pizza's on the way. They said they know you— Whoa. What's going on?" She took one look at Vic and her eyes went wide too. "Well. Hello."

"I'll be there in a minute," Lacey said.

"Hi, I'm Vic Donovan. Friend of Lacey's." He put his hand out for her to shake, and Cherise noticed the flowers Lacey was holding.

"Ooh, flowers! You must be the boyfriend we haven't heard about!" She stuck her head back in the apartment and bellowed, "Mom!"

"In a minute, Cherise. Go," Lacey pleaded with Vic, but it was no use. Her mother appeared at the door.

"What's going on out there?" Rose said. "It's getting lonely in here."

Lacey, her eyebrow raised dangerously high, shot a warning look at Vic. But he was entirely too pleased with himself. "This is

Victor Donovan." Lacey made introductions. "My mother, Rose Smithsonian, and this is Cherise, my adorable little sister."

"Well, what's everybody doing out in the hall?" Rose said. "Come on in." She snatched the flowers out of Lacey's hands. "These are beautiful; they belong in some water." She hustled them all inside and told Lacey to get a vase. "How nice of you to stop by, Mr. Donovan. Victor."

"Call me Vic."

"We're having pizza, Vic. You will join us, won't you?"

"He already told me he hasn't much time," Lacey said. "He just wanted to meet you."

"That's so thoughtful," Rose said. "Won't you sit—"

"But now he has to go," Lacey added, shooing Vic back toward the door. The last thing she wanted now was the dreaded boyfriend interrogation.

"A piece of pizza sounds good, Lacey." He shot her his sexy, appealing smile, but she wasn't buying it. "I'm sure I could stay for that." He put his arm around her shoulder. *I give up.*

"Cherise," Lacey said, "would you set the table, please? I want to show Vic something important. On the balcony."

"Oh, no problem."

Cherise and Rose looked terribly interested in the balcony, but Lacey said, "Alone." She opened the door, pulled him out, and shut the door behind them.

"It's a beautiful night, Lacey. And you know, they seem perfectly normal. Even charming. Imagine that."

"You're so funny." Through the glass she caught her mother and sister chatting companionably. "Thanks for giving them another topic of conversation, not that they needed it."

"It can't be all-killers-all-the-time, you know. What's the problem, Lacey? I like them. And they'll like me. After all, you like me."

"Oh, be quiet," she begged.

"Come here." He moved her to the secluded end of the balcony, where they couldn't be spied on. "That's better. I guess I really picked the wrong weekend to spirit you away."

"If I survive this visit, how about next weekend?"

"Sounds good to me. So, Stella spilled the beans?" He looked amused.

"Radio Free Stella. I'm trying not to blame her. Gossip is in her blood; it's what she lives for. She really should be on the air instead of in my hair."

Vic drew Lacey to him, wrapped his arms around her, and kissed her. "I also came over because I need to know that you are safe while this nutcase is running around loose."

"As you can see, I'm here, safe and sound, wrapped in the bosom of my family."

"And you can promise me that they aren't . . . well, prone to getting into trouble?"

"Like me? Is that what you mean, Vic? Don't worry." She broke away from him. "My mother has already informed me I am not to play around with killers or other unsuitable companions this weekend, which probably means you should leave now."

"She's my kind of gal." He kissed her again. "How long can we stay out here before the pizza arrives? Will they miss us?"

Lacey looked through the window. "Oh, no!"

"What?" Vic was on alert, ready to protect her.

"They're rearranging my furniture!" She opened the door, ready to lay down the law to her would-be decorators, when Vic put a restraining hand on her arm.

"You can move it back when they're gone. Why raise a ruckus?"

"You don't understand. Paint chips will be next, then wallpaper samples, and then kidney-shaped coffee tables."

"They're just having fun."

"How come you are never such a diplomat when it comes to me?" Lacey stepped inside, followed by Vic. Her mother was shoving a chair into a new place. She stood up, put her hands on her hips, and smiled brightly at Lacey.

"See. An intimate conversation area. Isn't this fun?"

Aunt Mimi's trunk, her pride and joy and the centerpiece of the room, was now shoved behind the sofa, which was no longer against the wall but set at an angle to the room. Maybe the trunk was safer out of their way. Luckily, someone knocked at the door.

"Pizza!" Cherise announced brightly. The table was set with plates and forks.

Vic answered the door and picked up the tab, which was only fair, Lacey thought. He was getting along amazingly well with her mother and sister. So well, she was seriously reconsidering whether he was the man for her.

Rose wasted no time bonding with Vic over the issue of Lacey's safety and the importance of staying away from people with murder on their minds. In her own defense, Lacey just nodded and smiled and visualized putting her furniture back where it belonged. She mentally cataloged the patterns in the trunk, promising she would have another outfit made out of the emerald-green crepe, as a reward for not screaming. After he downed three pieces of pepperoni pizza and a glass of milk, Vic announced he had to leave. He departed to a flurry of good-byes from the Smithsonian women, and a furtive kiss from one of them.

In their brief respective visits, Vic and Stella had brought a tidal wave of speculation to wash over her family. But Lacey wasn't in the mood to supply any answers.

"My, your Vic seems nice," Rose began. "And he's from Colorado too?"

"He's just a friend, okay?"

"I see," her mother said with satisfaction. "Well, your friend has excellent taste in flowers."

Lacey longed for peace and quiet. Watching a PBS pledge drive on television sounded too exciting for her. But Cherise's engine was still running. "We're only here for a few days, Lacey. Let's go out. Do the town. Run amok."

Only here for a few days was all that kept Lacey in a civil mood. She was so exhausted after this week that she felt a stiff breeze would knock her down. The last thing she wanted to do was go out. She groaned involuntarily.

"I'd settle for a trip to Wal-Mart, Lacey. Come on, I've been cooped up in a plane all day. I have to get out of here. Get your blood flowing, sis."

Whatever flowed in Cherise's veins, it wasn't the thin red stuff that Lacey's were full of. But she made a lightning decision. "There's this little jazz club I've been hearing about. Velvet's Blues. You game?"

Velvet's Blues suddenly seemed like the perfect compromise. One, it was close by, near the river on King Street in Old Town, above a pricey restaurant. Second, and more important, it was the club where Turtledove played with his band. With any luck, she could catch a few minutes alone with him to see what he knew about the shootings. And, she admitted to herself, Forrest Thunderbird—Turtledove to his friends—was an unusually attractive man who always seemed pleased to see her, without any of the awkward complications that always came along with Vic. And a little sweet jazz on his trumpet might help drive this awful week out of her head. "We can have a drink there, okay? Just one. And it's in Alexandria; we can walk there. It's not far."

"Cool! Sounds great; I need a walk. What should I wear?"

Cherise made a dash for her suitcase. Rose begged off, saying she was tired, but Lacey suspected she was more interested in rearranging the furniture and inventorying the kitchen cabinets without any interference.

"You're going to walk? Downtown?" Rose said. "But it's after dark."

"It's safe, well lit all the way, not even a mile. We'll catch a cab to come home," Lacey explained. "And Mom, don't touch my bedroom. It's off-limits. And really, the living room is fine the way it is. And the kitchen—"

"I wouldn't think of doing anything you wouldn't like." Rose's eyes glittered dangerously. "I'll probably be in bed by the time you get back."

"Just leave a light on so I don't stumble over everything you've moved."

chapter 21

Lacey exchanged her black sweater for an emerald-green cashmere that fit nicely and enhanced her blue-green eyes. But no matter what she wore nothing really seemed to fit right when her mother was around. Cherise freshened her pink lipstick and put on a baby-blue sweater and matching chandelier earrings. She let her blond hair down. *Geronimo High girls: Ready to party!*

The walk downtown to King Street was pleasant. The smell of wood smoke danced in the air, and Lacey took in big gulps of it, glad to be outdoors. She loved her apartment, but when it was full of visitors she felt as if she had wandered into some wonderland where it grew smaller and smaller. Cherise was happily gawking into the front windows of the elegant old town houses that fronted the sidewalks on the way to downtown Old Town. The beautifully appointed front rooms were kept uncurtained and well lit, often showcasing large oil paintings of distinguished Colonial (or *faux* Colonial) ancestors in lighted frames. But they were empty of humans, even on a Friday night, as if the aristocratic owners wished to show passersby that their taste and breeding were superior and as such, they had no desire to mingle. Vic liked to tell Lacey that they were all swilling gin and playing pinochle in their undershirts in the back room.

Velvet's Blues lived up to its name, with its smoky-blue velvet settees and velvet drapes framing the tall windows overlooking King Street's eighteenth-century buildings, only a block or two from the river. The lights were low and the ambience mellow. As the Smithsonian sisters arrived, the musicians were taking a break. The place was just filling up for the ten o'clock set.

Turtledove was nowhere in sight, so Lacey trailed Cherise to a table and ordered a ten-dollar gin and tonic that she planned to nurse until they left.

"Oh, I like this place, sis. It's so jazzy." Cherise smiled invitingly at Lacey. "So, tell me about this cute Victor Donovan of yours."

"There's nothing to tell."

"Ha! He brought you flowers. And he's gorgeous. And I saw him looking at you with those big green eyes. You're an item. You must be."

"Not yet we're not." Lacey shrugged. "He was just showing off for you and Mom. What about you? You're the popular one. Weren't you dating some waterskiing dentist?" That would be the perfect match, Lacey thought, for Cherise's big white smile. To be fair, most of the Smithsonians had good teeth. But Cherise seemed to display hers a little more ostentatiously. *Like those illuminated oil paintings in Old Town.*

"He's history." Cherise blew softly into the palm of her hand. "Gone with the wind. But there is someone new. And you know him. Remember Thomas Rutland from Geronimo High?"

"No way! Tommy Rutland? The quarterback you knocked out at the big game?" Lacey said as the drinks arrived at their table. "Wow. Kick me, Lethal Feet!"

Cherise wasn't smiling now. "Why would you ever bring that up? It's ancient history." She took a long sip of her drink, something with a huge sprig of celery, for fiber, no doubt.

"No, I think it's great. And you know what to do if he ever steps out of line." Lacey playfully socked her sister in the arm. "Or needs a lucky break. In the jaw."

"That's not funny, Lacey. That was a total fluke. It would never happen again in a million years."

"Come on. Don't tell me you've forgotten how to knock a guy out with one kick? What about the Code of the Geronimo High cheerleaders? Go, Lethal Feet!"

"Lacey. Don't go there."

"Gimme a G, gimme an E, gimme an R, gimme an O—"

Cherise returned the sock in the arm, harder than was absolutely necessary. "I could probably remember how to do it," she said in warning. "It could all come back to me in a rush."

"Ouch. You've got a strong fist."

"Geronimo."

The musicians started settling in with their instruments—sax, piano, drums, stand-up bass—and to her relief, Lacey saw Turtledove step forward into the spotlight, cradling his trumpet. Cherise was instantly at full attention.

"Ooh, look at that guy. He's beautiful. And big. Wow, I bet he played football."

"Always the cheerleader." Lacey caught his eye, and he gave her a slight wave and a lift of one eyebrow. Cherise's mouth fell open.

"You *know* him? And that other babe too, Vic Donovan? No fair, big sister. Time to share."

"I never share, and besides, you've got that old broken-down ex-quarterback of yours. What's he doing now?"

"He's in insurance."

"Good career choice." Lacey smiled as the music started, a low, slow blues she didn't recognize. She sipped her gin and tonic. Though her nerves were thoroughly jangled, she closed her eyes and tried to get in tune with the music. Cherise would be ogling all the men and smiling too broadly, Lacey knew.

Summertime was long gone, but the band played the song by Gershwin, Turtledove soaring into the lead on his trumpet, and then moved into "Rhapsody in Blue" for an appreciative crowd. She opened her eyes and saw a different side to Turtledove, a man in complete concert with his instrument. He was smooth—she had assumed he would be—and somehow his horn had the same warm, rich tone as his voice. The blues eventually subsided to a whisper, and the band took a break. Turtledove made his way through his fans, including several stunning and very statuesque women, to the table where the Smithsonian sisters sat.

"Ladies." He waited for his cue to sit down.

"Please join us," Lacey said. He pulled an empty chair from another table and sat down. A waitress scurried over with a tall frosted glass of beer that Turtledove accepted gratefully.

Lacey and Cherise were both aware of the envious looks they were getting from the other women in Velvet's Blues. Lacey made the introductions, using Turtledove's "real" name, the one on his business card, earning her another one of his winks. She said, "I wanted to see how you were doing after the other night. Did you tangle with Broadway Lamont?"

He shook his head and took another long slug of cold beer. "Broadway's a kick in the head, isn't he? We go way back. That was a hell of a night. I go chasing after that little freak at just the moment the shooter picks to attack Miss Amanda. Not my best night, professionally speaking. My apologies, ladies, I don't mean to sound cold. It's a damn shame about Amanda."

"You think the stalker was a setup, to get you away from her?" Lacey asked.

"The thought crossed my mind. But the cops shook him loose."

"Are you talking about the model who was killed right in front of you?" Cherise asked. She had been listening wide-eyed.

"Don't say a word to Mom," Lacey warned.

"Of course not," Cherise promised. "Golly." This evening was exceeding her expectations.

Lacey turned to Turtledove. "You must feel terrible."

"It doesn't do much for my reputation, letting a client get whacked while I'm on duty."

"Hey, even if you'd been with her, you know there's nothing you could have done."

"Nah, but I'd feel better if I took a bullet. It's written in the code."

"That's just macho talk, Turtledove. I'm glad you didn't."

He looked at her and laughed. "I guess so. The little guy was pounding on Amanda's trailer, throwing rocks at it, yelling at her to tell the truth about something. She told me to get rid of him. I said I wasn't leaving her alone; I'd just call the police. But she said it was an order: Get rid of him; he was ruining her prep for the shoot." He stopped for another half glass of beer. "I stepped outside and he ran. I gave chase. He's a fast little bugger; I give him that."

"I think anyone who had you chasing them would set his personal record," Lacey said.

"Unless it was a woman," Cherise opined. Now it was her turn to get the Turtledove wink.

"Anyway, I chased him for about two blocks before I caught up with him and persuaded him to accompany me. Meanwhile all hell breaks loose. Damn."

"Really, Turtledove, there was nothing you could do."

He focused on Lacey. "Did the bastard really steal your car for the shooting vehicle?"

Lacey nodded. "Looks that way."

She turned to Cherise, but her sister said, "I know, I know, don't tell Mom."

"Then someone tries to whack the doctor," Turtledove continued, "the guy Amanda was convinced wanted to kill her. Damon thinks it's a government cover-up."

"He thinks a cloudy day is a government cover-up," Lacey

protested, remembering her hissy fit reading DeadFed dot com that morning. "He's not always on the same planet we're on."

"He's not always wrong either. I just wish the whole mess hadn't happened on my watch. So are you working on this, Lacey?"

She shrugged, not knowing what she could safely say in front of Cherise. "Just working on a story."

"Uh-huh. You need protection on this, you call me. No charge, no limit," he added gallantly. "The truth is always worth protecting."

"I don't know what to say."

"Don't say anything. I gotta reclaim my dignity. If you need help on this case, you can count on me." He rose from the chair and emptied the rest of his glass. "Gotta get back to business. Ladies, it's been a pleasure." He made his way back to his trumpet. Cherise's eyes followed him.

"Lacey, I had no idea your life was so interesting."

"Thanks for the vote of confidence."

"You know what I mean. Writing fashion stories all day, I'd simply lose my mind. But who knew there would be all these stunning guys! And all this, you know, *drama*. Who knew journalism was about all this?"

"Indeed. Who knew?" Lacey sipped her gin and tonic. Turtledove began to play again, one of her favorite Gershwin songs, "Someone to Watch Over Me." She felt a little chill go up the back of her neck. He was playing it just for her.

Lacey took a deep breath before opening her door. It was just as she had expected. Her mother was still awake, and the room was completely different. Again. She had to control her face to keep from expressing any shock, and she reminded herself she could put it all back the way she liked it. *After they leave.*

"Hello, girls. Did you have fun?"

"Oh, fun's not even the word for it," Lacey said. "And it looks like you've been busy."

"Mom, it looks great," Cherise said. "I never would have thought of putting the dining room table up against the wall like that."

"Neither would I," Lacey said.

Rose beamed. "You see, dear, you have so much more room now in that teensy little dining nook of yours. Dining rooms are really a thing of the past. We'll find you some nice TV trays, so

much more practical. And Lacey, if we have any extra time tomorrow after the museums, let's stop by the Home Depot—you
do have a Home Depot here?—and pick up some paint swatches.
And maybe some wallpaper? Wall-to-wall carpeting would be
nice; these old wood floors of yours must be so time-consuming to
keep properly polished. And you know, we could always re-cover
that old sofa of yours. . . ."

Lacey Smithsonian's

Fashion Bites

Clothes That Bite—and Ties That Bind

In a perfect world your underwear would not attack you. In a perfect world your clothes would support you, comfort you, protect you. And in a perfect world you would not still hear those whispering voices in your head every time you go shopping or get dressed, those little voices telling you that color is too bright, that fabric is too cheap, the price is too high, the style is too young, too old, too whatever, or *it's really just not you, dear! Who do you think you are, anyway?*

But this is not a perfect world. This is a world where the underwire in your bra stabs you, your skinny straps fall down, your designer label gouges the back of your neck, your panty hose dig into your waist, and your shoes? Don't get me started on shoes! Fashion isn't for sissies, is it?

Do we want too much? Clothes that fit, fabrics that feel good and are easy to care for? And outfits that help us look our best, that make us feel . . . well, smarter and prettier than we would feel if we were naked? Is it too much to ask for?

Quit whining! Other centuries have had real backbone, or whalebone, in their garments. You think your outfit du jour bites? Wear a Victorian corset every day. Underwire attack? Imagine underwire running the length of your torso. Corseting requires real fashion fortitude, not to mention someone to pull those laces *really* tight. Remember to exhale, ladies! You say your stylish sky-high stilettos are instruments of torture—and the innocent victim is you? Fashion history has two words for you: *Foot binding.* Walk a mile in that ancient Chinese beauty's fashionable shoes? Not this barefoot girl.

And gentlemen, bow before the sartorial torment of the

well-dressed sixteenth-century dandy. Henry VIII's manly
tights, the even more manly codpiece, the doublet and jerkin,
the manly ruff around the neck—I take that back; I'm not sure
manly is the right word for a ruff. And you complain about
tying that torturous four-in-hand knot in your silk necktie?

As the antiquated torment of getting dressed has dimin-
ished, the small remaining torments loom larger. We have
become wimps about what we wear, here in the twenty-first
century, the Casual Friday of centuries, where we're all in a
huff because there's a wrinkle in our permanent press.
Denizens of previous centuries didn't need Mom's little voice
in their heads; they had something worse: sumptuary laws,
which criminalized your fashion choices. No silk or purple or
jewels for poor little you, you commoner. Maybe this isn't
such a bad world now, after all.

Yet still we hear those little voices of family, friends, and
the Mean Girls from seventh grade who create our own
sumptuary laws, tailored lovingly to our own peculiar dys-
functions. Do these voices sound familiar?

- "You're not really wearing *that*, are you?" (No one crit-
  icizes better than Mom.)
- "That's not exactly *slimming*, is it, dear? And doesn't
  your sister look nice?"
- "Why can't you just dress like everyone else, for a
  change?"
- "No. I like it, really. It's just . . . well . . . *you know.*"

So what's a Stylish Reader to do? Get dressed and go
shopping without your critics. Leave the invisible voices
home. We're grown-ups; we can handle an occasional underwire attack, and those beautiful shoes aren't going to kill
you (just don't fall off them). Rise above the petty annoyances
of fashion. And remember one thing: Grown-ups do not
have to dress for their mothers.

chapter 22

Driving the rental car the next morning with her mother chattering and Cherise frantically scanning stations on the radio, looking for something remotely like a Colorado station, left Lacey in a frenzy of distraction. She felt like a victim of circumstances that were poised irrevocably against her: a lightning bolt, a dead woman extracting a promise, her car stolen, her romance derailed, and her mother and sister with only one desire—a hostile makeover of her life.

"Radio sucks here," Cherise said. Lacey agreed that Colorado had much better radio stations. They weren't all yammering political chatter or shock jocks or oatmeal-flavored smooth jazz, like radio in D.C. "Hell has better radio," her sister said grumpily.

Lacey had brought CDs of Ella Fitzgerald and Duke Ellington to play in the car. She popped one into the CD player. She knew Cherise was more of a classic-rock girl than classic jazz, but it would have to do. Ella always did it for Lacey.

Lacey needed time away from her family to accomplish something. So she did the only thing she could think of: put her mother and sister in the car and headed for Stylettos. Since meeting Stella, Rose and Cherise had somehow decided they needed a total makeover so they could hit the nation's capital in style. They were taking Stella up on her offer. At least, Lacey thought, it would keep them out of Home Depot.

They urged Lacey to join them at Stylettos, but she convinced them she had an interview scheduled that she couldn't avoid and just needed a couple of hours alone.

"I thought you hated to work weekends," Rose said.

"This is different; trust me. I could always just drop you at the museum and meet you at noon for lunch," Lacey said, maneuvering the clunky rental car over the Fourteenth Street Bridge.

"No, no, no, we want to see Stella," Cherise said. "That way we can hit the Mall looking like chic Washington natives and not like tourists, so we don't embarrass you."

"You don't embarrass me," Lacey protested. "And you should be immensely thankful you'll never look like Washingtonians." Both her mother and sister were wearing jeans and white shirts, with sweaters looped over their shoulders. They had left snow and cold weather in Denver, and were amazed that the day was so temperate. They were dressed to blend into the D.C. scenery, except for the excitement and openness on their faces—a dead giveaway that they were from somewhere else. Lacey wore a pair of dark green slacks and a matching sweater, fitted around the midriff. She looped a scarf around her neck. She assumed that Rose and Cherise would be fine as long as she was with them. However, she was much warier of the danger of Stella spilling her guts to her mother. Last night was just a taste of what Stella could spill.

"I just want to get one thing straight," Cherise said. "When you write about a 'helmet head,' that's sort of like a bubbleheaded bob that's hair-sprayed till it won't move?"

"Yeah, it was very big here, but it's on the wane."

"I was confused, because back home, 'helmet head' is what you've got when you take your bike helmet off, or your white-water kayaking helmet, or your rock-climbing helmet, or—"

"Are you sure you can't join us?" Rose asked. "A new look would do wonders for your outlook, dear."

"I wasn't able to adjust everything in my schedule."

"People back home aren't so proud of working themselves to death."

"Sorry, Mom. You surprised me with this visit, you know."

"Really fun, huh?" Cherise said. "Who knew we could be so spontaneous? Oh, look, the Capitol and the Smithsonian Castle!"

"Last chance," Lacey said.

"Keep driving, dear," Rose said. "Stella's expecting us. We'll spend the afternoon at the museums."

Lacey drove on up Fourteenth Street while her mother and sister gazed expectantly at the glories of the city captured most beautifully on the National Mall, from the Washington Monument to the Capitol. The trees were turning in autumn glory, but the lawn was still emerald green. The sight always thrilled Lacey, and it seemed to work on her family as well.

"The leaves are almost all off the trees back home," Cherise said, amazed. "We had an early snow."

"You always have an early snow," Lacey said. "And I imagine

you'll have another one soon, the traditional Halloween storm. So all the kids can trick-or-treat in their down parkas."

"Well, we have the Rocky Mountains," her mother said as if that ended it. In Rose's world Pikes Peak trumped everything.

Lacey pressed on to Stylettos above Dupont Circle and miraculously found a parking spot two doors down, just as it opened up. She hesitated as they entered the salon, but she lectured herself that everything was under control. *A simple wash and blow-dry for them, Stella talks their ears off, and I get an hour or two to myself. What could go wrong?* She sighed.

Lacey waited for Rose and Cherise to be shuttled off to the shampoo bowls, and she briefly envied them their easy rapport and companionship. They had always been buddies, and she was the outsider. If only she lived through this visit without a hole eating through her stomach, she'd be happy.

Lacey was startled to see that Stella and the whole salon had gone prematurely Halloween. Stella was wearing her Bride of Frankenstein wig and makeup, and Lacey was afraid for a moment that her family might back out of the session. But no, Rose and Cherise seemed to be charmed by the extreme wig, the lightning bolts, Stella's matching manicure, and the painted-on blood dripping down the side of her mouth. As long as the blood wasn't real, it was apparently okay with everyone. The other hairstylists were coiffed as Marie Antoinette with a gory red line around her neck, Medusa with a headful of snakes, and Blackbeard the pirate with a long braided beard. *This would be such fun at* The Eye. *Mac could be Napoleon; Felicity could dress as herself, the Gingerbread Witch. And I'll be the Invisible Woman.*

"Oh, Stella? Come here for a minute." Lacey crooked her little finger at her.

"They are totally adorable, Lacey," Stella cooed. "Just wait till I get through with them."

"Hold on, sport. Nothing radical. They have to go back to Denver Tuesday, and they have to look like normal human beings."

"What? You think I'm gonna punk out your family?"

"Another thing. I am begging you here, Stella: Do not spill any more information about me."

Stella grinned, with a wicked twinkle in her eye. "You can trust me. Your secrets are safe with me." She crossed her heart.

"Secret or otherwise, do not gorge my mother and sister on the juicy gossip of my life, such as it is." Stella briefly looked glum and suspicious. "But feel free to ferret out any counterintelligence from them, if you like," Lacey said. "You can be my little spy for a change."

The stylist brightened noticeably. "What do you want to know?"

"I don't know—who my sister is dating, does my mom plan to run off with the golf pro, is my dad teed off about it, whatever. Their plans and dreams. Besides, they're a clean slate for you. I'm old news. I gotta go."

Rose glanced up from her chair and waved. "See you at noon, Lacey," her mother called.

"Not to worry." Stella smiled brightly and shooed Lacey out of the salon. "Have fun."

Lacey walked through Dupont Circle on her way to the hospital, which was only about a dozen blocks away down New Hampshire Avenue. It was a beautiful day, and she needed the walk to clear her head. Near the fountain in the Circle she noticed a crowd of people milling around an impromptu memorial of flowers for the late Amanda Manville, as well as a camera crew with a reporter positioned in front of it, obviously shooting a news bite. She also thought she caught a glimpse of John Henry Tyler, Caleb Collingwood's last friend, in the crowd. He was a small man wearing a white button-down shirt and khaki slacks held up by green suspenders. He looked owlish in his little horn-rimmed glasses and thinning hair.

Tyler hadn't responded to her e-mail. She would have stopped to buttonhole him, but unfortunately she had to get to Spaulding first. His strength, and his goodwill in allowing her to visit, might go only so far. Lacey wondered whether Tyler could be the shooter, a would-be killer who hadn't counted on his victim being surrounded by medical colleagues. *At least the bastard didn't use my car this time.* She walked faster, burdened by Stella's fear of the shooter. *Would he be here watching this little memorial scene?*

Lacey suddenly lifted her head at the edge of the Circle. She was about to cross the street, but there was something in the air, a seductive aroma. *Doughnuts?* The Washington, D.C., Krispy Kreme store was on Connecticut Avenue, just steps away. From behind her came a voice that made her jump.

"Hey, Smithsonian, how you doing?" Office jinx Harlan Wiedemeyer shoved a flat box of Krispy Kreme doughnuts at her. "Here, have a doughnut." Lacey backed away from him.

"No, thanks, Harlan. I'm in a hurry."

"Take one with you." He stepped closer and opened the box. A wave of hot doughnut aroma encircled her. He pushed the box in her face and she pushed it back. *Oh, no,* she thought, *I touched the Krispy Kreme box! I've been Wiedemeyered. I'll get a booster shot of the Harlan Hex!* Then she told herself to knock it off.

"Uh, no, thanks, really. What are you doing here?"

"Doughnuts." He pointed out the obvious. "See, I got a half dozen of the chocolate with little orange sprinkles; they're the special Halloween doughnuts. And I got a half dozen of the pumpkin. For the newsroom." She looked at him like he had two heads. "Oh, you mean what am I doing here in the District today? Just putting in a few hours at the office."

"I didn't think you worked on the weekends." But actually, she realized she didn't know much about other reporters' schedules at *The Eye.* On the fashion beat she got to take most weekends off.

He looked a little embarrassed. "Well, you know, I thought maybe Felicity would be there. There aren't too many people in on the weekends, and sometimes she comes in. I've seen her there. From a distance. I think she likes the peace and quiet. Such a sweet thing."

Sweet thing? The Gingerbread Witch? Lacey wondered what kind of drug Felicity was slipping into her brownies now. *A spoonful of sugar helps the hallucinogens go down?*

"And you thought you'd ask her out?" Lacey asked hopefully. Maybe it would get Harlan out of her hair. *And into the witch's clutches.*

"Gosh, I can't ask her out just like that. I mean, I kind of like to simply be around her. But if I got my nerve up . . . well, it would be easier on a day when the newsroom isn't packed with reporters."

"Ask her out, Harlan. Offer her a 'hot doughnut now' at Krispy Kreme. She'd like that," Lacey urged, but he shrank away at the suggestion.

"Oh, no, I've got a hot lead on a story today."

"Don't tell me; it's about some poor bastard."

"Exactly. Poor bastard died while posing as a human piñata."

"You're right, Harlan, that happens way too often. I'll read all about it tomorrow," she said, edging away from him. She was grateful that there was no rain in the forecast, no threat of lightning strikes.

"Don't you want a doughnut?" Harlan held a doughnut out to her, one of the special ones with sprinkles, but as she backed away, he looked at it and shrugged and took a bite.

Lacey picked up her pace, speed-walking down New Hampshire until she reached Washington Circle, which she crossed, and turned down Twenty-third Street to the George Washington University Hospital.

Lacey didn't particularly like the new hospital, with its preposterously dangerous entryway just outside the escalator to the Metro. Ambulances had the enticing opportunity hundreds of times a day to mow down commuters on their way to work. *Must be good for business at the ER.* It was a miracle no one had been killed yet. She walked through the security station into the shiny circular lobby, and the antiseptic reek of the hospital hit her. It was vaguely oppressive, but the walk had restored her spirits, and she felt more like herself again. At least she was free for the moment from her would-be redecorators and remodelers. And Harlan Wiedemeyer.

Her first impression of the hospital was that it was intensely beige, from the blond-wood paneling to the cream-colored polished floors with splashes of dark taupe. The medicinal smell caught Lacey in the back of her throat.

Even though Spaulding had agreed to talk with her, however reluctantly, Lacey felt she should show some manners. She dashed into the gift shop and bought a small flower arrangement in a ceramic vase, wondering if she could get *The Eye* to reimburse her, and stuffed the receipt in her pocket. She continued down a labyrinth of hallways to his room and checked the door: Spaulding should be in the far bed.

Lacey expected Dr. Spaulding to be hooked up to machinery, tubes, and monitors, and not looking his best. But she did not expect the Grim Reaper himself in a long black hooded robe to be standing by his bed, complete with decorative scythe—and a fat pillow, which he or she or it was just about to press down over the doctor's unconscious face. But that was what she saw. She would swear to it. It certainly wasn't the latest advance in medical technology.

"Hey! What's going on?" she hollered, and the figure in the black robe spun around, stopping momentarily what he or she was in the act of doing. A ghastly grinning white skeleton mask gazed calmly at Lacey. Then the Reaper resumed the task at hand, the pillow heading inexorably toward Spaulding's face again.

"Stop that, you freak," she yelled, and tossed the only thing she had: the vase of flowers she carried. Lacey made a direct hit on the Reaper's back. She screamed for help, furiously pounding the call button on the empty bed next to her. The figure turned and came toward her, shaking its hooded head and waggling a black gloved finger at her as if to say, *Naughty, naughty!* She could dash for the door, she realized, but then the Reaper would simply finish Spaulding off. She calculated that perhaps she could stall while help was coming. After all, unlike Spaulding who was helpless, she was ambulatory, and fast on her feet. *Except I'm just standing here like an idiot.*

Lacey backed slowly toward the door. The Grim Reaper approached, scythe in gloved hand, as if it were enjoying this game. Lacey looked around for something else to use for her defense when she heard footsteps rushing toward the room. The hooded figure glanced back at Spaulding, who lay there quietly, and the grinning skeleton mask seemed torn between finishing off the job, attacking Lacey, or bolting out the door.

Nurses and doctors reached the doorway and stood staring at this odd little Halloween tableau. The Reaper gave the empty bed a vicious shove toward Lacey, slamming her hard into the wall. The bed cut off her air, and when she hit the wall she was aware of a sharp pain in her hip. Two doctors stood blocking the doorway, but the Reaper growled and charged straight at them scythe first, and they parted like a flimsy hospital gown. Lacey caught her breath and raced to the door just in time to see the tall black-robed figure disappearing down the hall. She never did get to talk to Spaulding.

"The good news is, you saved Dr. Spaulding's life," Detective Broadway Lamont said, though he sounded a little cranky about it. "The bad news is, I still don't understand what the hell you're doing messing around in this case. I don't like how people get attacked just when you come calling. You got the jinx on you? You been hoodooed or what?" Lamont had caught the 911 call to respond to the second attack on the doctor. They were sitting in an unoccupied waiting room. Lacey sighed again.

"I told you, I'm innocent. I was just following up on the Amanda Manville story. It's what I do. Spaulding said he'd talk to me today, but all I got was a silent encounter with the Grim Reaper."

"And that's another thing I don't like. How do you think it feels to put out a bulletin on the Grim goddamn Reaper? I feel like a damn fool. But you're in luck. At least two doctors, three nurses, and one candy striper corroborate your story."

"A candy striper?"

He rubbed his nose. "Could have been a med student. They all look like babies to me. So what's the damn deal with this Grim Reaper of yours?"

"A fashion clue?" Lamont grunted, but she persevered. "It was a pretty good disguise, don't you think? Got him into the hospital, anyway. Lots of people start wearing costumes at work this close to Halloween. Maybe there's a children's wing with a Halloween party today?" He didn't look convinced. She thought about Stella and her costumed coworkers at Stylettos. "There's this place, Back-stage Books, where they rent costumes. Maybe our Reaper got it there. It used to be near Dupont Circle on P Street. They moved near Eastern Market a while back."

"I'll check it out, Smithsonian. Got that? The *detective* will fol-low up on the *civilian's* information. Because that's the detective's *job*. Backstage Books."

"No problem. And now I have to pick up my mother and sister at the beauty salon."

"Well, that sounds pretty damn civilized, but I'm sure you'll find some way to get the cops involved," he said. "Get out of here. I have your word that you'll be with your family and do touristy stuff for the rest of today?"

"Unfortunately, yes."

"You gonna stay out of trouble?"

"You have my word, Detective Broadway Lamont." She stood up and moved slowly, rubbing her hip, which was probably black and blue. She winced.

"Are you okay, Smithsonian?"

"Peachy." She smiled. "Just peachy."

"Then I won't be seeing you again soon. Be safe, you hear?"

"Likewise," she said. She limped out of the waiting room and out of the hospital. Walking had lost its appeal. She took a cab back to Dupont Circle.

When she opened the door at Stylettos it seemed that two com-pletely different women greeted her, wearing new hair, makeup, and clothes, their tourist togs stuffed in Ann Taylor Loft shopping bags. She looked at Stella.

"Who are these women, and what have you done with my mother? And my sister?"

"Just a little makeover. You were gone a long time, so we threw in some extras. Don't they look great?"

They did, in fact, look great. Stella had coaxed Cherise out of her perpetual blond Barbie-doll ponytail and into a sexy, swinging cut that skimmed her shoulders. It was a little too close to Lacey's own style, she thought, but she held her tongue. Stella had also ap-plied her magic touch to Cherise's makeup. Her sister was a knock-out, looking far more worldly than when she got off the plane the day before. She wore a navy-blue turtleneck with a short and sassy Black Watch plaid skirt and dark tights with comfortable flats, a sophisticated blond-cheerleader-next-door look.

And Rose Smithsonian looked alarmingly unmotherlike. She looked like a more knowing and alluring woman of a certain age. "You waxed your eyebrows!" Lacey said. Rose was wearing a brown skirt and tights, and a brown turtleneck that set off her ash-blond hairstyle that was now a bit shorter with a sleek blowout. Around her neck was a gold silk scarf. *My God, she almost looks French.* Sacre bleu!

"What do you think, Lacey?" Stella asked. Lacey was at a loss for words.

"Isn't Stella a living doll?" her mother asked, in a tone that implied Lacey was not.

"I don't know what to say."

"Speechless," Stella said, beaming. "I'll take that as a compliment. Come here." She pulled Lacey back to her styling station, out of earshot, and waved to *les femmes* Smithsonian, who were picking out expensive hair products at the front desk. "I gotta tell you, Lacey. They did this all for you."

"Huh? How is what you did for them really for me?" She stood there, waiting for Stella to divulge the priceless intelligence she must have gathered in the last two hours.

"Gosh, your mom is so proud of you. They want to fit in with you here." Stella sounded so wistful, Lacey wanted to believe her.

"No way."

"Absolutely, they want to live up to you, because you're the famous Washington fashion expert."

"They never said that."

"I swear they did!" Stella crossed her heart for emphasis.

"Very funny, Stella. Tell me another one."

"They are in awe of you. I know I am."

"You're all in awe of me? No doubt in that smack-Lacey-in-the-head, tell-her-how-to-live-her-life kind of awe? Like they don't know exactly which planet I come from?"

"It's like you're psychic sometimes, Lacey."

"But did you pump them for information that I might need to know, like I asked you?"

Stella started to stay something, but then she stopped, distracted by the new client who was being escorted to her station by the shampoo boy. Lacey turned to follow her gaze. Even with wet hair and a towel over her head the woman's walk and presence seemed familiar to Lacey. She was tall and aggressively busty. When the towel came off, she was revealed as a blonde, though her dark roots were showing.

"Stella, who is that woman?" Lacey asked quietly, but then she and the woman locked eyes in the mirror. It was Montana McCandless Donovan Schmidt, Vic's ex-wife, in the rather voluptuous flesh. *Does she remember me?* Lacey wondered. They said nothing to each other, but Montana lifted one eyebrow in recognition before Stella cut off their eye contact.

Okay, she recognizes me. But what on earth is she doing here? In my hair salon! With my stylist!

Stella turned her back to Lacey and addressed the woman professionally. "Hi, I'm Stella. So what are we doing today?"

"Something sexy," Montana purred. "I'm getting my ex back this weekend." As if Montana knew what Lacey was thinking, she confided to Stella, "He recommended you."

Oh, Vic, Lacey moaned to herself, *why are men so stupid?*

Stella laughed. "Don't worry, hon; when I'm through with you, he'll be a goner."

Lacey felt her heart plummet to her toes, but she bravely lifted one eyebrow in scorn to the woman in the mirror. Lacey fervently hoped Stella would give Montana one of her over-the-top, Halloween-special, goth-princess-on-gasoline-fumes looks. But no, Stella would just camouflage the blond man-eater's telltale dark roots with a gallon or so of 'Brazen Blonde' hair color and cheerfully send her out to stick her knife in Lacey's back. *What if I whispered just the right words in Stella's ear?* Lacey mused. *What if I said, "Stella, if you were ever my friend, remember that game of yours: Salon of Death?"* But someone tugged at Lacey's arm.

"Lacey, let's go; I'm starving," Cherise said.

"Lunch, of course." Lacey tried not to limp as she walked to the door. Her hip ached, and her heart was broken. She could hardly wait to see what would happen next. *A plague of locusts?*

"Whoa, who was that cheap package of goods?" her newly elegant sister sniffed, referring to Montana.

"Sometimes, Cherise, you know exactly the right thing to say." *Who knew my little sister could ever make me feel better?*

chapter 23

"But I want to see where it happened, Lacey," her mother said over her cappuccino after lunch at Kramerbooks, the little bookstore and café down the street from Stylettos.

"Where *what* happened?"

"Where Amanda Manville was shot," Cherise said. "It's right around here, isn't it? That's what Stella said."

"What did she tell you?" *I knew I couldn't trust her.*

"Everything! And it's impossible to miss all of your stories that she has posted in the salon. She thinks you're brilliant. She, like, quotes you all the time," Cherise said, highlighting the downside of having a fan like the inimitable Stella.

"And while I'd much rather you weren't involved with this whole murder mess, your family is here for you," her mother intoned. "And we are going to help you." Her mother was calm. Too calm. Rose might as well have added, *whether you like it or not.*

"Help me?" This was the worst possible suggestion.

"With your investigation, of course. That's what you're up to, isn't it? I recognize the look on your face," Rose said.

Lacey tried to make her face as blank as possible.

"It's that I've-got-a-secret-and-I'm-not-telling-Mom look," Cherise explained helpfully. "Yeah, like that. Right there. The Lacey look."

"You don't have to be so smug, Lethal Feet," Lacey snapped back.

"Hey, that's not fair. It was just that once, but you're always—"

"Girls, girls, girls. Don't bicker," Rose refereed.

"You two don't understand what my job is all about. I don't make up stories; they just happen. I only ask questions of people. That's all."

"Questions that lead to stabbing people with scissors and . . .

and sword thingies." Her mother sniffed. "I must say, I never
raised you to do that sort of thing. It must come from your father's
side of the family."

"Like Aunt Mimi?"

"Exactly. In any case, we're here to see that you're safe this
weekend. After all, there is a killer on the loose," her mother said,
as if this were the most natural subject for the family to be discussing. "And by the way, are we going to see any more of that
nice Victor Donovan? Such a gentleman, bringing you flowers like
that."

"No, we're not." *Though I may have to kidnap him to keep him
from being hijacked by Montana, the Venus Mantrap.* "He's very
busy. Homeland Security and all that."

"Let's go to the Circle and see where Amanda was shot,"
Cherise urged. "Mom's taking an interest in you, Lacey. You are
the eldest child, after all."

"I take an interest in both my girls." Rose smiled at both of
them and gave each a quick little hug to indicate the equality of her
affection. "And their little problems."

"I give up; let's go. One scene of the crime, coming right up."
Lacey paid the bill, stashed their bags of clothes and new Stylettos-
brand hair products in the trunk of the rental car, fed the parking
meter again, and led them down the street to Dupont Circle.

"It must have been right there," Rose said, marching over to
where the large pile of flowers lay, the hodgepodge of grocery-
store bouquets and stems of roses that Lacey had seen earlier. The
blooms were accompanied by signs of remembrance to Amanda:
WE LOVE YOU, AMANDA. WE'LL NEVER FORGET YOU. THE GOOD DIE
YOUNG. FAREWELL, BEAUTIFUL BUTTERFLY.

The small man Lacey had seen earlier was still lurking about,
though it looked like he had gotten a takeout lunch and eaten it
there. This time he wasn't going to get away from her. "I'll be right
back," Lacey said. "I have to talk to someone." Without another
word, she headed swiftly for John Henry Tyler, who seemed to
know who she was. He headed in the opposite direction around the
fountain, which, being dead center in the circle, impeded a straight
getaway. Tyler was speedy for someone so small, Lacey thought,
and she picked up the pace. She noticed that Cherise had loped off
counterclockwise around the fountain to head him off at the pass.

Rose followed, and soon Tyler was surrounded by three Smithsonian women, his back to the fountain. To escape, he'd have to

take a dip in the water. He was barely taller than Lacey, maybe five-foot-six at the most.

"Hello, John Henry Tyler. I am Lacey Smith—"

"I know who y'all are," he said, cutting her off short and glaring at her through his round horn-rimmed glasses. Tyler spoke in a quick, flat staccato, brushed heavily in a West Virginia accent and cadence. Even in his khakis and old tweed jacket, he had a fastidiousness about him that surprised her. His skin seemed to shine with an extra scrubbing. "I know who y'all are, and did you have to bring your whole posse to round me up?" He took off his glasses and polished the lenses with a handkerchief from the breast pocket of his jacket. The first time Lacey saw him, he had been sweating. Was he calmer now because Amanda was dead?

"Whatever it takes. Pardon my manners. Mom, Cherise, this is John Henry Tyler." And to him, she said, "This is my mother, Rose Smithsonian, and my sister, Cherise Smithsonian."

"All Smithsonians? I'll be damned. Why don't y'all hang around those musty old museums of yours instead of harassing peaceful citizens?"

"Our museums? Gee, they're not really ours," Cherise said, "but we are—"

"And my daughter is not harassing you, but if that is what you want, we would be happy to arrange it," Rose said in a very matter-of-fact tone. "However, all we ask is that you answer a few civil questions." She gave him the universally understood "mom look."

"Very well, ladies, if you must." He heaved a dramatic sigh. "Y'all may proceed with your interrogation."

"It won't take long," Cherise said. "We have better things to do. We have to see about our museums."

"By all means, do so then," he said.

"I'll do the asking, if you don't mind, Cherise, Mom," Lacey said before addressing Tyler. "They're just visiting. And you could have avoided this whole scene if you had merely e-mailed me back."

Tyler sat down on the lip of the fountain's edge and put his hands up in surrender. "Y'all can see I am unarmed, and I am sitting here peacefully for yet another interrogation and disparagement of my good character, even though you are not an officer of the law, but a mere tradesman in the Fourth Estate."

Lacey was sorry she didn't have her tape recorder with her. He promised to be a good quote. Instead she pulled out her notebook and tried to keep up with him.

"I merely beg you, Miss Smithsonian, not to stab me, as I believe that is where your particular expertise lies. I assure you, I am not a danger to you."

"Maybe not, but you are a smarty-pants." *Smarty-pants? Good God, I'm already talking like my mother.*

Tyler put his glasses back on and made a face at her.

"Lacey, you have to be careful about this stabbing habit," Rose said. "You'll get a reputation." Was that a snarky comment? From her mild-mannered mother, the archenemy of snarkiness? Lacey was surprised, if not downright shocked.

"It may be indelicate of me to say so, but she already has a reputation," John Henry Tyler interjected. "It is not terribly ladylike and might be said to betray a lack of decent upbringing."

"Young man, you hush up when I am talking." She looked at her daughter. "Maybe you should switch to baseball bats or something, Lacey honey, instead of knives." Tyler shuddered visibly.

"If you think Lacey's dangerous," Cherise said to Tyler, "you should see what I can do with my feet." Tyler looked startled, and for Lacey, this was another earthquake. Old Lethal Feet never mentioned that particular episode of her own free will, and certainly not with pride.

"Ladies, please," Lacey said.

"Yes, please, let us just get on with this," Tyler pleaded.

"Are you the one who was stalking Amanda Manville? Did you sign those letters 'Johnny Monroe'?"

"I am hardly a stalker, although I suppose I can understand how that mistake could have been made. I did write a number of letters to Amanda Manville, and I did sign some of those letters by the name Johnny Monroe, which I found easy to remember and conducive to the concealment of my true identity."

"Why, and what did the letters say?"

"I merely asked in a most civil manner for some moments of her time. I had written her before using my true given name; however, she never gave me the courtesy of an answer. Her publicity people merely sent back a photograph, which I found gratuitous and insulting. She never answered any of my previous letters in which I politely asked what happened to my friend Caleb."

"Like the open letter to Amanda that you posted on your Web site?"

"Exactly so."

"And the Johnny Monroe letters?"

"I decided to write her some letters that took a different approach, from a name that held no untoward associations for her. I merely asked for a few moments of her time. Like a lovesick fan. I thought if she simply would talk with me in person, she would soften and give me an explanation. Hah!" Tyler shifted slightly and stretched his back. "Instead she sicced that huge bodyguard on me. As if that was fair. I am a nonviolent and entirely nonthreatening person."

"He said you were throwing things at her trailer."

"Was I?"

"I saw you spit at Amanda Manville after she was shot."

"Yes, I did, and I'm not terribly sorry she is dead." Rose gasped at the audacity. "You must understand, Miss Smithsonian, I wanted to know what became of the best friend I ever had in this sad world, Caleb Collingwood. And now I'm afraid I will never know, which pains me a great deal."

"You're saying he never got in touch with you?"

"He dropped off the planet about three and a half years ago." Tyler folded his hands together in front of him and put his head down for a moment with his eyes shut. "Y'all write this down now. His last words to me on God's green earth were, 'I'm going to see my girl now. I have to talk to Mandy. Take care of yourself, John Henry.' And then he was gone, never to be seen again."

"Do you think he could have killed himself? That's what Amanda said happened."

The little man started and opened his eyes. "Lord have mercy, no. Caleb was no self-murderer, even though he had no family, just a no-account drunk of an uncle he lived with after his daddy died, and his mother left when he was a boy. Caleb would not kill himself, even though he had lost the love of his life. And as far as I'm concerned the real Mandy Manville died on the operating room table during that plastic surgery, and in her place an alien was being born."

"But couldn't something else have happened to him?"

"I blame Amanda Manville, because she took away his manhood in front of everyone's eyes on national television, and he did not deserve that. Caleb may have been neglected by God in the looks department, but he had as great a heart as anyone who walked this earth, and when he fell in love with plain little old Mandy Manville, that was it. He would be true to her unto death. I believe he is dead. I believe where there is smoke there is fire, where there are rumors there is some truth, and where Miss Amanda Manville Supermodel is concerned, there is no good to be had. Caleb Collingwood is dead, and she murdered his soul, if not his body."

"And now Amanda is dead. She was murdered—both body and soul—by someone who hated her."

"Well, don't y'all look at me. I didn't do it, and at the time of her demise I was being manhandled by her moose of a body-guard."

"Did you divert him on purpose? So the killer would have a clean shot at her?"

Tyler was momentarily speechless, but he recovered. "No, upon my honor. I fear we will never know the truth. We cannot be set free from this mystery."

"I have to say you show precious little compassion," Cherise said.

"My compassion is for my lost friend Caleb."

"Did you know Mandy before she was Amanda?" Lacey asked.

"I had met her several times. I was to be Caleb's best man. Mandy was a fine lady, not beautiful, but of sweet disposition. I never saw her after that terrible television show."

"What do you think of Dr. Greg Spaulding?"

"Who?" John Henry Tyler squinched up his face.

"Her plastic surgeon. The one who transformed Amanda Manville."

"Him? Why, I don't give two hoots in hell about him. I wouldn't know him if I ran into him on the street."

"Somebody tried to kill him the other day. Someone who did run into him on the street. And whoever it was tried to finish the job today in the hospital." Her mother and sister looked at her in surprise. Lacey's experience at the hospital that morning had somehow escaped mention over lunch. She knew that John Henry Tyler was too small to have filled the Grim Reaper costume, but perhaps he had friends who were involved. *Perhaps the same friend who gunned down Amanda?*

"That so? Well, I cannot say I am surprised."

"Really? Why?"

"It is a miracle anyone's walking around alive in this crazy murder capital of yours," Tyler said. "Drive-by shootings, killings on every corner, and no matter what you might believe, Miss Smithsonian, I did not shoot Amanda Manville, nor did I have any-thing to do with the attempted murder of her devilish surgeon." He looked somber. "Is that all?"

"I'll be writing about this."

"You feel free," said John Henry Tyler. "I have nothing to hide. And now if you ladies will excuse me."

Lacey stepped back. He hopped off the edge of the fountain, collected his dignity, and walked right out of Dupont Circle. Lacey closed her notebook. Rose looked very pleased with herself.

Cherise announced that she wanted to go back to the makeshift memorial to Amanda and read all the signs, because they might contain clues. She and Rose sauntered over to the floral mound. Lacey sat on a bench to jot down notes on her conversation with Tyler.

"Lacey Smithsonian?"

She looked up to see the blonde she'd spotted before at Stylettos. Lacey was right: Montana's roots were nicely colored, and the blowout looked quite respectable. In fact, she looked far more polished than Lacey remembered ever seeing her. It was clearly a look for the city. However, her T-shirt was as tight as a drum, or rather two drums, and her jeans were even tighter. *Good thing Levi's are constructed so well,* Lacey thought, *or she would split a seam.*

"Montana McCandless Donovan Schmidt, I presume," Lacey said.

"For the moment. I'm dropping Schmidt. He's ancient history."

"So I heard." The women sized each other up. "And what about current events?"

"He mentions you occasionally. Vic, not Schmidt. I understand you're friends." Lacey said nothing. Better to keep Vic's ex talking. "I think it's only fair to warn you: I'm back in the picture. In the present."

"That's not what he says, but I appreciate your boldness."

"And you're moving out of the picture."

Lacey put her notebook back in her bag and stood up. She came up only to about Montana's nose, but she looked her right in the eye. "Why don't we let Vic decide for himself?"

"Oh, we are. I'm just letting you know you should get out of the way before you get hurt."

A preemptive strike to make me think it's over when it's not? She had to give Montana credit for trying. But she was also getting on Lacey's nerves.

"Your hair looks great, Montana, thanks to Stella. But you shouldn't wear your jeans cowgirl-tight in this city, unless you're planning to rope and hog-tie your man. Or is that the only way you can keep one?"

Montana lifted her chin. "Consider yourself history. Like Schmidt."

"No, thanks. I consider myself the future."

Vic's ex snorted and stomped off. Lacey gathered her wits— and her mother and sister from the Amanda memorial—grateful that she didn't have to explain Montana or reveal anything else complicated about her relationship with Vic Donovan. *If I still have one.*

"Find anything interesting?" Lacey asked.

"Maybe. There are lots of clues here," Cherise said. "We just don't know what they are."

Lacey gazed at the flowers. There were so many, jumbled in a rather disturbing clash of colors, put there by people who had never met Amanda, and yet somehow felt they knew her. They felt as if they had lost a friend. "If you can find a clue in that mess, good luck."

"What do we do now?" Cherise wanted to know, looking ex- pectantly at Lacey as if she were the cruise director on the S.S. *Smithsonian.* Lacey knew very well what the Smithsonian women wanted to see most of all in Washington, and she was going to give it to them, till their feet were screaming for mercy. After all, even John Henry Tyler had said, "Why don't y'all hang around those musty old museums of yours?"

"You wouldn't want to see the museums, would you?"

chapter 24

They agreed their first target of choice at the Smithsonian Museum of American History would be Lacey's personal favorite, the First Ladies' gowns, the ever-popular display on the wives of the Presidents. "And the shops, don't forget the shops," Cherise said. "I need something that says Smithsonian all over it."

"Okay. I need to stop by the office for about half an hour, but I can drop you at the museum and then meet you later."

"No, Lacey," her mother corrected. "We have half an hour to spare. We'd love to see your office."

"But I have to write a story and check my messages. You'll be bored. Really bored."

"We will be fine. You can do your work, and we won't make a peep."

"I can't work with you there peering over my shoulder."

"You used to do your homework with me peering over your shoulder. And you always got excellent grades, except, of course, in math." Rose was firm on the subject, presumably suspicious that Lacey would be off investigating without her freshly made-over backup team.

"You won't like it, and it's a perfect waste of your new clothes." Lacey said, giving in. *Tuesday, I just have to make it till Tuesday.*

The Eye Street Observer's newsroom was quieter than it was during the workweek, but there was a low-key hum of activity when Lacey arrived with her family. She passed by Mac's office. His lights were on and he was in, no doubt working on a heart attack.

As a general rule, Lacey tried to keep her weekends free of the office. But the second attempt on Spaulding's life was worth a story. In fact, she was sure Mac would send the Grim Reaper after her if she failed to turn in this story. She could write a few paragraphs and hand it off to the weekend city editor, or Tony Trujillo, the cops reporter, if he was around. She was trying to compose the story lead in her head.

"Smithsonian!" Lacey turned to see Mac at his door glaring at her.

"Hi, Mac." *Don't start.*

"Did you not promise me you would stay away from here and do family things this weekend?"

"I am." She indicated her two companions. "This is my mother, Rose Smithsonian, and my sister, Cherise Smithsonian." They waved and smiled. Lacey just hoped they wouldn't say anything incriminating about her.

Mac looked skeptical, as usual. "Nice to meet you." To Lacey, "What are you doing here?"

Lacey sent her mother and sister to the staff kitchen to see if there was fresh coffee and then turned to Mac. "I went to G. W. Hospital this morning. Someone tried to snuff Spaulding. Again."

"And you know this because . . . ?"

"I was there." She saw his face cloud, and she rushed on to say, "I had already set a meeting with Spaulding. But when I got there, someone was in the act of smothering him. For the record, we never got to speak, what with the police report and all."

Mac trained his eagle eyes on her. "And how does this connect to your beat, to fashion?"

Wow, good question, Mac. Wait, I know. . . . "He, or she, was wearing a costume, the Grim Reaper, at least by my interpretation. Black robe, skeleton mask, pale eyes? Big scythe? It's a fashion clue."

He grunted, put his hands together, and cracked all ten knuckles in a rapid-fire motion. "How is Spaulding now?"

"He's alive. If it helps, Detective Broadway Lamont said I saved the guy's life." She knew she was treading water here. Mac still did not look happy, but he was resigned.

"I'll see if Detective Lamont will give us a quote to that effect. And Lacey . . ."

"Yes, Mac?"

"Go write the story, and get out of here."

"No problem."

Lacey found her mother and sister wandering around her desk and conferring about the surrounding decor. Her desk was in its usual state of barely controlled chaos. Paper, press releases, and notes were stacked in semiorganized piles. Luckily, she also had a pile of fashion magazines to distract them.

"If you turned your desk to a forty-five-degree angle, Lacey, you'd be able to take advantage of the natural light from the window and avoid the glare of the afternoon sun on your computer screen," Rose suggested. "And your feng shui would be so much—"

"Mom, I'm sure it would. But if you start rearranging my newsroom, my editor will kick our feng shui right out of here." She adjusted the blinds to dim the afternoon glare. "Now please sit down, and I'll write my story as quickly as possible."

"All right, but I don't know how you could work in this environment," Rose complained. "It's simply bedlam."

To Lacey, the newsroom looked the way it always did during the week. Except with much less bedlam. But the feng shui was certainly a little chaotic. Most of the reporters had their own system of filing. Tony Trujillo called it "archaeological," meaning piles of newspapers, notebooks, and documents were stacked up to several feet high on their desks, filing cabinets, and the floor space all around them. Lacey's desk was not nearly that bad, but she could tell the ambience made Rose nervous and Cherise bored. She turned back to her story.

The assailant wore black, Lacey began. *The victim wore one of those awful hospital gowns. . . .*

She was happy Rose and Cherise were drowsing over their old copies of *Vogue.* As she finished her story, she received an e-mail note from Trujillo that the memorial service for Amanda Manville would be held the next day at the new Bentley Museum of American Fashion, at two in the afternoon. *Oh, my,* she thought, *there's that name again: Bentley.*

Lacey looked at her fellow would-be investigators. "By the way, I have to attend the memorial service for Amanda tomorrow. It's quasi-public, by invitation only."

"Then you can get us in, right?" Cherise asked, rousing herself.

"Don't get your hopes up."

"By all means RSVP for all of us," Rose said. "Do you think the murderer will be there?"

Lacey did think so, but she wasn't going to say yes. It would only encourage them. It had to be someone close to Amanda; maybe someone who carried a grudge, someone who had been the victim of her abusive temper. *That doesn't narrow it down much.* She wondered if Caleb Collingwood would be there, if he was still alive. He'd be pretty easy to spot, she thought. Lacey e-mailed her acceptance for a party of three from *The Eye* and hoped they would buy it.

"Aren't you through yet?" Cherise's foot was tapping and Rose had finished a cup of *The Eye*'s coffee, remarking on how loathsome it was. Lacey finished with the last paragraph then sent the file, turned off her computer, and grabbed her keys.

"Let's go," she said. "If the Smithsonian will not come to us . . ."

chapter 25

Her legs were screaming, Lacey decided. They had every right to scream, after spending the entire rest of the afternoon marching back and forth and up and down and hither and yon on hard museum floors behind Cherise and Rose.

Everything interested her sister and her mother, it seemed. At the Museum of American History they raced through popular culture, oohed and aahed at the Presidential collections, kibitzed cattily at the First Ladies' gowns and the ample figures that had been shoehorned into them, wondered as they wandered through early home building in America, and drank in every delicious detail of Julia Child's kitchen. And now they wanted to play Clue with Amanda Manville's death.

"But the motive, Lacey, don't we need to discover the motive?" they kept asking. "Who wanted her dead the most?" They were determined to make this murder a bonding experience. "What do you think, Lacey?" they asked over and over. *I think I want to sit down and take my shoes off.*

But it was really the shopping spree through the five—count 'em, *five*—gift shops at American History that was the crowning glory of their trip. Cherise loaded up on pink Smithsonian Cherry Blossom Festival T-shirts, navy Smithsonian sweatshirts, Smithsonian mugs, Smithsonian shot glasses, Smithsonian pencils, Smithsonian pens, Smithsonian memo pads, Smithsonian caps, and more, much more, all boldly emblazoned with the name Smithsonian.

Rose indulged in several sets of GREETINGS FROM THE SMITHSONIAN gift mugs and matching tote bags. She also picked up several other styles of Smithsonian tote bags, Smithsonian sweatshirts, tins of Smithsonian cookies and candies, and a host of small stocking stuffers, including Smithsonian change purses and key rings. Lacey picked up a Rosie the Riveter WE CAN DO IT mug and skipped the rest.

The more they bought, the happier they were. "This is so great, Lacey; half my Christmas shopping is done, and no one will be able to forget who this stuff came from," Cherise said. "If I didn't get enough, I'll call you and you can just run over here and get more, right?"

"You're not tired, are you, dear?" Rose inquired.

"I've lost the feeling in my feet."

"As long as it's not your head," Cherise said.

"I think I'll need crutches." Lacey did lower-back stretches while they were in line to buy their loot at the last gift shop.

"You're not petering out on us, are you?"

"Sorry, the cheerleader genes skipped me." Lacey checked her watch and was grateful to see the doors would be closing in ten minutes. "Oh, darn, they'll be chasing us out of here."

"Can we come back tomorrow after the memorial service?" Cherise suggested. "Or we can do Air and Space, or Natural History. Or both."

"That would be a treat," Rose agreed.

"Wouldn't it? But the service will probably be boring for you. I could bring you here and duck over to the service myself. It's only a few blocks, really."

"Nice try," Rose said. "Remember, we're a team."

"What are we doing tonight, Lacey?" Cherise was still not showing any signs of fatigue. "Last night at your little jazz club was a kick and a half."

"How about some supper?" Rose said. "You will want something to eat. Then we can make a list of everyone Lacey thinks had a motive to kill Amanda Manville. We can cross-check means, motive, and opportunity, just like on TV."

To Lacey's relief, Cherise thought that sounded "cool." Even better, they agreed to Lacey's suggestion to retreat to Old Town for a steak dinner at the brew pub on King Street, which she always found restored her strength and good spirits. A medium-rare steak, she felt, was better than a bottle of vitamin B. She also felt she deserved it, after a rather trying day. She thanked heaven there were no vegetarians in her family. And even better, the big dinner finally had the appropriate soporific effect on Cherise, who agreed to go home and watch television for the rest of the evening. Oh, yes, and list all the potential murderers and analyze their motives.

Montana, murder, makeovers, and mayhem were on Lacey's mind for the rest of the evening. She didn't know if there was anything she could do about Montana, or that she'd even come to a conclusion about the murder of Amanda Manville, but she was pretty sure that she would not escape mayhem with her family around. *Broadway Lamont told me it's always your nearest and dearest you've got to watch out for.*

Visions of falling leaves and crisp walks in the woods with Vic and a cozy fireplace had fizzled in the glare of family togetherness, but they kept flirting with her imagination. She wondered if it would ever happen. And Rose and Cherise kept chattering happily away about poor murdered Amanda, like the three of them would come up with a major breakthrough on "the case." But it was too early to give up the game and go to bed for the night without seeming antisocial.

"How did you first get involved in solving murders, and do you think you can make any money doing it?" Cherise asked. "Do you think it's, like, a talent that runs in the family?"

"There are many talents that run in this family," Rose said. "And I'm sure that Lacey would never charge for her investigations." They were taking up all the space on her sofa. There was no room for her. She had to drag a chair over from an "intimate conversation area" where Rose had stationed it. They glanced up at her with interest. "If you sit there, dear, we won't be able to see the movie."

"It's not time yet. Right now I need your attention, Mom. Your full attention, Cherise."

"Oh, wow, have you figured it all out?"

"No. But we're going to have a chat. And we have to come to an understanding about what I do. I am not a detective. I am not even an investigative reporter. I cover fashion. That's it. Sometimes in the course of what I do, I notice something that leads to a discovery. What people wear reveals something about them. Maybe it's just their standard of living, or that they are a designer snob, or their profession, or whether someone is a Democrat or a Republican, a student, a goth rebel, a soccer mom, or the neighborhood busybody. Things like that. Sometimes it reveals things they're trying to hide. But I am not trying to do what the police do. Are we clear on that?"

They seemed to agree. "But how can you tell a murderer," Rose wanted to know, "from what he's wearing?"

Lacey thought. "Usually it's the details, small things. Paying attention to things that other people miss." *Like a man whose hair gets thicker—because he's wearing extensions made of his victims' shorn locks,* she remembered, thinking about the "Razor Boy" murders she had gotten involved with that spring, those dead hairstylists with their missing hair. "I merely ask questions. I am a writer, not a freelance righter of wrongs. I do not willingly put myself in danger."

"Of course not, dear, and we're here to make sure of that," Rose said. "But how did you end up having to stab all those—" The phone rang, and Lacey ran for it gratefully.

"Hi, it's Brooke. I'm downstairs. Can you buzz me up?"

"No need. Door's broken, just push. Come on up. Where's Damon?"

"With a source. Not with me. Just us girls. I thought you probably needed reinforcements; am I right?"

Do I ever. When Brooke arrived she introduced herself as Lacey's friend, so Lacey was spared making the usual introductions. Brooke brought a fresh bottle of gin and a sack full of limes and made herself right at home.

"G and Ts all around?" she asked. Cherise revived instantly.

"Who's Damon's source?" Lacey asked when she got Brooke alone in the tiny kitchen.

"I knew that would get you. But I don't know. He says it's too dangerous to tell me yet."

She slipped off her jacket and took over Lacey's kitchen to play bartender. Lacey pulled the tonic from the fridge, while Brooke sliced limes and squeezed juice into glasses. Lacey opened the gin and gave an extra shot to her mother's and sister's glasses.

"No doubt it concerns the top secret Bionic Babe project," Lacey said drily.

"You'll be sorry when it's true, babe."

"Astonished at any rate," Lacey said, but her skepticism did not deter Brooke. It never did. They moved into the living room with the drinks.

"My, that's strong," Rose said, taking a sip.

"Mine is perfect," Cherise said.

"We're all going to the Manville memorial service, right?" Brooke asked. "I'm going with Damon. My man in the know. You'll meet him."

"Of course," Cherise said. "We wouldn't miss it. I read that several major supermodels are going to be there, like Heidi, Gisele, Claudia, Laetitia, maybe even *Tyra*." She sounded as if she knew them all, just old friends of hers from Geronimo High. "And maybe even some movie stars." She had been paying attention to the television news, as well as to her big sister. But her attention was now held by something else.

The movie was *Now, Voyager* with Bette Davis, just coming on sans commercials on WETA, the PBS station, and Cherise and Rose shot to attention. It was the ultimate sentimental makeover movie, Lacey had promised them, featuring Bette Davis's transformation from frumpy spinster to sassy single heartbreaker with a fabulous wardrobe.

"Isn't that the movie that's all about cigarettes?" Rose asked. "Where that guy from *Casablanca* does that corny lighting-two-cigarettes-at-once thing and then gives her one?"

"Ooh, that's so disgusting," Cherise said.

"Actually, it's pretty comical. But forget about the cigarettes," Lacey said. "This film is completely about how a diet, chic new clothes, and a great eyebrow waxing can change your life." The only problem was that the designs by Orry-Kelly, particularly the fabulous suits, which she was anxious to gaze upon again, made Lacey long to stretch out on the floor, open Aunt Mimi's trunk, and look for similar patterns from the same era. She particularly remembered a gorgeous and perfectly simple black dinner dress that Bette Davis as the newly chic Charlotte Vale wears in defiance of her horrid mother. The dress was made even better by pinning camelias in the décolletage. But Mimi's trunk had been relegated to a deep dark spot behind the sofa, and besides, it was Lacey's personal trunk of dreams; she didn't want to share it. Her mother and sister wouldn't understand.

"Okay, then, I know," Cherise offered. "We could do shots every time someone lights up."

"We'll be sloshed before the movie's half over," Lacey said. "But look out for that great outfit the first time she steps off the ship, when the camera pans up from her spectator pumps to her smart traveling dress to her big straw hat that shadows her eyes. It's a real movie moment."

Rose and Cherise didn't want to miss a minute of it, so Brooke and Lacey were free to take a break on the balcony. It was slightly brisk but brilliantly clear, and the moon was rising over the Potomac River. They grabbed their jackets and gin and tonics, and Brooke took her new Burberry tote.

"Damon is going to find out whether those supermodels are part of the Babes project."

"And how can he tell that?" Lacey asked.

"His source has a very classified piece of equipment, a handheld GPS detector, which should be able to pick up and decode the distinct frequencies that their implants transmit."

Lacey nodded sagely, just as if she had the slightest idea what Brooke was talking about. "What if they don't have implants?"

"Please. They're models, with busts as round as grapefruit. About as natural-looking as their cotton-candy hair."

"Okay, I'd love to see Damon prove that," Lacey said. "Does the machine beep when he gets close to the implants? Louder and louder? Like a Geiger counter?"

"We'll have to see. Maybe he can put it on vibrate mode so it doesn't interrupt the eulogies." Brooke reached for her purse and withdrew her latest Spy Store toy. "Night-vision binos. Generation Three. Check these babies out."

It was fun watching small furry critters near the water's edge and seagulls sleeping on the pilings, but soon the binoculars lost their novelty. And the full moon illuminated the whole scene and decorated the Potomac with a glittering swath of moonlight. They needed a really dark night, Brooke said, for a proper test of night-vision binos. Lacey handed them back just as something close by caught her eyes, a movement on the other wing of her own apartment building, the wing that met hers at a right angle.

Standing on the far balcony was a black-robed figure, looking at her. His face was hooded and shrouded in shadows. She couldn't make out whether the figure was wearing a mask or not, but her heart froze. He stood still in the crystal night air for a few moments, and Lacey was glued to the spot, blood pulsing in her temples. She reached out to tap Brooke's shoulder for the night-vision binoculars, but Brooke was engrossed in watching a possum in a tree.

The French doors of the other apartment opened, and a Gypsy woman in flowing scarves came out. She said with a distinctly Brooklyn accent that carried on the still air, "Whaddaya doin' out here? We're gonna be late. You're always makin' me late."

The hooded figure replied in another nasal New York accent. "I'm comin' already. What would the party be without the Scythe Man? Hey, babe, you seen my scythe anywhere?" He gave the Gypsy a friendly pat on the butt and stubbed out his cigarette.

Lacey felt a rush of relief and anger at herself for jumping to the conclusion that the Grim Reaper was stalking her and had followed her right to her home. *And right to my mother and sister!*

"Let's go in, Brooke. I'm chilled to the bone."

FASHION BITES

Life Is Not a Dress Rehearsal:
You're the Star; Don't Dress
Like the Understudy!

Shakespeare said, "All the world's a stage, and all the men and women merely players."

If that's true, why are you dressing like the understudy and not the star? There are players and then there are *players*. It's your life. What are you waiting for? Your big break? Brad Pitt? Rumpelstiltskin at the door to spin your over-processed, strawlike hair into silken gold? Maybe you're waiting for next week, next month, next year to get that winning wardrobe together. Or maybe you prefer being an extra in the story of your own life, an extra who fades into the background. Like so many of the drably dressed in the District of Columbia, their eyes downcast on the Metro, invisible in their dull-gray polyester suits with the baggy seat in the skirt, clutching the knockoff Louis Vuitton bag in a death grip in one hand, the chirping cell phone in the other. Extras in one of those bad Washington thrillers that can't even get the Metro stations right.

Wouldn't you rather be dressed like the leading lady?

Believe it or not, D.C., some people enjoy what they wear. For example, spotted on the Metro: a young woman with short, spiked burgundy hair, wearing a faux-leopard swing coat, fishnet hose in black boots, and dramatic kohl-rimmed eyes, and a look that said, *The movie of my life is French!* She may not be your cup of tea, but she has a definite idea of who she is, and how she looks, and she's not afraid to show it. You can bet she has a starring role in her life, whether it's the movie we'd want to be in or not. Unlike those of us who are waiting for life to hand us a script and a wardrobe to go with it.

Some of you will say there are more important things to do than think about clothes while there is hunger and poverty and despair in the world. Why, then, are you reading this column?

Have you ever noticed how well people onstage or in the movies dress? Okay, maybe not the postmodern films that dwell on the gritty underbelly of society and depress the living daylights out of you, like English or Swedish films where no one is happy and quiet desperation chokes the plot into grim despair, where lank, greasy hair and bad skin are an artistic manifesto. No, not those. I wouldn't even want to be an extra in those.

I'm thinking about how the stars were turned out in the great, big, classic Hollywood films, in stunning black and white or glowing Technicolor. The films that inspired women to follow their dreams in wonderfully tailored togs. Granted, stars like Bette Davis and Katharine Hepburn had designers like Edith Head and the incomparable Adrian, but they had something else: the attitude to carry it off. When Bette Davis in *Now, Voyager* is transformed from the frumpy, dumpy Charlotte Vale into the alluring and mysterious "Miss Renee Beauchamps," she makes an unforgettable entrance that instantly makes her the star of her own life, though she doesn't know it yet.

You and I may not have Bette Davis's fabulous wardrobe (courtesy of Orry-Kelly) to help us shed our ugly-duckling shells and reveal our beautiful inner swans. But we can borrow Bette's attitude, an attitude that says, *I'm not the understudy. I'm the star.*

chapter 26

St. Mary's Church, a few blocks from her apartment, was the only place Lacey knew she could get some peace and quiet Sunday morning. Lacey remained the only Catholic left in her immediate family. She knew that Cherise and Rose would prefer to let her go alone, and for that she gave thanks. "You could always go to some Protestant church," she had pointed out. "Christ Church, for example, George Washington's very own church, it's very pretty—"

"I'm on vacation," Cherise said sleepily, and hit the pillow again. In return for an extra hour of sleep in Lacey's trundle beds, they promised to have breakfast made by the time she returned.

At St. Mary's she slipped into the very back pew, knelt down, and closed her eyes. She heard the small, comforting noises of other worshipers filling up the pews. When she opened her eyes Victor Donovan was kneeling next to her.

She felt her eyes pop open. Vic generally looked like a wayward altar boy, the kind who might be caught fencing in the back of the church with the candlesticks and racing through the "Our Father" so he could go play baseball, or catch frogs, or tease girls, or whatever boys did after church. He grinned, knowing he had caught her off balance. With a name like Donovan, she had always assumed he was Catholic, but with his personal history, she also assumed he didn't have much to do with the Church, at least not anymore. She raised her eyebrow at him.

"You can't give me that look in church, Lacey; it's some kind of sin. Mortal? Venial? Skeptical. That's it; it's a skeptical sin." He sat right next to her, not as an answer to her prayers, because she wasn't praying about him. *At least, not exactly.* However, his white smile and the twinkle in his eyes teased her. He took her hand and squeezed it.

"Why are you here?" she whispered.

"Praying for your safety. Move over."

Notes from the organ signaled the beginning of the Mass, leaving her to wonder about him for the next hour. But she was bemused to notice that he knew all the words, and he knew when to rise and when to kneel. *He's done this before,* she concluded. She assumed he wanted to lecture her about something, and when they emerged into the sunshine with the rest of the parishioners she asked him.

"What made you show up here?"

"I called and your mom said you'd gone to church. How come they're not here?"

"They turned Protestant. It's easier. Leaves more time for golf."

He laughed out loud. "But easier has never been your way, has it?"

"I don't do it on purpose. It just happens that way." He gave her a look. "Don't say anything. And why are you here, really?"

He squinted in the sun and reached for the sunglasses in his pocket. "I had it on the best authority, a responsible reporter I know, that you were going to be safe this weekend. And then I saw *The Eye Street Observer.* I shouldn't read it, but I can't help myself. It detailed your run-in with the Grim Reaper. Luckily, you escaped the scythe."

"You can't get mad at me; we've just been to church."

"Like I said, I was praying for your safety. I lit a candle for you." He put his arm around her shoulder, and they walked down South Royal Street back to her apartment. His arm around her shoulder felt very nice and, for once, uncomplicated.

"I ran into Montana," Lacey said. "We had a sweet little chat. She warned me she's getting you back."

Vic sighed. "One thing you need to know. This is Montana's last stand, and she knows it."

"I think you're wrong. She doesn't know it."

"Well, I know it, Lacey. And that's the important part."

"And is everyone still standing in Montana's last stand, or has she laid you low?"

"Still standing." He took a beat. "I was never married in the Church, Lacey." She looked at him. "Just thought you'd like to know. For future reference."

"And where were you married, if not in the Church? Aboard a tramp steamer?"

"Las Vegas, Nevada, a justice of the peace. So, from certain angles, it never even counted as official in the first place—although it sure as hell seemed official when we went to court to break it up."

"Oh, Vic." *Las Vegas? Not Las Vegas.* "Couldn't you have just shacked up, as my mother would say?"

"Would have been easier, that's for sure. Maybe somewhere in the back of my mind, I knew it wasn't forever."

He walked her home, but couldn't stay for brunch, much to her relief. She didn't want to press the subject and ask for his intentions. She wasn't even quite sure about her own intentions, and trying to spell them out would just ruin the mood. She just smiled. It simply meant that Vic could be married in the Church. If he chose to. Someday.

chapter 27

"It must have seemed like a good idea at the time," Lacey said in response to her mother's harrumphing disapproval of the circus-like atmosphere at Amanda Manville's memorial service.

Mourners of all stripes gathered before the Bentley Museum of American Fashion, tourists, fashionistas, Amanda groupies, puzzled locals, all gawking at the media and one another, trying to spot the rumored celebrities in the crowd. News trucks blocked the museum entryway, and a slow-moving line was passing through security while guards cleared names on the invited-guest list. Lacey was relieved to find the name Smithsonian was on the list for a party of three.

Once they were inside the Grand Lobby, the media were blocking nearly every view of the podium. Lacey spotted the broadcast reporters, rehearsing their opening bits with their camera crews. Cords snaked willy-nilly through the room, making an obstacle course between the folding chairs and the memorial display, creating hazards that would earn them frowns of disapproval from safety inspectors. The focal point was a group of enormous photos of Amanda on easels and a podium for the speakers. A tableau of plastic mannequins posed among the photos, dressed in outfits from the Chrysalis Collection.

It was mere chaos and confusion now, but it threatened to be pure pandemonium later. People were jockeying for position, and the Smithsonians, under Lacey's experienced leadership, selected their seats immediately in self-defense, to avoid the ruthless game of musical chairs later. There were far too many people invited for each to have a seat, so a disgruntled mob would end up lining the walls. Lacey was sure that was deliberate. *A packed house always looks better on camera.*

Rose and Cherise were wearing their new outfits from the day before. They looked fashionable and chic, and their clothes were dark enough to be respectful at a memorial service. Lacey decided on a vintage navy wool crepe suit from the war years with gold buttons and full sleeves ending in tight buttoned cuffs. It fit her perfectly, and she always marveled at how clothes from the Forties fit her as if they were tailored for her. Her mother merely raised an eyebrow at the suit, but Cherise swore she loved it, which was just weird.

Judging from the funerals Lacey had been to in Washington, D.C., she assumed the mourners would be wearing a perfect hodgepodge of clothing. And they were. The simple rules for wearing dark clothing that did not evoke a party atmosphere were gone.

A trio of lanky models strode past the Smithsonians. They looked a little like aliens: too tall, too thin, too much eye makeup, giving them that big-eyed look that alien chicks dug so much. They wore pointy-toed stilettos and a little too much bare skin to show any actual respect for the dead. Their fashion statement seemed to be, *Look at me! I'm alive! And nearly naked!* Or as Rose said, "A strapless dress at a memorial service! Well, I never."

"Not only that, it's cold enough in here to store cadavers," Cherise said, although with hot television lights, the room was bound to heat up soon. Lacey asked her sister to watch her seat while she circulated. "Fashion clues, you know." Lacey moved through the crowd, taking in faces and clothing, not knowing exactly what she was looking for. She knew only that she needed to keep her eyes and ears open.

Cordelia Westgate, the former spokesmodel for the famous House of Bentley fashion empire, stopped dead in her tracks when she saw Lacey. They had met before, and there was no love lost between them. Cordelia had been involved with the Bentleys when intern Esme Fairchild disappeared earlier that year and was later found murdered. When Lacey's stories for *The Eye* brought down the house, so to speak, Cordelia had been swept out of her position.

"What are you doing here?" Cordelia demanded.

"My job, and I could ask the same of you, Ms. Westgate."

"If you must know, Amanda was a dear friend of mine," she said without the slightest sincerity. Though only twenty-eight, Cordelia was in her waning days of modeling. It wasn't the years, but the mileage, as they say, that was destroying her looks. Hard living and late nights were traced in the lines of her face and the bags under her eyes. Nevertheless, the fading beauty's bones were still marvelous, and her ravaged looks were far more compelling than those of any interchangeable trio of younger models.

"Have you found a new gig yet?" Lacey inquired.

"Like I'd tell you," she said. "You're nothing but trouble."

"I try not to cause it, but it does seem to cross my path," Lacey admitted with a small smile.

Cordelia lifted her perfect nose and sailed on past to join the knot of supermodels, who tried to ignore her. Slightly worn, a little shorter, and not as anorexic as this year's models, Cordelia was still truly beautiful. They were just the flavor of the month, and they would soon be out of fashion in their turn, like she was. But Cordelia Westgate was also notorious; partying, posing nude, and sleeping with rogues and killers would do that for a girl. Photographers crowded around Cordelia, who smiled serenely for the cameras.

Lacey recognized Hansen's long lens among them. He was one of the still photographers wearing press credentials. She also caught sight of Tate Penfield with his video camera, with a throng of models and wannabes vying for his attention. She waved to him.

"Hey, Lacey, how are you doing?" His brown eyes were bloodshot, his hair was falling in his face, and he was sallow, as if he hadn't slept in days.

"Tate, are you all right? You look worn out."

"I was up all night editing the rough cut. I'm showing it tonight."

"Your documentary on Amanda? Really, Tate, your subject isn't going anywhere now. You shouldn't kill yourself to finish it."

"Very well put." He favored her with a big smile. "But this is my own memorial to Amanda. Tonight I'm showing it at Brad and Yvette's house. You'll come, won't you?"

"I don't think the Powerses will ask me."

"It's my guest list, not theirs. And you're invited." Penfield pulled a card from his pocket that read, TATE PENFIELD. PHOTOGRAPHER. On the back, he wrote the time and the address of Brad and Yvette's Georgetown home. He also wrote, *You're invited! Tate,* and he underlined it for emphasis. He handed it to her.

"I don't know. I'd love to, but I'm saddled with my family this weekend."

"Bring them along, I'd really appreciate it. Believe me, we'll be overloaded with supermodels." He grimaced. "I could use some real human beings in the mix, for balance. And it's being catered. Lots of food."

"Catered food? For supermodels? Don't they just consume lettuce leaves, caffeine, and cigarettes?"

"And vodka." Penfield laughed, and his weary features regained some of their chiseled beauty. "So there'll be plenty of leftovers. Please be there. You'll be the only reporter." He pointed his camera at her and clicked the shutter. He started moving toward the podium.

She hated it when people seduced her with the promise of being the only reporter. An exclusive: It was a bait she found nearly irresistible. And his invitation would give her something unique to offer her mother and sister. She had been planning popcorn and a couple of old movies from Video Vault. "What time?" Lacey asked before Penfield was out of earshot.

"About eight."

"I'll try."

Hansen approached leisurely, cameras slung from his shoulders. "Hey, Lacey, I'm having a problem with my old Peugeot wagon; can I trouble you for a lift to my studio on your way home? It's not far out on New York Avenue, and you can catch Two Ninety-Five back to Virginia."

She shrugged. "Sure, but you're tall, and you'll have to deal with my family in a dreadful rented Echo."

"No problem. I once drove to California nonstop with two buddies in a Volkswagen Beetle."

"Great. Catch me after the service." Lacey turned around and almost tripped over Brooke Barton and Damon Newhouse.

"Lacey, can you sit with us?" Brooke asked, hoping, no doubt, to share her latest conspiracy theory about the skinny models who looked like aliens. In Brooke's world, Lacey thought, they *were* aliens, progeny of the secret beings that survived a spacecraft crash in Roswell, New Mexico. Damon looked very intense and said nothing.

"Can't. I'm with the family. They're holding my seat for me." She perched on a seat and pointed over to Rose and Cherise. Brooke waved. They waved back. Brooke was wearing a lawyerly gray pantsuit and gripped her Burberry tote, and Damon was in his usual black cyber-beatnik attire and his small black glasses, looking very serious. They made a very attractive couple, though beneath their sleek, polished exterior, Lacey knew, they were just conspiracy-addled adolescents playing "I Spy" with high-tech toys.

Brooke tapped Lacey on the shoulder. "The Grim Reaper? With a scythe? Lacey, how could you not tell me last night? I am seriously disappointed in you."

"I'm sorry. I couldn't tell you with my mother and sister hanging around. Besides, you always find out everything anyway."

Brooke was only slightly mollified. "Damon says you nearly caught a rogue government assassin in the attempted murder of Dr. Gregory Spaulding."

Lacey glared at Damon. "You didn't put that on your Web site, did you? Tell me you didn't."

He smiled and waved the peace sign. "You know, Lacey, in certain circles, GR stands for an officially nonexistent group of assassins and thieves known as the Government Repossessors. Their unofficial logo is the Grim Reaper. Coincidence?"

Do not smile, she told herself. *You know how you are, if you smile, you'll laugh, and this is a memorial service, for heaven's sake, and your mother will hear you laughing, and you will never hear the end of it, so do not smile!*

"I see. And what does this have to do with the death of Amanda or anything else?"

"Ah," he said, knowing he had her attention. "They are sent to wipe out debts. Spaulding owed a debt because his Bionic Babe was a spectacular failure. First the GR repossessed her, and now they're repossessing him. Or trying to. Be careful, Smithsonian; you're not on the repo list, but you could get caught up in the net."

"And this is all secret, right?"

"Not anymore," Brooke jumped in. "Not with Conspiracy Clearinghouse on the job." She proudly stroked Damon's arm.

"I thought so. So how's the other little project going," Lacey asked brightly, "detecting whether these supermodels have clandestine GPS units in their breast implants?"

Damon shushed her. He looked a little crestfallen, and Brooke hastened to explain. "We think they have a jamming device. We haven't been able to get a clear signal in here, although you wouldn't believe how many cell phones we're picking up. We're hoping to get a lot closer to one of our targets later."

Lacey bit her lip to keep from laughing at her mental image. "I have to go find some people. Okay? We'll talk tomorrow." As Lacey stood to go, Damon and Brooke both gave her the thumbs-up sign. *Just a couple of crazy space cadets in love.*

She decided to take just a few minutes for herself in the Bentley wing. She slipped away from the crowd and made her way back down the main hall. She wanted to revisit some of the magnificent pieces from Hugh Bentley's early collections that were displayed there. Maybe it would help her to take a breath, let her mind relax. The effortlessly elegant dresses and suits from the Forties that had made Hugh Bentley's reputation were beautiful. She admired them for some minutes, recalling that Hugh, the old bastard, had once yearned to enshrine her own one-of-a-kind Gloria Adams suit in this very display. But she knew she had to get back before the service started. She turned at the sound of voices coming from a side hall that led back to the far end of the museum's Grand Lobby, which appeared to be the staging area for the memorial service.

Lacey saw Zoe in profile, leaning against the wall. Yvette was standing still beside her, and from their vantage point they seemed to be able to check on the crowd and time their entrance for the main event. Lacey stepped back and found that by gazing into a mirrored display case at the corner of the hallway, she could see all the way down and still remain hidden from their view.

Zoe was dressed in a black wool crepe from the Chrysalis Collection, with perfect princess lines and long, roomy sleeves with satin trim. It was an appropriate dress for the event, and it slimmed and flattered her. She drank designer water from a plastic bottle, then set it down on a side table. She checked her watch and sighed while Yvette bounced lightly on her heels, anxious to get the show on the road.

With her hair in a shiny chignon, Yvette was looking her Grace Kelly best, beautiful and sophisticated. She wore a chocolate-brown wool suit with a shawl collar and gold buttons. The acoustics were so clear over the polished surfaces of the hallway that Lacey could hear her every word. Yvette told Zoe she would be out in a few minutes to start the program.

"It's best to wait for everyone to arrive," Yvette said. "For the cameras."

"I'm so tired, Yvette."

"Just a little while longer and this will all be over."

"I didn't want her to die," Zoe lamented. "I just wanted my life back."

Yvette lifted Zoe's face with her hands. "And fate stepped in and gave it to you. She changed, Zoe; she wasn't the Mandy we knew. Now you have to be strong and get through today. Tomorrow will be easier."

Zoe took a deep breath. "I'll try."

"Good. It's time. Go take your seat. I'll be there in a moment."

Zoe nodded and started walking toward the podium. Lacey lingered to see Brad Powers emerge from the shadows and kiss his wife on the back of her neck.

"Now all you have to do is your part," he said.

"Hopefully the last in this ugly melodrama," she said. "Goodbye, Amanda. For a while, I was afraid she was going to make it."

Was that just an incredibly nasty thing to say? Lacey caught her breath. *Or did Yvette just allude to a possible involvement in her death?* Lacey checked her position to make sure no one knew she was there and moved farther back.

"It's all over, Yvette. She can't hurt us anymore."

"Or sleep with one of us anymore."

"Would you just forget that? She's dead. It's what you wanted, isn't it? Now go on out there. Chrysalis is going to be a huge hit with you and Zoe at the helm. And Amanda's beautiful, tragic face to sell the line."

"I just want to get out of here till the circus subsides."

"You please the cameras today, and we'll be on a plane to California tomorrow. Now, go out there and break their hearts." He gave her a swift kiss on the forehead, and she held on to his hand for a moment before moving down the hall. Powers stood watching his wife, arms crossed.

Lacey's shoe squeaked on the polished floor, and she froze. Powers spun around quickly and peered down the hall. He saw her reflection in the display case, and their eyes met. Lacey decided this was a good time to make tracks back to her seat. As she turned to go, he rounded the corner in a hurry and roughly grabbed her arm.

"Oh, no, you don't, Smithsonian. What the hell were you doing spying on us?"

"Take your hands off me."

"What did you hear?"

"What do you think I heard?"

"You answer me, or I swear to God I'll—" But Powers didn't finish. Somehow Turtledove had materialized behind her. He calmly removed Powers's hand from Lacey's arm and twisted it around behind the smaller man's back, deftly sliding between them and slamming Powers face first against the wall. Powers looked tough and fit, but next to Turtledove he looked like a little boy with a shaved head.

"Or what?" Turtledove asked, and Powers closed his eyes, trying not to grimace in pain. Lacey realized his arm must be hurting where Turtledove was gripping it. Powers said nothing. "Right. Then why don't we all take our seats for the service. Zoe's about to speak." He gave Powers his arm back. Powers opened his eyes and started breathing again. He was flushed right to the top of his bald head.

"Sorry, Ms. Smithsonian—Forrest. . . . We're all a little on edge. I'm, um, I'm a little protective—about my wife. I guess I misunderstood. . . . Sorry." He straightened his tie and left, shaking his arm.

Her heart thumping, Lacey willed it to slow down. "Wow, thanks. I didn't know you were still on the payroll."

"I'm not."

"Then what are you doing here? Not that I'm complaining."

A long, slow smile lit up his face. "Just keeping an eye on things for Damon. And watching over you."

"Thanks, Turtledove. I'm glad you're here."

"My pleasure." He escorted her back the way she came and left her at her row of seats. He gave Cherise a big wink and slipped back into the crowd. Several people stood so Lacey could reach her seat in the tightly packed row.

"Where have you been?" Rose asked. "And who was that big man?" Cherise also looked at her questioningly.

"I'll tell you later," she whispered, her heart still pounding. She was surprised to see that she knew the handsome rascal sitting next to her. FBI agent Gary Braddock, a well-known fashion plate in his own right, was cool and elegant, perfectly groomed, nothing remotely resembling Lacey's image of a typical nerdy FBI guy in a rumpled tan suit and a bad tie. He was wearing a charcoal suit and a black turtleneck, which enhanced his piercing blue eyes. *Is it true he was once a model himself?*

He acknowledged her. "We really must stop meeting this way. Nice outfit."

"Agent Braddock. How'd you know I'd be sitting here?"

"Lucky guess." *Liar,* Lacey thought. *How flattering that the FBI follows me around, looking for trouble.*

"So the FBI is on the case now?"

"The Bureau is officially being asked to join the investigation as we speak. So have you uncovered any fashion clues, Lacey?"

Braddock was teasing her, her mother was staring at her, and Cherise was poking her in the ribs, trying to ask silently who this latest cute guy was. Lacey tried to Zen out, but she was struck by the irony of being surrounded by so many attractive men this weekend. Normally in Washington she found herself in the midst of a mob of bland, interchangeable, wonky men who wouldn't even look at her. All this unusual male attention would give Cherise the wrong idea, not to mention her mother.

"You didn't read *The Eye* today?" she asked Braddock.

"Your run-in with the Grim Reaper? I'll keep my eyes open for that black robe and the scythe. Sounds scary. Of course, a scythe in your hands would be even scarier."

"If you think that's scary, have you met my family?" Lacey said quietly so that only Braddock could hear her. "They want to help me investigate a murder, whether I want to or not."

He did not look amused. He was about to say something when the service started.

Amanda's parents were conspicuously absent, apparently preferring to keep their grief private. Zoe had taken her place up front and looked far more composed than she had the other day, and Brad Powers had pulled himself together by her side. Lacey spotted the much-put-upon Fawn, her Burberry scarf in place, looking unexpectedly cheerful, as if the slaves had been freed at last. She saw Lacey and waved.

Yvette acted as the emcee for the event. There was no minister to lead the prayers because there were no prayers, and there were no hymns. However, there was a throbbing multimedia slide show of Amanda's unusual and briefly dazzling career, set to driving runway fashion-show disco, all of it moderated by Yvette Powers with an awful lot of composure for being such a close friend of the deceased. And there were various testimonials from Amanda's friends and colleagues, including some of the famous supermodels whom the crowds of the curious outside had come to ogle. Their remarks were called eulogies in the memorial program. Lacey thought they resembled real eulogies about as much as the woman they described resembled the real Amanda Manville. The supermodels read their parts like actresses reading scripts they had never seen before, some of them possibly in a foreign language. Yet there was a common theme. They all loved Amanda Manville.

Who wrote this thing? Lacey wondered. *It's like a bad play at the Washington Theatre Festival.* It dragged on, riveting and tedious at the same time.

Yet Yvette proved to be a clever actress, who convinced many in the audience that she was devastated by Amanda's loss. And she seemed to display a real concern for Zoe Manville, whose tribute to Amanda was saved for last. Zoe started to read a poem by Christina Rossetti, "When I Am Dead, My Dearest." She said it was Amanda's favorite. But she broke down, started again, and choked up and could not finish. She looked helplessly at Yvette. Yvette comforted Zoe and led her back to her seat. Yvette finished the sentimental little verse and wowed the crowd. Finally it ended. Tate Penfield was still shooting the crowd as they signed their names under a giant photo of Amanda.

"Yvette must've gotten an A in Oral Interp," Lacey whispered to Cherise while Rose flashed them a disapproving look.

"With friends like that, Amanda didn't need any enemies," Rose said later. Suffice it to say, Rose found the poem in questionable taste, but it was the multimedia show that really stuck in her craw. "Someone could have offered a prayer for the poor thing, for heaven's sake."

Cherise loved every minute of it, and she supplied Lacey with a running commentary on the seamy scandals of the various models in attendance.

Lacey put her hand in her pocket to make sure that Penfield's card with his invitation was still there. She was determined to go to that viewing of the rough cut of his documentary, whether she had to drag her family along or not. All the usual and unusual suspects would be there, up close and personal, and maybe the vodka Penfield mentioned would loosen a tongue or two.

At least I'll get my family fed. And it'll make a great story to tell Mrs. Dorfendraper back home.

The mood in the cramped Echo was subdued as Lacey drove Hansen to his photo studio. The warehouse neighborhood looked a little bleak in the fading October light, but Hansen swore it was fine. It was actually too deserted around there at night to be dangerous, he said, unfolding his long limbs as he exited the car.

"How are you getting to the Powerses' party?" Lacey asked.

"I'll catch a taxi. Or Tate will drop by here. He's got his car today. No prob. You want to come in?" he offered, obviously proud of his little side business. "I'll show you the studio."

Rose and Cherise weren't interested, but Lacey took the opportunity to ask to use the "ladies' room," and she was a little curious to get a quick glimpse of his and Penfield's photography digs.

Hansen was such a part of the furniture at *The Eye* that she was be-mused to discover he had another life outside the office.

"I'll be right back out," she said, as her mother and Cherise locked all the doors and huddled suspiciously in the Echo.

She didn't learn anything interesting. The space was sparse, decorated in what might be called comfort deprivation, with an at-tempt at civility in the tiny office. Lacey was in and out quickly.

"Back so soon?" her mother inquired as Cherise fiddled with the radio again, trying to find something halfway listenable.

Lacey jumped back in the car and turned up the heat. "It's as warm in there as an outhouse in January."

chapter 28

Lacey found it hard to believe that with Amanda's memorial barely over, the rough cut of Penfield's documentary could possibly be in shape to be screened. But then, he'd been working on it for months. The memorial service had left her cold, she reflected. Perhaps this personal memorial to Amanda from her photographer would be a warmer event.

After a break at home to unwind and change out of their memorial-service clothes and into something vaguely resembling casual-dinner-party-in-Georgetown clothes, Lacey packed her family back in the Echo for the drive into the depths of swankiest Georgetown, the legendary abode of the Cave Dwellers, the District's version of an old-fashioned social elite, now mostly just a memory.

Their destination, according to Penfield's invitation, was several blocks distant from the congested restaurant and nightlife strips of M Street and Wisconsin Avenue. But as usual in Georgetown, even on a Sunday night, Lacey concluded there hadn't been a vacant parking space since the Truman administration. She finally tucked the rental car into a barely legal scrap of a space near Georgetown University and led her little expedition the rest of the way on foot, as all Georgetown expeditions ultimately traveled.

Although Penfield had personally invited Lacey and told her to bring her mother and her sister along to the small gathering at the home of Yvette and Brad Powers, the female half of the couple seemed less than thrilled when they arrived en masse at the front door. Lacey was prepared to flash Penfield's card, but Yvette rose to the occasion and graciously ushered them into the front hall of her Georgetown manse on P Street Northwest.

"Lovely of you to join us," Yvette said. "Please go on into the theater, and there are some refreshments set up in the parlors. Find a waiter if you need anything. Do have some champagne, and we'll be seeing Tate's film in"—checking the wall clock—"oh, a few minutes or so."

Brad swept up behind Yvette and put a protective hand on her shoulder. He acted as if the ugly little scene behind the scenes had never happened. "Tate said you'd be joining us tonight. He's been wanting a fresh perspective on his work." He forced a bland smile and stared at them until Yvette cleared her throat. Lacey did not care for his emotionless blue-eyed gaze, which was as cold as his wife's.

The Powerses scurried off to attend to more important people coming through the door. Though left in the lurch, the Smithsonians, one and all, found the house to be its own ample form of entertainment. Her mother and sister were thrilled to be part of this particular event, partly because they assumed the murderer might be here, though they hadn't a clue as to who it was. Even better was being able to ogle the inside of a beautiful Georgetown home, an unexpected treat. The whole weekend was turning into a giant scavenger hunt for them. As a bonus, her mother hadn't mentioned the new-car-for-poor-Lacey problem all day. Lacey was perfectly content to let Rose and Cherise enjoy their own version of events. And the killer would be there in Penfield's footage, Lacey was sure. *Somewhere.*

On their circuitous way to the living room, Rose forged ahead, determined to take in the decor of the ultra-well-to-do. She even poked her head into the kitchen past the catering help and the solicitous waiters, followed by Cherise, who was happily on the hunt for the lifestyles of the rich and famous, and Lacey, who longed to be inconspicuous in the crowd. Cherise jabbed Lacey in the ribs and loudly whispered, "Would you look at that! They have locks on all the kitchen cabinets and drawers! What is up with that?"

"The rich are definitely different. Come on." Lacey prodded her mother and dragged her sister out of the kitchen.

"But we haven't seen everything," Cherise complained, craning her neck to look up the oak staircase, which was richly carpeted with an Oriental rug.

"We have to behave, Cherise, and all the good seats will be taken," Lacey said. She guided them back through the living room, the dining room, the parlor with the piano, and another parlor without a piano, into the home theater, splendid in black velvet drapes, vintage movie posters, and deeply cushioned chairs. The very idea of a home theater silenced Rose and Cherise. They were agog at the opulence and indulgence of it all. Lacey, meanwhile, was interested in all the folks who got to sit in the good seats. She was glad she and her family had changed into slacks and sweaters for the event. Lacey had assured her mother and sister their wardrobes would be okay, though she told her mother to keep the scarf and gave her sister a pearl necklace for that preppy look. She noticed Cherise fingering it happily as they took their seats. Pearls were in abundance.

Cordelia Westgate earned a place of honor as the one name model, though slightly less than super now, who had shown up. She looked right through Lacey. Zoe, who seemed fatigued, was in the center seat. Hansen, who must have gotten a ride in with Penfield, also snagged one of the deep, cushioned chairs, as did, of course, the host and hostess. The Smithsonians sat on extra folding chairs that had been set up for the less important. The crowd seemed somewhat subdued, even for old-money Georgetown. All had earlier been at the memorial service, which was more like an endless infomercial than a remembrance of a beloved friend and colleague. And now this. It had been a long day.

Penfield appeared refreshed. He seemed to have caught a second wind, now that he was in the final stretch of his project. "It's still rough, and there is a lot of editing to do," he explained, "but I just wanted to share this much with you, as my tribute to our own dear Amanda." The cut they would see had no credits, no musical score, little narration, and the final scenes were still to come, but Penfield welcomed their comments on this work in progress. "And now without further ado," he said, and he started the video on the enormous plasma-screen television.

If Penfield had really captured months of Amanda's private moments and the reactions of the people around her, Lacey presumed, there had to be something there for her to see. There would be a telling moment, a revealing look, a comment that took on a new meaning with Amanda's death. And even if there were no clues, perhaps the film would supply some closure for her. Amanda had laid her burden on Lacey's shoulders, and Lacey had not taken it seriously. She was working out her penance for that. There was nothing she could have done to save her, she told herself one more time, but it wasn't helping much. *I could have believed her,* she thought. *Everybody wants to be believed.*

As Penfield said, the film was a little rough, yet his handheld, intimate journalistic approach made it feel surprisingly personal. The first photo montage introduced a riveting time-lapse sequence

of the changing faces of Amanda Manville, from a round-faced
baby who looked like any other baby, to a cute, if rather strange-
looking child, to a gawky, geeky teenager whose features seemed
to be going through a Cubist period, to a homely young woman
with a sparkle in her eyes, and finally to the amazing beauty she
became. This last face cycled through its own set of changes, as
Amanda evolved from the *Chrysalis Factor* makeover darling into
the dazzling cover girl and runway sensation, a supermodel face
with an endless variety of looks, from sporty girl next door to sultry seductress. Amanda's many faces segued into interviews with
friends, relatives, models, designers, fellow *Chrysalis Factor* par-
ticipants, and her surgeons, among them Dr. Greg Spaulding, all
intercut with Amanda in action on fashion-show runways and in
photo shoots and interviews, both with Penfield and with the print
and broadcast media.

Seamlessly following a segment from *Entertainment Tonight*,
Lacey was shocked to see herself interviewing Amanda at their
first meeting at Snazzy Jane's on Tuesday morning. She hadn't realized Penfield had videotaped the entire exchange—and he
hadn't asked her for a photo release. His skillful editing captured
the screaming-bitch act Lacey had witnessed. She saw herself trying to reason with Amanda, then reluctantly agreeing to follow up
if anything should happen. Confusion and disbelief showed on
Lacey's face on screen, which she could now feel burning. *Thank
God the lights are out.*

Cherise poked her in the ribs. Her mother stage-whispered,
"Lacey, it's you, dear!" Several people turned around to stare. *Why
did I bring them here?* Lacey lamented. *I should have my head examined.*

Amanda's episodes of *The Chrysalis Factor* flashed by, with
quick behind-the-scenes takes of Amanda with her homely fiancé,
Caleb Collingwood, followed by the new Amanda with her new
love, Dr. Spaulding. Lacey thought she saw something in one clip
of Caleb in an unguarded moment, an off-center reaction, an odd
look, but she couldn't put her finger on it. *He was pretty odd-
looking anyway. And wait a minute! What on earth is he wearing?*
It nagged at her, but the clip was too brief; she couldn't quite catch
what was odd about it. She would need to see the entire TV
episode again. If Penfield had taken his clips from the originals, he
must have the complete episodes on videotape at his studio. But
she would have to watch them tonight, with everyone partying
here in Georgetown and not looking over Lacey's shoulder. *And*

I'll be able to fast-forward to the clip I need to see, she thought, *without the Snoop Sisters at my back—if I can just get them to stay put here.*

She told herself to pay attention. On screen she saw Amanda with her lovely sister, Zoe, Amanda swathed in bandages, and then the new Amanda revealed in all her glory. There was no narration to make the point, but the editing clearly compared Amanda's emergence with the emergence of the Chrysalis Collection. There were shots of Zoe and Yvette hanging up the first dresses in the collection, giggling while Amanda dictated where things should go, Brad Powers predicting success, toasting them with a glass of champagne at the premiere showing of the collection at Snazzy Jane's. A slightly disjointed sequence covered Amanda's final photo shoot at Dupont Circle, including candid footage from the photo setup and the hair and makeup prep, presumably shot by Hansen. Lacey was surprised to see Stella sticking her tongue out for the camera while blowing out Amanda's hair. Penfield's editing of Hansen's footage seemed rougher here, Lacey thought, more rushed, less polished; these must have been the segments he was working on right up to the last minute. There were a few of Hansen's chilling, blurred stills from the shooting itself. Lacey felt her face flush and her heart race. In the aftermath Penfield got an evasive comment from Detective Steven Rogers and a few blunt words from Broadway Lamont. He even had an interview with Damon Newhouse of DeadFed dot com: Local reporter Lacey Smithsonian was "a magnet for trouble," he said, but she was "committed to the truth, no matter the consequences." Lacey squirmed in her seat.

Finally a quick montage of the memorial service at the Bentley Museum led to a closing shot of beautiful doomed Amanda, pulled out of chronological sequence, perhaps from the *Chrysalis Factor*'s "big reveal" episode. Surrounded by mirrors, she repeated over and over, "It's what I've always wanted. . . ." The screen went black.

Following a few moments of silence, the applause started and people began to chatter in relief. Lacey overheard snatches of animated conversation all around. "Of course the collection will continue; it simply must. . . ." "Brilliant piece of work . . ." "My God, she was beautiful. . . ." "What a loss . . ." "So if it wasn't Spaulding, who was it?"

The lights came on. A number of people were wiping away tears, and Zoe was openly sobbing. Yvette looked drained but composed, and Brad, as usual, seemed angry about something. Tate Penfield was basking in the spotlight in his role as filmmaker. Women crowded around him, including the comely Cordelia. They made a stunning couple. Still, he caught Lacey's eye and winked at her. She waved and edged out of the room to find Hansen at the buffet table, chatting with her sister and mother. They were enjoying the Brie and pâté and other delicacies, for which Lacey had no stomach. She pulled her lanky photographer friend aside and asked if she could borrow the keys to his and Penfield's studio. She told him she had left her notebook there earlier and needed to pick it up, and without it she couldn't finish her story for Mac tomorrow morning.

It was a transparent lie, she hadn't even had a notebook with her at the time, but he didn't seem to notice. Hansen was such a mellow live-and-let-live kind of guy, he didn't find the request odd. Lacey suspected that if she told him she was going to throw an all-night rave party in his studio he'd simply tell her to "party on, dude." He dug into his pocket and handed over the keys, detaching a small ring from a larger one.

"I'll get them back to you tomorrow," she said.

"Hey, what's going on?" Cherise said.

"Nothing, I've got to go and pick something up at Hansen's studio. Won't take a minute," she lied. "I'll swing back to pick you and Mom up later."

Rose Smithsonian overheard and stepped between them. "You aren't going anywhere alone, Lacey Blaine Smithsonian; haven't we made that clear?" *Oh, no, the middle name again.*

"Yes, but you two are having such a good time; you haven't seen the rest of the house, and you've hardly had a bite to eat—"

"Eating canapés hardly trumps my daughter putting herself in danger. I didn't raise you like that." Her mother smiled. "Lacey, honey, face it, you are not getting rid of me until you take me to the airport and wave good-bye at the gate." Rose picked up an hors d'oeuvre for the road. "You've got something, don't you? Something on the murder?" she said under her breath.

"Maybe," was all she'd admit. "Cherise?"

"I'm coming too." She sulked at the idea of leaving the party, but then she brightened. "Is what that Damon guy said about you true?"

"Not a word. He's an Internet reporter. On the Web, it doesn't have to be true. Makes the job so much easier." Lacey rounded up their jackets and herded them quietly out of the Powers mansion.

No one urged them to stay or even came over to say good-bye, though Hansen waved from across the room. Cordelia was draped over Penfield, and he and Brad and Yvette Powers were in an intense discussion with another very Georgetown-looking couple. Penfield looked over at Lacey, then smiled and shrugged as if to say, *I'm all tied up,* which was perfectly fine with her.

Lacey drove east across the District again to the warehouse area out New York Avenue Northeast, where Hansen and Penfield shared studio space. The area had looked a little desolate in the late-afternoon light; after dark it looked positively creepy. She turned off New York onto the deserted side street full of grimy old brick warehouses covered with gang graffiti. Everything seemed calm, but Lacey's nerves were on edge.

"This dump again?" Cherise wanted to know. "We left cozy little Georgetown for this? This place is the pits. It's like how Lower Downtown Denver used to look a million years ago." Rose turned around from the front seat and flashed her younger daughter a meaningful look. "I mean, couldn't we just look for the killer during the day, when it isn't so spooky?"

"I have to find a videotape of that original episode of the makeover show that Amanda was on, *The Chrysalis Factor.* I noticed something in one of the clips tonight; I'm not sure what. There's a copy of it here at the photo studio. At least there should be, because Penfield used footage from it in his documentary," Lacey said. "And we're not looking for the killer. If I find anything, I'm calling the police detective I've been talking to. You saw him in the film. The really big one."

"You didn't tell us about the big detective," Rose said. Lacey knew that now she was getting the "mom look," but she kept her eyes on the road.

"I would have gotten the police involved last time I had a, ah, a confrontation, but they weren't around. This is just a little reconnaissance mission tonight, okay?"

"Who do you think did it, Lacey?" Cherise prodded, wanting at least an interesting story out of the evening.

"I have to watch the videotape," she said evasively. "But I want to hear what you two think. Any ideas on who the murderer is?"

Her mother leaned forward in the backseat and uttered a sigh. "That was a lovely home, but my money's on Yvette. She's as cool as a cucumber. I think she could do it without mussing her hair. Did you see how organized her kitchen was? And with company coming! And caterers running around everywhere."

"But could she drive my car and gun down Amanda at the same time?" Lacey asked.

"Her husband could have driven while she pulled the trigger," Cherise offered. "Or vice versa."

"They said they were having drinks with Zoe at the time," Lacey said.

"Well, duh, they could all be lying."

"What about that Zoe?" Rose asked.

"Her own sister?" Cherise was aghast.

"Cain and Abel," Rose said.

"Yeah, but Amanda was Cain, not Abel," Lacey said. "Wasn't she?"

"Okay, maybe Zoe was in on it too, only later she regretted it," Cherise chimed in, "and now it's, like, eating her up, in spite of Amanda being a holy terror? She's, you know, *torn.*"

"Very nice, Cherise, I like it," Rose said. "What do you think, Lacey?"

"The Powerses are icy characters, and Zoe does seem torn. But they only want to sell clothes. Whoever did this involved me on purpose. What for?"

"Do you think your father would like a red dining room? Like the one at the Powers home?" Rose mused, much more interested in decor than death. "I had hoped that we would discover the killer at that lovely Georgetown home, rather than in some dump of an industrial zone. But we will endure, dear." She patted Lacey on the shoulder. "A red room." She sighed.

Lacey was silent as she pulled the icky little Echo into the empty lot at the warehouse and parked under one lone light.

"Good grief, Lacey. Couldn't we have waited till tomorrow?" Cherise was moaning. "And that Hansen of yours is so cute. He is single, isn't he? Why didn't he come with us?"

"Don't you have a boyfriend back home? That wreck of a football hero?"

Her sister ignored her. "I've never been in a house like that before. I mean, a dark red room? How cool is that? Two parlors? Hot and cold running waiters? It's so cool."

"Black marble bathroom fixtures with gold faucets. Can you imagine?" Rose said. "And we didn't even get to see the upstairs."

"You guys didn't have to tag along with me, you know. You could have stayed. Maybe Yvette would show you her closets, and her wine cellar, and the butler's pantry—"

"You're the murder expert," Rose said.

"Murder expert!" Lacey choked. "I'm not—"

"I'm sure we are doing something more important here." Her mother got out of the car first as Lacey locked up. "You would actually come out here to this dismal place alone at this hour of the night? Tell me you would have called that nice Vic Donovan for help if we weren't here."

"I would have called Vic." *Of course, that would be difficult. He's a little hard to reach right now, between Homeland Security and man-eating Montana.* The thought of Montana gave her an uncomfortable pang in the heart, but she concentrated on the task at hand. *But maybe Turtledove? Maybe I can ask him to watch over me. Again.* Lacey checked to make sure that her cell phone was in her jacket pocket. She had coded Turtledove's number into speed dial, just in case. But it wasn't there. She remembered she'd left it plugged in at home again, charging the dead battery. *Damn.*

"Well, that's good." Rose seemed slightly mollified. "You know, you could always move back home to Denver, where it's safe."

"We'd be at each other's throats."

"No, no, no, you could live with your sister."

"Hand-to-hand combat, instead."

"Come on, it would be fun, Lace." Cherise thought everything sounded fun. "We could be hot-chick crime fighters together. We could write the book on it."

"I can see it now," Lacey said. *"Jumping Tiger, Kicking Dragon: The Cheerleader's Guide to Martial Arts."*

"Was that a smart remark, big sister? 'Cause it sounded like a smart remark to me."

"A smart remark? *Moi?*" Lacey said. "Why, I never."

chapter 29

Lacey fumbled with Hansen's keys and unlocked the warehouse door. Rose and Cherise marched into the studio's reception area, with Lacey bringing up the rear. She flipped on a switch. The fluorescent light buzzed unpleasantly and made them all look a little green. A small office lay behind the postage stamp of a reception area, which featured both an electric heater and a fan, indicating that it was always either too hot or too cold. Lacey figured that when all the studio lights were on it would get quite hot, but the cinder-block walls made it chilly this evening. Despite her leather jacket, she shivered.

Outfitted in the cheapest of put-it-together-yourself furniture, a desk, bookshelves, plastic filing cabinets full of files, and some folding chairs, the reception room was functional, but not at all inviting. It was an unpleasant contrast to the luxurious Powers home they had just left.

A side door led to the studio, which was long and narrow, with a makeup area up front, a curtained changing area, and the actual shooting stage at the back. She glanced briefly into the room: Open shelves full of props and equipment lined the walls. In the center of the room tripods, lights, and reflectors were set up, probably for Monday morning's first customers: actors, no doubt, in need of flattering head shots. Cameras waited on their tripods, a digital Nikon, thirty-five-millimeter SLRs, several video cameras, a Hasselblad, a big, old-fashioned Linhof view camera. A gray paint-spattered backdrop covered the back wall, behind stools and director's chairs facing the cameras. Nearby, other backdrops were folded, black and white and blue ones, and others in various shades and textures.

Her mother and Cherise watched Lacey as she quickly scanned the shelves. The props consisted mostly of sports equipment: baseball bats and tennis rackets, balls and caps. There was also a cache of toys for children, something colorful that would help them smile for those priceless photographs for Grandma and Grandpa.

"Just think, Mom," Cherise said, "maybe we'll solve Amanda's murder here, all of us together. Cool, huh?"

"That's asking a lot for one weekend," Rose said drily. "But nothing is impossible."

Ignoring their banter, Lacey decided she didn't see what she was looking for in the photo studio, so they all retreated to the reception area with its office and the tiny restrooms. The office was locked, but the key was on Hansen's key ring. They must share it, Lacey thought. One wall was covered with tear sheets from *The Eye* of Hansen's own work, plus some enlargements of head shots of local actors Lacey recognized.

Although it was small, it was more comfortable than the reception area. It had an ugly gray sofa, the unimaginative color of choice in so many Washington establishments, a brown-striped cushioned chair, and two old wooden desks, all facing four or five TV sets and a bookshelf full of videotapes and DVDs showcasing Penfield's work. One desk was set up as a makeshift video-editing studio: an Apple computer, two monitors, speakers, headphones, remotes, and a stack of DVD, VHS, and Beta SP decks for editing and copying his documentary footage. Lacey knew this had to be where he'd put together Amanda's film.

"Just sit down for a minute, I'm looking for . . ." Lacey ran her fingers along the bookshelf until she laid her hands on what she was seeking.

"What?" Cherise sounded anxious.

"*The Chrysalis Factor*, the original episodes with Amanda Manville, before the makeover." Lacey turned on the biggest television set, fiddled with some buttons, found the right remote control, and popped the videotape into the VCR.

"Lacey, dear," her mother said, "you have not given us the background we need if we're going to help you solve this mystery."

"Let's just watch the show, and if I see what I'm looking for, you'll be the first to know. Besides, you'll like it; you'll get to meet Amanda again the way she was, the original, un-made-over Amanda."

"I don't think I should tell your father about our new red dining room."

"You know, Mom," Cherise said, "he's going fishing with the guys next weekend."

"That's brilliant, Cherise! I'll have it done by the time he gets back."

"Well, I, for one, am glad I haven't left you alone in my apartment," Lacey said. "Next week you'll be back in Denver, safe and sound, and you can paint the whole house fire-engine red. For that matter you can paint Dad fire-engine red too, if he'll hold still long enough." *And leave my apartment alone!*

"Not the whole house, dear, just the dining room. And not a fire-engine red. I was thinking of that nice deep red we saw at the house in Georgetown. Cranberry, or ruby. But maybe I could paint our bedroom navy? For a nice contrast." Rose settled into the gray sofa, folded her arms against the chilly air, leaned her head against the back of the sofa, and closed her eyes. "Something to show my bridge club."

Lacey turned on the videotape. She also switched on a small space heater she found under the desk to warm up the room. She closed the office door to keep the heat in.

"But what are you looking for that just has to be done tonight?" Cherise asked.

"Simple, a clue. A fashion clue. After all, that's my job. I saw something that someone wore in Penfield's documentary, but I can't be sure of what it was until I watch the tape. And we're watching it here tonight because I don't want to steal it and have someone miss it. And all the other interested parties whom I'd rather not run into are partying in Georgetown, out of our hair. And while we're talking about killers: Remember, we don't have to catch him. We have cops for that. I only have to uncover him. Or her."

"Her? You think it's a her?" Cherise was incredulous. "Yipes, I knew it was Yvette! Or Zoe! You'll tell me when you see whatever it is you're looking for, okay?"

The addictive little melodrama of Amanda's makeover journey finally started and stilled the chatter. It seemed to Lacey that Rose and Cherise should have had quite enough of Amanda by now, but they were riveted. And the first shot of Amanda before the surgery was startling.

"I don't need to be beautiful; I just want to look normal," were Amanda's first words for the cameras on *The Chrysalis Factor,* nearly four years before. Lacey had forgotten how gawky the bird-like girl nicknamed Ostrich had seemed, and yet, how charming, especially by contrast with the screaming diva she became. Even her vocal quality was warmer than the screech she had somehow attained at the height of her fame. But Lacey was looking for the interviews with Amanda's friends and relatives. She fast-forwarded, to yelps of dismay from Rose and Cherise, who wanted to savor every minute.

"Slow down! That is not the same woman," Cherise said, squinting at the screen. "No way." The younger Zoe had also arrived on screen with something of a shock. "That can't be Zoe Manville!" Cherise hooted. "I mean, it sort of looks like her, but I don't know; the Zoe we saw today would make two of her."

"It's her," Lacey said. "I think Amanda fattened her up in revenge."

They all listened intently as young Zoe spoke, not quite convincingly, about how hard it was to be "the pretty sister." "Oh, my God! She was a cheerleader too," a horrified Cherise protested. "What happened to her?"

"She broke the cheerleader's fit-for-life oath. They can't all be you, Cherise," Lacey said, returning her attention to the video. The interview with Caleb Collingwood, Amanda's boyfriend, came next as they sat side by side on the ugly sofa. This was the clip that Penfield's documentary had reduced to a quick flash of Caleb giving Amanda that odd look, a look that seen in full now seemed to say, "Please don't let the woman I love slip away from me." And then there it was in plain sight, Lacey's "fashion clue" to the killer's identity. She was stunned. She had to remember to breathe as she watched. She grabbed the remote and froze the frame for a long moment.

Caleb was wearing a heavy fisherman's knit sweater that Amanda had made for him in ivory wool. It looked brand-new. She had even cable-stitched their initials, A. M. and C. C., down the sleeves, entwined together in an intricate pattern, the same pattern Amanda had crocheted on the sleeves of the abandoned wedding dress Zoe had shown Lacey. It made the sweater unique. Caleb proudly showed it off for the camera and gave Amanda a kiss on the forehead. Together they spoke of their wedding plans and their lives ahead of them. The pre-*Chrysalis* Amanda had loved to knit; Zoe had shown Lacey some of her work. And the post-*Chrysalis* Amanda went ballistic when she saw the shabby old sweater that Tate Penfield claimed to love, his "sentimental favorite," Lacey remembered. *There it is: It is the same sweater.*

The scene switched to Dr. Greg Spaulding, who discussed what could be done about Amanda's looks. "Do I feel like Pygmalion?" he said. "A bit. But this is all about giving a young woman the normal life she wants."

"A normal life was the last thing she got," Lacey said aloud.

"Hush, we're watching." Cherise turned the volume up.

"Turn it off," Lacey said. "We can go now. Gotta call Broadway, bug him with this fashion clue. Come on."

"No!" Cherise cried. "I never saw this bit."

Rose put her foot down. "Lacey, dear, you simply can't keep interrupting us. We need to see all the clues. You may think you have what you need, but we want to see the whole show. I want to see how it ends."

"We know how it ends!"

"Yes, sadly, we do. But Cherise and I want to see the transformation, step by step. I never saw this the first time it was on TV. It was on opposite one of your father's bass fishing shows or something." Her mother returned her attention to Amanda. Cherise nodded and put her finger to her mouth to shush all the talk. They were engrossed; there was no moving them now.

Lacey sighed deeply. *Next thing they'll want to order a pizza and watch Penfield's entire videotape collection.* She stood up and walked softly to the door into the reception area. "Okay. Five minutes. I'll just go make sure I locked the front door." Rose and Cherise waved her on without looking up. She closed the office door behind her.

Lacey could see the front door was shut, but before she even tried the knob she had a sinking feeling she wasn't alone in the warehouse. She heard a sound from the photo studio. *It's nothing, he can't be here, he was busy being lionized by the Georgetown crowd.* She stepped through the studio door, hoping she was wrong. Her heartbeat sped up and told her she was right.

"Hello, Lacey. Alone at last."

No, she told herself and turned at his voice. He was standing in the shadows between the cameras and the backdrop.

"Hello, Tate," she said quietly. "Or should I say Caleb?"

chapter 30

"Caleb Collingwood is dead," he replied. "Hadn't you heard? Amanda Manville killed him."

Tate Penfield reached into his camera bag and pulled out the old, and now quite worn, fisherman's knit sweater that Lacey had admired when she first met him. The one she had just seen Caleb Collingwood proudly show off on videotape, his gift from Amanda. The one he'd worn to tatters. Lacey was right: It was the same sweater. Her stomach flipped, right on cue.

"I had heard that," Lacey said. "I even read it on the Web, so it must be true. But nobody seemed to know for sure how Caleb died or where he was buried, so I never quite bought it one hundred percent. Corpus delicti, and all that."

Penfield lovingly stroked the sweater. "That's what I like about you. You just keep going for it. DeadFed was right."

"When I left the party, you were surrounded by admirers," Lacey said, hoping her voice didn't quaver. She took a breath. "I thought you'd be busy all night."

"Yes, but I saw you chat with Hansen and then leave. As soon as I could shake off the groupies, I asked him where you went, made my excuses to the crowd, and here I am."

"How did you get here so fast?"

"Shortcut. I've been all over the District ever since college. You probably came up New York Avenue, right? That traffic's a killer."

"Why did you follow me here?"

"I wanted to see you figure it out." Penfield's smile lit up his beautiful face. "When Hansen told me you were coming here, everything was clicking into place. Just as I hoped. Even a day or two early."

"You've been baiting me. Why?" There was no answer. "I don't get it. No one would ever have known you were Caleb."

"They will now." Tate seemed pleased that she had unmasked him, and Lacey couldn't imagine why.

"How?"

"You'll tell them."

"Right." *If I get out of here alive, yes, I sure as hell will.* "Amanda knew who you were all along. That's why she was angry about you wearing that 'ratty old sweater.'"

"But you said you liked it," he said. "And that really pleased me."

"You said it was a sentimental favorite."

Penfield laughed and slipped the sweater over his head, stretching his arms through the frayed sleeves with their interconnected initials of C. C. and A. M. As tattered as it was, it looked richly textured over his black turtleneck sweater. He stepped toward her into the light so she could admire it.

Was it some kind of talisman, a good-luck charm? Lacey couldn't take her eyes off him. He didn't seem to have a weapon. He didn't act threatening. She told herself to bide her time, wait for the right moment.

He drew a deep breath and said, "That's better. It's always cold in here. Well, except when it's hot. Mandy made this for me as an engagement present, you know."

Lacey tried to imagine Caleb Collingwood's awkward face above the sweater instead of Penfield's beautiful one, but it was nearly impossible. "Plastic surgery?"

"Oh, yes, every bit as extensive as Amanda's. Different surgeons, though. Painful, ridiculous. The funny thing is, I never thought I was so ugly, until that night when I read it in her eyes."

She stared at him intently. "So I suppose you dye your hair and wear brown lenses to cover your hazel eyes."

"It's very Hollywood." He smiled. "The contacts are not prescription, though." With his index finger he flipped them out of his eyes, one by one. It was fascinating to watch part of Caleb emerge, although his eyes looked pale and strangely intense. *Could they mesmerize?* she wondered. *What the hell am I doing here, and how am I going to get out of this mess?*

"I'd better go, Tate."

He reached out his hand toward her, but she backed away. "I'm not going to hurt you, Lacey. Honest. I want you to help me. I need your help."

Icicles were crawling up her back. She knew she couldn't trust anything he said. She had been in the same room with killers before, and she knew what it felt like. *It feels like this!* She started scanning the shadows and the shelves for something, anything, to use in self-defense. Something that wouldn't involve blades, she hoped. She thought of her mother, who had suggested she switch to baseball bats. There were baseball bats on the prop shelves. She eyed the nearest one; it wasn't quite near enough. But at the moment, she decided, she needed to keep him talking. *Still thinking about the damn story, Lacey? Think about your life!*

"Why did you come here tonight?" she asked.

"The same reason you came, Lacey. For the story, of course. The documentary on Amanda isn't finished, and you are playing a major part in it. It's going to have a big climax."

You can't win an argument with a crazy person, someone once told her. "Why did you kill Amanda? Was it for your film?"

He laughed again. His manner seemed so warm and unthreatening that she was surprised to find he had reached out and put his arm around her shoulder before she could retreat. She flinched and stepped away, but he didn't seem to notice.

"Of course not. The film is just a way to . . . well, tell the story. That's what filmmaking is for, right? No, Amanda had to die because she was a monster. She turned me into a monster too. Bought and paid for the man you see before you."

"Amanda paid for your surgery?"

"Maybe you should sit down, Lacey."

"I'll stand, thanks."

"It's a very simple tale," Penfield said. "Caleb loved Mandy. People said she was plain, but she had a beautiful spirit, and Caleb found comfort there." He closed his eyes and remembered a moment. "To me she was always beautiful."

Funny how they always say that, Lacey thought. Everyone who sent their wives or girlfriends off to *The Chrysalis Factor* said, "I always thought she was beautiful."

"Amanda Manville came back to Caleb Collingwood a goddess. And a monster," Penfield continued. He reached out gently for Lacey's hand and moved her toward the cameras, indicating that she should take one of the dark-blue director's chairs that were placed opposite each other. His hands pressed down firmly on her shoulders, directing her down into the seat; then he took the other chair. Lacey must have looked like she was ready to bolt. He sighed. "Look, you can leave if you want, I won't stop you, but this is where I tell you what happened and why I did it. You do want to know, don't you? That's what any reporter would want, right? The rest of the story?"

It was pathetic, because it was true. But she didn't believe the part about letting her go. Lacey had to swallow and clear her throat before speaking. "Yes, of course I do, Tate. But do I call you Tate or Caleb?"

"You can call me Tate, because I've been a monster for so long. I'm used to it. Caleb was a goofy kid, a little gawky, but he was never a monster."

A little like Ichabod Crane, Lacey thought. But something dark must have lurked below the surface to make him change, slowly and surely. Did it begin with the first incision, or even before? Perhaps it started when Mandy Manville was first selected for the doomed honor of plastic surgery on national TV.

Lacey tried to control her breathing and remain calm. She angled her chair so she could keep an eye on the office door, behind which her mother and sister were still watching the video. "All right, Tate, tell me your story. And if I feel like leaving, I'm going to leave. Got it?"

"Fair enough."

He stood up, switched on a bright studio light, and adjusted it to bathe Lacey in a warm glow. He smoothed Lacey's hair back. She tried not to recoil under his touch. Her stomach was doing flip-flops, as if she were on the top of the high dive and was expected to do a double somersault, something she'd never actually achieved in swimming class. Whatever his game was, Lacey figured he could change the rules at any minute. After all, he had at least two identities and was capable of killing. *At least of killing Amanda; perhaps it's not such an exclusive club.* She told herself to be aware of every movement he made, every twitch indicating a sudden mood swing. Penfield had maintained his cool so far, but she couldn't believe this whole scene was meant to end with a cheery wave good-bye.

After switching on music with a remote control, Tate sat down again. The achingly sad and sweet notes of Ravel's "Pavane for a Dead Princess" filled the air.

"When I saw Amanda for the first time after the surgery, she looked unreal. Did you know that it cost almost a quarter of a million dollars to turn her into that bizarre creature? How many operations for Spaulding's poor third-world children would that pay for? But I digress. Amanda was a complete work of art and a complete piece of work." His voice was dispassionate. "Amanda turned and looked at me on national TV as if I had been swallowed up and turned into a frog. We both knew it was over. Although I have to admit she may have known it was over before then. And then she turned and ogled Spaulding, or should I say Dr. Franken-stein, with that indecent leer, which he returned. I realized that she'd already slept with him. And for the ultimate humiliation, of course, it all had to be on national television."

"It must have been really terrible for you," Lacey said, and meant it.

"I couldn't speak. But that insipid announcer filled in with something inane, like, 'Poor Caleb has been struck dumb by the sight of Amanda's beauty.' I felt as if my heart was trying to escape my body, strangling me. The tears you saw on TV were from rage, not happiness."

Lacey had no response. Under the Ravel, they both heard *The Chrysalis Factor* droning on softly in the closed office. Penfield cocked an eyebrow at her.

"My mother and my sister are watching it in the office."

"Really? A family affair." He mused over this fact. "Must be nice to have such a close family. You just take them everywhere with you, don't you?"

Against my will, she told herself. *Stay calm; wait for the right moment.* She shifted in her chair and noticed at least three video cameras that appeared to be taping the scene. "These cameras are on?"

"I turned them on when I got here."

Another photo ambush. Great.

"When did you decide to kill Amanda?"

"It's funny, that of all the questions I've asked myself, I can't answer that one. I don't really know when. Maybe it was after I'd allowed myself to be desecrated with plastic surgery. But at some point the idea just took hold."

"But you must have wanted the plastic surgery?"

"Amanda did. She talked me into it. She thought it would make up for everything, but of course it did not. Her mea culpa, her bank book. 'Here, be beautiful, be happy, have a nice life, now leave me alone.' Of course, I was at loose ends. I had no idea what to do with myself without her, so I agreed."

"Did you think she'd fall for you again?"

"It crossed my mind, but we'd gone too far for that."

"But look at you; you're gorgeous, talented, successful. You could have anything you want."

"That's what Amanda said." Penfield's look darkened. Lacey realized she had better not repeat anything that Amanda had said.

"You don't like being the handsome Tate Penfield?"

"The fellow in the mirror, you mean? It's still a bit of a shock to see someone else there. But I've gotten used to him."

She stared at his beautiful face, though it had lost some of its charm for her. "Women throw themselves at you."

"At him, the mirror man. Not me. It doesn't count. There was only one woman for me, and she left long ago."

"What about all the rumors that Caleb disappeared and she killed him?" Lacey wished she had her notebook. "What about all the murder theories on your old buddy Tyler's Web site?"

"She did kill him. That night in front of the world. I thought the least she could do was put up with a few little rumors. And I planted a lot of them myself with John Henry. Anonymously, of course." He smiled. "Amanda hated that, but I thought it was fun."

"What about Tyler? He cares about you. Was he part of your plan?"

"Not knowingly. I liked John Henry. But he's better off believing Caleb is dead. It's true, you know."

How easily Tate seemed to be able to compartmentalize things. Questions jumbled around in Lacey's mind. There should be a sensible order for them in the event she escaped from this nightmare intact and lived to write a story about it. "Why did you choose me? There are other reporters. With more important papers. Why not some hotshot from *The Washington Post*?"

"You're a hotshot. And this will make your career. I read about Lacey Smithsonian's escapades with killers on DeadFed dot com. I thought you would be up to the challenge."

"You didn't read my stories in *The Eye*?" She felt vaguely insulted.

"Oh, yeah, but they lacked that *je ne sais quoi,* that over-the-top abandon that DeadFed has. I am a country boy, after all. Where I'm from we always like a little sensationalism, a good tabloid story. Giant babies, green aliens, wolfman in my bathtub, that kind of thing. And it's got that wacky Washington angle we all dig here. Fun stuff."

Curse that stupid Web site! More proof that DeadFed is just for lunatics.

"DeadFed says there are two things you can't resist, Lacey Smithsonian: a good story and an invitation to trouble." His voice was taking on a slower cadence. *So is he Caleb again now? And which one is the dangerous one?*

"That sounds like another quote from Damon Newhouse. How flattering."

Penfield nodded, obviously pleased that she was being such a good audience for his story. But aside from his banter, she was worried about her mother and sister in the other room. No matter what he said about not wanting to hurt her, he was a liar and a killer. *And damn it all to hell,* she just realized, *he's a car thief too!*

"And another thing: Why did you have to steal my car?"

"To get your attention, of course. You tried so hard to dissuade Amanda from believing a killer was after her. And after I had so diligently planted all those clues and letters I couldn't let that happen. I was the one who told Amanda about you and how I thought you could help her."

"You set me up from the beginning. You set us both up. And she trusted you completely." Lacey realized Amanda's trust had made it so easy for him. Amanda's letter to her, the one she received after her death, even suggested that Lacey go to Penfield with questions.

"Oh, yes. I'd turned into her pet photographer, her little in-house cameraman. She was always comfortable with me, and she liked being the only one who knew my real identity. Our little secret. And then when you met her that day at Snazzy Jane's, she had to go and act like a complete psycho bitch. I could tell you thought she was a lunatic. So I had to make it personal. I already knew what kind of car you drove, because I dropped Hansen off at the paper that day and he pointed it out. He was surprised; he said you never drove it to work. Did you know I used to build fast cars for a living? When I realized I could take yours, it was a sign. It seemed that everything was going to work out, in spite of Amanda's lunacy."

"You used my car to commit a murder." She could feel her voice cracking with emotion, and her eyes teared up.

"Cars don't commit murders, Lacey. People do. Besides, if you're going to blame the weapon, blame the gun, not your car." He had the temerity to smirk. "It got your attention, didn't it? And really, Lacey, take it from a pro, that car needed so much work, you really are better off without it. Fun to drive though. Zoom, zoom."

"You bastard." He laughed, but she couldn't just sit there. She stood up, looking around for something to beat him with. Unfortunately, there was nothing to use as a club within arm's reach. She faced him. "Wait a minute. If you're Caleb Collingwood, who the hell is Tate Penfield? He graduated from a high school in West Virginia. He was shy. Said so on the Web. Is he alive? Did you steal his identity like you stole my car?"

"Sit down and I'll tell you." He waited for her to resume her seat. "Tate was pathologically shy among strangers. High school was hell for him, even though he was as attractive as all the girls said. To answer your question, yes, I did steal his identity, and he is dead."

"Did you . . . ?"

"Did I kill him? No. He hanged himself." Caleb shifted in his seat. "Tate Penfield was my first cousin on my mother's side. Closest thing to a brother I ever had. My handsome cousin. Ironically, this face looks quite a lot like his. So it is Tate Penfield I see in the mirror. We were the same height and weight. He was reclusive by nature. Had a rough childhood. And like me, no relatives left to speak of by the time we grew up."

Lacey was aware that Penfield's—or Caleb's—voice was now shifting into a West Virginia accent, sounding a lot like the younger man on the taped show that her mother and Cherise were still watching.

"Tate didn't associate much with other people, and he was considered an odd duck. But we were pretty close. His folks dropped him off at our house one day when he was just a kid, and they never came back. After we grew up, he lived alone up in the Blue Ridge in his folks' old cabin. He called me here one night to say good-bye, which was funny, because he never went anywhere. It was after Amanda dumped me and before my surgery. When I finally figured out that he might be talking about suicide, I jumped in the car and drove through the night to talk him out of it. I arrived just as the sun was coming up. He was hanging from the apple tree in the front yard. His body was still warm."

Questions would only stop the flow of Penfield's story, so Lacey kept quiet. Perhaps the deeper he got into it, the more he would forget about her. Her gut instinct, in spite of all the confessing-killer scenes she'd seen on TV and in the movies, was that if someone really wanted to kill you, they would just kill you, and not talk your ears off first.

"I cut my cousin down from that tree and I buried him back in the hills where no one will ever find him. That was what the note said he wanted. He wrote it on the back of a paper grocery bag and left it on the kitchen table under his coffee cup. He washed the dishes so there wouldn't be any unnecessary mess. I think a person's last wishes should be respected, don't you?"

She didn't really know what to answer, so she said nothing.

"After I buried him, I stayed another day or two. I chopped down that apple tree. It was heavy with the smell of rotting apples. I loved my cousin, but he had a side that no one could reach. He claimed he was of no use to the world because his family threw him away. But I saw how he could be useful to me. His Social Security number. His driver's license. We would even have some of the same DNA passed down through our mothers. I knew everyone he knew, and none of them would be expecting Tate Penfield to be very sociable. As I burned what remained of that tree, I decided to take Amanda up on her offer to change my life. It was very useful to have valid identification that no one would question. So I became Tate, and Tate came out of his shell." Penfield sighed. "Now, we were discussing the end of the story. I'll give you your cue, Lacey." He turned to check on a video camera.

She jumped from her seat and ran toward the door, but Penfield was quick; he closed the distance between them easily. He spun her around and grabbed her hands and pulled her back to the cameras. "No. It's not over yet. Listen to me: Don't be afraid; this is your Pulitzer prize, your ticket to the big time."

"Tate, just let me send my mother and my sister home."

"They're not in any danger. Tonight we'll finish this sad story. And it'll be your story, too. To tell the world." He steered her away from any avenue of escape. He didn't release her; he pushed her back down into her seat and held her wrists firmly in his hands.

What is he waiting for? Lacey wondered. She could always scream, but she would have to choose her moment carefully. And she would have to yell her lungs out to alert Cherise and Rose, glued to the TV, behind the office door.

"What do you want?" She was determined not to use the words *kill* and *me*. There was one thing that Lacey knew: She did not want her blood splashed garishly on any television screen, pandering to the prurient interest of the television audience, if not on the nightly news, then later on Court TV. In no case was that acceptable. Maybe she could grab a camera tripod and smash him over the head with it; she briefly wondered how much it weighed. She made a move. He blocked her, still holding her wrists tightly.

"You have it all wrong, Lacey."

"That would be nothing new, Tate."

He tightened his grip on her arms. "You seem to think I mean to do you some harm. I don't. Really, really, I don't," he crooned, is if to soothe her as one would soothe a crying baby.

"You're not?" *And that means Mom and Cherise are safe?*

"No. It's time to dispatch the monster. And that's not you. It's me. It's my turn to die."

"Oh, my God. You're not planning to commit suicide on camera?" *That's a mortal sin. But then, so is murder. I can't look.*

"No, no, no, that's not the scenario for the final scene. The scenario is this: You are going to kill me."

chapter 31

"No!" Lacey felt the air escape her lungs in that desperate denial. He released his hold and she jumped up and backed away from him. "No, no, no! I can't do that!"

"You have to," Penfield said. "Lacey, please."

"Please what? Kill you? What universe am I in?"

"I've tried and I can't."

He followed her until she reached the shelves, bumping her hip painfully against a sharp edge. "Oww. Back off, Tate."

"Careful, don't hurt yourself," he said, as if he cared. "Lacey, I can't pull the trigger. Amanda, yes, but I can't kill myself. The truth is, I'm a god-awful coward. I still remember how lonely it must have been for Tate. I can't forget cutting my cousin down from that tree."

"Take a pill! Anything, only don't do this to me."

"What I have done demands a blood sacrifice."

"Not from me! I'm not a judge, jury, or executioner." She tried to sidle down the wall toward the door.

"I'm a monster and I must die." There was a tone in his voice, a wildness in his hazel eyes that warned Lacey he was sliding into dangerous territory. She wasn't sure he was a monster, but certainly he was mad, she thought, and he could transform at any moment. After all, he'd already transformed once.

"You could turn yourself in. Virginia will execute you," she offered hopefully. "So will Texas," she added, wondering even as she said it what on earth Texas had to do with it.

"Unfortunately, the District of Columbia will not. Years on death row are not what I'm after. 'The man had killed the thing he loved, and so he had to die.'" Lacey recognized the quotation from Oscar Wilde's "The Ballad of Reading Gaol." He paused; he sounded quite rational. "I have left instructions on how to finish the documentary. It's all yours. Hansen will be able to help you. Should be a hot property after I'm dead." The music had stopped, and Penfield fell silent again. She was aware of the buzzing from the overhead fluorescent light. The television in the next room was blaring, "Go with Amanda now as she shops for the fairy-tale dress for her big reveal! Who is this vision of loveliness? And how will her fiancé, Caleb Collingwood, react when he sees the new Amanda . . . ?" *Good God,* Lacey thought, *are they watching the entire series?*

"I have only one regret, you know," Penfield said. "That bastard Spaulding did not die."

"It was you I saw in the hospital."

"The Grim Reaper. Yes. I always liked Halloween. I would have finished him off, if not for you. But that can't be helped. Other than that, your timing on this entire venture has been impeccable. And just so you know, I'm sorry I hurt you, Lacey. I was a little irritated with you at the time."

"If you planned it, how did you know I would be there when you shot Amanda?"

"I didn't. That was such a good omen. A sign that everything was going my way. Did you ever get a sign from above?"

Yeah. Mine said, HOT DOUGHNUTS NOW. "You don't have to do this, Tate. And you can't ask me to commit murder."

"I suppose you're right." He sighed; then he bared his teeth in an unnatural smile. "Well, then, there's always self-defense. Your specialty, right?" He yanked her back to the center of the room. "One way or another, this is my day to die. This is a cautionary tale. It needs a moral. The monster must die at the hands of the beautiful heroine."

"Are you crazy? You want me to kill you on camera so I can go to prison? That's your moral?" The illogic of it stunned her. "Turn off the damned cameras," she pleaded, hoping that he would turn his back on her just long enough.

"Live fast, die young, and I certainly don't care about leaving a beautiful corpse." She realized Penfield's stunning features were beginning to get on her nerves. "Nevertheless, the cameras must stay on. Don't worry, Lacey." He reached behind his back and pulled out a gun from the waistband of his jeans as she watched in horror. He offered it to her. "I have written a full confession, including how I coerced you. I figured it might come to this. Actually, it's a video confession. I'm not much of a writer."

"No! I'm leaving, Tate. And I'm taking my mother and sister

with me." She could hear *The Chrysalis Factor* winding down back in the office. She turned around and took a step before he grabbed her with one arm and with another thrust the weapon at her, butt first. It looked like a nine millimeter; she had fired Vic's, and she didn't like it.

"Take the gun," he growled at her.

"I'm not going to kill you, Tate." *As God is my witness.* "And I don't like automatics."

"Do it!"

"No!" She struggled to get away from him.

He took both her hands and pressed them around the gun. He looked her in the eyes and spoke very clearly. "I can kill you, Lacey, and your cozy little family, and commit 'suicide by cop.' A messier ending, but it works for me. We already know that I'm a murderer. You have no choice. So now it's either you or me." Something had switched on in Tate's face. He was serious.

Lacey told herself that she had not been clever enough; she had let her damned curiosity bring her to this point. She had wanted to get the rest of the story on Tate Penfield. *Well, be careful what you wish for.* Adrenaline pounded through her veins, and she realized she would have to do something she hated more than anything in the world. Something that went against every fiber of her being, everything she believed in and held sacred.

God help me. I'm going to have to ask my mother and sister for help. She was struggling with him, nose-to-chin. The gun was now over her head, pointing at the ceiling, and he was squeezing her hands, wedging her finger in the trigger guard. "You're hurting me!" she yelled into his face. Penfield pressed his finger over hers on the trigger—the pressure was painful; she felt the trigger move—and together they squeezed off a shot. The report reverberated in the cement-block studio, and the bullet nicked the fluorescent light and set it swinging. It surprised them both.

"Okay," he growled. "That was a start. Next time aim for my head." Penfield's face was gleaming with moisture.

"You're sick," Lacey said.

"Yes. Crazy, insane, depraved, vicious, vengeful. All of the above. You have to slay the beast. Come on, Lacey, you've been face-to-face with killers before. That's why I chose you. This part was made for you, damn it; now shoot!"

Lacey could feel a trickle of sweat drip down the middle of her back. And then she heard the familiar voices that always seemed to be there to witness her most humiliating moments.

"Lacey, what the hell are you doing?" It was Cherise, the perfect sister.

Her mother's voice chimed in, but Lacey couldn't take her eyes off Penfield. "Lacey Blaine Smithsonian, what in God's green earth is going on? I never—"

"No time. Help me. Hey! I need some help here!" Lacey felt Penfield turn his attention to the other women, his hands still imprisoning Lacey's around the grip of the gun.

"Welcome to my good-bye party, Mrs. S. and Cherise. Just to bring you up to speed, I'm a filthy murdering beast and Lacey is going to be a hero for killing me."

"Oh, my God," Cherise wailed. "Oh, my God."

"Perhaps you've got more guts than your sister, Cherise. Would you like to try?" He waved the gun at her, Lacey's struggling arms still attached to it.

"Stop harassing my daughters!" Lacey could see Rose out of the corner of her eye, but was pretty sure Penfield couldn't.

"Maybe you'd like to take a shot at me, Mrs. S."

"Maybe I would. Just maybe I would." Rose's mother-tiger instinct was rising.

Her arms aching, Lacey concentrated on keeping the gun from pointing at anyone, but with one eye she could just see her mother stride to the wall of props. Rose saw the golf clubs and selected a nine iron. Lacey knew her sister must be somewhere nearby as well.

"Hey, there, Lethal Feet," Lacey said, mentally urging her to get it. "Where are you?"

"Don't call me that." Cherise's voice quavered. "Oh, man, Lacey, what are we gonna—"

"Give me some of that Geronimo High spirit you're so famous for, Lethal Feet. Geronimo, remember?"

"I don't think I can," Cherise moaned.

"Don't think, do it," Lacey commanded her. "Give me a cheer!"

While Cherise squirmed in indecision and Lacey struggled with Penfield, Rose Smithsonian crept up behind them, hefting the nine iron. "Let go of my daughter, you bastard."

"Oh, I will, as soon as she does what we came here for." Penfield tightened his hold on Lacey's hands and swung her around for a better camera position. "Shoot, damn it," he commanded. He concentrated all his energy on Lacey, but he warned them, "If you interfere with this, Lacey could get hurt. She could die; you could all die!"

"Mom, what are you waiting for?" Lacey asked.

"I don't want to hurt him." Rose tightened her grip on the golf club and squared her feet in the correct LPGA position, assuming the golf ball was at shoulder level. Penfield swung Lacey around to put himself out of club reach.

"Hit him, Mom! He wants me to kill him!"

"Why, that's just insane." Lacey's mother squared her shoulders. "I can't believe this is the kind of person you've been getting involved with."

"Mom! Just do it!"

Rose stepped briskly around behind Penfield and smacked him directly across the back with the nine iron. It knocked the wind out of him, and with a grunt he let go of Lacey's hands.

The nine millimeter dropped from Lacey's now stiff and very cold fingers, and she kicked it across the floor, out of anyone's immediate reach. She took a few steps back, away from him, and felt the cold cement-block wall of the warehouse at her back. Penfield was staggering. Rose gave him another firm whack with the club, lower down, just at kidney level. He yowled in pain.

Penfield pivoted toward Rose and tore the nine iron from her hands with a low growl. He turned back and staggered toward Lacey, grinning maniacally, his breath ragged, the bent golf club waving menacingly in his hands. Cherise was clapping while jumping in place, counting out half-remembered moves from her old Geronimo High routine. As she had once promised Lacey, it was coming back to her.

"Gimme a G," Lacey yelled. "Gimme an E! Gimme an R! Gimme an O!" Cherise was back in the cheer zone now, but there were too many letters left. Penfield rocked woozily on his heels; he lifted the club. Lacey cut to the chase. "What's that spell? Geronimo! What's that spell?"

"Geronimo!" Cherise shouted with all her might. Penfield spun around to look at her. He leaned forward and shook his head to clear it. At the same moment Cherise delivered her stunning high kick to his jaw. Lacey had never seen her in such perfect cheerleader form. Cherise's new tan pump connected with Penfield's jaw at the very apex of her kick, knocking him out cold. He crumpled to the hard floor, and the nine iron went flying.

Cherise looked down at her handiwork, or rather footwork. Three Smithsonian women crowded around the fallen killer and spoke in unison.

"Geronimo."

chapter 32

"It's so nice to see you two working together on a project for a change," Rose said, as Lacey and Cherise busily trussed up Tate Penfield like a Thanksgiving turkey, using a roll of duct tape from his camera bag. They left him in a sitting position on the floor, leaning against the wall. He was still unconscious, but except for a cut lip, he seemed to be physically all right, as near as they could tell.

The sisters looked at each other and rolled their eyes. "Toss me the tape, Lethal Feet; you missed a spot," Lacey said. Cherise stuck her tongue out and threw her the tape.

Lacey finished double-taping his wrists and ankles just as he came to and started thrashing around, but the duct tape held. Penfield was conscious now, in pain and furious. He seemed to have completed the transformation that Lacey had feared. He wasn't Tate or Caleb anymore. His language was so vile that it took all of Rose's patience not to stop his bleeding mouth with another piece of duct tape. But when Lacey picked up the twisted nine iron and told him to shut up, he stopped talking and sulked.

"For the all-time record, game-winning high kick, Cherise, thank you," Lacey said. "Both of you."

"That's what families are for, dear." Her mother gave each daughter a quick hug. Penfield said a bad word, and Rose almost kicked him, but she stopped herself.

"Don't get close to him; he's tricky," Lacey cautioned them. "I need a phone. I left my stupid cell phone home."

"There's one in the office," her mother pointed out.

Lacey located Penfield's gun, where it had come to rest under a stool in the makeup area. Nobody seemed to need it at the moment, she thought, so she upended an empty wastebasket over it for safekeeping. She backed into the office carefully, keeping her eyes on Penfield, even though Rose stood sentry with the nine iron in her hands—and a new spring in her step. Lacey called the private D.C. police number that Detective Broadway Lamont had given her. It seemed well past the moment to call 911. Lamont was off duty, a dispatcher told her. Lacey started to explain the situation, but she realized it wouldn't be easy to put it into a sound bite for a bored police dispatcher. Would another detective do? she was asked. Did she want to transfer her call to 911?

"I want Broadway Lamont," she said. "Find him, page him, track him down, wake him up. He'll want to see this for himself. Tell him it's Lacey Smithsonian, and I have a killer for him." She gave the address and hung up. If that didn't get her Lamont, she decided, she'd have to call Agent Braddock at the FBI. Her next call was to Trujillo.

"Lacey? Hey, man, what's up?" He sounded groggy.

"Did I wake you up?"

"It's okay; my eyes are open now."

"You alone, Tony? I'd hate to interrupt anything."

Trujillo laughed. "I'm sure you're calling about something important, so I'm waiting already."

She took a breath. "I'm in Hansen's studio on New York Avenue."

"Yeah, I've driven him over there a couple times. He needs a new car. So?"

"We've got the guy who killed Amanda Manville."

"Dude! No way!"

"Way. The thing is, I know Mac won't let me write the news story. At least not without you. He's got this thing about objectivity, and I don't have any on this subject." The truth was that she felt torn. Penfield had seemed like such a good guy before he morphed into the hostile-makeover killer.

"I'll be there in twenty." Trujillo hung up. Back in the studio Lacey studied the elaborate video-camera setup Penfield had arranged to capture the final scene of his documentary. The cameras were still whirring softly. "I wonder how we turn these damn things off."

"Don't touch my cameras," Penfield ordered gruffly, but they ignored him. Lacey decided to let the tape run out on its own.

"And don't you ever call me Lethal Feet," Cherise said firmly, "unless you are in mortal danger. Again." She took a quiet moment to comb her hair and refresh her makeup.

"I'm very impressed, Sis. I wasn't sure you still had it in you."

Cherise tossed the comb at her sister's head, but Lacey neatly caught it. "You'll always be Lethal Feet to me."

"And what," her mother demanded, "about me?"

"That's a wicked swing you've got there, Mom."

"I've been practicing," she said proudly. "Wellshire Municipal Golf Course."

"I suppose you're mad at me for messing up your visit?" Lacey asked.

"Mad? Why would I be mad? You needed your mother. And I was there for you."

"*We* were there for you," Cherise chimed in.

"Do you suppose we'll be on that Web site of yours?" Rose's eyes twinkled. She was growing younger with her enthusiasm. "That'll give Mrs. Dorfendraper something to talk about!"

"Oh, I can practically guarantee it, Mom."

"It's been a wonderful trip, Lacey," Cherise said. "Of course, you kept all the cute guys for yourself."

"And I got to see how they decorate a house in Georgetown," her mother said. "Although I think a black bathroom is going a bit too far."

Cherise was staring at Penfield. His eyes were closed, but even tied up, disheveled, and clearly deranged, he looked like a sleeping god. "Are you sure this is Caleb Collingwood? That ugly guy who was in love with Amanda? I just don't see it."

The unlocked front door of the warehouse slammed open, and Lacey expected to see Tony Trujillo or the cops burst through it, but instead it was Hansen loping through the office into the photo studio.

"Smithsonian, you there? Sorry, I need my keys—" Hansen was going to say something else, but he was riveted by the sight of Penfield decked out in duct tape. He looked at Lacey and her mother and her sister.

"Whoa. This isn't some kind of weird sex thing, is it? 'Cause I could just leave—"

"Don't be ridiculous, Hansen," Lacey said.

"Please stay," Cherise said, training her big baby blues on the tall blond photographer, who melted a little bit under her gaze.

"Hansen!" Penfield roared to life. "Help me out of this, buddy! She's a lunatic on the loose, and so's her whole damned family. You gotta help me—"

Everyone started shouting at once. Lacey was afraid Rose was going to have to use the nine iron again, and she wasn't sure who would get it first this time.

Lacey looked up and saw Vic stampede through the door, dark curls flowing over his forehead and green eyes blazing, with a look somewhere between relief and fury. Trujillo appeared in the studio doorway behind him, looking as cool and collected as if he'd been planning this entrance all day.

Vic took in the room and saw only her. "Lacey." He closed the distance between them and held her in his arms.

"You two have met, I presume," Trujillo cracked.

"How did you find me?" Lacey asked Vic.

He brushed a piece of hair out of her face where it had fallen. "I couldn't get you on the phone." She thought of her cell phone, safely plugged into its charger where she left it. "So I called Slick here."

"Yeah, just try to get some sleep on a school night," Tony said. "He called right after you did."

"I followed him over here," Vic said. "Why didn't you call me?"

Her mother and sister and Hansen and Penfield were mercifully quiet, and Lacey temporarily forgot all about them. "I thought you'd be busy. With Montana." But the truth was that she didn't know how to explain the whole situation to him. And she knew he couldn't quite explain Montana to her. Maybe they both needed to clear the air.

He threw her a look that said he couldn't believe it, but he reached out and hugged her instead. "Okay, what's going on here?" He looked over at her mother and sister, and at Penfield trussed up on the floor. "I'm sure there's some kind of good explanation for this, or an interesting one, anyway."

Vic was waiting for an answer, but Hansen was confused. He made a move toward the duct-taped assassin, but Lacey blocked his path.

"Penfield killed Amanda," Lacey said. "He attacked Spaulding, twice. And me."

"Tate? Is that right, man?" Hansen asked. "What the hell—"

"The documentary. No matter what happens," Penfield said hoarsely, "you must finish it. Hansen, promise me." His voice was punctuated by sirens screaming through the nearby city streets and stopping at the warehouse. The group stood still. Penfield's head dropped as everyone listened to car doors opening and shutting.

Three D.C. cops with their guns drawn stormed through the front door and streamed into the studio.

"Police! Nobody move," one policeman ordered, though no one was moving.

Lacey held her breath. To her relief, Detective Broadway Lamont ambled into the studio behind the uniforms. "Smithsonian, what in hell is going on here? Trujillo, you part of this madhouse too?"

Trujillo just smiled and tipped his head toward Lacey.

"Looks like a damn party going on here." Lamont's eyes settled on Penfield. "This the guy? You're telling me this guy did it? Nice of you to wrap it up, Smithsonian, but I am waiting. Speak to me, madam."

She explained the whole scene to Lamont as best she could, watching the storm clouds of skepticism gather in his furrowed brow. The thunderstorm abated somewhat once he was convinced that Penfield was Collingwood; Amanda's sweater proved it. And Lamont was assured that a full confession from the killer was on videotape. Lacey lifted the wastebasket and showed him the gun. Lamont laughed out loud. He ordered one of the uniformed cops to sit on the wastebasket until the forensics team arrived. But he was still irritated.

"Smithsonian, you are a nuisance to public safety, and you piss me off."

"Now tell me something I don't know, Broadway." The D.C. homicide cop pretty much rounded out the chorus of people who would be singing the same song, including Douglas MacArthur Jones, the editor who would blame her for his high blood pressure. And then Vic's full reaction was still to come. She hoped he would save it for some private moment. *A very private moment.*

"I thought the District would be secure with you hanging around with your mother and sister. I thought I told you to stay safe."

"Well, I was safe. Ultimately."

"You had nothing to worry about, Detective," Rose put in. "We managed very nicely by ourselves. We Smithsonians stick together." She hugged her daughters.

When he had moved Lacey out of earshot of her formidable mother and suspicious boyfriend, Detective Lamont finished his lecture and gave her a bit of unsolicited advice. "As soon as I have statements from every last one of you, I want you to send your Smithsonian posse home."

"Why, Broadway, you mean this town ain't big enough for the four of us?"

"It's barely big enough for the two of us, Smithsonian. And do it before Halloween. Halloween is one of my busy nights."

"Don't worry, they're out of here"—Lacey looked at her watch. It was nearly one o'clock on Monday morning—"Tuesday."

"Now tell me, did your sister really knock him out with one kick?"

Lacey smiled. "Back home, we call her Lethal Feet Smithsonian."

Broadway Lamont whistled through his teeth. "And I thought the cheerleaders at my school were tough."

Monday went by quickly. Lacey slept late, put her mother and sister on a boat cruise to Mount Vernon for the afternoon, and stopped by the office to face Mac Jones. He held up the front page of that morning's *Eye Street Observer* as she passed by his office. The headline: "*Eye Street*'s Smithsonian Snags Supermodel Slayer." She saw the byline: Tony Trujillo. She stepped inside.

"The best part of the story for me, Smithsonian, was that you were so certain you weren't going to get into any trouble this weekend." He dropped the paper and made a show of reaching for his big bottle of Maalox.

"Not my fault—" she started.

"We've gone down that road before. Three Smithsonians? Trouble times three." He shook his head and raised his eyebrows. "Now get out of here. Keep your mother and sister out of any more of those sticky situations that you specialize in. Got it?"

"Yes, but—"

"I don't want to see you back here until your coconspirators are safely on a plane back to Colorado where they belong. Do you read me?"

"Loud and clear. And Mac . . ."

"What now?"

"Thank you." She left his office and stopped at her cubicle, where she noticed a large, flat manila envelope lying on the seat of her chair. The office mail cart had just come by. She opened it and a note tumbled out.

Dear Lacey,
    If everything goes according to plan, I'll be dead by the time you read this, and you'll know the whole story—

*because now it's your story too. I hope you don't hate me
for it. I'm enclosing the best photograph of you that I took
the other day, and the negative. Please use it for your
column. It's quite good. And you're genuinely beautiful.
   Farewell.*

It was signed *Caleb Collingwood*, which was crossed out and
replaced by *Tate*.

She pulled out the eight-by-ten, black-and-white matte photo.
She thought it was perhaps the best photograph that had ever been
taken of her. Penfield had caught a searching look in her eyes and
the faintest hint of a smile. Lacey tucked it back in the envelope
and set it back down. She knew she would never use it. *And I'd
better not let Mac see it. I'll put it in Mimi's trunk. Tomorrow.*

She noticed Felicity returning to her desk with a platter of gingerbread cookies. She glanced at Lacey with a big smirk on her
face.

"Better be careful, Lacey. Sooner or later someone's going to
polish you off."

Lacey was going to ignore Felicity today, but that smirk—and
the cookies—made it impossible. She turned around and saw Harlan Wiedemeyer peeking out at the chubby object of his desires
from behind a filing cabinet down the hall. He had a Krispy Kreme
Halloween-sprinkles doughnut in his fist and a lovelorn look in his
eyes. Something had to be done. Lacey needed to wipe that smirk
off Felicity's face, and she needed to confront the little jinx and
throw all this stupid superstition off her shoulders. It was time to
flip the switch on the accursed Wiedemeyer Effect. *Like a lightning bolt hitting a mirror,* Marie had said. She rose from her chair,
marched down the hall, grabbed Wiedemeyer by his free hand, and
dragged him bodily back to Felicity's turf.

"Wait, Lacey, what're you doing? You want a doughnut? I've
got some back at my desk. . . ."

Felicity just stared at the two of them, dumbfounded. Lacey
shoved Wiedemeyer to within inches of the food editor. No one
said anything, so Lacey finally took Wiedemeyer's hand and put it
into one of Felicity's. He gulped in sheer terror. Felicity's eyes
went wide, and her face turned fuchsia.

"Okay, this is the deal," Lacey said. "Harlan likes you, Felicity.
And you like him. Why? God only knows. I can't explain it. A
mystery of the universe. Just deal with it, both of you. Have a
doughnut. Have a cookie. Have a nice life. Together." She gave

Wiedemeyer another little push toward Felicity and slung her purse over her shoulder. Lacey announced, "My work here is done."

Lacey strode away, leaving Felicity Pickles and Harlan Wiedemeyer looking foolishly at each other. They still held each other's hands. Wiedemeyer slowly reached out and offered Felicity his chocolate-glazed, sprinkle-covered delicacy. She stared at the doughnut and then into his wondering eyes. She smiled.

"Oh, Harlan. Thank you. Have a gingerbread cookie?"

chapter 33

"Lacey, I feel terrible that we're leaving you before we've solved your car problem."

"It's okay, Mom; I can take care of it myself," Lacey said. She had neglected to tell Rose that all of a sudden it seemed to be raining cars, or at least car offerings.

First, Miguel Flores called from New York the day before to compliment her on nailing Amanda's killer without, as he put it, "having to actually nail him *to* anything, as it were." He mentioned that he still had no place to put his car in Manhattan, didn't really need it there, and he couldn't possibly keep it in storage in the District anymore. Storing it was frightfully expensive, and seeing as how Lacey was minus a car since losing her beloved Z, he would make her a sweet deal on his precious yellow Volkswagen Beetle that he adored, with the FLORES vanity plates and the yellow silk rose in the dashboard vase. He wanted to make sure it would go to someone who would love it. Lacey was too stunned to speak, but finally she said she would think about it and call him back.

Then Brooke called. It seemed that her law firm was unexpectedly in possession of a number of properties from a client who didn't have the cash to pay his legal fees. Now they wanted to dump the barter and were willing to take a loss for a quick sale. Barton, Barton, & Barton was looking for a new home for a brand-new, arrest-me-red Nissan 350Z, unfortunately *not* vintage, Brooke noted, and it certainly wouldn't blend into the background like a proper Washingtonian's car. But she assured Lacey that the title was clean, as was the car, and she would have first dibs on it at a greatly reduced price. Lacey drew a deep breath and said they'd talk over drinks later.

Finally, Detective Broadway Lamont called to tell her she wouldn't be seeing what remained of her old Z for quite a while.

Forensics had linked it to Amanda's murder; her car was now trial evidence. He suggested that she check into the D.C. police auction of the current confiscated and impounded vehicles. They were a good deal, some primo big-bucks drug-dealer cars, he said, fresh D.C. titles, and locksmiths were standing by. Lamont could show her around personally. "Just bring cash."

"Oh, that's sweet, Detective. Just what I had in mind, some drug lord's land yacht," she said. "Have they all been checked for bodies in the trunk?"

He laughed. "No telling. You pays your money, you takes your chances. Might be a little bonus for you."

Lacey thanked him for his concern. She said she would call him back. Finally, she had missed a call from her psychic friend, Marie Largesse, who left one of her cryptic messages.

"Lacey, *cher,* y'all are just never around when I call, are you? You'd think I'd know, being psychic and all. Thought you should know, dear, that nasty little jinx you had stuck on you? That dark cloud, with all that thunder and lightning? All gone. Poof. Whatever you did, it did the trick. I'm getting the all-clear on your astral-vibration frequency, and I'm seeing blue skies headed your way, *cher.* Now you call me, you hear? I want to know your secret. 'Bye now."

"Lacey?" Her mother's voice brought her back to the present, Tuesday morning. They were at Reagan National Airport, and Lacey was walking her mother and sister to the security gate. "We'd stay longer, but it's just that I always host the big Halloween get-together for all the neighbors."

"No problem. Just be sure to serve Mrs. Dorfendraper an extra helping of gossip along with her doughnuts and cider."

"Oh, I don't plan to brag," Rose said seriously, even though she had carefully packed a dozen copies of *The Eye Street Observer* with Trujillo's front-page story on the fabulous Smithsonian women and their killer catch.

"I *do* plan on bragging," Cherise said. "Are you sure the police won't give us a copy of the videotape? You know, just the part where we hammered him and laid him low?"

"Not in time for the party, I'm afraid," Lacey said.

"Well, I want a copy as soon as you get one. Okay, Lace?"

"You bet. VHS or DVD?"

"You know," Rose said, "there's so much we didn't get to do on this trip."

"We'll come back soon," Cherise promised. "Now that you have trundle beds."

"Better practice your cheers, then," Lacey said. "I may need the help."

"I could always teach you my routines," Cherise offered. "How are your high kicks?"

Lacey wanted to laugh, but her sister was serious. "I'll keep that in mind." Lacey gave her a quick hug, and Cherise strutted toward the metal detectors, her sleek new blond haircut swinging confidently.

Rose gave Lacey a big hug and a kiss. "Now remember, I can come anytime you need me if you run into anyone like that crazy Tate Penfield or Caleb Something or whatever his name is again."

"Mom, I do not make a habit of this sort of thing."

"Of course not, dear. I'll call you the minute we get home."

Lacey watched as they put their luggage on the conveyor belt and Cherise flirted with the TSA guards. And she watched as they turned around and waved. She waved back and smiled.

She was exhausted. The scent of heavily caffeinated coffee was calling to her. She was dead tired, and she felt as if her limbs would fall to the floor. That is, until she was jolted wide-awake by the sight of Vic Donovan walking through the terminal with Montana McCandless Donovan Schmidt at his side. They were headed to the security gate where Lacey had just left her mother and sister. *Yeah, he's been busy with work,* she thought. *With that piece of work.*

Lacey didn't think they had seen her, so she ducked into a bookstore, where she observed them from behind a tall rack of best sellers. Her heart skipped a beat. She was, quite frankly, fed up with this particular involuntary response of hers whenever she saw Vic Donovan, no matter what he was up to. Lacey felt devastated to see them together, but she couldn't tear her eyes off them. She had to see their good-bye.

Vic looked just as tired as Lacey felt. He made an easy target when Montana lunged at him, throwing both arms around his neck. It looked as if she were hanging on for dear life and giving him mouth-to-mouth resuscitation. Lacey was in agony, and only her pride kept her from crying; or maybe it was the white-hot fury she felt. She saw Vic break free from Montana, taking both her arms gently from around his neck. He then spun her around and gave her a little shove toward security and beyond. *Oh hell! Was that the big kiss-off—or the big kiss-on?* Lacey wondered. *I could just ask him—No, I can't.*

Montana must be on the same Frontier flight to Denver as her mother and sister, Lacey realized, and she hoped the blond barracuda wouldn't be seated anywhere near them. *On the other hand, never underestimate a Smithsonian woman.* They could certainly take care of themselves.

Vic put his shades on and strode back down the terminal. Even weary, he looked so handsome with his broad shoulders, narrow hips, faded jeans, and leather jacket. She thought he would walk on by, but he stopped. He'd spotted her.

"Lacey! What are you doing here? You following me?"

"You should be so lucky. I just put my mother and sister on that plane. I don't have to ask you what you were doing."

"Me? I was working all weekend. You're the one who was getting into trouble."

"Working?! Working on what, Montana's self-esteem problem? And don't change the subject. You've been with Montana most of the weekend. Or was it every second of the weekend? The weekend you were supposed to spend with me."

He let out an exasperated sigh. "You know it isn't like that. And we have got to talk about the other night at the warehouse too. It wasn't exactly easy on my heart, seeing you there with a killer trussed up on the floor. You and the Amazons." Lacey and Vic hadn't had any more time together that night, after he made sure she was safe. Detective Broadway Lamont and the D.C. police took over, and then Rose took custody of her adult daughters like the mother hen she was, insisting there would be time for explanations later, but now they all needed their beauty sleep.

"I saw you kiss Montana good-bye."

"She kissed me, Lacey. I didn't kiss her. There's a difference; you told me that once."

"She kissed you? You were just an innocent victim? You could have fooled me."

"Could I? Really, Lacey? You want to see what a real kiss is like?"

"As a matter of fact, I do." She stood her ground and stared him down.

"Well, then, madam, allow me." Vic swept her into his arms, bent her over slightly, and kissed her till her toes curled. She heard appreciative laughter from the coffee shop across the way, but she didn't care.

It was a good thing they were at the airport, where kissing in public was no big deal. This kiss was definitely different from the kiss she had witnessed between Vic and Montana. This kiss was *on*. Lacey responded, circling her arms around him. She felt a little dizzy. Finally he released her.

"Now *that* was a real kiss," he announced with a swagger. "What do you think?"

"I don't know, cowboy," Lacey said with a slow smile. "You'd better show me that again."

A **Crime of Fashion** Mystery
by Ellen Byerrum
Designer Knockoff

When fashion columnist Lacey Smithsonian
learns that a new fashion museum will soon grace
decidedly unfashionable D.C., it's more than a good
story—it's a chance to show off her vintage Hugh
Bentley suit. And when the designer, himself, notices her
at the opening, Lacey gets the scoop on his past—which
includes a long-unsolved mystery about a missing
employee. When a Washington intern disappears, Lacey
gets suspicious and sets out to unravel the murderous
details in a fabric of lies, greed,
and (gasp!) very bad taste.

Also in the **Crime of Fashion** series:
Killer Hair
Hostile Makeover
Raiders of the Lost Corset
Grave Apparel
Armed and Glamorous

**Available wherever books are sold or at
penguin.com**